Saga of the Dead Men Walking

Insanity's Requiem

Book IV of the Auramancer's Exorcism

JOSHUA E. B. SMITH

Sing for the Saints.
Cry for the Condemned.

I0524098

© 2022 Joshua E. B. Smith
Published: February 28, 2022
ISBN-13: 978-0-9990590-8-1
ASIN: B09QNSTGQ3
Imprint: Independently published
The right of Joshua Smith to be identified as author of this Work has been asserted by him in accordance with sections 77 and 78 of the Copyright, Designs and Patents Act 1988.
All rights reserved. No part of this publication may be reproduced, stored in retrieval system, copied in any form or by any means, electronic, mechanical, photocopying, recording or otherwise transmitted without written permission from the publisher. You must not circulate this book in any format.
Publisher: Joshua E. B. Smith
josh@sagadmw.com

DEDICATION
& ACKNOWLEDGMENTS

Sometimes, this is the hardest part of the book to write.

Honestly?

Most people skip this. In fact, they skip it to the point that I've been advised to move the dedications to the back of the book. Honestly though? If I move it to the back, nobody's going to see the most important part.

The thank you.

I can't do this on my own. Between my designer, my editor, my girlfriend, my family, God, and ALL of my fans – take your pick, they all have a hand in it in one way or another. All of you have saved my life and kept my career going even when I'm ready to quit. I love you all.

But this time?

To Trinity.

My companion of 21 years. My fluffy mother. The cutest of cute little black cats. You've helped me with every book I've ever written, and closing this tale without your tail on my lap hurts more than you'll know.

I miss you and love you, my little floofy princess.

Your absence in my heart is felt.

Sincerely, your giant kitten,

~Josh

CONTENTS

PROLOGUE
Evening of Staddis, 11th of Firstgrow, 513 QR

"There once was a Daemoness so twisted, so vile, that some named her the Mother of Sin," the man in the blood-red robe intoned. "She had hair of flame, eyes of stars, and by all accounts, she may have been the most beautiful creature in all creation. Yet," he warned, "her beauty alone was a trap. Her skin was made of the fabric of the void itself, such that even gazing upon it for more than a few moments would be enough to lose your soul to the realm of perdition."

In the dim stone-and-clay room, his guest didn't say a word. He couldn't even if he wanted. Nastavol had made sure of that. A quiet, ethereal fire burned all around the struggling soul trapped in the room by spellwork and outright willpower even as the necromancer held a tiny, oily black skull in his hands.

The Sycian looked down the chacos in his grip and smiled wistfully. "If I could be, I would be envious. I do remember a time when such a feeling would have crossed my mind – but that was a long time ago," he admitted quietly.

The ethereal form across from him twitched. He'd *been* twitching. It was hard to say at this point if he twitched in response, or twitched from pain. The flames blazed all around him, but they were dark. Muted. They burned, but they didn't burn on this plane. Not... entirely.

"Yet you note I said 'once.' She was a consort of Arch-Duke Belizal, you see. Not his wife, no, that honor befell another demented creature. A consort. Part of his harem. More importantly, one of his generals. The Mother of Sin had a gift – a very special, very intent gift. She could consume an object, or person, or creature. Consume, and then regurgitate it. When she did... oh, when she did. It was not glorious. It was a thing of awe."

Beside him, Rishnobia chuckled. The black-furred mote bounced up and down and crooned. "[Give an object of men/be granted object of damnation.]"

Nastavol nodded slowly. "Yes. As my Acolyte says. Whatever she consumed returned tainted. A human child would return as a gremlin. A dog would return as one of the Hounds of Perdition. Food would return rotted, toxic. She took great delight in consuming part of a man, or half of a woman – and would then watch as the ruined, mutated flesh would war against its host.

"None of those things made her a general, of course. A monstrosity, yes. No. What gave her power and rank were men. Men like weapons. Men use them. It is one of the reasons men are so populous in the pit," he continued before he gave the shaking, blue-and-black figure hovering in front of him a grin. "You would know that, would you not? But I digress.

"She served as Belizal's armory. She would swallow the weapons of men and return weapons effectively forged in damnation. One could argue that she was the reason that the Arch-Duke was able to win his battle against the Adelins. I am not sure that is correct. It is a reasonable argument."

"[Hubris of men/think themselves wise,]" Rishnobia countered. "[Adelins were damned/because of ego.]"

Nastavol entertained a brief flicker of a smile. "Ego and open wounds, yes. However, I return to as I said: 'once.' After Agromah fell, she decided to give no heed to the agreement struck between the Duke and the Heavens. She left the continent to spread her devilish delights to the world at large. As punishment for her ways, a group of simple men were empowered with knowledge and spine to track her down. They named themselves the Sons of Veritas – after the last city of the Adelins. Later, they would become known as their actions."

His guest continued to wordlessly struggle in the flames. His skin melted and reformed between licks of burning torment. His bones charred and reconstructed themselves with each flicker of agonizing incineration.

"They hunted. They found her. With the aid of a Master Artisan – and the 3rd Granalchi Dean-Adept himself, Shol'val Xabraxis Mulvette – a vessel to capture her was created. Men being men – and not exactly creative – they named it as plainly as they could: the Urn of Xabraxis."

"[Lack of imagination/lack of standards.]"

"I did say that were simple men," the man in the blood-red robe answered dismissively. "The history of the Urn from then on is muddled, as such things are when they are two centuries past. You know where it landed. Your efforts helped me find it. The Lovers have it. That was my initial conclusion, and where you came in. You and your assistant proved it."

The figure in the flame thrashed even harder and tried to reach through the flames to grab a smoldering chunk of bone and flesh on the floor. It couldn't make it. The fires prevented him from touching his anchor. The lumpy skull stayed out of reach no matter how hard he tried.

"It was the mace. Abyssia created it. That is why I had Anais deliver it to the Lovers. The Mace of Insanity's Rapture would be drawn to the Urn and let her – let *me* – know if it was truly buried behind all of those wards. It all worked perfectly." His demeanor changed. The bland expression on his face soured. It did worse than soured. It carried the weight of an eternity of rage.

His guest recoiled away.

"Until you grasped for more power than I had decided to offer. You disappoint me, Donta. I resurrected you. I pulled you from the pit. I gave you new life. New peace. New hope. Permission to be free of perdition, if only you served me as I said. You did not. You went beyond your station."

Rishnobia chittered eagerly and bounced up and down on the floor. "[Given chances/took failure! Gambled for strength/gained only weakness!]"

"I cautioned you upon your rebirth: success would grant you salvation, of sorts. Failure would grant you other." Nastavol picked up the toxic, deformed skull that had served as the assassin's anchor and looked down at the mess with a sneer. "I do *not* reward failure. My title is not 'The Man of Crimson Delight,' you know."

The chacos erupted in a sickly green flame. Donta's spirit screamed in agony as the flames around him flared to a bright blue light. Claws of fire ripped from the center of his chest and began to rip and tear his essence – and as they tore, the claws pulled his spirit into the gaping hole they had ripped open. As he imploded, Nastavol crushed the chacos in his grip and let the debris crumble to the floor.

"I am the Man of the Red Death," he intoned as his minion returned to damnation. "I shall I leave such trivial concepts as 'forgiveness' to my brother."

Not that his brother knew that this red-robed murderer was his kin.

Nor was he in a forgiving mood.

***

"I never liked you," Akaran remarked dryly. "You were an ass when I first met you, you were an ass when you threw me out of the Manor, and you've apparently been an ass to my associate."

"Friend," the pudgy man beside him corrected. "Associate makes it sound like we only have a business relationship. I do greatly value our time together."

The priest let Riorik's comment slide. The recipient of their conversation, however, just kept his head down and took their accusations like a champ. He didn't have much choice in the matter – he couldn't go anywhere. Stockades had a way of doing that.

"So. Here's my problem. You allowed a vampire to prey on the residents of Medias Manor – a haven for the lost, the broken, the mindless. You *directly* allowed for the torture of one of the guests *and* the murder of one of the staff."

Riorik cleared his throat. "Not to mention I suspect you had involvement in getting this good gentleman removed from his room at one point, didn't you?"

Ronald Telpid, the former Sergeant-at-Arms for the Manor clenched his fists and shifted in his chains but otherwise didn't say anything.

"As I'm sure that Henderschott told you," Akaran continued as he slowly circled his prisoner, "you are in *deep* shit. The charges laid against you include 'Cavorting with the Dead, Betrayal of Office, Betrayal of Oath, Betrayal of Station, Accomplice to Murder, and Accomplice to Torture,' and… honestly? Those are just the charges that the *Crown* has hit you with." The priest looked down at Telpid and couldn't stop the sneer on his lips. "As far as the *Order* is concerned, I'm going to get in trouble if I don't personally cut your head off before midnight."

"Then do it, you bastard," the half-naked former guard grumbled. "Please, just end it already."

The exorcist snorted in disgust as his friend chortled. "Oh, dear man. I don't think you understand where he's coming from. His people are… irritated. The same monster you helped actually succeeded in killing one of their paladins that served this fine city. Murdered in battle. Painfully, if I understand correctly. To say that they are angry…"

Telpid shuddered in the stocks and shifted his chained feet on the rough stone floor. Of all the things that you could say about the city dungeon, a place of creature comforts it wasn't. "Killed one of the Harlot's cunts. Maybe they're not all bad," he spat with a rough laugh. "Go on. Kill me you fisk."

"Believe it or not, I don't actually want to," Akaran countered as he rubbed his hands across the fresh stubble growing back in on his scalp. "I honestly think you have more to offer alive than dead."

"I'm not going… going to tell you anything… while I'm like this," his prisoner retorted. "If… if I help you, Annix… it's going to be worse than death."

The exorcist shook his head as he painfully squatted down to look up into Telpid's eyes. "I have spent a great deal of time, very recently, learning about what things are worse than death. Given your current litany of sins, I'd say you're in line for most of them if I do to you what you allowed others to do," he whispered in a hushed, almost horrified voice. "I would be very, very careful in what you ask for."

"He's right," Riorik happily pointed out. "I haven't had quite the same experiences but I have no cause to think that the boy doesn't speak anything but the truth. It is very much in your best interests to atone for your sins now before someone else atones them *for* you."

The gravely tone in Akaran's voice – and the cheerful one from Riorik – gave the former guard a pause. "There's no such thing as the Abyss. Even if… even if there is, I did what I had to."

"To paraphrase a refrain my friend has offered me in private many a time: 'The road to perdition is crowded by those that believe what they had to do was right.' He's quoted it to me quite extensively."

"Has it done anything to stop you?" Telpid mocked quietly.

Akaran glanced over at the thief, who merely shrugged. "His Order has a saying about 'velvet gloves' and 'gauntleted fists.' I assume that since it works for them, that well, maybe some of my excesses can be excused if my heart is in the right place."

"Your heart is in your coinpurse," the exorcist countered.

"Which I have been very liberal with opening to aid you."

The boyish priest rolled his blue-gray eye and adjusted the patch covering his other. "After you've stuffed it with crowns you've stolen."

"I do not steal crowns," Riorik countered, "I exist firmly in the lines of what is business, ethical or not. Yes, it's true; I do make arrangements to obtain them that some find inappropriate."

"Either way," Akaran sighed as he turned his focus back to the Saa, "that doesn't help *you*. I understand you're afraid of Annix. I don't blame you. I'm sure he threatened to turn you into one of his spawn if you didn't behave."

Telpid coughed and spit up a bit of thick spittle onto the floor.

"Couldn't be so lucky. Think I had a choice? He showed me what he could do. I *had* to. If I didn't…"

The priest glanced over at his portly friend and nodded once. Riorik pulled out a small scroll of parchment and a chunk of charcoal. "So let's get to that," he began. "I'm going to be honest with you: I don't think I can offer you a way out of this, but I'll ask. I firmly believe you that *you* didn't think you had a choice. The larger concern right now, for you and only you, is what happens after we talk. If you're not honest with me, I have to hand you over to people that won't be as gentle when they repeat my questions."

The disgraced Saa shifted in the stocks and tried to look up at his tormentors. "I'm dead either way."

"Yes, but I should express the importance of *how* you die," the Master Thief of Basion City countered. "Do you die by a sip of hemlock? Do you die at the headsman's block?" he asked as he opened his vest to show off a very curved, very serrated, very sharp blade. "Or do you die without feet?"

Telpid's reluctance crumbled. "So Annix tortures me… or you do."

"True, I guess. Except he's not here, and if you're hung before nightfall, he won't get to touch you. I mean I could simply let you go and we can see if he thinks you've betrayed him…"

"You wouldn't."

Akaran grabbed the Saa by his chin and painfully twisted his head up so he had to look into the priest's one good, furious eye. "I need answers more than I need to be concerned about your health, safety, or comfort. One way or another, I'll get them tonight."

Resigned to his fate, Telpid talked.

Nor was he the only one who did.

***

A little girl kicked her feet in the surf as little blobs of sea-foam splashed against her legs. She wore a simple little white cotton dress, and she had a bright yellow bow in her auburn hair. At least, it looked auburn. A few silent minutes later, it turned blonde. Then raven. Then it turned a color that couldn't be described. It was just a matter of time before it changed again.

"They say that time doesn't exist on this side of the Veil," the little girl said suddenly, as if she could hear the thoughts from the woman beside her. "That's not true. It just lasts as long as you want it to. Want a moment to last a mortal lifetime… human or other? Then it can. Want to hurry up and meet your grandchildren? Then blink. They'll be here."

"I don't… I don't have children," the woman lamented. "Illiya didn't… bless me."

The little girl smirked in idle bemusement. "She really didn't, did She? Of course, you could've adopted. Imagine how different your life would've been if you had," she replied as she gestured with her hands. The view beyond the bay shifted, and instead of crashing waves, a scene unfolded of three small children – two girls and a boy – as they ran around underfoot of a woman with jet black hair and soft green eyes.

Everyone laughed, and laughed, and laughed.

Except for the woman on the beach, who watched with tears brimming in her soft green eyes as the wind brushed her jet-black hair across her naked shoulders. "I served the Empress. I did what I thought was right."

"Looks like you were wrong. That could've been yours."

"This is worse than the Abyss," Rmaci quietly sighed. "It doesn't make you wait for the ever-after."

"You would know, wouldn't you?" the little girl charged with a smile that quickly faded to nothing at all. "Brings us to a very interesting question about what to do with you."

The former spy nodded sadly. "I know what I want."

"Do you? That's not a hypothetical question; answer me. Answer me truthfully. *Do you* know what you want?"

"Not to go back to the pit."

The girl snorted. "Well that makes you special, doesn't it? All you want is to not rot away in the dark. There's been very few people on this side of eternity who have said, 'Then just kill me and send me to the Abyss!' and actually *meant* it."

Rmaci blinked at the venom in her voice. "I… I don't know about special, but that's what I want…"

"Well, you ball of formerly-torched-sunshine, there's a really big question about *if* you've earned it. You didn't exactly do a whole lot after the Boss's thug gave you an out, did you?"

"I planned to do more…"

"Yeah yeah," the little girl said with a dismissive wave of her hand. "You have any idea how many people say that? 'Oh no, I was going to repent! Oh no, I was going to make something of my life! Oh no, I was going to build a home, or spend my life with my wife once we could be together!' *Everyone*," she said as she answered her own question. "*Everyone* has a *thing* they wanted to do before they got a shiv up their ass. You think you're special?"

Rmaci bristled and started to turn to face the brat, but she couldn't turn her head all the way to the side. She vaguely remembered Akaran having the same problem when they were on a beach in his dream… no. Not his dream. His… memory. "I'm… am I dead? Am I… really dead this time?"

The little girl nodded. "Don't feel bad about not catching on. It's the nature of the realm. You relax once you're here. Relaxed people don't always think things through. Ignorance, bliss. You're not in pain and the sand ain't abrasive and it's easy to just lose yourself for a bit when you get here."

She swallowed nervously and looked out into the rolling waves. "That means I made it here though?"

"Figured that was obvious at this point," the otherworldly brat retorted. "Question is, do you get to stay here? Do you get to walk off the beach and head on up to the Boss's estate or do I get to throw your ass into the ocean and watch you sink?"

"That's… that's still an option?"

"Oh, you poor thing," she replied with a sigh. "That's *always* an option. Let's not kid ourselves here. You've got more blood on your hands than a cat in a birdhouse. You're a liar, a thief, a manipulator. You've tortured people – and be honest, at least one of them you did just for the fun of it. You've broken up marriages, spread your legs for anything that you thought could get you ahead, and you even tried to charm your way out of Zell's chamberpot after you died for all the good your efforts did," the girl lectured. "Weren't you married, too? How did that end again? Remind me? You know that our Lady takes a very dim view of people that break their vows of marriage. She's the Goddess of blessed Love, if you haven't forgotten."

The spy winced and tried to swallow past the lump in her throat. "I uh… I hadn't put those thoughts together quite that way."

"Liar," the girl scolded. "Do better than lying, you burnt-up little dead woman. I'm giving you an opportunity to make your case before Someone Else decides to make it for you. If you can't find it in yourself to find even a sliver of *honesty* that you can explain *why* you should be allowed to stay here, *you won't.*"

Rmaci looked down at her hands and couldn't help but watch as they started to shake. "Does that mean I'm going back?"

The long silence that filled the air grew so suffocating that the spy thought she was going to choke on it. "It means that your future is cloudy," the child admitted. "However, I do have something good to tell you."

"What... what could you possibly mean by that?"

The girl turned to the dead woman. Her irises caught fire and her pupils turned into sinking black vortexes that Rmaci could *feel* pull at her flesh. The *Void* was in her eyes and it *wanted* her. "That the decision isn't up to me," she said before she blinked twice and the haunting storm of damnation vanished to be replaced by brilliant golden eyes that pierced her heart.

If the spy could've pissed herself, that would've done it. "Then... then who?"

"Then who? *Who* do you *think* I mean?" she replied just as a hand gripped Rmaci's shoulder and squeezed so hard it felt like her bones were going to break. "I mean *Her*," the little girl said as she gestured at a figure that had suddenly appeared behind the dead woman.

Rmaci made a strangled scream of pain as impossibly strong fingers dug into her flesh. *[We need to have a talk,]* the figure growled so harshly that the waves retreated away. *[You played with something that didn't belong to you, and **I** would like a word.]*

"You asked to earn your forgiveness, oh murderess you," the girl taunted as the spy screamed in wordless terror at the Divine figure. "I figured you'd learned by now — *holy* does not mean *nice*."

The dead woman clutched at the fingers digging into her arm and tried to pull free. Any objections she had were silenced with a single wave of the Goddess's finger that forced the spy's lips to slam shut.

The little girl just chuckled as the Goddess picked the sobbing soul up off of the sand and marched into the ocean until both the spy and the Divine disappeared from view.

There weren't any more screams. There weren't any more complaints. Everything settled back into the perfectly peaceful realm that it was made to be. Just the little girl, the surf, and the sand. Once she was content neither of them would make it back to the realm anytime soon, she stretched and turned around to head back to her other duties.

"Every single one of 'em. I swear," she sighed. "They come up here, lounge on the beach, take in the sights, think everything is fine. Blessed lot of 'em mope and piss in someone's yard and then they get all kinds of stunned when the Lady decides to do something about it."

No responses came forth from the waves, and she sighed again.

"Humans. I swear to the Origin, if they weren't so blessed *adorable*..."

I. MEETING OF MINDS
Morning of Zundis, 12th of Firstgrow, 513 QR

A few days prior, Akaran had suffered what he had not-so-lovingly referred to as a 'gathering of headaches.' If he ever learned the secrets of reverse-chronomancy, which nobody had yet cracked, he promised that he'd go back and apologize to them. They – that gathering of Ishtva, Telburn, Karaj, Alverach, the Oldstone, and more – had absolutely *nothing* on the handful of people he had ordered gathered together in Overseer Hannock's meeting room.

Absolutely *nothing* at *all*.

"So now that you've gotten the outbursts out of the way, let's get down to figuring out how we are going to deal with it – because we *are* going to deal with it," Akaran stressed as he leaned forward with his weight on his hands atop the large oak table in the middle of the room.

"Do you... seriously... expect this body to believe... that there are... *vampires*... loose in my city?" Hannock growled through clenched teeth. He was a big man with a deep voice, and the way he made the floor vibrate with the accusation was somewhat impressive.

"Yes. Not just your body but also these other people," the priest replied as he gestured at the others present. Lieutenant-Commander Henderschott choked back an inappropriate laugh while Elsith Gorosoch, Huntsmatron of the Basion City Hunter's Guild, continued to give him a nearly-unblinking and utterly withering glare.

She wasn't alone with that glare. "I don't mean *my* body you uneducated buffoon," the Overseer rumbled. "You demand a meeting. You walk in here. You empty your bowels and shit lies all over my estate and then you have the *gall* to stand there and threaten *me* if I don't believe you?"

"It's light on the lies but accurate on the rest," Akaran answered with a shrug. "It doesn't really matter how much of it you believe. I'm giving you as much truth as I can part with but at the end of the day, you're stuck with the decision."

"He might be but *I* am not," Paverilak replied. The second-in-command to the Provincial Maiden had a habit of throwing his weight around whenever it wasn't welcome, and he seemed content to live up to his reputation. "With respect to the Maiden-Templar, she doesn't outrank *my* Lady – Maiden Sanlian Esterveen. As she has ordered me to –"

The exorcist cut him off with a wave of his hand. "With respect, Betrothed, Sanlian isn't *here*. Catherine has issued an Order of Inquiry. I'm just as happy to have you arrested and put in a cell until Sanlian comes to bail your ass out than I am to put up with people getting in my way."

"You don't have that authority," Hannock snarled as Paverilak's jaw dropped to his chest. Then, as he turned his head to Henderschott, repeated the statement – as a meeker question. "He doesn't, does he?"

Before the Commander of the 4th Garrison could answer, he was firmly interrupted by a fuming woman in a dark green cloak. The hood had been pulled down across her shoulders, and her golden-blonde hair had been angrily tied into a rough ponytail. "How about we start with what evidence you have rather than what you plan to do about it," Elsith demanded.

It wasn't phrased as a question, and the tone in her voice made the (much) younger exorcist-turned-temporarily-paladin decide to take heed of the Huntsmatron's *suggestion*. "If we can keep the interruptions to a minimum, I'll explain as much as I can."

A request that might be harder than not to adhere to. In addition to Overseer Hannock, Lieutenant-Commander Henderschott, Huntsmatron Elsith, and the man that amounted to the provincial governor, the meeting room was packed with a few other wonderful people as well. That list included recently-promoted Upper Adjunct Acti Risson of the Temple of Stara – a man that Akaran had met weeks ago, and thankfully, hadn't been overtly hostile to his claims so far.

There was also Consort-Blade Sua. Sua was not the kind of man you ignored, but he was the kind of man you hoped ignored you. Consort-Blades were rarely seen away from their Maidens, and if there was a more-skilled fighter in the city, you'd be hard-pressed to say *who*. The best part of Sua's presence was that he didn't seem to like to *talk,* though it was just as terrifying to realize he was *listening*.

Everything they said was going to get relayed back to the Provincial

Maiden within hours of whatever they decided. If she didn't like what she heard, then Sanlian herself would be in the city proper before the week was out. It was in *everyone's* best interests to make sure that she *liked* what she heard.

He was joined by another man that the exorcist had some recent experiences with: Adept Lolron Essinge from the Basion City Granalchi Annex. His presence was a bit redundant. After all, the Headmaster of the Annex was married to the Huntsmatron, which the priest was sure made for *all* kinds of interesting dinner conversations.

But, Akaran quietly assumed, *she's going to have her hands full dealing with the shit I'm about to feed her...*

Speaking of feeding shit, there was another woman in the room that was of moderate importance to note. Akaran didn't know – and didn't want to know how she'd been included in the meeting – but he knew her fairly well. She sat with her arms crossed over her more-than-ample bosom and smirked at the priest every time he opened his mouth.

That was Celestine "Cel" Navarshi, the Innkeeper for the *Drunken Imperial* down in the district of Lower Naradol. She was also an unabashed and very obvious member of the Fleet-Finger's Guild of Basion City, and answered directly to the new Guildboss – Akaran's 'friend,' Riorik the Hobbler.

One person surprisingly – though maybe not very – missing was the Lady of Medias Manor, Lady Ridora herself. Apparently, she'd had her fill of dealing with the dead and damned and the politics around them after the exorcist had carried out one of his duties right on her doorstep. However, just because the Manor didn't have a representative present, it didn't mean that Akaran hadn't been saddled with a new handler.

His name was Brother Levathil Pilatti, and before he'd been designated as the holder of the exorcist's leash, he had been the Head Archivist of the Repository of Miral. The rank was impressive: both for his age (fewer than sixty years – a feat in and of its own self) and because he was second in academic rank only to Maiden-Templar Prostil herself. In all of Akaran's visits over to the Repository, he'd never met the silvery-bearded and bald-headed man.

That was, until this morning. The stories about him had painted him as a strict, by-the-book type, but so far most of what he had done was take notes and glare at people. All things considered... well, it was either have someone with their hand on his neck or be locked away in the Vault somewhere, he was sure of it.

All told? It'd been a rancorous mess to deal with.

He only expected it to get worse.

"Alright. This mess starts before the death of Odern Merrington, an Instructor-Adept at the Granalchi Annex. Unfortunately, I don't have names to put on the dead and missing prior to him – so that's where we're going to start," he began. "Everyone here knows that he was murdered on the 4th of Greenbirth – so a little more than two months ago. His death was later compounded by the gruesome slaughter of Livstra Oliana. Before we go on, I have to give up a little bit about her that some of you aren't going to like," he said as he glanced over at Cel.

The innkeeper looked back at him like she was going to strangle a rat.

"There's been a rumor that she had some dealings with *unsavory* people," Risson interjected.

"They're not... *all* bad," Akaran replied as he tried to discretely smooth things over with Celestine. "As it turns out, Livstra was living a double life. By day, she was the Administrator of Medicine at Medias Manor. By night, she was also known as Liona Reanage – or otherwise entitled, 'The Gambling Mind.' With that rank, she was the head of the Fleet-Finger's Guild."

Henderschott blanched and nodded in agreement. "He's right on that. The Guard had ample suspicions that she was involved with the Fleets."

"Ample payoffs, you mean," Cel muttered under her breath just loud enough for Akaran to hear.

Grumblings aside, the exorcist went on. "Instructor-Adept Odern owed money to Livstra. The assumption we're working with is that Liv was supposed to be framed for his death, arrested, removed from position, whatever. When the Guard didn't take the bait, she was subsequently murdered to get her out of the way."

"Out of the way for who? Why?" Lolron asked with a frown. "The thieves?"

"No, actually," Akaran replied with a shake of his head. "Livstra was directly overseeing the care of a woman being treated in Medias Manor. Her name is Bistra Enil – a former exorcist with my Order. An exorcist that's been targeted by an inhuman; the same one responsible for these murders. Our best guess is that Liv was on the verge of realizing that, and he killed her."

"The so-called vampire, you mean," Hannock proclaimed with a dismissive wave of his hand.

The priest clicked his tongue against his cheek. "That'd be the one. His name is Annix. You'll have signed testimony and a description delivered to each of your offices by the time this meeting concludes. He's responsible for their deaths and a host of others. Either by his own hand or by his spawn."

Risson cleared his throat and straightened up a little. As he did, his Signostica of Stara — a crystal vial filled with sand, soil, ash, and air — clattered on his chest. "Spawn? Exorcist, I don't like the implications of that word."

"You shouldn't."

"I like the way you say that even less."

"After Livstra and Odern, it appears that Annix thought it had covered up his mess. It seems that he was right, too. He targeted one of our *other* murderers loose in the city walls — one most of you know: Lady Anais Lovic. I honestly don't know why, but, that was when he and I first crossed paths."

Several people in the room suddenly looked *very* uncomfortable at the accusation against Anais's honor. Not the least of which were Hannock, Lolron, and Paverilak. Elsith and Cel just looked disgusted. Risson was the only one that didn't blanch, flinch, or suddenly try to look at anything else in the room but the exorcist.

"*Other* murderer?" the Upper Adjunct asked.

"I'll address that bitch myself once the boy is done," Elsith interrupted before he could continue.

Akaran caught himself before he could make a quip about it, and decided to stick to the facts just this once and save the witty remarks for later. "We've come to the conclusion that he liked to feed on the lower-station citizens in the city; the ones that wouldn't be missed by anyone of importance. After he attempted to — and failed — to kill Lady Lovic, she sicced her bodyguard on his scent. If you don't know him, his name is — was — Donta."

"Was? You mean Donta's dead?" Lolron interrupted before he realized what he was saying. The outburst (and recognition of the name) didn't go unnoticed.

"Donta was already dead," the priest explained in a way that provided next to no explanation at all. "Again, I'll let the Huntsmatron explain."

That only vaguely pacified the Adept, but that was good enough.

"One thing lead to another, and Annix had one of his minions make a play for Donta. We have a name for her, too — Sherril Inyadine, a former battlemage attached to the 5th. She is directly responsible for the massacre at Flynn's Landing."

"The Guard can confirm that one," Henderschott added. "That slaughter, and two others of note."

"At least you have a suspect," Paverilak replied with a glare. "Why is she working with him?"

"She's tied into an exorcism that Bistra carried out several years ago. The same exorcism that lead Bistra to be targeted by Annix. Sherril had assisted her, but was eventually kidnapped and subsequently turned against the Crown."

The Overseer leaned forward and drummed his fingers on his desk. "You're expecting me to believe that one of the Queen's own would be somehow seduced and corrupted to pledge fealty to a *vampire*? That's madness."

Akaran just shrugged at him. "Turned her against the Crown and turned her into another creature like *him*. It likely wasn't by choice. I'd be lying if I said she was the only one we knew about, but, I'm not here to lie and make you feel better."

Hannock flinched and glanced over his shoulder at a painting hanging on the wall behind him – another movement that didn't go unnoticed. Neither by Cel, nor Akaran, nor Henderschott. Sua, too, but the Consort-Blade didn't react even as the Overseer took a trembling breath and got ready to ask a question he didn't really want to know the answer to. "Who... who else?"

"There seem to be several," the priest answered. "I'll get to them momentarily. Shortly after the Landing, Sherril moved on to her next target: Upper Adjunct of the Order of Stara and High Priestess of Basion City, Lexcanna Jealions."

"I thought she was murdered by some... well, battlemage? A... Badin, wasn't it?" Paverilak asked with a frown.

"So did the order of Stara," Risson interrupted. "We have since been provided with evidence otherwise, and we have humbly offered our sincere apologies to Specialist-Major Badin for the accusation. We will make it up to him in the future."

"Thank you, *Uppa-junct*," Akaran replied earnestly. "I know he'll appreciate that."

Risson nodded gravely as Henderschott spoke up. "We can also tie that murderous little slitch to Kee Tessamirch and the slaughter at the Advensi's base."

The Betrothed and the Consort-Blade both perked up at that statement. "So it wasn't one of yours? How certain are you?"

"As reasonably certain as possible," Henderschott admitted. "With Malik's abduction, and the description of that fight, it seems that this Annix bastard has moved on from just tormenting some nut at the Manor to outright trying to turn the city into the site of the next Dawnfire-Midland Border War."

The silent-so-far Brother Levathil cleared his throat and rapped the end of his old grizzled walking stick against the stone floor. "I would strongly advise the esteemed Lieutenant to speak respectfully of Missus Enil. She has neither earned nor deserves scorn from any of the assembled."

"Lieutenant-Commander," Henderschott corrected, "but my apologies."

The interruptions out of the way, Akaran continued on. "So Sherril is responsible for Flynn's Landing, Lexcanna, and Kee. Those are just the ones we know about. It's also presumed that Annix has turned several other individuals in the city – though we've managed to cull a few."

"So you have caught his minions?" Hannock asked. "This isn't just… ravings of a lunatic? We all know you've recently spent time in the Manor yourself."

"We have, but at a cost. Five days ago, there was an attack in Port Cableture. We believe that it was another assassination attempt on Anais. Several citizens were killed, as was one of our own: Paladin Faldine Golanstav. As tragic as her loss is, she was able to kill one of her attackers. We aren't able to conclusively identify that one, but we were able to put names to the others before they were excised."

"Who were they?" Paverilak asked. "Anyone of importance?"

"Important to someone," Akaran countered. "The first was man believed to be named Ettaquis. He's a known associate of Lady Lovic. The other was a former medicannia at the Manor – Raechil Lamar."

The mention of Ettaquis's name made the same people that had been uncomfortable over the suggestion of Anais's crimes flinch all over again. "Are you implying that Anais was employing a vampire…?" Adept Lolron asked with his eyes wide.

Akaran shook his head 'no' before he offered his stance. "I'm saying that it's likely Annix caught him, murdered him, and then turned him against her. That's a very common trait among his kind."

"But Ettaquis is dead, yes?" Lolron pressed. "*Dead* dead, not this… walking abomination you're accusing him of being?"

"Dead dead," the exorcist confirmed before he let a grim smile decorate his lips. "I carried out their executions personally. Raechil had a sister – Kiasta Lamar. They both went missing at the same time. If Kiasta wasn't turned, we presume she's been eaten."

"This story is turning very convoluted," Hannock said with a frown. "You're claiming that Livstra Oliana, a well-respected pillar of the city, was secretly leading the Guild of Thieves. You're claiming that she, and Odern, and supposedly this Raechil woman, have all been killed by one man?"

The priest flicked his tongue against his cheek again. "Not a man, not… not as you know it. But yes, still responsible for the three of them, and Ettaquis. He's also is likely responsible for ordering Sherril to wipe out the Landing, murder Kee, murder Lexcanna, and that he ordered three of his spawn to attempt to assassinate Anais for good measure."

"But *why*?" Risson asked with a frustrated gesture. "These are very serious accusations! Mass murder. Kidnapping. Presumably necromancy? Or at least, demonic liaisons? If you're suggesting that he's behind Malik's abduction… just… why? How could he even turn these people, as you've suggested?"

Henderschott cleared his throat and stopped leaning idly against the wall. "I can't speak for demonology, but I think I can answer that question. May I?" When Akaran gave him a nod and turned to get a drink, the Lieutenant-Commander went to work. "The 4th was able to independently verify some of this. About three years ago, the 5th Garrison requested assistance from the Order of Love to find a few missing men in and near the village of Squistal. In the process, the woman at the center of this nightmare – Missus Enil – encountered and banished a demon. Over the next few months, a small trail of destruction erupted across the northern border. It was presumed, at the time, to be little more than skirmishes and bandits. As this new evidence has suggested, there was some kind of relationship between the beast she banished and this Annix bastard."

"That doesn't explain *why* they're doing this *now*," Paverilak complained. "Why *here*, why *now*?"

"Annix is responsible for more than Akaran has let on," Brother Levathil threw in. "The Order carried out an exorcism on the 7th of this month – that one at the Manor. It seems that this vampire has been using advanced chaos-tainted magic to bewitch, bewilder, and torture Exorcist Enil for some time. Once his spell on her was broken, we were able to ascertain that the monster she excised in Squistal was his 'wife,' if you believe such a creature can hold one."

"That's the gist of it," the exorcist added. "Bistra killed his wife, the army helped, and he's been torturing her ever since. Now that the heat is on, he's moved from just tormenting the poor woman to trying to embarrass the Crown. And now us in the Order, too. The more he works against the city, and the more obvious he's making it? Well, it makes people doubt we can save them. By 'we,' I mean every single person and organization represented in this room."

Hannock curled his lip in a disgusted sneer. "Embarrass us by murdering everything in sight? That is one way to go about it."

"It actually is," the Betrothed replied. "There is very little right now that would serve to unsettle the Queen as much as having one of her safest cities fall into riots, bloodshed, and a forced interruption of the largest political alliance in the last decade. Not to mention that it would stir dissent against the Lovers once the fact that a demon has been laying siege quite literally right under their noses is brought to light." Paverilak frowned and rubbed his hands together. "That's quite a remarkable mind."

"Unfortunately, it really is," Akaran agreed. "Everyone looks like shit, the faith in the Crown gets shattered, we end up with a potential war with the Odinal Wartribe and probably some of the other Midlanders. *Then* your Maiden comes down hard on Catherine and the Repository, *and* he gets personal revenge against the exorcist that banished his mate. Didn't the 2nd Imperium War start under *better* circumstances?"

"If I was attempting to disrupt the social system of an area, I don't think I could have come up with a better method myself," Elsith lamented. "Which brings us to Anais."

Lolron cleared his throat. "Yes, what about her? As dangerous as this Annix creature is, I'd like to know more about what you think her involvement is."

Akaran knocked back a flagon of water and answered with a shrug. "Well, that's one thing we don't know. I don't believe that she's involved with the vampire – in any way other than pissing him off. Our problem with *her* is that she's *also* inhuman, as was her bodyguard."

"Perhaps you could clarify what you mean by 'inhuman,' please?" Hannock asked as a few beads of sweat appeared on his forehead.

"She isn't human. *What* she is we're not sure. Donta was detained a few days ago before he was murdered in captivity – and by our witness accounts, by Anais herself. He was some kind of sentient animate."

"A sentient animate?" Paverilak pressed with a single eyebrow raised.

Brother Levathil took over for the exorcist for that question. "There are ways to resurrect the dead from the Abbhorent Place of Perdition that hide the nature of their cursed existence. They are very difficult, very rare, and always dangerous. When a necromancer or other unholy abomination seeks to re-animate a corpse for their use, it's often just a mindless rotting husk. In this case, we could not be so lucky."

"Think of it like a golem. A construct," Akaran added, "but instead of being a creature that is brought to life by a mage to do a menial task, it's the soul of someone dead and damned brought back to life with his or her mind intact."

"One cannot stress how dangerous such a creation is," the Brother pointed out. "To even create one is to wield great power. To presumably create two? For their minds to be so intact that they have been able to operate in plain sight without being identified? To do business like any one of us? I daresay that the Order hasn't seen such a thing on the mainland in the last half-century."

Adept Lolron reached into his robes and pulled out a small leather-bound journal with a title of, *The Sixth Remnant* written on the cover. "Correct me if I'm wrong, but isn't such a creature referred to as a so-called 'Black Resurrection' by your Order?"

The title caught the exorcist's eye in a hurry. 'The Remnant of the Sixth School,' as it was known, was the school of Necrosia — all things necromancy. The study was strictly forbidden by the Academy and banned by order of the Crown. Of course, *strictly forbidden* was always up for interpretation... and the laws of both the Midlands and the League to the North weren't as unforgiving on the subject.

Akaran looked at his handler and confirmed it after Levathil gave him a faint nod. "It is. Until we catch her, we won't know for certain. She's either a necromancer of vast power, or she's working for one. We don't know which yet and won't until we can shove a spike through her head and see what falls out."

"She is also the second-most valuable name on my wall at the Guildhall," Elsith interrupted. "I've never liked the woman and she has gone out of her way to corrupt every organization she's come into contact with. Mine included. The Guild has agreed to work closely with the Lovers to make sure she is brought to heel for her crimes."

"What crimes would those be?" Hannock asked. "All I've heard of the woman is that she's loose with enough coin to get her way around town."

The exorcist shrugged. "Loose with coin and employed a murderer of her own. Donta was responsible for nearly wiping the Fleets out of the city, he's killed a Huntsman, and bribed another to try to kill me."

"We also found evidence that ties him to a few of the dead refugees that turned up last week," Henderschott added. "I'm glad he's gone. Wish we'd been the ones to do it."

"We also think she's personally responsible for the poisoning and stabbing death of a man named Raes — a local innkeep."

"More than that," Cel interrupted, "Raes was on the Fleet's Council. That son of a bitch Donta... what he did my to friends... whatever burning pit awaits him ain't deep enough."

The Overseer cleared his throat. "You are levying a host of accusations with very dangerous implications. The crimes you are suggesting are far from ones we can ignore."

The priest blinked. "I don't think you should ignore *any* crime," he replied even as Cel huffed in irritation. "But you're correct. That's what we're dealing with," Akaran replied earnestly as he pointed at a pile of tightly-bound papers and scrolls on the large table they sat at. "That mess of paper contains signed statements, testimony, and formal accusations against and by numerous individuals and recognized organizations in the city. We've already brought charges against the former Sergeant-at-Arms of Medias Manor and an Adept from the Annex. Name of Ishtva, if anyone would like to offer testimony against him. Turns out he'd spent time with Anais. We expect more to be added to the list."

"As much as I appreciate the standards of sworn testimony, do you really expect me to believe that there are *vampires* loose in the city? It all sounds like your people pissed off some monster that's come to roost, and you're trying to blame it on... old myths," Paverilak declared with a haughty sneer.

The priest looked back at his handler, and when Brother Levathil nodded his head, he reached down into a pouch at his waist. As everyone watched, he quietly fished out a pair of small objects before he flung them onto the desk. The teeth clattered and bounced into the stack of papers. "You act like you're the first person I had to convince."

Paverilak's sneer slowly turned into a thin frown. "Are those..."

"Fangs," Akaran answered. "I have fangs. Lolron can tell you that they're inhuman. Risson can tell you they're Abyssian. Elsith can likely identify the creature they're from," he replied to the Betrothed, giving a slight nod at each of the three in turn. "Those are from the one that murdered Paladin Faldine. One has been sent to the Headmaster Adept to help develop a tracking method. The other has been sent to... a friend... to help convince some people to work with us. We presume that the other two belonged to Lady Sannah Hosheck."

"SANNAH?!" the Overseer exclaimed. "You can't POSSIBLY mean to –"

"Her signet ring was found at Cableture and she matched the descriptions of one of the vampires that attacked Faldine," the exorcist countered harshly. "She hasn't been seen since and we don't know what her arrangements were with Annix or when she was turned. I have people trying to find out about her even now."

The flush across Hannock's jowls was as bright as the sun, but the rest of the room took the news in stride. "You know, as of late I've only seen her after dark…" Risson interjected.

"When I've seen her at all," Elsith agreed with a growl. "If she was one of Annix's, then she wasn't a recent turn."

"I still can't believe it at all. I won't," Hannock countered. "I've never seen any indication that she's ever been anything but a model citizen of the Queen."

Akaran shrugged his shoulders and gave Levathil a questioning look that the elder priest matched with a nod of approval. They hit a nerve, and that was interesting. "We're still trying to ascertain that she was one of Faldine's attackers, or if she's just one of the missing. We'll let you know when we know more."

Maiden Sanlian's political manager pursed his lips while Hannock scooted back in his chair and the other three reached for the teeth. Elsith had already been convinced before the meeting, but they had decided that it was important to have her proclaim it to the others. "You play hard, don't you," Paverilak mused under his breath. "So let's assume – or at least, entertain you – in your presumption that it is a vampire. What do you intend to do about it?"

"I think the bigger question is: What about Malik?" the Huntsmatron interrupted. "If we buy into the Lover's theory that this creature is trying to spread chaos, then our missing groom may be a bigger problem than the Overseer suggested."

"Oh, the diplomatic incident is finally being addressed, is it?" Henderschott grumbled from the corner. "I don't want to think about what happens if Akaran is right. We just hung the head of the Woodmason's Guild and wrecked half of Lower Naradol looking for him," he vented as Cel made a very nasty gesture in his direction.

Hannock shifted in his seat and tried to straighten his red fox-fur jacket. "It's safe to say that the whole city is already looking for him. No matter who has him, we'll find him."

"You may want to find him faster," Akaran murmured. "Because I know I'm right – and if Annix has him? What would be more embarrassing than doing to the Son of Odinal what he did with the battlemage? Can you imagine if he was turned…?"

The Lieutenant-Commander lost all color in his face. "You don't… he wouldn't."

Risson straightened up and his eyes went wide as the same thought dawned on the Betrothed. "Good man, that is a horrific thought."

"I don't get paid for pleasant ones."

"I've worked with your people," Elsith grunted. "You don't get paid."

Akaran started to make a retort, but he let it slide.

The Upper Adjunct looked down at the fangs and quickly coerced a streamer of light from his fingertips. The spell lightly caressed the pieces of bone before the tendril *flinched* and vanished into thin air. "I cannot say what manner of beast those belonged to with certainty, but it isn't of this world. Overseer, I'd listen very closely to this man."

"He can listen while you answer me," Henderschott interrupted as he addressed the exorcist. "It's bad enough that Malik is missing. I cannot begin to tell you how much blood would be spilled if he ends up dead. If he ends up like one of those *things* that ripped up Cableture?" he hypothetically asked before he cracked his neck and looked down at the floor. "Akaran... this whole city. Whatever the Odinals don't tear down the resulting riots... what are we supposed to do?"

Paverilak let out a breath he didn't know he was holding. "I cannot begin to fathom the measures that Sanlian would take to restore control. Nor do I want to imagine how irate the Queen would be in such a situation."

"Or the Holy General," Akaran added. "If this gets any worse than it is right now, there isn't a single person in this room that wouldn't be better off getting on a boat and going to Golden Empire of Matheia *tonight*. Even the assholes in *Ogibus* would be preferable, if it comes to that."

A very uncomfortable, incredibly miserable, and painfully crushing silence filled the room as everyone digested the warnings. Finally, it was Lolron – of all people – who spoke up. "I only speak in interests of the Annex. I recognize that city security is not something that the Granalchi are often interested in, outside of what you contract us for," the Adept began as he slowly worked the thought out, "and with that statement made, as painful as it will be for the city at large, I am sure, I strongly recommend that you listen to the priest."

"If the priest says something worth noting, then –" the Overseer began before Paverilak cut him off.

"This is no longer a matter of mere city leadership nor local security. I understand that your superior has issued an Order of Inquiry, has she not?" the Betrothed asked with a flat, disgusted tone to every word that left his lips.

"She has."

"That does grant her specific powers over the Grand Army and any civilian enforcement. I suspect that she has included a sworn statement transferring a portion of that oversight to you?"

"With some exclusions," Brother Levathil clarified, "though I will confirm that she did."

Paverilak made a disgusted guttural noise from low in his throat. "Then what would you have us do?"

Akaran looked around the room and took a very long, very deep breath. He had the attention – if not the support – of almost all of the most powerful people in the city. He had the blessing of the Order, the support of the Guild, and a conversation with Henderschott earlier had secured the backing of the Guard. All he needed now was to live to his rank in the temple.

Be a Messenger of Love.

For once, the message wasn't 'fisk you.'

"Well, Hannock. It was a nice city you had here."

The Overseer blanched and placed his hand just below his throat nervously. "What do you mean by had?"

"I think he means he plans to burn everything down," the Lieutenant-Commander quipped with a resigned smirk. Nor was he wrong. In fact, he was closer to being right than he'd realized.

The exorcist sent a short prayer and then laid down the temporary sigil of rank his boss had given him. Paverilak growled under his breath at the sight of it and Elsith shot him a raw look of disbelief. "I've been told to do this regardless of if you like it or not. So learn to like it and it'll go easier on all of us."

Cel had a comment for that which suggested he'd never had an evening with a woman that he hadn't paid for. The Huntsmatron had an equally scathing retort that she kept under her breath. Even Lolron bristled a little.

Their objections to his borderline-insolent comments aside, Akaran tore into the setup he'd worked on with Badin, Henderschott, and a few others over the last day. He'd assembled a surprisingly effective war-council of his own, both in-Order and out. They all had their reasons to help, although at the end of day, it resulted in the same long-term goal.

Fortunately, a few recent events worked in their favor – the first of which were the refugees from Mardux. "We had to shove them in so many places that half of the basements, cellars, warehouses, *and* a third of the tunnels have been packed to the brim. Aside from a couple of deaths, nobody has gone missing… or reported any kind of nest."

"Those deaths have mostly been declared natural and accidental," Henderschott added while Akaran took a drink. "Except for three. Two of them are now suspected to be the work of Donta and Anais, and the final one is up in the air – but not the vampire. The Guard and the Order did a combined investigation on it. Donta, probably – asshole left bone-shards at the scene."

With fewer places to hide, that made their work easier. The next argument was less pleasant and a bit more circumspect. The exorcist laid out some of the work he had arranged with the Fleet-Finger's Guild and heaped ample credit in their direction. "They don't want us digging through the city any more than we want to do it," he explained, "so they've gone to great measures to work through their territories. They've found a few locations that suggested concern, and there are Order Wardkeepers and Messengers of Love currently dealing with those situations."

When pressed, he'd only say that every city had 'bottom-feeders,' and 'leftovers.' Brother Levathil took a moment to speak up from under his thick wool-and-fur coat to suggest that they would all be happier not knowing. They both stressed to Risson that he'd need to have extra tenders at the Pyre before the day was out.

Asked again, neither of them would clarify *why*.

However, when Hannock dared to ask *how* the Fleets were supposed to track down or identify *problem* areas, Akaran jumped on it with gusto. "The same way that the Guard is going to," he replied as he fished out a small trinket from his utility pouch. "These gems are imbued with a couple of enchantments. They won't last long. Few days, a week at most. They'll glow when in the presence of Abyssian influences."

Upper Adjunct Risson took that moment to speak up. "Exor... excuse me. *Paladin* DeHawk, while I freely admit that I am no full scholar on the machinations of the condemned, it is my understanding that vampires are not true beasts of the pit. If those stones are attuned to Abyssians, wouldn't they miss the aura of a more worldly, Kora-born creature?"

He was actually correct, to a point. "You're right – the old lore says that the Abyss actively loathes them and that there is a special place in perdition for creatures of that ilk. What was it..."

"I believe it goes, '*In the place of the Quiet where Wrath is Silent, the Sire of the First Fang burns evermore, a light in the sky to bathe the muted damned,*' which... it does paint a picture of punishment," Levathil replied. "It is long said that the first vampire is the son of Covorn, the God of Wrath. His realm – it is said – is simply called *Covorn's Quiet*."

"So, there. The Abyss hates the child of wrath. Now that you know that – the answer is that our Messengers and Scyers can track them specifically, but it takes corpse-ash... and we were only able to recover a minimal amount at Cableture."

"However," the representative from the Granalchi Academy offered, "regardless of the true nature, Headmaster Gorosoch developed a way to craft an enchantment that will identify places and persons steeped in death. The void left behind in the ether when a soul passes on is soon filled by energies both holy and not, regardless of the… shall we call it, *disposition* of the individual in question. We must assume that the nature of this monster is to feed, and feeding does not leave behind living husks for very long."

"Same way that wild magics and Abyssian taints normally enters the world. Open a door and you get a draft," Akaran added. "Lolron, Elsith, please give my thanks once again to Telburn."

The Huntsmatron gave him a wolfish grin. "I should thank you. That idea bought us a new house."

"Bought you a…" Hannock began as a few more beads of sweat erupted on his forehead. "Boy? The Granalchi don't work for free. How, exactly, are you paying for this?"

"After he leaves town, I'd put a new lock on your treasury door," Henderschott answered with a bemused grin of his own.

Akaran didn't bother to answer the question. "It's important to get the darker places checked out first. That's why I made arrangements with the Fleets instead of the Guard. With full respect to Henderschott, the thieves know where all the best hiding places are."

"With respect?" The Lieutenant-Commander quoted. "That's a first."

Undeterred by the sarcasm, he went on with his plan. Telburn and the rest of the Academy were hard at work producing as many gems as possible, but it would take time before the guard could be outfitted with them even at a rate of one stone per five soldiers – and there were only so many men available to the Order. It was going to take a few days for Catherine to complete her sweep of Cableture, although once she was done?

"Not only will the Repository be brought fully to bear on the hunt for Annix, Admiral Maddon will be dispatching as many Fleetsmen up the canyon as he can spare," Akaran confirmed. "Henderschott's going to have more men keeping the peace than he knows how to deal with."

"Do you mean to suggest that the Repository is more interested in the events in the port than they are hunting down a supposed vampire?" Paverilak interrupted. "That makes a very strong suggestion that Maiden-Templar Prostil isn't being as forthcoming as to the nature of the *other* assault as she claimed."

Before the Exorcist-turned-Paladin could answer, his handler very loudly – and very ominously – cleared his throat. "Uh. It was pirates, good sirrah. *Sycian. Pirates,*" he stressed.

The Betrothed flattened his lips into a razor-thin smile. "Of course. I would never doubt the *validity* and *accuracy* of *sworn testimony* from one of the Queen's own Maidens."

"I think it's a wonderful thing that you don't," Akaran admitted.

"All of that aside," Henderschott interrupted, "you still haven't explained exactly how you think this is going to unfold."

"Because I don't know. This son-of-a-bitch has significant magic at his fingertips. It's also *fisking* smart. Smart enough to out-play the Order. Smart enough to out-wit Ridora. Smart enough to hide itself from *you* for *years*. We start by trying to flush it out – and use every mage capable of putting down wards to be alerted if it goes into any of the territories we've pushed on."

Elsith snapped her fingers and suddenly sat up straight. "Oh! I meant to tell you – my lovely Telburn was able to decipher the spell you found at the Manor; the one you attributed to this fang-faced bastard. He said, 'Tell the boy there's a good reason he didn't understand it; it was written in *Ameggenon,*' though he didn't say more than that. He did confirm it was a masking spell, and you were correct in the assumption that it was based in a call to the, and I quote, 'the raw elemental unmanageable, the essence of chaos itself,' end-quote."

"Ameggen–?" the priest began to ask before Lolron interrupted with a shocked gasp.

"Oh! Well that's *absolutely* troubling. I'll save you from speaking the inquiry; that's the language of the elves."

Akaran blinked. "Elvish? I didn't... look I'm not a scholar, I think we can all agree on that, but I didn't think anyone spoke...?"

"People don't. Nobody has. Not since they were exterminated."

"A dead thing speaks in a dead language," Risson dismissed with a wave of his hand. "I have to say that of all the accusations laid, that is the least shocking."

The Adept, however, just shook his head. "It's more than 'speaking' in a forgotten tongue. Any child can learn a word and repeat it, but it takes someone of great intellect or control to be so fluent and have such a command over it to use it as the basis of magic – especially in Ameggenon. The Elvish *moyapods,* as they were called, were truly etheric savants. They were beyond the understanding of ether that we have as humans. Their connection... it was a crushing blow to the world when they were lost."

"Not as lost as you'd want," Sua grunted from his corner.

He had a point, and it hurt to consider it. "So not just smart, but *fisking* smart," Akaran grunted.

Lolron shook his head again. "Ah, no. Let me be clear: there isn't a soul in this city that has the power to channel their spells in *any* tongue, let alone the base of elven spellcraft. We could only be so lucky to assume that it is merely *fisking* smart. I would dare suggest it means that it is fisking *old*. I would also caution that any magic that you plan to use against it to trap it or ward it away is only as good as the lack of interest he has on whatever is behind it – I would not count on a ward to save a life in this case."

"Oh that's bloody wonderful," the priest groused under his breath. "Brother, can you make sure...?"

"Catherine will be notified at once," Levathil grumbled. "The idea of a vampire is poor enough. The suggestion that it may have existed since before the time of the Crusade of Suns is intolerable. The possibility that it can undo our magic? Preposterous, under circumstances, but these times are far from. That is a warning well-taken. We won't ignore further ones handed to us."

The younger Lover had to give a quiet agreement to that. "So right now, we get as many Guardsmen ripping through the more affluent areas as we can. We've established it isn't stupid, so it might try to hide out in plain sight somewhere. Or just as likely, it has more than one nest so it isn't forced to retrace its steps every night. The Fleet-Fingers are going to turn out the gutters, and the Order is going to respond to anything either group finds," he reiterated. "That leaves dealing with the night – and that means that Risson? I need to put the Staras to work."

"The souls under my preview are always at work, Sir Exorcist."

"Paladin," Akaran corrected, "and if you call what they do work, then sure. What I need is to have your men blanket the city. Consider it... outreach."

"Interim," the Uppa-Adjunct countered. "Do I dare ask what you mean by *outreach*?"

The temporary-Paladin pursed his lips and scratched at the stubble growing back in on his chin. "Well. The Guard isn't welcomed in certain areas, and the thieves can only do so much. What I want your people to do is to start spreading the Good Word. I don't care *which* word but I want them out and about in the city. Talk to people. Bring food. Bring water. Check people for injuries."

Risson frowned and tilted his head to the side. "We already do all those things."

"Maybe once a month," Akaran returned, "though we're not saints in that regard either," he admitted before the Adjunct could argue. "Spread wide. Spread far. Set up extra outposts in the city — small shrines, waystations, whatever. Encourage people to come by. Ask questions about the missing. What I need most from you is to be eyes and ears."

"You want us to interrogate the good people of the crown under the guise of providing aid and comfort? That doesn't feel... morally acceptable."

"Well it's that or it's feeding more bodies to the pyre when we find them — and we *will* find them. Maybe not today, maybe not tomorrow, but we'll find them," the Lover countered as he pointed over at the Adjunct. "Besides. It'll give you an opportunity to help calm down the locals, spread the Words of your Gods, and try to improve the overall health of the city. Healthy and happy people are people that won't want to riot."

"And I do like it when people *aren't* rioting," Paverilak interrupted. "I will see to it that the Staras are appropriately assisted in establishing checkpoints for you. Do you have a preference...?"

Akaran thought on it for a moment and shrugged. "Upper and Lower Naradol. The merc district. The ones over near the Ellachurstine and the Stara shrine are already well-covered. The tradesman's district too. The Fleets have the merchantile sections."

Maiden Sanlian's Betrothed slowly nodded his head in agreement. "I do have to say, for a young one, you have a head for this. As much as I detest that you have brought this to my doorstep, I admire your conviction."

"That makes one of us," Henderschott grumbled from the side. "What about Malik? The Odinals are in the street *right now* trying to find him. I nearly got *stabbed* by one of their Warmaidens this morning when I told her I didn't have any news."

The Lover took a deep sigh and looked down at his hands. "I'm going to take personal responsibility for his safety. Please have anyone that knows anything about it talk to me about his abduction. He's a friend," Akaran added, "and I've already had to execute one person I knew. I don't want to make it two."

"I don't recall the Lovers declaring an execution," Hannock slid in. "That sounds almost like a disregard of the law."

Akaran pointed at the two fangs and glared at the Overseer in disgust. "Those teeth didn't fall out of the sky. Raechil Lamar, if you knew her."

Henderschott cursed under his breath. "I did. She was kind. Her sister, not so much, but she was kind."

"I will agree on the sister issue. Are you sure it was her?" the Adjunct asked.

"I'm sure neither of them will be a concern for you anymore," he answered with a pained sigh. "If we don't find Malik before Annix turns him, he'll go on the list."

"The enough chatter," Hannock rumbled. "I may not approve of what you plan, but something must be done. I suggest that if we wish peace, then we must move quickly."

Akaran turned his attention back to his handler and frowned. "Brother Levathil? A favor to ask you."

The Lover smiled warmly, almost like he was someone's grandfather looking down at his children's children. "You know no favors need to be asked of the Order. What is it you need?"

That was a lie, and they both knew it. "If Annix is this... mega-mage..."

"Moyapod," Lolron interjected quickly. "It isn't that they are of such greater skill than us but if the books are accurate in their description –"

"If Annix is a *moyapod*," Akaran interrupted, "and that has the Granalchi in a fit, I'm worried about our people. Make sure anyone that might be a target gets a burn-bag. That includes Bistra."

Henderschott rolled back on his heels as a troubled look crossed his face. "Burn-bag? I recognize the fact that you're planning on setting fire to the city but if we're going to hand patients in the asylum something with that kind of name, I want to know more about it."

"It's nothing you have to worry about," Akaran downplayed. "It's just a trick we have."

"Illiya assumed fire was a trick when She first handed it down from the sky, child. I'm with the Lieutenant-Commander – tricks from your Order do not always work well," Lolron interjected.

Levathil's smile faded almost immediately as he ignored them entirely. "That would be more than a few spells to prepare. Those kits are not quickly crafted."

"Which is easier? Growing and training a new Maiden-Templar or shoving some silver and sulfur in a burlap sack and yelling Words at it?"

The Lover laced his withered fingers together and cracked a single knuckle. "I do hope the rest of the room understands that our work is more involved than merely just... *yelling Words* at things."

"Oh, yeah. They also know we *mutter* words at things, too," Akaran grunted as he looked around the room. Reluctantly, the other headaches and assembled leaderships signed off on his plan one after another. "One more thing," he added as the last of them agreed to his plans. "I need to find someone – the Tidesinger. Anyone have any idea where he went?"

"Quinchecco?" Risson asked with a confused blink. "Now that you mention it, he hasn't been by the temple since yesterday morning. That's quite odd for him."

All the exorcist could do was just utter a simple, heartfelt, "Shit," under his breath. "Find him. I've got it on good authority that Anais is looking for him. I don't know why, but... it's safe to say that *all of us* should want to stop her from getting to him first."

Everyone agreed with certain levels of irritation, grumbles, and concession. Even the Overseer made a choice remark about '*Being sure that she doesn't get what she wants.*' The protests were noted, acknowledged, and promptly ignored.

Shortly after – and after an impassioned request for a prayer from Risson to bless them all in their journeys – the gathered assembly broke away. The newly-minted paladin left before just about anyone else, though he was cut short in his efforts to leave the estate. As soon as she was out of the old musty meeting room, Henderschott got his attention.

Forcefully.

The Lieutenant grabbed Akaran's arm so hard that he almost pulled the priest down to the floor. While the younger man protested the rough treatment, the reason was stated with such blunt crassness that it shocked everyone that overheard. "What the fisk did you do to Seline?"

The priest shook him off and gave the soldier a bewildered-yet-disgusted look. "Not a damn thing. Why?"

"Don't fisking bullshit me, you asshole," the L-Comm seethed. "Last I saw her, she was drunk, pissed, and scared. Since I have *never* seen her drunk *or* scared, *and* your name was all over her lips, I want to know exactly what the fisk you did to her. Or with her."

"Nothing, Hender, I swear," Akaran offered in return. "Last I saw her was at the docks. Last I know, she got away safe when Darin... when the *pirates* attacked."

"Don't even shit me on the *pirates*," the guard growled. "I don't care what bullshit you peddle to them, or *why*, but to me? No. You don't get to do that. I also don't give a damn. She was upset *before* that, and you were *why*."

The exorcist tugged his arm free and rubbed at what he was sure was going to end up being an ugly bruise on his upper arm. "Annix was at the Manor. I broke a spell he was using. It got ugly. She was okay when I left her. She was okay when I saw her at the docks. I *swear it*, Henderschott."

"Then where is she now?"

"How should I know? I'm not her keeper."

The Lieutenant didn't blink. Didn't flinch. Didn't bother giving a warning. Instead, he hauled off and *punched* Akaran in the gut. The rage-filled blow connected *solidly* against the wound that Raechil and Ettaquis had opened up before they'd been excised in the hold of the *Shatterstorm*.

Akaran doubled over with a loud groan of pain and wrapped his arms around his stomach. Henderschott caught him and pressed himself up against the priest with a growl. "She was *yours*, you ungrateful piece of shit, and whatever she saw you do *really fisked with her head*. I don't care *what you did* at the Manor, or what fisking shit you did at the docks, the *only* fisking thing I care about is where she is. You don't know? Then you're *going* to find her."

The priest gagged and spat up something unpleasant as he hugged his gut and leaned against the wall. "Didn't think... you two... liked each other..."

"That's not any of your damn business. So help me, if she doesn't turn up safe, it's your head. I'll take it myself." Henderschott grabbed the priest by his throat and shoved up upright with more strength than Akaran had given him credit for. "Do you fisking understand me?"

As the room emptied, Risson and Lolron stumbled into the argument and watched the exchange with their eyes wide – and mouths shut. "Hender, I like her. She's... mostly wonderful. I want her safe as much as you do."

"Oh I doubt that," the Lieutenant grumbled. "In fact, you better like her *less* than I do or there's going to be even *more* grief on your head than what you've got. *Find her* or I'll find *you*."

"Jealous prick," the priest managed to mutter under his breath.

"In ways you wouldn't understand," Henderschott spat as he stormed off without another word.

Akaran rested against the wall in silence as the representatives from the Staras and the Annex decided that, maybe just this once, that discretion would be a better part of valor and moved along without comment. Brother Levathil, however, had no such interest in silence. "My boy? I recognize that we are often tasked to get to the blunt truth of a matter, but you'll have to learn to find ways to use your tongue in a way that doesn't entice people to want to remove it."

"Not the first time I've been punched this week," the exorcist sighed in resignation. "Probably not the last."

"A statement that is all-but assured," the elder Lover agreed. "You're bleeding again... I sense a call for the seamstress is in order."

"Seamstress? I need a healer."

"Child, as often as you suffer gashes and worse, it's best you learn how to tend to your wounds as a tailor. You'll be able to apply the skill in many ways, not just to flesh."

While he waited for that, an unfortunate set of truths was about to be uncovered, by the one person responsible for two of the city's prominently missing.

***

"Before we begin, I want you to understand that I have a great deal of respect for a man in your position," the bewitching, graying, and thin woman intoned from the basement doorway, "although I most assuredly do not have envy."

Her captive looked up at her from the corner of the poorly-lit, very flooded, basement dwelling. He had no idea where he was at, though judging by the smell, he assumed they were somewhere near the Orshia Overflow in Lower Naradol. The only blessing was that it was still in the city; the way that her thugs had jumped him last night, he was grateful that he was still in Basion. She could've had him anywhere by now – and he didn't realize that's exactly where her employer wanted him to be. "Everyone envies me," he croaked, "it's my wonderful singing voice."

Anais looked down at him with what he had to hope was a bemused smile, though in the dim, he couldn't tell. "Oh, Quinchecco. You don't mind if I call you that, do you? 'Tidesinger Quinchecco, High Priest of Aqualla,' doesn't exactly roll off of the tongue."

The Aquallan shook his head – which was one of very few things he *could* move. She had him tied down to a rickety wooden chair so thoroughly that his head, toes, and maybe two fingers were all he could safely get to budge. "Madam, I don't think that you invited me here the way you did to exchange pleasantries."

She nodded and slowly sauntered toward him across a few dry floorboards. Half of the basement was badly flooded, to the extent that he was reasonably sure he could swim away if the back wall was half as rotted as it looked. It wasn't uncommon for some of the buildings in Naradol to be designed *to* flood whenever the Overflow crested. In fact, some of the richer merchants would even set up crab traps and only block

32

a lower wall out with rusted bars or thin slats of stone.

The downside was that it smelled like a sewer. A moldy, musty, dank sewer laden with rot and a thin sheet of sickly-yellow algae. "I am afraid that I did not, no. Should I assume that you know who I am, or must I...?"

"Anais Lovic, isn't it?" he croaked. "Disgraced broker of secrets, stories, and conniver of coin?"

"Conniver of coin?" the aging woman mused with her tongue planted in her cheek. "I daresay that's a new one. Merchant of Secrets is the usual title – or Broker of Secrets. Conniver... hmm," she mused as the faint smile turned into a much larger one. "I am suddenly beginning to wish that our circumstances were much different."

Quinchecco looked up at her with his auburn eyes as the ends of his pointed, elf-like ears twitched. "If anyone can change them, it would be you."

Her smile faltered as she took a single step back with a resigned sigh. "No, I'm afraid it isn't. For what it's worth, you're not here for any reason of mine and I personally bear you no ill-will, despite how it must seem."

The priest lowered his head to his chest. "Hunted by the city, you exchange jobs from secrets to kidnapping? With respect, Lady Lovic, it seems you've had a fall from grace."

"Oh my dear man, you have no idea the depths of which I have fallen and risen in my time," she admitted as she pulled a piece of flint out from a dirty brown robe she'd found and struck it idly against the base of a small sconce on the wall. A few strokes later, and she'd successfully lit the one lamp in the entirety of the ruined room. "Though others have recently fallen even lower than I," she added as she glanced towards the far wall. With a gesture, a small candle caught fire and a squirming, gagged, and hooded young woman came into view.

The Aquallan looked at the huddled lump in a filthy dress and then cast his eyes back at their captor. "I try to keep a peaceful, respectful tongue even in the face of great discomfort, Lady Lovic, but..."

"Which I do truly respect and appreciate, believe me. You are one of the few. Most at this point would have tried to scream for help or fill the air with enough invectives to set my hair on fire. "

"Would it do me any good if I did?"

"No," Anais admitted, "though a few choice bouts of vile words does tend to alleviate minor stress. That said, I am aware that you likely don't feel that this is a minor event. Though, I will add before we begin, that this isn't personal."

"Such a relief," the priest drolly replied. "Not to place a fine point on the situation, but I sense that you intend to do more than tie me up and idly chat...?"

The broker nodded sagely. "Yes. I'll cut to it: I am employed by a very powerful man whom you have unwittingly had dealings with as of late. You know something that he doesn't, and I've been tasked to collect you."

Quinchecco blinked and looked around the dilapidated basement again. "There's more to it, isn't there?" he asked slowly. "If this was simply... well, *with respect*, a simple kidnapping... you wouldn't even talk to me."

"I had heard you were a wise man. I appreciate that you live up to the reputation," Anais confirmed with that faint little smile on her gaunt, wrinkled face. "You know something that my benefactor would like to know and I would like to know what that is. It might even be safer for you if you told me."

"There's easier ways than abducting me to get answers."

"No, I'm afraid that there aren't," she countered. "In all honesty, I should already have you well on your way out of town by now, and not safely stored under it. Understand the quite literal 'grave risk' I place us both in by having your extraction put to a pause."

The priest glared up at her and tried to twist his hands in the ropes behind his back. "You abducted me and say that I'm in even more risk than if you had just handed me over?"

Anais nodded as she slowly began to take her hair down. "Yes. Now. I have questions, and you have answers. The problem is, I'm not sure which question is the right one – or what answers you may know. Plus... to be honest, I must imagine that your people are busy turning over every rock and log in the city to try to find you right now. Time is not my friend, which means it is not *your* friend."

Something about the way she said that made his damp skin grow cold. "I suspect the time for good manners is over?"

"No, please, no. I welcome this change of polite, even if strained, dialogue," she countered as she walked over to the quivering, muffled lump in the corner. "What I mean to say is that this interrogation will be short, in one way or another."

"Tell you what I want to know or you'll kill me? I don't think your Master would approve."

"He wouldn't, but he has his ways of getting answers even past the Veil," Anais admitted. "As do I. We are both very practiced hands with Deadcall – you're aware of that particular method of magic, are you not?"

Quinchecco blanched. "To commune with the dead..."

The broker shook her head and grabbed the burlap bag covering her other captive's head. "To force the dead to not just speak of this world and the next, but to speak and be truthful."

He swallowed nervously as he sized her up all over again. "You would've killed me already if you needed it that badly. Unless you really need me alive."

"Contrary to popular belief, I have enough blood on my hands. I do not look to add more – and yes, your life is very important to me. I was not tasked to send you to my benefactor in a box. I was tasked to deliver you alive, and mostly well," she answered as she touched her throat and tried to fondle a necklace that wasn't there anymore. "His *pet* even demanded that I turn over a relic from the Stonehewn – just in case it might make me *tempted* to do unkind things to you."

"Then why suggest it? I do not think that you need much temptation."

"I know more of temptation in death than I ever knew to use in life," the broker countered. "Just because I do not *wish* kill doesn't mean that I am not *able* to kill, or that I *won't* kill if you force my hand," she countered. "So: pleasantries aside. The Urn of Xabraxis. Do you know it?"

He blinked in confusion. "The Urn of...?"

"That would be no," Anais said with a disgusted little curl of her lips. "Abyssia? Do you know of her?"

"Abyssia...? What sort of name...?"

"A demonic one, so no, not that," she mused. "He did give me such a list back at first breath," she muttered under her breath. "Perhaps the Axe of Nightmares – or the Diamantic Blade? Would either of those ring a bell in that rather fluid skull of yours?" the broker asked as she untied a rough stretch of rope she'd fashioned into a makeshift leash for her other captive.

Quinchecco struggled against his bonds and tried to move the chair to no avail. "Lovic, I have no idea what you're talking about. Let us go. Please."

Anais pulled the hood off of her other captive and sighed as the young blonde looked up, her sweet-brown eyes brimming with tears and terror. "I've already expressed that your wish in that regard is much less than possible, and warned that I don't have much time. My benefactor already attempted to discover what you knew once, and many people died with the effort. One more, if I must, will not add much to that tally. Seline would object but he wouldn't care either way."

The Aquallan's eyes went wide. "Sel... that's Missus Valdin! What did that girl do to you?!"

"Nothing," Anais replied hastily. "As far as I know, despite an alliance with someone that wishes me harm, she's done absolutely nothing that would cause her to deserve any of this."

"Then let her go!" he demanded at the top of his lungs.

The broker wrapped her fingers at the base of Seline's hair and pulled her over to the water's edge almost effortlessly. "I'm afraid I really can't. I *cannot* harm you, or my benefactor will do things to me that defy the Laws of Normality. However…"

Quinchecco could see where she was going with this, and for the first time since waking up in her clutches, suddenly felt utterly powerless. "Whatever you're getting ready to do, don't."

"Then give me a reason *not* to," his captor retorted. "Rishnobia, by chance? Have you met that disgusting little mote? Or are you harboring secrets of something much more based in the waves – you wouldn't happen to know where Admiral Roschell is, by chance? The Graveyard would be a very big prize, all things considered."

"What would anyone want with that cursed flotsam?!" the priest shouted even though his eyes narrowed defensively. "He's not even *real*! He's a *myth*!"

Anais flinched and nearly dropped the blonde-haired healer. "Oh please don't say something so stupid. Not when I hold you in such high esteem," she lamented. "There are many things in this world that people like you believe to be myths that are not. Would you like to see one?"

Seline screamed and shook her head so violently that she caused the broker to inadvertently pull a chunk of her hair out, and a chunk of her bloody scalp with it. She desperately tried to tell the priest not to ask that, not to agree, not to say yes. Anais gripped her tighter and marched her on her hands and knees to the flooded floor.

Her pleas fell on deaf ears. "A liar, kidnapper, and murderer? If you think you can surprise me more, you're not just a monster – you're *deluded*."

"Monster?" she replied with a laugh. "I suppose this means that the time for pleasantries really has ended, hasn't it? Very well. But first: it is true, isn't it? True that the Tidesingers are blessed by Aqualla to be able to hear anything in the water? That your sense of hearing beneath the waves is far greater than anything you have on land?"

Quinchecco looked at her and then down at her bloody, terrified prisoner. "Don't do it. You don't have to drown her. *I don't know what you want*."

"I believe you, and that's unfortunate. I also can't risk her screaming while I try to convince you, which she will, but if she screams when I do this?" Anais returned with an aggravated sigh. Before he could even begin to beg her not to do it, the broker shoved Seline's head into the brackish water and held her down. "Then *only* you hear it. Hopefully, that will serve as your motivation."

The healer *did* scream. She screamed, she thrashed, and she buckled in Anais's super-human grip. Seline couldn't do anything else with her hands tied behind her back and her legs bound together at her shins. Floodwater splashed all over the broker and ruined her already-filthy gown.

"I know torture. I know suffering. I have no delight in causing it, but she *will* live. *How* she lives is up to you."

"Anais, no! Stop it!"

But as Seline screamed and the Aquallan tried to order Anais to stop, the broker went a step further. Her glamour faded and unveiled who she really was to his terrified eyes. "Now. About 'myths' and 'monsters,' I think you may understand you're very much in the lair of one of both – so let's try this again."

The medicannia couldn't hear the questioning. She struggled to breathe, and swallowed air every time that the broker let her up from the awful water. Her chest felt like it was about to explode and her eyes burned from the toxic watery waste, but none of that scared her as much as the scorpion-like tail that slowly unwound from Anais's neck...

...right before her head was pushed back under the surface.

***

To her well-deserved credit, the seamstress did an absolutely wonderful job. To Akaran's credit, he kept the screaming down to a few muted curses. A special mention should also be made to the maid that found him a clean shirt after he was pointedly told that he, "would not be permitted to enter the city at large with the appearance of being tortured by the Overseer's assistants," despite how appropriate that may have felt.

What he ended up with was a delay that he didn't want to deal with. For a change, it was a pause that ultimately worked out in his favor. Once he left the Overseer's estate, the next stop on his list was a long hike towards Thesd Villa – one of Anais's former bases of operation. It wasn't likely to give any leads on the vampire, but he long-ago decided that any new information was going to be good information.

Even if he didn't like it.

Nor did he like it when it found him.

He liked the messenger almost less, although the feeling was mutual.

He hadn't even made it halfway to Thesd before a grumpy, muscular, absolute *weapon* of a man chased him down and called out his name in the middle of the street. The only thing that kept the priest from drawing his blade and getting into a fight on the spot was the sole fact that it was still light out – and he didn't think that anyone was ballsy enough to try to kill him in broad daylight… in public.

Though after he thought about it, he realized it might be more likely than he'd want to admit. This man didn't have murder on his mind – or if he did, not Akaran's – but he did have a message. He looked somewhat familiar, though it wasn't until the exorcist noticed the hateful *look* that this walking human wall gave his cane that he pieced it together.

"Didn't I hit you with my stick a few days ago? When I was trying to find the Oldstone?"

The bodyguard-apparent growled low and slow in the back of his throat but didn't rise to the bait. "He wants you."

"That's a first," the exorcist replied quickly. "Why?"

The Oldstone – otherwise known as Altund Obermesc – was the resident Speaker of Stone for the city. The Order of the Unders wasn't exactly a *popular* religion, and their patron God, Stilamatheric, the Stonehewn, rarely gave a solid shit about what humans were up to. Still, their Order had some sway in a city sunk into a pit and surrounded on all sides by stone walls and more tunnels than you could find your way through on a drunken bet.

His bodyguards, however, were not as stony as their looks would have you believe. When he'd had to go get the Speaker's attention, they'd tried to stop him. A few embarrassing (for them) moments – and some crafty stickwork – later, and he'd disproved their reputation of being a cadre of well-trained fighters.

It was unfortunate that Altund had the personality of a slug, and the girth to match. He was one of the absolute least pleasant people that Akaran had met so far in his time in Basion, and that included at least three different dead women that were still milling about in the world despite their lack of a pulse. *Or at least two dead women. I wish I knew what happened to Rmaci*, the priest wondered to himself as the Oldstone's bodyguard lead him out of the main thoroughfare.

"Behind the Falls," the gruff and scruffy soldier grumbled in hushed tones. "Found something you'd want."

The exorcist frowned and leaned against a nearby wall. "I know he's far from my biggest supporter in the city. Why would he give me anything?"

"Don't know. Don't care."

"Did he at least say what it was?"

"A perversion."

That wasn't the answer he had hoped for. At the same time, he had a sinking feeling it was the best one he was going to get. "No offense to the Speaker, but anything that meets his standards of *perversion* doesn't give me warm and fuzzy feelings."

The jab earned him a smirk from the tanned, dark-haired, and very armored guard-turned-courier. "Shouldn't. He found bodies. Bring your friends."

"He found bodies and sent you to me? I assume the Guard is already there?"

"No."

Any hope he had that he could take his time vanished in a heartbeat. "He found bodies, sent for me, and *hasn't* told that fool with the right hook about it? I'm going to ask again: why?"

The handsome mountain of a man just shrugged. "Fourth stop up on lift. Ask for Ethod. He'll take you there. Bring your friends," he stressed. "Lots of work to be done. The Stone says these graves belong to you to dig."

There was something about the way he said that... "The Oldstone, you mean?" Akaran asked with a little trepidation. "Or..."

"Stone speaks to Speaker. Speaker speaks. Stone is Stone."

When Altund's man left — and was well out of earshot — the priest unleashed a series of profane invectives that caught the attention of a random passer-by. He didn't particularly care, and he didn't stop unleashing them, but he did take a moment to explain himself to a frightened young woman who looked at him like he had two heads. "All I'm saying," he tried to explain, "is that the Istalla twits keep ranting about how 'Ice preserves' and 'ice protects.' And the Pristi types? All about how, 'With Light comes a cleansing.' Now apparently it's 'The Stone speaks and the Speaker Speaks of the Stone Speaking,' from *these* idiots," he groused.

The poor girl just smiled nervously and nodded along in agreement.

He ignored her painfully obvious discomfort and wrapped one hand around the hilt of his sword and the other around the head of his cane. "Elemantalists. Gods help all of us if they ever get to a damn *point*."

***

The Safest City in the Kingdom.

It was a misnomer.

The corpse at her feet would agree. As would the one beside her. The soon-to-be-a-corpse a few yards away would agree, too, if his lips hadn't been sewn shut. He was too busy digging grave after grave to care about such idle thoughts regardless. Yannis, by name. A gardener in life, a gravedigger at the end of it. It was a fate that was oddly fitting.

The city was called safe only because it was hard to break into – if you were an army. It wasn't uncommon to see people who had suffered from idle bands of raiders or bandits seek refuge here. It wasn't uncommon to see men weary of war retire on the buildings packed in tight rows under looming cliffs. It was safe because few mundane threats could be bothered to take the effort to invade – and it would take a great deal of effort.

Except that was for threats of mundane. There were other threats. Worse threats. More insidious. To be sure, the presence of both the Manor and the Repository had their own effects on the safety of the population. A lost soul, a wraith, a remnant of the deceased? You'd find plenty in most cities.

The presence of so many guards, guardians, and priests – the 'not-nice kind,' as a certain one in particular often says – reduced both the rate and duration of any such abomination. That wasn't to say that the Order (any of the Orders) dug around in every nook and cranny, but they had a way of dealing with hard-to-ignore and sometimes hard-to-find threats.

Yet for all of their efforts, darkness did prevail. If it was smart.

Which was the very crux of their current failure.

All of the dead hated the day. Some because it reminded them of the lives they once had. Others because the curses of the Abyss made their power wax and wane in the direct light of the sun. Some still hid because they had no desire to be seen, no interest in being caught, no will to be returned to the other side of the veil.

One species of Abyssian hated the sun for other reasons. They hated it because they were such an affront to both the light *and* the dark that the Gods above *and* below had cursed them to immolation if they even *attempted* to come near such purity. It was the price they had to pay for being damned yet unpunished, dead but alive, and capable of granting eternal life but incapable of causing growth.

You'd never find one in Sycio. The sun beat down on the Golden Sands longer there than nearly anywhere else in the world. It'd be rare to see one in Civa; the Burning Empire enjoyed setting things on fire a bit *too* much. Dawnfire? Too unpleasant, as a whole, given the Crown's grudging reliance on the Lovers to enforce the peace.

Yet even in places where one would not expect to find a vampire? You might be mistaken. Another failure of the Order; another failure of the Hunter's Guild. Another failure of the 4th; no matter how ineffective they'd be. Because for all of their efforts, because for all of their security, because for all of their platitudes and haughty names and designations and spells and more? In their holier-than-thou minds and attitude, there was one concern that was never addressed.

In a city sunk deep into the ground, sometimes you didn't need to wait for the dark to move outside of the light. You didn't need to wait because in a city thriving into a pit, shadows reigned night *and* day. When the sun cannot cast its light unobstructed except when it lords over the top of the city for a few scant hours out of the day...

...it becomes a place where darkness can thrive.

A place where darkness can *breed*.

Breed it did. Breed it had been doing.

Malik was safely secured away in Madam Pramidi's House of Hides, well outside of prying eyes and searching hands. Magic had been put in place enough to dissuade the mundane from approaching, and warnings had been established enough that the vampire would know if someone with pathetic mortal skill somehow stumbled across it. That left the next idea, the next play. The next way to sow chaos.

Sherril had done such a wonderful job of destabilizing the city. The battle in Cableture — an amusing development, to say the least — had further pushed things to the edge. But the factions of power weren't at war with each other yet, and the Lovers were the glue that held them together.

"Humans fear us," Annix had told his sired battlemage. "They fear the death we bring, and they fear the gift of life we offer after. You feared me before you bent the knee and tilted your neck."

His minion had bristled at the accusation — and the memory. She'd submitted alright, but not until after he'd had his way with her body and mind. Not all of the scars had healed after she had turned. The ones that hadn't never would. It was as constant of a reminder of the sadistic pleasures he delighted in as much as the pointed teeth he'd gifted her with.

If he cared about her feelings, he didn't show it.

She knew better than to assume he did. "They fear that we become more."

"Yes, they do. You have learned," he said with a smile that she couldn't see. Ever since the fight at the Manor, he had gone out of his way to stand in any shadow he could as if there was something there he was missing now. "It is only by the curse of life granted us that our brood grows so slow. Days by three for a meal to become a servant; weeks by six before they can learn to speak once again. Months by nine before they can blend as you do."

Every word he uttered was the truth. Every word he uttered failed to carry the weight of his statements. Once resurrected, there was little a newborn could do but be trapped in a torrent of emotions, a fog of thought, and a horrific hunger. Unless their sire was present, it was not unheard of for a fresh broodling to become so unstable that they would find a way to kill themselves – the sun being the typical.

Annix didn't let his children throw themselves away so easily. Their use was defined by his interests. Not theirs. Never theirs. If they survived those three days? Their minds would have returned enough to be able to focus. They'd be little more than human-shaped goblins at best, but once that period was gone, they had so much more potential.

She thought back to the handful of slavering, drooling, mindless cretins that her Meister had chained to the basement wall. "Weak and befuddled as they are, that is not to say that even the youngest of us cannot be given worth." He lifted a clawed hand and drew a sigil in the air that crackled with blood-red and black sparks before it faded away. The twitching mass of broodlings quieted and turned their dominated eyes to him. "Worth of single use when aimed correctly; yet still use."

"My use was single when you claimed me," Sherril remarked slowly. "Mayhaps one of them may be of use later."

"Mayhaps, if they serve well. If they don't, the next will. Or the next after," he remarked as the body at her feet twitched in a post-death tremble. "Or these, if needed. So many have been rushing to leave the city as of late. They won't be missed until we are long gone; and the Guard is too busy to patrol the roads as they should. However hard they look, they fail to find the places we thrive."

She quietly nudged the corpse with the toe of her boot and wiped blood off of her jaw. "Why do you need so many? And here, so far away from home?"

Annix chuckled. His voice had a constant, gravely rasp to it. Every time he laughed, it felt like he was raking his claws across the bones of her ribs all over again. Just like he had before she'd bent the knee. "Because I need you to demonstrate your love to me. Because I need my line diluted. Because I need my line confused. Because I *need*," he replied slowly.

The way he said the last word made her stomach fall and caused her toes to curl in revulsion against her own will. "I just… I just want to know how I can serve… and if I know your idea then I can serve better."

"Be more concerned over the task you have yet to begin," the elder vampire replied with a poisonous tinge to his voice as the moons shone through the trees overhead. "A task of three. Do you know which three it shall be?"

"I do. A priest, a thief, a mage. I will deliver their souls to the next."

Annix laughed quietly and slowly. The noise boomed with an irregular throb that made her skin crawl to listen to. "Then I shall bring the Order of the Harlot suffering. A magnitude less than what they have delivered unto me – but a start. A taste. A taste I shall tinge with blood. A taste of justice, as only my people know it."

II. MIRROR, MIRROR
Afternoon of Zundis, 12ᵗʰ of Firstgrow, 513 QR

From the eastern part of the city to the Falls, the trip wasn't that bad. It was faster if you could reliably walk, but the exorcist couldn't. Just to save his strength, he was granted a simple, horrible, rickety wooden cart to make his life easier.

And it did.

Until it took a stop in the Abyss.

One heartbeat, he saw the city going by on all sides at a not-quite leisurely pace. The next? The sun was gone. The sky was pitch black. His eyes were filled with smoke.

He had a heartbeat to scream before he fell face-first into the Everburning Pyre. Flames licked at his face as he inhaled a lungful of burning ash. People howled in agony all around him. Voices he recognized. Voices he didn't. The fire coursed across his flesh and left streaks of charred skin behind.

A fierce blast of *cold* quieted them down. Ice shuttered his eyes.

When he opened them again, he saw Rmaci as clear as day... as day gets on a moonless night in a field of black sands and pools of molten glass. The Pyre was gone, and she had her back to him. All she did was point to the distance at a figure under the rolling clouds above.

Rolling clouds. Thunder. Lightning that raked across the sky and struck at his feet. Lightning that a man in a blood red robe directed with his hands towards the Repository.

"Him. There will be sparks. There will be thunder."

"What? I know him. That's —"

"He will be the cause," she accused as she pointed a gaunt finger at the

distant figure. *"Even as lightning is forced to betray friendship."*

Akaran took a rough step forward and realized he was sunk to his knees in muddy water. It was strewn with bodies, bricks, stone columns and… "Where did these… this come from?" he demanded. "Rmaci, where am I? Are we in the Abyss? What's going on? Where in the thundering damnation have you been?"

"I have been where time isn't. You are where time will be," the dead woman warned as she turned to face him. The fires were gone from her face, and the ice had melted away. Still, she was anything but healed. She was *shattered.* *"I have been where messages have been written. I have become paper for a bleeding quill with a truth you need to know."*

Her face held itself together by force of will alone. Pieces of her skin moved like loose glass hovering in place. In that one moment, she was more terrifying than she'd ever been in life. "What truth? Where are we?"

"The truth is that Love is an act of defiance," she cautioned before a streak of blinding white light obliterated her from his mind all over again. He swore at the top of his lungs as a rolling shockwave lifted him up off of his feet…

…and he felt the cold damp cart under his ass again. With a shake, Badin grabbed his friend's shoulder and shook him awake. "You alright in there? You're cursing in your sleep."

The exorcist slowly opened his eye and tried to take in his surroundings. For a moment, he would've sworn he felt frost in his eyelashes, but he shook the feeling away with the rest of the weirdness from his dream. "Now I'm cursing as I wake up. We here?"

"We're here."

In the distant corners of his mind, he swore he heard Rmaci say, *"And you are the most defiant of all."*

***

Ethod, Akaran determined, was the kind of man you either trusted with your life or trusted to make your life miserable. There was no in-between with him. He was a half-foot shorter than the Lover, with slightly graying hair and eyes the color of the mud caked on his leggings. He was quiet, reserved, soft-spoken, and most importantly, he radiated the kind of peace that came from someone that was either *exceptionally* holy…

…or exceptionally *dangerous.*

There was no in-between. It was just a matter of trying to figure out which was which. Ethod had greeted them warmly enough, and he didn't seem concerned either way with the group the exorcist had assembled – an Order Wardkeeper by the name of Hadraie, a pair of mercenaries from the Guild, Badin, and an extra guard from the 4th that happened to be in the wrong place at the wrong time. It wasn't as heavy a crew as Akaran had wanted, but the Oldstone's message hadn't left him with a lot of time to waste.

Hadraie was a little interesting herself. He'd only caught a few glimpses of her in his time in the city so far before now, although she'd never said a word to him. Ever since he climbed out of Cableture, however? He would've sworn the silver-eyed girl had been behind his every step. She hadn't shut up either – always asking where he was going, why he was going there. She always had a word to say or a comment to make.

It was beginning to be unnerving. *She's worse about it than Rmaci ever was*, he groused quietly.

As it turned out, Ethod wasn't at the mouth of the caves. Instead, that honor had been left to a scampy kid that was almost as tall as the exorcist's leg. Maybe. The kid was more than happy to lead the band of impromptu (and barely willing) adventurers into the mouth of the cavern.

The only thing that made Akaran think that maybe he wasn't wasting his time was the dead undja he'd found days ago out along the stairwall. It was as clear of a sign as any that Annix would have a nest around here, and in the ensuing chaos, it had mostly slipped his mind. Mostly, but not quite. He'd taken… pains… to get Riorik to place eyes on the cave entrances… which explained why Austilin had joined them a matter of minutes after arriving at the Wallmen's Lift.

He hadn't been summoned, he hadn't been asked for, but there he was. It was almost by magic. He was, sadly, of no real help at all. A few minutes into their journey into the side of the city and the mountain of a man was bested by the actual mountain itself. In short?

He couldn't fit.

While he waited outside, the rest of them realized that for people that *weren't* the size of boulders, the caves weren't that bad to travel through. The front end of the majority of the caves – and there were dozens along the wall – had sconces and braziers at their mouths and further down their halls. Several of the larger ones received plenty of traffic, and there were all manner of claymakers, miners, stonemasons, and more who worked tirelessly through the systems.

All good things tend to come to an end, however. It didn't take long before smooth walkways and wide tunnels gave way to jagged floors, sharp walls, and low ceilings, and blood-streaked stone protrusions. The twisting pathway didn't make it easy to crawl through with arms and armaments, but the sheer frequency of the blood splatters encouraged him to pick up the pace.

He wasn't at all happy that he did.

When they finally met up with the Oldstone's gray-cloaked contact, he was smiling from ear to ear – despite a puddle of blood no more than three steps away from where he was sitting. He was leaning up against some kind of glistening-wet mud wall that looked decidedly out of place for the cave, even though the system was exceptionally damp everywhere they'd traveled so far. The older man happily slapped his knees with a pair of mail-covered hands and greeted the party with a smile. "Ah! Good men! I was starting to be concerned if you were going to arrive in time!"

"In time for what...?" Badin asked slowly as he looked around the cramped chamber. There were a pair of barrels with the old man, one of which had its lid off and a pool of festering water sitting in it. Aside from that, a strangely-shaped sconce, and a bedroll, there wasn't anything of note at all.

Ethod shifted his shoulders and his cloak brushed against the stone with a strange metallic scrape. The cave was barely wide enough to fit half of their party, and the unlucky sod from the 4th was stuck in the hallway behind them. "In time for things to take a course more natural than what's behind this wall," he explained without explaining. "Please do allow me to say how much I appreciate the speed of which you took. It may be best for all of us."

"Wasn't best for someone," Akaran pointed out as he gestured at the glistening red pool. "Altund wanted me here. Why, and who does that belong to?"

"Ah. A man in a rush – not a trait that I have. Stone is... well, one that follows would not say slow, but it only moves with haste when other forces are pressed upon it."

The Lover bit his tongue and stopped himself from saying the first thing on his mind, and managed to soften the comment that slipped out of his lips. Barely. "I'm pressing. Explain."

Ethod chuckled softly and nodded his head in understanding. "The brashness of Love. Eternal, enduring, when nurtured. Yet, while it may be slow to grow at times, others it arrives in a hurry and burns with light brighter than Lumin Herself."

Akaran felt his patience crumbling and replied to him through clenched teeth. "Ethod..."

"Yes, yes. I do apologize. The blood belongs to the ground now, but before the dust claimed it, as dust does in the end, it had been within the Oldstone." The revelation drew a startled noise from one of the Huntsmen behind him, and the wardkeepers exchanged nervous glances between each other. "Before you ask, no, he did not join the ranks of the city's other recently departed. His wounds are not grievous, though they are painful."

"Well, that's good. Where'd he go off to? For that matter, what was he doing down here, regardless? I thought he'd gotten screwed out of his contract for the tunnels behind the Falls."

Ethod answered with a short nod of his head. "Yes, yes, he had gotten… screwed, as you so crudely state it. Yet while he is a man of ill-luck with business as of late, he does listen to the ground. The ground has been rumbling for days about an illness within the stones."

"An illness in the stones?" Badin interrupted. "Illness? If you even suggest that the Circle is —"

"The Men of Rot?" Altund's man quickly interrupted. "By the tunnels, no. No, nothing of the sort. Rock does not grow 'ill' as illness is 'spread.' But rather, there is something in the ground that should not be. He felt it here, and felt it radiating from the northern lip of the city. As for what he's doing now, I cannot say, but for here? He had been attempting to find the cause."

Akaran pursed his lips and frowned. "I assume he did."

"He did. He also didn't waste time in leaving."

"Honestly surprised that fat bastard even made it this far," Badin whispered under his breath to his friend.

The Oldstone's man heard it anyways. "Yes, he is a… mountainous figure… I shall grant. It is sad to have to say that while he only gave the dirt the wet of the body, the ground was given three of our own. This is why you were sent."

"Shit," the exorcist grunted under his breath. "I offer my respect to the departed. I'll see to it that they are granted a peaceful passage to the next life. Where are they?"

Ethod reached over and patted at the muddy wall. "Behind this, for now. It is not a permanent burial, as one expects you may need to use other methods."

Badin glanced at the wall and then at his one-eyed friend. "I don't think I like the implications of that."

The priest pursed his lips and sucked in a sharp gulp of stale, musty air. "I know I don't. Explain what happened, please, and be as detailed as you can."

The Stonehewn-worshipper was only happy to do so. In relatively short order, he laid out what had brought Altund to the caves – and what happened after his arrival. The Oldstone had come to the decision that since he had been manipulated by a dead woman and her bastard of a bodyguard, that maybe there was something more behind the Falls than he knew. It was a stretch, but after the deal had gone south, he came to the conclusion that she may have been lying… and that there was more than just the precious gems and ore enough he'd been promised.

Technically, the caves had been bought out by the Overseer after she had made her arrangements, but as Ethod explained, "The Speaker of Stone does not think highly of the Blackstone Traders. He feels that they take the name of the God of the Unders in vain by merely existing." As such, Altund went digging without permission granted or presumably even asked for. "Nor is he fond of Lady Hosheck, whenever she deigns to poke her nose about."

"He's not? Then he'll be happy to know she's dead. Annix turned her. The Order culled her."

"Death is rare to be celebrated by honorable men, good Lover," the stoneworker replied before he let a brief smile dance across his lips. "Still. It may ease his discomforts if but for a moment."

With that said, Ethod returned to his tale and he was circumspect, at best, about the number of claimable materials that the Oldstone may have discovered and would only say that, in his words, "Anais hadn't been entirely untruthful." That aside, he went on to add that there was an odor from the ground that didn't seem to be of natural bent. Further exploration discovered another set of caves beyond where Altund had been searching – leading to the hall they stood in right now.

And more importantly, what was behind the wall the self-declared Stonekeeper kept giving subtle, albeit nervous, glances at. "He did not have much time to say what exactly it was he discovered. Healing is not a skill that blesses the followers of the Stonehewn, I am ashamed to admit. We can bind a broken bone in stone that will keep it from twisting, yes, but to patch flesh?" he shook his head in resignation as he posed the question. "Our bodies are not made to rejoice or respond well to clay."

What he found was another chamber – maybe two or three – and a creature in it that rabidly assaulted the Oldstone and his bodyguards. "It is not uncommon to find a menagerie of monstrosities that inhabit the Undertunnels. The realm beneath the soil is a harsh place to survive in; to adapt, many things have grown teeth sharper than what our flesh can easily withstand."

"That's a lot of blood for teeth. How big were they?"

Ethod blanched from the battlemage's question. "Big enough to inflict much pain. Except that it was not just teeth; and it was of a creature both native to the Unders, yet not natural to this realm."

"So Altund threw up a wall of mud and ran off?" Akaran interrupted. "I can't say I blame him, but he has to know that won't last long."

"He does," the sagely follower of Stone agreed. "The spell he used? His words: 'If the one-eyed brat can't get past it, then he's less a man than I thought,' and that I was to resolve the circumstances myself."

Badin shook his head with a flat, resounding 'no' as he backed away. "I am not blowing up a magically-conjured wall in a cave."

While the priest sized up the conjured defenses and scratched at the stubble growing on his chin, Ethod did his best to calm the Specialist's nerves. "There will be no need. I presume that a man that hunts magic has ways to disable it. Of course, I also have ways to ensure that should the magic that you hunt turn about and hunt you, that no other lives will be lost."

"You don't look like a fighter," Akaran replied idly as he began to dig around in the pouches at his waist.

"No, I am not. However, your Goddess has a way to fill the hole in a man's heart. I do respect that, and respect the holes you fill elsewhere. Yet I too know how to fill a hole, and how to seal a void."

One of the Huntswomen — a tall, pale woman with short cut auburn hair and a frown that could've depressed a parade — cleared her throat. "Ask him what his title is."

The exorcist looked away from the wall and raised his eyebrow slowly. "Ethod...?"

"I am a Tunnelbore."

"He means he's a sapper," Badin realized as the lover blinked in confusion. "Got a feeling that if this goes bad, none of us will see the sun again."

Ethod smiled warmly over at the mage with the coal-black beard. "It is such an over-rated blot in the sky. Yes, your friend is correct. We will not be tanned by the light of the star, nor be blessed with the glimmer of the moons. But..."

"...but?" the exorcist asked with a raised eyebrow.

"I suspect that the shift in flow and shift in origin of the Orshia-Avagerona Falls would be a great sight to behold, and it would pain me not to be able to see it," he admitted with a warm-but-not-really smile.

The admission fell on Akaran's shoulders like an ox, and it took him a moment to clear his thread of the very vivid picture that popped into his mind. "I'm reasonably sure you just threatened to collapse the entire back wall of the city."

"Only a portion," Ethod replied with a wave of his hand. "I do take pride in my work, but I do not wish to discover if this cretin has more of its own brood deeper inside these caves than the depths of which we have been blessed with the ability to explore."

"Did Altund at least say what it was that attacked him?"

"No, he didn't seem to have care to give detail. Loss of blood, shock of lost friends. Such things do tend to dominate a mind when a situation does not resolve itself in a way one would want."

Badin let out a gruff snort. "So he called for help, sealed a wall, set you in charge of destroying the Falls if you think you have to, and then didn't bother to say what he found?"

The Tunnelbore nodded his head and made an opening gesture with both of his hands. "Yes, that is the sum of it."

"Akaran, do you...?" the battlemage asked as the hunters and the guards all exchanged knowing, nervous, and unhappy quiet looks between themselves.

His friend ignored him and ran his fingers over the mud again. After another thoughtful stare, he quietly whispered a single word: "**Kormatpat**," under his breath. Quiet or not, the moment the spell left his lips, he recoiled away in disgust.

"What was that?" one of the Huntsmen demanded.

"Tracking. Altund wasn't wrong to call, that's for damn sure."

Ethod looked down at the puddle of gore and then back up at the exorcist. "I would have assumed that was a given, considering."

"Not all help is created equal," Akaran grumbled before he worked his tongue around the edges of his mouth and spat in disgust. "Can almost taste it now. It's not a vampire, I can say that much."

"What is it?" the huntswoman asked before Badin could make another sarcastic quip.

He shook his head and began to roll his sleeves up off of his forearms. "I don't know. It's not... it's not *powerful*, just..."

Ethod smiled knowingly. "Offensive?"

"Very," Akaran agreed. "Okay, it can't be left intact. Hadraie?"

The Wardkeeper stepped forward and bowed her head. Her robes did their best to flow with her movements, but the honest truth? The trip into the cave had left them so tattered that she was doing her best to pretend they hadn't been reduced to rags. "Yes, Messenger?" she asked with a soothing voice – and the new title that the Maiden-Templar had given him before he'd left Cableture.

'Messenger of Love.'

Often given to Paladins or the ranks higher, to be a Messenger meant more than just being an exterminator to the Order. You were on a higher calling, a more righteous one. It meant you were concerned with more than just the desires of the dead and damned; it meant that you were shouldering the burden of trying to rid the world of the cause of their evils… and those that exploited them.

So far, she was the only person that had called him that and he didn't think it was going to last. Still, a Messenger included more than those who took up a sword against evil. It meant any of those willing to spread the Words of the Goddess through thick and thin and to defend against perdition at any cost. And every cost.

"Find the tightest choke point in that hall, and lay out a Ward of Dissuasion. Nothing deeper than twenty yards back. Don't want it to get far."

"You expect it to get loose?" the Tunnelbore asked with a surprised tilt of his head.

The temporarily-named Messenger of Love shrugged. "Don't want to risk it. It's already killed three people. I might be the fourth."

"I'd appreciate it if you'd not be," Badin interrupted.

"I'd appreciate it if you got ready for a sparkcall," Akaran shot back over his shoulder. "When this wall comes down, it's going to notice. It's not close, but I'll be shocked if it doesn't want to come over and find out why."

The battlemage pursed his lips. "You're not going to have Ethod here blow it up, are you?"

"No," the exorcist answered much to his friend's relief.

"Speaking of which," Altund's man interrupted, "Gentlewoman Hadraie? May I request that you please be so kind as to watch for the inscriptions I have already placed in that hall? I do not know what your magic might do when mixed with mine, and I would hate to have the tunnels change their shape without warning."

Akaran and the Wardkeeper exchanged very concerned stares back and forth between them. "I… I shall be very careful," she replied slowly. "Messenger? By chance, would you have any sulfur on you?"

The exorcist paused and reached down to unhook a small bag on his belt. "Yeah, why?"

"A trick I learned in an earlier deployment," the red-haired woman replied as she took his pouch and carefully poured it into one of hers. "Mixed with flakes of silver and a vial of sap, should the ward be activated, it will also disperse the mix into the air. It both burns and causes a distortion in the ether of a demon exposed. Might make it easier to track, if it escapes."

His eye widened as he pursed his lips. "I *like* that trick," he exclaimed as he worked that idea through his head. "I think we just became friends." *A trick that a Wardkeeper **shouldn't** know. Who **is** she?* he quietly mused as she took the pouch from him.

Hadraie bowed her head slightly and turned to find an appropriate spot to work her magic – but not before she replied with a parting remark. "Mayhaps if you spent more time with the Order than with the thieves, you'd have more friends than just I." Then she paused and lingered for a moment before vanishing into the tunnel. "Of course, it would be a failure if you needed more than I."

Once she was out of earshot, both Hunters and Badin all turned their eyes to the exorcist. "Did... you know, it's been a long week, but I'm pretty damn sure she just made you an offer you shouldn't refuse," the sparkcaster offered slowly.

"She did," the huntswoman confirmed as Akaran stood there with a dumb look on his face. As he tried to protest the remark – and everything it suggested – the mercenary cut him off. "That's her. What do you want us to do?"

"Send one of you out, and take Hadraie with you after she's done her work. Find Austilin. Just because he's too big to walk back here doesn't mean he can't be useful blocking the way in. Or out. If this fails, Hadraie's either going to need an escort or a bodyguard to let Catherine know what happened. The rest of you?" he called out as he worked his fingers and willed a small blob of magic in front of him, "If this fades before I get back, run."

The spell had a limited lifespan. Exactly *how* limited he wasn't willing to admit, but it should buy enough time to root around in the caves and find whatever had attacked the Oldstone. "I think I haven't said how much it's a relief that you're able to use magic again," Badin offered. "You've got much more of a pep in your step now that you can... you know."

"Walk?" he asked. "Yeah, I get that."

Ethod tapped at the wall with the back of his hand. "I daresay you haven't expressed how you intend to move this wall yet. Did you need my services?"

"That?" Akaran asked. "No."

"Then how...?"

Rather than answer directly, the priest just pulled his sword out of the thin sheath on his waist and placed the tip against the mud. He slipped two inches into the wall before he reached forward and pressed the palm of his other hand against the dirt. "**Disenchant!**" he rumbled from deep in his throat.

As the spell rolled off of his tongue, a brilliant sheen of lavender light rolled down the edges of his shortsword until it sank into the wall. The mud immediately began to dry up and crack; a heartbeat later, chunks of it broke free. By the time everyone could take their next breath, the barrier disintegrated into a pile of dust and loose stones.

"Ah," Ethod quipped as the others marveled at the sheer efficiency of the spell, "I see the Oldstone spoke correctly of you. He'll be pleased."

"No he won't," the exorcist replied with a faint grin. "He's gonna feel feedback from that. Hope he wasn't doing anything important."

Across town, Altund roared as pain blossomed behind his eyes. The shout made the medicannia working on his gut wound jump back in surprise – and she stabbed him with the tip of her needle by accident. As the slug of a man swore about *that*, Akaran looked down the exposed passageway with a sigh.

The sigh was frustrated. The steel in his voice was not. "Wait here. I need to go murder something."

For a change, it really was that simple.

Regrettably, murder was what had caused the problem to begin with.

***

The magical scent left behind from *kormatpat* was strong enough you could find it with a bloodhound, and at the moment, that's exactly what Akaran felt like. An underfed, underappreciated, hunting dog wallowing through the muck to find his master's prey. With all of the tortures and torments that had befallen his life recently, the winding walk – almost a crawl – through the cave system was an odd relief, in a way.

But not so odd that he was blind to everything laid out in front of him. The tunnel was littered with clues and worse, though more of the *worse* than the *clues.* It didn't take long for the jagged rocks to melt away into smooth pieces of stone that were almost like butter to touch. In fact, they were so smooth, they were simply unnatural.

Someone had a mage go through here and slag the edges down. Almost like they wanted to make the trip into the caves as unpleasant as possible, and once you get far enough in, it's no longer an inconvenience, he realized as he rounded a short bend. *You make it this far, you're not going to give up.*

The stone was one concern. A torn piece of a Guild cloak he found in the profoundly sharper section of the cave was another. *Since Ethod didn't say anything about Hunters accompanying Altund in here… oh. Wait. Didn't they lose someone near these tunnels? Cassanol?*

As he wracked his memory, the little bit of the story that he could remember came to mind. The Guild had suffered a loss at the base of the falls a few weeks prior. A lone Hunter, with a hole in the center of his face. Huntsmatron Elsith Gorosoch had eventually put the blame on Donta, Anais's former bodyguard. *Could be other reasons to find a torn cloak here, but that's the easiest one.*

He paused for a moment and shuddered as he briefly entertained the idea that he might be wrong. *Let's hope that's why, at least. Begs to wonder though… why?*

It was a question without an immediate answer, and when it dawned on him nobody was going to reply, it brought him up a little short. For what felt like the first time since he had left Toniki and Gonta, he was alone. Entirely, utterly, by himself, alone. Nobody was walking with him in case he fell over. Nobody was trying to keep a watch on him to make sure he didn't take more cocasa than he should. Even the handful of times he'd ducked down one alley or another for a few minutes of quiet in the bustling streets of Basion, there had always been someone within earshot.

Nor did he have a voice in the back of his head offering a mix of lectures, torments, insults, and suggestions. Strangely, that was the part that made him the most uncomfortable: the loss of Rmaci's voice. And oddly, the loss of her terrible, disfigured, yet strangely comforting face. Knowing she was there and ready to pop out at any given moment had left him on edge, focused, and ready to move at a moment's notice.

Now that she was gone… in a way, it almost felt like he'd just lost a pair of eyes he didn't believe he could trust. *Soon as I finish this, I'm finding her*, he swore. *She couldn't have gotten destroyed with Daringol. I'd have felt it. I know I would have.*

Thoughts about what he would've felt and when quickly subsided as memories of a tortured woman gave way to something worse: a torture chamber. An actual, unquestionable-in-design, torture chamber. Only it wasn't just for torture. It was for… living. Living in the middle of a nightmare.

A nightmare with a very bright light.

One that was blocked by a wrought-iron gate that had been ripped off of its hinges and bent almost in half. *Oh. I love a good sign*, he grumbled to himself as he carefully tried to work his way around the bars. Not only were they warped, they glistened with blackened oil that had the same stench his spell had picked up on.

As soon as he rounded one last twisting bend, the tunnel abruptly gave way to a cavern with a recessed pit with walkway ledges along the side that were taller than the average man. It gave anyone entering the chamber the ability to walk around its perimeter with free reign to look down at the ghastly contraptions below. The ledge's height also served as another defense in and of itself — because the moment Akaran stepped across the threshold, the roof of the chamber lit up with a shining white magelight that damn-near blinded him where he stood.

It was only by luck or by grace that he caught himself before he fell into the mirror-lined pit. He didn't get time to consider the ramifications of a dungeon full of mirrors — of all the damnable things he could've found — before a pair of greasy and oily hands grabbed him by the back of his neck and flung him back into the hallway.

He landed so hard that had the rocks not been (strangely) blasted smooth already, he would've split his skull open and lost the fight then and there. By the grace of the Goddess, all he ended up doing was bruising his upper back and shoulders on a slightly-curved chunk of stone. Once he got a good look at his attacker, sudden death was a preferable option.

The 'good look' wasn't, though it got the general gist of the fight out of the way in a hurry. It most *definitely* wasn't a vampire, and it most *definitely* wasn't a wraith. It *had* been human once, but that 'once' was not anytime recent.

It was a woman; or least, it had been one. It was naked, greasy, and rotted. The defiled monstrosity quickly dropped from the cavern ceiling and landed on all fours. It skittered across the rock floor, with a mix of elongated nails and bits of finger bones that made a haunting clacking sound with every hand-and-foot step it took. Her joints had been twisted and distorted to an extent that she no longer even appeared human.

Instead, she seemed to be more like a cricket with human flesh.

For one brief heartbeat, he thought he recognized the eyes that were mostly hidden behind strands of slick, oily, bloody hair that dangled in front of her face and her impossibly-wide jaw. But only for a heartbeat. Because that's all the time she gave him.

The magelight he'd had in his hand faded as the impact left him stunned and dizzy on the floor. There was enough light coming from the ghastly chamber behind her that he could make out details here and there before she attacked again. He tried to will chains, or another light, or *something* with magic around him, but the ringing in his ears dampened his ability to call for a boon.

The beast didn't speak. A gash in her neck had robbed her of that ability, even if she'd been able to use it. After she landed on the floor, she dove straight for him. It was all he could do to kick her away, and even that didn't help for long.

Ultimately, the only real saving grace was that he hadn't lost his grip on his sword when she'd flung him to the ground. She jumped and landed astride his chest, pressing her rotted carcass down on his body. Slick with gore and Goddess-only-knew what else, she dug her fingers and toes into the stone and anchored herself on the floor.

Each time she bent down to bite at his face, he was able to bat her drooling jaws away with the back of his left hand. Each time she tried to slam against his body to knock the wind out of his lungs, he doubled up and drove his forehead against her chin.

After the third impact, she jumped off and attempted to rip at his right foot. Even as the world spun around him, he had the wherewithal to pull his good leg back and planted a kick in the center of her face so hard that it shattered her nose and dislocated her jaw.

The creature recoiled, but even in obvious pain, it didn't make a sound. It bounded away from him which gave him a little time to catch his breath and push himself away from the ground. She moved from the floor to the wall in a single jump, and then from the wall to the roof of the short cavern.

If it'd been higher, it would've been impressive. As it was, it just put her head at the same level as his chest – which was the last place she should've gone. Simply put, even the most dexterous warrior couldn't swing a sword in a hallway very well.

But you didn't have to be dexterous to thrust with one.

Her mouth flopped open in a silent scream of rage, and he rammed his sword down her throat with all the force he could possibly muster. The tip of his blade punched out the back of her neck and severed her spinal column in one single stroke. She lost her grip on the ceiling and fell in a mangled, disgusting gray-and-black heap on the ground.

Except the defiled *thing* didn't stop moving. Her arms and legs twisted in uncontrollable spasms. Her mouth worked and gnawed on his weapon like she was trying to chew it in half. One of her eyes looked up at him, while the other rolled around to look at the wall. A harshly screamed command of, "**PURIFY**!" ripped out of his lips and caused her wretched body to arch up.

A cloud of grungy smoke rolled off of her torso, but she didn't quit trying to struggle free of his weapon's bite. He repeated the edict a second time, and that blast sent a cloud of evaporated rot off of her flesh. The fog of tainted steam made his eye water and elicited a sickly cough out of his chest, but didn't seemingly do a damn thing to put her out of her misery.

It wasn't until the smoke cleared and he summoned a fresh ball of light into his hands that he realized what this monster really was – and as monsters went, it wasn't a good sign. He shook the last bit of disorientation away and bound the poor creature with phantom chains so thick and tight that there was no chance she could get away.

Several long, difficult, and exhausting minutes later, he returned to the rest of his party with the damned thing in tow. As they all offered started gasps and most of them gagged from the smell, he walked over to the Hunter and took a warhammer off of her belt. Without uttering a single remark, the exorcist drove the blunt edge into the defiled woman's face.

Each strike was met with a dull, wet thud. Each crack of her bones was met with a grunt from her crushed lips. Each time he pulled his arm back and drove the flat of the hammer against her face, more of the sickly oil melted away from her skin.

A crushing blow obliterated her eye as Ethod moved away from the brutality and made a holy gesture across his chest. "Good man! The beast is already slain, isn't it? What madness…?"

Akaran ignored him.

Another heavy *crunch* echoed through the tunnels as he systematically went for the other side of her face. "Gods, Akaran, what are you *doing*?" Badin groaned as he covered his mouth with a gloved hand.

His third strike bounced off of the edge of his sword and sent sparks flying across his chest. The impact jostled his wrist enough that he had to pause. He met their disgusted, horrified gazes and shrugged in a mix of resignation and defeat. "What must be done," he answered before he returned to his task.

It took eleven hard, violent, *wet* blows across her face before she quit twitching. It took four more to break her hands and feet. Another four to shatter her shoulders and knees. By the time he finished, there was little left to identify the woman as anything more than a flesh-bound bag of meat.

When he was done, he dropped the hammer to the ground and sagged against a stalagmite. The remaining huntswoman, Ethod, Badin, and the guard from the 4th – who had spent the entire time silently trying to pretend he wasn't even there – couldn't get the revulsion off of their faces. Whether it was from the smell, or the gore, or just the way that the exorcist had methodically broken her body down into a pureed blob? That was hard to tell.

"Sorry," he muttered to the hunter before he closed his eye and took a long, ragged breath. "I needed the hammer."

"Are… are you done with it?" Ethod managed to croak out. "I… I cannot say that I have ever…"

"No," Akaran said with a disgusted glance at his gore-streaked chest and thighs. "No, I'm not done. The good news is that we don't have to burn it."

His battlemage friend swallowed back a mouthful of bile. "I've known how you work for long enough that I'm not as happy to hear that as you think I'd be. What *do* you need to do with it?"

The Lover looked down at the mangled heap and let his magical chains fade away into the ether where they came from. "Stick the corpse in a barrel. Wrap chains around it. Real ones, not mine."

"…and then?" Badin slowly asked.

"Load it onto a ship and pitch it into the high seas. Might get away with dropping it into the Overflow, unless it floods. It always floods though, right? Maybe we can dump it in the Repo. Wonder if there's some kind of sewer or something that she won't make a mess in…"

"A burial in water? You must excuse me good… I think good… priest. You should understand how offensive that even sounds – let alone to be party to such an act! – would be to one such as myself," the Tunnelbore interrupted.

Akaran just shook his head. "Burning it will take more than a week and it'll spread enough toxic smoke to choke half the city. I had an argument about this very subject with the Tidesinger a few days ago – but honestly? Water. Water will dissolve it. Whatever bones are left won't harm anyone or anything." He looked down at his clothes and carefully peeled his gloves off. "My tabard, on the other hand, that we can burn."

"That was a ghoul, wasn't it?" the hunter interjected before Ethod could raise another complaint. "Did you deal with the remnant…?"

"It was, and no," he answered with another sigh of resignation. "We're not done here. I don't know if it was guarding the rest of the shit I found, or if it was attracted naturally. But…"

"But what, Akaran?" Badin asked as his eyes slowly went wide. "What *shit* did you find *now*?"

***

His first thought about the room had been correct.

It was made for torture. You couldn't walk ten feet without seeing a shackle, a hook, or a bonesaw. Bloody, thick chunks of rope adorned every fixture. He counted at least two racks, a cistern halfway filled with oil, a raised bed of coals, and cages. *Multiple* cages. In the middle of the massive cavern, a small pillar had been raised up off the floor with a large wooden chair in the center.

Not a chair, he realized, *a throne*.

The throne was the only thing that wasn't stained with blood and only the Gods knew what else. The equipment had been used – repeatedly, he imagined, and he absolutely hated his imagination for the thought. Aside from the obvious and gratuitous violence, two things stood out under the harsh light from the magelight imbued into the chamber. The first?

Well, that was the question on everyone's minds. "Good priest, I am not the least-learned man in the world. Yet, I am confounded by this. The brutality? That, I understand. I am… horrified… but I understand. The rest…?" Ethod asked as he looked around the room – and as the room looked back at him.

Badin cut the statement to the quick. "What the fisk is up with the mirrors? How do you even *make* this many mirrors?"

"If you're asking me how they make mirrors, I don't have a damn clue," Akaran admitted. "Some… Granalchi thing. I think. I've just never… never seen this many. Ever."

"Some good money to make if we can get these outta here," the specialist quipped as he tried to look at anything *but* the implements of terror and pain.

Ethod slowly turned around to face the soldier with his eyes wide and face absolutely aghast. "Are you daring to suggest that we would steal these and attempt to make a profit from the misery?"

"The mage has a point," the Huntswoman offered. "Elsith's gonna want paid for the escort. This might do."

"It's a city-wide emergency," Badin countered. "She gets paid directly from the Overseer's –"

"Would you three shut up?" the exorcist interrupted as he ran his hand across one of the smooth, reflective surfaces. "The only thing that's more murderous than this cave is the headache I have. This place… it's like I'm *swimming* in *death*. I can barely fisking breathe."

The Tunnelbore walked over to the fuming, unbalanced priest and placed a hand on his shoulder to help steady him. "An oddity, now that you mention. I can hardly smell a thing."

Badin stopped and took a deep breath. The hunter and the guard followed suit, and each of them looked as perplexed as the Stonehewn's follower. "Okay, this shit-hole should reek. Why can't I smell anything at all?"

"The Huntsmatron mentioned that whatever has been at the heart of the city's grief knows how to use magic. A spell of some kind?" the Guild representative offered.

"It's the ether. It's repugnant," Akaran groaned and stepped away from Ethod. With a wave of his left hand, he carved a quick design into the empty air with his fingertips and spoke a pair of simple words: "**Illuminate**," he demanded, "and **unmask**."

As the spells slid out from between his lips, he felt his finger ice over for a moment and a matching cold chill pulsed through his most recent scars. The coldstone shard in his eye throbbed with the surge, like it was *offended* by the impurities he felt in the room. Once the feeling faded and he saw how much magic was being used in the cave?

Any doubts he had about forcing someone to *pay* that cost were gone with the wind. Small runes etched into the walls, ceilings, and floors took on a dark red sheen, while the very magelight illuminating the cavern took on a brief pink hue. "A spell of a lot of kinds," he answered with a disgusted mutter. "Huntswoman? Badin? Any of the runes you see – tell me if you recognize any. Guard?"

"It's Sergeant, if you must," the soldier argued with a pained sigh. "Sergeant Allmerge, I told you –"

"I don't care, honestly," Akaran interrupted with a dismissive gesture that only served to piss Allmerge off even more than he already was. "You and Ethod know this city better than I do and this shit came from *somewhere*. Find out where."

"Ah, do forgive me, good sirrah paladin, but... how? I am not an investigator. I... I honestly want to leave very badly," the Tunnelbore implored with one hand over his mouth and the other shaking uncontrollably at his side.

The Lover picked up a pair of rusted tongs and looked them over before he threw them down to the floor in disgust. "Unless the bastard that built this place is a blacksmith and an oresman on top of being a mage, *someone* made these. Someone made that table. Someone made that chair. Someone made these mirrors," he said with an increasingly angry tenor. "Someone put their traders-marks on these. I want to know *who*."

Badin peered into one of the mirrors and shuddered involuntarily as he tried to count how many different Akarans they displayed. Staring into one of them was like looking into a universe full of pissed-off priests. At this point, it was hard to say what was going to give him worse nightmares – the sight of the room, or the idea of a multitude of exorcists. "I've never seen anything like this shit on these mirrors."

"If it's in Ameggenon, we've found Annix's lair," he muttered, "not that there's any doubt. We're gonna need a whole damn slew of people. I can't imagine we've found anything else."

"Start with the Granalchi," the Huntswoman called out. "I can't read half the runes in here, but *someone* from the Annex made this magelight."

"How sure are you?" Akaran called up at her. "What's your name, anyway?"

"Colosa," she replied as she rolled her pale-golden eyes. "I'm glad you finally thought to ask. This magelight though – it's not just an invocation. It's powered. Someone spent a *lot* of crowns buying the charge-stones to keep it active."

The exorcist kicked a loose rock over and rubbed his eye in aggravation. "Violent, sadistic, self-absorbed, and rich. Now if I could explain the mirrors, I'm sure I'll never want to sleep again," he added as he looked up at his reflection and felt the words die on his lips.

Badin walked over and put his hand on Akaran's shoulder. "I've seen you make that look before. Don't crack on me again. I'm not dragging you out of here."

"The mirrors…"

"What about them?"

Akaran reached over and pressed his palm against the glass. "They don't reflect everything."

"What?" the mage asked as he looked around in confusion. "Are… are you okay? Because I can see everything. I can see the tables, I can see the pit, I can see the floor, I can see *you* even though you've got that scary look in your eye again."

"Except you can't see Annix," his friend pointed out as he tried to turn away from the mirrors and failed in every direction.

"What? No. I mean, he's not here… right?"

The exorcist shook his head so violently that it made his throbbing headache pound even harder. "It's not that he isn't here, it's that you *can't see him* in the reflection. Lumina? The God of Light? She *abhors* vampires. Light itself refuses to acknowledge them, so She refuses to carry their visage any more than what our eyes must. A reflection? You can never see one. Not in water, not in ice, not in crystal."

"If you can't see a reflection, then why would it go to all this trouble...?" Badin wondered as he looked around in bewilderment.

Colosa figured it out before he did her calm exterior broke down on the spot. "They don't need light, either, do they? If light abhors them, they can see in the dark?"

"So sayeth the lore," he confirmed.

She hopped down off of the ledge and looked around the dungeon with her mouth wide open. "He wanted them to see it. Didn't he?"

"Goddess... I pray not," Akaran replied as he started to tremble – out of anxiety or rage, he couldn't tell which. Probably both. "But yeah. He did. He did all this so they could watch. So his victims could *watch*."

"Worse than watch," she added. "They'd see everything from almost every angle..."

Badin felt his stomach lurch up to the back of his throat and but by the grace of the Gods kept from emptying his stomach on the floor. "They'd see it but they'd never see the reflections."

"It gets worse," Akaran added as another revelation hit like a brick. "He could manipulate his own shadow. Turn it into an avatar of sorts. He could have someone spread out on one of these crosses and torture them until their hearts gave out and they'd never even see what was doing it. The pain would only be half of it... can you imagine the terror? Being ripped apart by an invisible...?"

The words left his lips and everyone, absolutely everyone, stopped what they were doing and slowly looked around the room like they were seeing it for the first time. It was Allmerge who broke the silence first, and he was joined by semi-silent agreements from the Huntswoman and Ethod both. "So... uh. Exorcist? Paladin? Whatever you are? You uh... you need help killing this thing or...? Because uh... I don't think I'm gonna be able to sleep 'till you do."

"Answers," the Lover replied with a profane curse. "I need *answers*."

Answers that he was going to get very soon.

Answers he wouldn't like.

***

Answers he really, truly, wouldn't like.

Digging through the torture pit was bad enough, but it was what they found in a side chamber that turned the exorcist into a livid pile of priest. What he hadn't admitted to anyone else was what Colosa had asked about... that there was more to a ghoul than just a ravenous, corrupted corpse. The monsters were something a little less than 'undead,' but worse than 'animated.'

They also never traveled alone, but they didn't hunt in packs. No, it was an entirely different manifestation – though just as important to banish along with the physical form. While he let the rest of his group dig through the mountain of evidence with the mirrors, Akaran invoked the same Word he had used to find the ghoul to track down what was left behind.

That's what ghouls were, ultimately. They were the 'left behind.' They were an unnatural result of natural occurrences. People died every day. Usually no more than one or two in any given area at any given time. That was normal. Natural. Large-scale death, however? A sudden die-off? Disease, disaster, or mass murder?

Disease and disaster are natural, and every now and again a human would find something a little higher on the food chain that they shouldn't have crossed paths with, but outright murder was not. *Mass* murder absolutely wasn't. Mass murder and no care given to the remains?

There was a reason that the Order made sure to police every battlefield they could. There were reasons why the Queen's Law dictated how remains of her fallen were disposed of. Wild magic – wild *abyssian* magic – always festered in areas of great strife and loss. Add terror, torture, and supernatural forces *causing* the strife to the mix, and you had a perfect breeding ground for an imperfect creation of the Gods.

Although which God to blame was a question for someone else.

Ghouls weren't the only bottom-feeding abomination that tended to visit places of grief, but they were... complex, even in their simplicity. Be they drawn to the slaughter, or be they raised by natural occurrences, ghouls had one purpose and drive in life. They ate. They devoured corpses. They fed on whatever death left behind. They were mindless. Dangerous. Single in thought, and never quite the same twice. They didn't always appear, but when they did, they *had* to be destroyed. Once they were finished with corpses...

...they'd make new ones.

The tracking spell led him through a wandering, wavering path that eventually terminated in a room that left him spitting in anger. Badin had decided to follow along, though at Akaran's direction, he'd split off and had gone to check out another passageway that didn't feel *quite* as offensively *wrong*. The sparkcaster had gone without argument when he realized that his friend had willed a blazing chunk of etheric silver chain around his hand again out of habit.

He'd been right earlier: someone had carted in all those decorations, just not by purely physical labor. Someone had meticulously carved out a perfectly square, perfectly smooth room out of the mountain and in the middle, they'd dropped an intricate etching in a slightly depressed pit on the floor. The etching crackled with magic, was charred around the edges, and if there had been any doubt, the signature of the Academy was baked into the spell.

It wasn't just your run-of-the-mill 'let's make a thing do things' spell, either. This was one of the ones that had made the Granalchi a household name and the favorite of every merchant guild across the world. It was what they simply called a transport rune – a short name for a complex spell that let the caster move an object from one location to another. Love them or hate them, yet for all of their faults, the Granalchi were honestly the linchpin of large-scale modern commerce.

It also required someone that knew what they were doing. From Akaran's understanding, a simple Adept could activate one, but to place one? Or to place one this large? That took someone that had studied the schools of magic for a *very* long time. For a moment, he entertained the thought that it might be the Headmaster, but he dismissed the idea almost immediately.

Either way, between this and the light in the other room? Even if the idea that he was directly involved was completely absurd, Telburn was going to have a *lot* to answer for. However, out of necessity, he'd have to wait in line.

"You can come out now," the priest called out. "I know you're here, and I don't mean harm. I'm here to help."

"*Help*?" a woman's voice called out. "*The same way you helped my flesh*?"

Akaran shrugged and made a show of letting the light fade from his hands. He didn't need it anyways – the same magelight that kept the torture chamber illuminated permeated every room, nook, and cranny he'd walked past since entering the underground lair. "It might've been your flesh, but it wasn't you. Do you have a name?"

"*One you know*," she whispered from all around him.

He grimaced and tried to make out where she was speaking from to no avail. "I don't like knowing the name of dead people. Especially if they haven't been dead that long."

The voice almost wavered in the air and he could hear ripples of distress emanating from the closest corner. *"Nor should you be blamed for such. Yet you are who you are, as I am who I was."*

He sucked on air and let his shoulders sag. "You know, in training, we don't 'talk' to dead things as much as we just 'banish' them. Do people just... I don't know. *Learn* to be cryptic after they die or is it a more, 'the Gods say we can't speak direct,' type of deal?"

"Death..." she began after a moment of uncertainty he could almost feel, *"death... changes... the perceptions one has. I... I do not mean to be a cause of... consternation."*

"You're not, and I'm sorry," the Lover apologized with a sigh. "I've had... well I'd say I've had a long week but I imagine it pales to yours."

"You would be correct."

Akaran turned around and faced the corner. With a small word, he pulled a ball of phantom energy into the air and let it settle against the floor. "I do need to help you though," he added as a feminine form began to struggle to avoid appearing in the air above the illuminated sphere, "and I promise that I will be as gentle as I can."

The spirit let loose with a sigh and quit resisting the light. After a few heartbeats of flickering in and out of sight, she finally manifested as the broken shade that she was. *"Love, pain. Light. Ice. It radiates from you. I couldn't see that before. I can now. I expect that you see the death that radiates from me. There are men dead now, men dead at my hand. I must imagine that is how and why you have found me."*

He let himself feel a brief moment of relief – just a brief one – that he wasn't looking at Seline. Or Rmaci. Or anyone else he'd been close to. Not that the woman in front of him didn't invoke feelings of sadness... but it could've been worse.

Kiasta Lamar. Bodyguard to the Mother Eclipsian. They'd met briefly in what felt like years ago. She'd been missing for weeks – and when her sister turned up as one of Annix's spawn, it was assumed she might've been turned, too. Instead? Finding her like this?

"I'm sorry."

"Why should you be?" the spirit asked. In life, she'd been short, thin, but always had the look of a woman capable of tearing your tongue out and nailing it to the wall if she wanted. In death, she wasn't much different. It was just harder to see the details, and parts of her body were blurry, almost like they were out of focus. That wasn't unexpected. Not every spirit had the strength, or even the will, to make their presence fully known. *"You were not the one to cast me to such form."*

"In that case, should I wager a guess and say that you're not interested in being the vengeful, wrathful, hateful type of spirit?" he asked with a little hopeful smile. "If you're not upset with me…"

The ghost shook her head and tried to float away from the ball of light at her half-visible feet, but she found she couldn't without a struggle. *"Don't confuse my inability to wreak havoc with the lack of desire to do so,"* she countered. *"A lack of anger towards you does not mean I have a lack of anger."*

Akaran managed another faint smile but added a slow nod of his head. "From you, of all people, I will respect that. As the Mother Eclipsian's bodyguard, I'd expect nothing else." He looked up at her again and his smile cracked. "As Raechil's sister…"

Kiasta's shade bristled and her hair billowed behind her in a sudden spike of anger. He felt the ether *boil* in the air between them. *"My fate was monstrous. That it was forced at her hand? Do not mention her name!"*

"Forced at her hand…? What do you mean?"

"As if you don't know," she charged, *"Her blood screams your name — be it in parts thanks and hate both."*

The exorcist cringed and took a step back as he bowed his head. "I'm sorry. Again. I am. She wasn't –"

"I know exactly what she was, for she is why I am in this state," the shade snapped back as her hair continued to billow around her and her body continued to shake and twist as if it was being blown about by a wind from another realm. *"I do know what, and who, and how. I know the night decries the truth of what you did, how you did, and for why you did."*

He bristled and let a trace bit of power ignite along his fingers. "Is that why you attacked me or…?"

"What that was – was not I. What you should be attacked for, I will not."

Akaran let the energy fade again, though it left flakes of gore-streaked ice across his fingertips in passing. "Kiasta. I'm sorry. I am. May I ask you about your death?"

Her lip curled and showed more teeth than would have been humanly possible, had she been alive. *"You ask permissions to ask the dead? I wasn't aware your ilk did such."*

"Normally we don't, but I know you and…"

"…and you ache to know what I know, yes? To satisfy morbid curiosity, or to hunt the one responsible for so much pain?"

"Both," he admitted. "Would you like to know more about what you are?"

"What I am? I am Kiasta Lamar. Sister to a woman you murdered after she died, much as you murdered my flesh after I died. That even in death, it seems I have chosen violence. What more is there for one such as I to know?"

The exorcist made a show of sitting down on the ground with his legs out. The trip through the caves hadn't done his knee any favors, and the gut-cut he'd suffered in Cableture had been protesting the entire time through the caves. "How about that you aren't at fault for the violence, as you put it. You haven't moved on yet because you couldn't. For whatever reason, your body got corrupted. You, on the other hand, your essence... the *you* I'm speaking to? You're not responsible."

The shade looked down at her hands and slowly, tiredly blinked. *"How do you know? I watched what I did."*

He shook his head and tried to clean off the bloody gunk that had caked onto his skein of water. "No, you saw what your *body* did. I'm not my body. I'm a soul. I'm a soul trapped in a bag of flesh and meat and bones. My soul is me. My essence is me. You... the real *you*, you're *your* real essence. You're what was inside the flesh you had when you were alive. You left your flesh – and not by choice. *You* did nothing wrong."

"Yet still my own body. I watched it rip those –"

"Kiasta, no," he scolded. "Just because I own something, doesn't mean I control it. I had a cat once, back at the Grand Temple. Loved it. It liked to bite my hand. One day? It scratched the shit out of my instructor. Steelhom *still* has the scar on his wrist. I got yelled at, yeah, but it wasn't my fault." Akaran took a drink of not-as-fresh-as-he'd-like water and tried not to gag at the smell of the gore on the leather. "Just because something is *yours* doesn't mean you're always able to control it. If you can't control it, you can't be held accountable for it."

She looked around the room and started to slowly come into better focus. With focus came grotesqueness. The parts of her form that had been blurry and shifting were shown to be covered with scratches, rents, and bites. *"Are you... are you comparing me to a cat?"*

"Do you want the honest answer or the respectful one?"

"Is there... is there one that says I am not the monster I seem to be? For I look..."

"You aren't a monster, Kiasta. I don't know who you were in life. You may have been some secret dog kicker or maybe you liked to piss in the local brewer's ale cask. Right now? In death? No, you are not a monster."

"Then... if it is not my fault, why... why do I look this way?" she asked as

she gestured down at the phantom wounds on her flesh. Etheric bones and gore began to appear under her skin and around the wounds. She bore the marks she had been given before she died, and the more she focused, the worse they began to appear.

Akaran slowly rubbed his fingers together and tried not to think about what Annix could've done to her to cause those wounds. "I've been told that a lot of ghosts display the wounds they had when they died. I don't know why. You just... it's the last thing your mind remembers. You see it with clothes a lot, too. Sometimes."

"So as it is then... just a curse of being dead?"

"Afraid so," he admitted. "You can take solace that it won't last long."

"Will it not? Do you know what happens to me once I pass? You claim I am not responsible for the followers of Stone, yet it was my body. You claim it is not my fault that I died, but it was by my sister's hand. Both of these things are mine and you claim I do not carry the weight of their sins? Had I not wronged her, she would not have brought me..."

The exorcist raised his hand and shook his head firmly. "No. Let me stop you there. I think I'm getting a feel for what happened: Annix turned your sister, and she...?"

"They. He, her, and the others."

His eye narrowed in both anger and concern. "How many others?"

She let the question linger in the air before she finally answered. *"I cannot say what I do not know. Do not ask me names. I do not know. I do not wish to think of it."*

Names would've been helpful, but he had an idea already. *So between her and Rmaci... I guess the dead need to cross over before they learn the secrets of the world...* "Okay. I won't ask for details. You don't want to relive it and I don't want to know. I promise that I will do everything in my power to get justice for you."

"Justice, you promise. Revenge; retribution. Those are what you bring. Justice comes in the after. Without justice, there can be no rest. Without rest, I am no better beyond the veil than I am on this side of it."

"Again with the cryptic commentary," he muttered under his breath. She heard it anyways and growled, but he tried. "I've said all that I think I can. Let me help you pass over."

As he stood up, she pulled away and almost curled up in on herself. *"I have no wish to stay but must I go? The Mother of Night has many children that live in the shadows. I may wish to commune with them for a time. See the things the Mother Eclipsian spoke to me of so many times."*

He willed another ball of light into his hand and let shifting lavender energy course around his palm in a swirl. "Your body was corrupted and your soul was stuck in this world because of it," he replied with a little shake of his head. "In time, it might corrupt your essence, too."

"Might is a possibility, but I might not?"

"It'll be easier this way," Akaran answered honestly. "Go now while you still have control over your will. You've suffered enough in this world, and Erine wouldn't forgive me if I let you endure any more torment than you already have."

Kiasta floated up to the roof of the small chamber and pulled away from the wisp of power radiating off of his hand as it crept up his wrist. *"She has more reasons than that to not forgive you."*

Before the exorcist could ask what she possibly meant by that, the battlemage stepped into the room with an announcement – which died on his lips as surely as the phantom woman that caught his eye. "You found another dead woman. At this point I'm not even sur..." he started before he realized *who.* "KIASTA? What in the name of the Gods happened to you...?!"

"Annix," Akaran replied, "with help."

"Some of that mess in there... was you... oh, Gods," Badin uttered as he felt his stomach roll up all over again. "Oh I'm so fisking sorry."

"Apologies do nothing for my loss when you are not the cause," she countered before she let her eyes settle on the priest. *"Or the only cause. Tell me – will I see my sister on the other side?"*

Akaran opened his mouth and started to answer with something reassuring but decided honesty might do better. "I... I don't know," he had to admit. "We don't know what happens when they change. Or what happens when they're slain. Do vampires have souls? We... think so. Are they the same soul as they had before they changed? I don't know."

Erine's bodyguard hovered in silence as he explained how little he actually knew. *"I suppose it matters not. She and I went on paths much different. I expect not to see her in the Moonlit."*

"The Moonlit?" Badin asked. "Erine's mentioned that a few times..."

"And you listened?" Kiasta asked. *"I see why she cared for you so."*

The exorcist stepped forward while they talked and reached up into the shade with streaks of radiant light. The energy on his hand crackled and spread through her spiritual body. "She cared for you, too. She was afraid this had happened. I'll let her know you passed over when I see her next," he added as he whispered, "**Disperse** and **purify**," to trigger the rest of his magic.

Kiasta jerked away from his hand even as her essence began to lose cohesion. *"I shall see her before you – why assume you'll see the dead as the living? Do you not know…?!"*

It was too late. "Know what?" Badin thundered as his eyes went wide.

Akaran wrenched his hand away, but the damage had been done and the spells had been uttered. Kiasta managed to say simply, *"That she's –"* before a mix of pink and purple light coursed through her like miniature bolts of lightning and made her dissolve away in a cloud of pale fog and ether.

"That she's *what*?" the mage shouted at the fading mist. "Know *what*?!" he demanded. When the ether didn't respond, he whipped around and grabbed his friend by his shoulders. "Bring her back! She was trying to tell us something about Rine!"

Akaran blinked and looked down at the fading, frost-tinged magic on his hand. "Rine?"

"*Erine*," Badin stressed. "My *Rine*. How fisking hard did you hit your head?"

"Hard but not…" the exorcist tried to explain as the battlemage started to shake him by his shoulders. "Stop that. I can't bring her back. I don't know what she was –"

The mage cuffed his arm. "You made her go away. You can make her come back. Use a spell. Draw a rune. Say a prayer. *Something.*"

"I can banish them, Badin, I can't bring them back!" Akaran shouted. "Listen. She was disoriented. She was stuck on this plane and couldn't cross over. I'm sure she was just confused."

Badin looked back in the corner and the last of the magical fog as it vanished into nothingness. "How sure? Because she didn't sound like she was confused."

His friend wiped the frost off of his hand and took a couple of steps back. "We'll have to get out of this shit-bucket first. Soon as we do, we'll tell her all about this and mourn the sisters properly."

"Damn right we've got to get out of here. Akaran, I haven't heard from Rine since before I had to bail your ass out at Cableture. If something's happened to her… Akaran, if something's happened to her…"

"Nothing's happened to her," the exorcist replied slowly as he looked at the raw fear etched all over Badin's face. His eyes were huge and bloodshot, his lip was trembling, and the mage would never admit it, but there were the hints of tears around the edges of his eyes. "You don't know what she went through. Worse than anything you can imagine."

"I don't know. Ever since I've met you, I've had to imagine a whole goat's bladder *less*."

There wasn't any kind of argument to be made against that particular observation, so the Lover deflected as carefully as he could. "As soon as we leave, we'll go find Erine. We can't yet."

Badin took a moment to wipe his eyes and try to compose himself. "I don't want to talk about what you just did to Kia, either. I'm starting to think that I need to owe the Gods all the thanks I can manage that I don't have your calling."

"You kill people. I help people move on."

"No, Akaran, you kill people too. Just your way means they don't come back and I hate that I can even say those words and have them make sense," the battlemage lamented. "You'd do the same damn thing to me if you thought you had to, wouldn't you? You won't say you're killing me. You'll say you're releasing me or helping me 'find my way.' But you'd do it, wouldn't you?"

His friend just shrugged.

The older man let out a tired breath and slowly tried to rub his hands clean on his tunic. The blood on his fingers was just the wrong shade to blend with the red on his uniform, and would've stood out worse if it wasn't already so filthy. "Let me guess. You've got Order bullshit to do in here?"

"I wouldn't say bullshit but... yeah..." Akaran answered as he gestured at the runes on the floor and then at the spot Kiasta had been inhabiting. "I need to pray for her. I need to disrupt this rune. Look at the size of it. It's Granalchi. An Adept put this here. It's a transport –"

"It's worse than transport. You're going to need to send a few more prayers than just for Kiasta," the mage warned.

Before his friend could even ask what he meant by that, the mage turned around and gestured for the priest to follow. A few minutes – and several more twisting turns later – and they ended up in another room. Ethod and Colosa were already there. It was a scene almost out of the exorcist's nightmares... and to the extent that he flashed back to Rmaci and the dungeon cell where she'd been set on fire.

The women in this cell hadn't been burned alive. It looked like they'd starved to death. In the dark. In a cold, damp cell. Alone except for their own screams.

There were seven of them. Akaran had to count twice to make sure he wasn't seeing things. Two of them showed signs of torture. The bars of their cell showed signs of decaying grease and ichor. "I think the ghoul tried to get at the corpses," Colosa whispered as she tapped her fingers against a warped chunk of iron. "I don't know if I should be happy it couldn't... or not."

"This is more than food," the Lover uttered under his breath. "Annix has been careful until now. He wasn't killing this many at once. If he did, the whole city would be crawling in wraiths and shades."

"You don't think he was just playing with them?" Badin asked slowly.

Akaran turned away from the bodies and clenched his fists. A sudden, familiar *rage* started to boil around his heart. For a moment, his vision started to turn red around the edges until he could force the anger back down. "I think... I think that Annix has been trading bodies for favors... or... crowns. And I thought the shiverdine was a bastard..."

"Don't you dare tell me that there's someone worse pulling the strings," the mage growled as he bent down to check one of the corpses for anything that might *somehow* be a clue.

"Worse? No. As bad?" the exorcist offered with a slow shrug. "This son of a bitch needed a place to hide. Then he needed money. So he makes a deal with someone. He gets magic in this pit, he gets the crowns he needs for his toys, and all he has to do is keep some of his collection alive to be shipped off elsewhere."

Ethod cleared his throat and very slowly walked out of the room. "I daresay I liked it more when I knew I could merely bury things that were an affront against nature."

After he left, the remaining three − mercenary, soldier, and priest − stood in silence as they looked over the naked bodies. Finally, the battlemage broke the haunting quiet. "Akaran? You don't get to decide what happens to the peop... creatures... that you kill, do you? You don't get to put in a bad word or anything to really... make it hurt, you know? Do you?"

"No," the priest answered slowly, "but we both know someone that can make them wish I had."

"Boss Hob?" Badin asked.

"Boss Hob."

His friend stood up and pulled the broken iron door away from the cage. He'd shattered the lock with a single bolt of lightning when he'd found the prison, and the Huntswoman had gone after the hinges. "Think Riorik'll let me help?"

"I think there's a limit to shit even he's willing to tolerate, and this is going to push past it," Akaran replied as he swallowed back another fresh mouthful of bile. "This is going to take a while to deal with. Get out of here, tell Brother Levathil that I need help. A lot of help. Then go find Ri... I mean, Erine. I'll catch up when I can."

III. A BROKER'S BET
Evening of Zundis, 12th of Firstgrow, 513 QR

The mood in the city had changed. Weeks ago – days even – people were as jovial as they were angry. They were eager for a fight, but just as eager to pound back a flagon (or ten) of ale. Kids were singing, people were hanging decorations, and merchants were hawking everything from fine wines to finer women.

They weren't doing that anymore.

With Malik missing and the city guard flooding the streets, any pretenses of 'celebration' had been thrown out the window. Merchants were quiet and subdued, and many had taken great pains to stash their more expensive valuables. Decorations were still up and plastered over every wall, street, and hanging clotheslines, but it seemed as if every window had a pair of furtive eyes peering out from them. It made getting supplies difficult to say the least.

Supplies she didn't give a damn about, but her captives did. *There are times when I miss being able to taste food. At least that bastard gave me the ability to enjoy wine,* Anais sighed to herself as she cradled two different clay jugs against her chest. *Though this yeshal smells delicious. I wonder what would happen if I tried some...*

Seline seemed oddly adamant against wanting any, for reasons unknown. Something about Cableture. Madwomen. Hard to keep track of their delusions.

She didn't wonder about either for long.

The streets along Lower Naradol were notorious for letting you go from one point to another without being molested – if the locals knew you. Or knew of you. People knew of her, and others knew her personally, and neither was working in her favor. In the past, Donta's presence had been enough to ward away the random urchin. Now that he was off in Nastavol's hands doing damnation-only-cared *what*, she had to spend far more energy dealing with the locals than she wanted to.

It was a worthwhile trade-off to be rid of him, though she planned to rip into Rishnobia the next time the mote bothered her. *How dare that little beast saddle me with even more labor but take my help. Little monster expects me to fail.*

There was no way to avoid the eyes on her back as she vanished into an abandoned house, though those eyes didn't see her as she carefully moved through a semi-concealed passageway into the next building over. Or down the tunnel she had learned of months ago. It made little sense to hide in plain sight if there wasn't a place to hide below it

She made it into the basement and let her guard down for just a few brief moments that nearly cost her everything she had to give. "Now that I've brought you two food, shall I expect that you'll likewise change the topic of your complaints? I'm under no obligation to keep either of you fed; I only do it out of consideration for the time you've so graciously donated to speak myself and my employer."

"Ah, dear lady, or should I say *dead* lady," Riorik called out as he stepped out of the shadows behind her and smiled, "I daresay neither of them have much to say to you at the moment."

Anais dropped the food and all of her haughty pretenses at the same exact time and she spun around faster than she had any real right to. Her fingernails extended into claws as she realized that not only did she have an uninvited guest, she was missing the others. "Who are you — what do you want? Where are —"

"Where are, indeed. I'll admit that the efforts you went to covering up your tracks were monumentally impressive. You should be commended for your efforts," the thief replied, "though I would've expected men more loyal to guard the way. Or... did you lose the last of them? Is that why you're all alone?"

"You didn't answer either of my questions," she spat back. "Where are they? I *need* them."

The Guildboss looked around the flooded basement and tried to step over a pile of something that stank to no end. "I hope your needs didn't require them to be in good health. Neither looked like they felt halfway decent, I have to admit."

"The Tidesinger. How much for him?"

Riorik shot her a mirthful grin that went from ear to ear. "I do appreciate a woman that's willing to cut straight to the chase. You must truly want him to be willing to open up the coinpurse so readily." She took a few strides toward him but stopped when he lifted his hand and shook his head. "You can put a hold on the threats and the indignation. Yes, I have him, no, he's not for sale, yes, your day is worse now than it was a quarter candlemark ago. I'm only here as a courtesy."

Anais looked up the way she came and looked around the room for any sign of any other intruders. "A... courtesy? Are you a brave man or a mad one?"

"One could say a touch of both, but the same could be said of us all. Before I add anything further, I do ask that you keep one thing in mind," he cautioned. "Missus Valdin is someone I consider a friend and I am far from impressed by the way that you have handled her while she has been in your care. With that clear in the air, do note that my care for your personal safety or comfort can be measured in the volume of a sprig of honeysuckle that you might use to measure the quantity of piss you could measure from a mosquito."

Her jaw flopped open as she stared at him in utter disbelief. "You come into my home and interfere in my business and threaten me? Who do you think you are?"

"Your home?" he scoffed as he gestured at the decaying building. "Hardly; don't be insulting. You may be on the outs but even in times of strife you have taste. No, Madam Broker of Secrets – as you've spoken of yourself before – I am offering no threats. I am only explaining what your new life looks like."

"My reality looks like I am about to claim another mark on my soul before I burn this shitty hut to the ground," she snapped as she bent down and pulled a blackened, gore-streaked, twisted steel dagger out from the back of her boot. "You will tell me where you hid the Tidesinger before I do!"

The thief smiled at her. Then he spread his arms open wide and opened his vest along with it. "I wouldn't," he cautioned as he touched a glowing set of runes that had been stitched into his pure white tunic. "As I said: you have a new world to face. You can either do it with your head held high, or your hand charred to a stump. Either way makes no difference to me, but I do beseech you that you should take the time to hear me out."

Etched into the fabric, the runes had been specifically crafted by one of the more brilliant minds at the Repository. The reasoning was that nobody wanted to hunt a vampire unprotected, but the bastard had figured out a way to keep a step ahead of Hunters (of mercenary and priestly breed alike) as they walked around in otherwise-identifiable uniforms.

The solution? Start adding Order sigils and runes into clothing and bless them extensively. The spells wouldn't last long, and it was another duty for the Repository scribes that they weren't trained to do. Levathil had taken the idea of the burn-bags to another level, and the thief had made sure his name was on the top of the list to be blessed by both a tailor and a spellsmith.

It wouldn't do much. But it might just work to save a life. His, or possibly even hers if she decided to play nice. "I'll tell you whatever you want to know in exchange for Quinchecco. That's the deal," Anais offered.

If she didn't, that was perfectly acceptable, too. "No, that's not. I recognize that he's important to you, but he's off the table. I frankly couldn't care less as to the *why* he is, so please don't bother. Other people can figure that out."

"No Tidesinger, no deal."

"No deal, no head," Riorik retorted with a hasty promise. "If you happened to think I came alone then you aren't worth a tenth of the rumors I've heard about you. As I said: I am here *now*, in this *brief* moment of time, only as a *courtesy*. To give you a chance to do the sensible thing before the sensible thing is done unto you."

Anais seized up and looked up the stairs from where she came. "I wasn't followed. I couldn't've been."

"You weren't. Though yes, you did cover your tracks well – just not well enough. Not with the whole city up in arms over the Malik situation. I shall assume the bodies I found in the other room were the men you hired to secure the Tidesinger…?"

She didn't bother to offer an explanation or a retort.

The thief gave her the faintest hint of a smile. "No matter either way. You have two dice to roll. One says that you should tell me where to find this supposed vampire lord… master… monster… meister? …whatever pretentious name it calls itself. The other…"

"The other being that I tell you nothing and you have someone strike me down?"

Riorik shook his head, almost insulted. "Oh, dear. No. No, the other option is to tell me what your benefactor wishes to learn from the Lovers. And yes, I know you have answers to both. You passed as much on to the my friend's singed wraith." He straightened his vest and fastened it closed. "The question of if you're struck down or not does have bearing on your responses to either. I'd love both, but I'll take one."

The world suddenly seemed to shrink down on the broker, and the basement didn't feel like a safe haven anymore. It felt like a prison. When she heard people moving in the halls both behind her and upstairs... "Do I have any guarantee of safe passage?"

"I guarantee you don't have a lot of time. Less the longer you stall."

She glanced up the stairs again. There were at least three different voices speaking in hushed whispers that she couldn't make out. There were at least two more behind her. Almost certainly more in both directions.

When she let her eyes linger a little too long on the underground pool, Riorik cleared his throat, then picked and dangled an empty glass bottle in the air that had been sitting on the floor beside him. "You can risk it if you wish, but a couple of very insistent Oo-los assured me that pouring this vial of... honestly I have no idea, but a vial full of it... pouring it into any small tract of water would be incredibly uncomfortable for anyone of a less-than-living persuasion should they jump into it. It probably won't kill you, but I can't help but think that it'll slow you down and piss them off even more than they already are if they have to put on their wading boots," he cautioned.

Anais looked back at him and let part of her glamour crumble around her eyes to show him the extent of her disgust. "I hope you rot."

"It is likely," he admitted. "Though I'm working on changing that particular end-of-life arrangement. You, however, don't have that much time. Pick now, or take a gamble. Which is it?"

Purely out of habit, she took a long, slow breath. "I don't know where Annix rests his head," she admitted, "but I know someone who does: Lady Sannah Hosheck. She is Overseer Hannock's right hand. Does all of his dirty work. She's done more dirty than work as of la-"

"Yes, she's quite dead," Riorik interrupted. "I do hope you have more information than just her name."

"Dead?"

"Very. She attacked one of the Lovers. She didn't make it out of the situation as more than ash."

The revelation didn't go down easily, and she rocked back and forth on her heels. "Well, dead or not, I know that she was involved in the smuggling trade – trade of flesh instead of traditional wares. Worse a cunt than the shiverdine."

Riorik rolled his russet-brown, ever-so-slightly bloodshot eyes to the ceiling. "Missus Lovic, if you think that *anyone* is going to be persuaded to allow you to keep... well, doing whatever it is you do in lieu of breathing...

by offering the name of a woman that's already been reduced to dust and suggesting that she's skimmed coin from the Fleets, then I am sorry to say you are sadly mistaken."

"I didn't say anything about crowns," she hastily pointed out. "I said she was skimming off of the trade. As in: I know the Order has been looking into the disappearances of the downtrodden. Given her less-than-human nature, I'd say she found a way to make things work for her benefit. Food in one hand, coin in the other."

"Are you implying that the missing are meeting ends other than just as a snack? Interesting," the thief remarked. "Yet, it does not put anyone one step closer to finding Annix or, may he still be intact, the groom to be."

"But if you trace the steps of –"

"Except she's quite dead, deader than you at that, and without her still heart giving truth or clues, it will take time to find out what she may or may not have known and known where," he countered. "Time which I unfortunately admit that none of us have. You included, it seems."

Anais flinched as he turned to leave. "It's not my fault she's moved on from this world."

"If only I could be sure of as much," he lamented. "Yet I'm shocked you thought you could buy me off with such insignificance. You were *at* the battle in which she lost her life, and I can't imagine you didn't know her fate. Do you find me so simple? Because if you do, that's insulting."

The broker clenched her teeth and felt one of the rotted pieces of bone crack in the back of her mouth. "You don't want to know what I think of you. *Fine*," Anais seethed, "then give me an assurance that they'll let me leave and I'll tell you what my benefactor has me searching for."

"So I would speak quickly – because I assure you, you will be allowed to leave," he promised as he turned back to face her. "Oh, and do speak honestly. Neither they nor I are in a mood to have our giblets twisted."

"What do you know of the Urn of Xabraxis?"

"Nothing," he admitted after working the name over in his head. "I know of the Bejeweled Vessel of Shadazeen and the Copper Urns of the Burning Empire. Tacky things, the copper ones. Had opportunity to see a drawing of one once. I'd hate to be interred in it."

Anais smoothed out her robe as a short-lived feeling of relief washed over her. "The Order knows it well, though I doubt they would know it as well as they'd like. They won't want to part with it, but that's what he's searching for. That, and what's in it."

Riorik raised his eyebrow. "And what, pray tell, Missus Lovic, is in it?"

"Power."

"Power is in many things, I assure you. You of all people should recognize that. What kind of power, exactly? What would a... I presume a necromancer? ...want with an urn? My understanding is that those with knowledge of necrosia prefer to work with bodies that are... intact, as opposed to ash."

She shook her head. "That's a different secret — the mother of all secrets, you could say. You asked what. I told you. Everything I have done has been done in service to further that goal in one form or another. The Order won't part with it willingly and I think it's obvious that I wouldn't have been able to go digging around even under the most fortunate of circumstances."

The thief nodded in begrudging agreement to the sentiment. "Yes. I have come to understand that it's a literal gold mine in there, yet one so secure that even my reach would find it difficult. So as I can understand: the death, destruction, and the deals? They were all done to obtain this... glorified chalice?"

"Find, not obtain. If he intends to recover it, I do not know how." When he started to argue, she cut him off with a quick wave of her hand. "You asked for truth in exchange for an exit. I honor my deals."

"That is what your reputation claims, I acknowledge. Though I ultimately do know that objects of power draw the attention of men of the same. Very, very intriguing. So I suppose the question becomes: how sure are you that the Lovers have it?"

Anais touched the gaping hole in her face where her eye used to be. "To trade in secrets, one must be able to verify that they are there."

He chuckled slowly. "Well then. Obvious puns aside, I cannot begin to imagine how much effort it must have taken to root through their belongings through intermediary after intermediary. I suppose you'll next tell me that the crowns you've earned from one deal or another were very truly done in such service...?"

Her pale face took on an ugly flush that haunted her eye. "I... was placed... under a palace grander than any that *any* human has *ever* dreamed of when I first left this world. I assure you, Master Thief, that I would sooner lock myself in a cask and plunge into the deepest depths of the Nightmare Sea than allow myself to go back there."

"Between us I would be careful whom you mention such ideas to, all told given the circumstances," he cautioned as he sucked at the musty air. "Cask in the Nightmare Sea. Interesting."

She continued on as if he hadn't interrupted her. "I will *never* serve in that ditch of flesh below Lust's own tower of screams again. So allow me to assure you that I have no intention of retiring in discomfort once I am released of the one that currently has my neck fastened by a chain."

"Oh, such a shame that. Life is full of tremendous disappointments," Riorik replied with a sad little shake of his head as any relief she felt drained away. "Before I let your leave be taken, there is one thing that interests me. Purely personal, of course. Not of any grand plan or whatever have you."

Anais bristled and looked up the stairs again as more of her glamour faded. "You promised..."

"I did, and I am a man of my word. Who were you?"

The broker blinked her remaining eye and tried to hide her confusion. "You know who I am. I am Lady Anais Lovic. The Merchant of Secrets."

"*A* merchant of secrets, not *the*," Riorik countered. "It's just that in the limited time that I've had a friendship with a certain foolhardy young exorcist, I've picked up a few things. The dead don't always go by their God-given names, or at least, the ones they were born with if they came to... well, if they came to possess a soul, I suppose... from this realm. That means that 'Lady Lovic' is as much of a creation as your illusory magics are of your face. Not the real thing, but a thing worn to trick others. So... who were you?"

Anais slowly lifted her knife and pointed the tip at his throat. "If you know enough to ask... Madeline Hummadalt. It won't do you any good; she's been dead for a very, very long time."

"That is a fair answer," he agreed with a sad nod of his head. "Despite our differences, I have come to earn some respect for you as I clean up your messes. I imagine I could have learned a lot from who you once were," he said with a resigned sigh. "Thank you. Oh, and I should suppose then that the business with Quin is entirely in relation to this Urn you seem to be so desperate to find?"

She blanched and looked over at the chair she'd held him captive in. "It's... it's not just about the Urn. That's what I was after. What he's after... no. He's after more, and between us, it terrifies me. If I speak of it, he'll do more than kill me."

Riorik rolled his shoulders and straightened his back a bit with a groan and a grunt of relief. "Ah. I do understand that. I suppose if I renege on my word and kill you after all, I'll never know?"

"You'll know. Too damn late to do anything about it, but you'll know."

"Interesting. Well, that aside. It would be very satisfying."

"Except I know your reputation. First Gonta, then Basion. You are a man of your word. You promised that I can leave, so I trust that you'll tell your goons to allow me passage unmolested."

The thief gave her a look like she'd just grown a second head. "Who said anything about those fellows being *mine*?"

Anais took a sudden step back as the rustling from the stairs above grew louder and the distinct sound of steel rubbing against could be heard echoing through the rooms above and behind. "What? You said —"

"I did say that I was here as a courtesy, I just didn't say *whose*. Your actions have allowed me to profit quite handsomely and while it was my men who found you, I've recently found it advantageous to strike an alliance with some very interesting people. If you thought that I cared about whatever Urn your so-called *benefactor* is after, you are quite wrong. I couldn't give less of a shit. There's very little I'm gaining from this conversation, except a measure of satisfaction."

"What satisfaction, you disgusting oaf of a man?" the dead woman seethed as the hand holding her dagger began to tremble — and the coiled scorpion tail around her throat began to unwind.

Riorik crossed his arms and snarled in disgust as Paladin-Commander Spidous stepped into the poorly-lit room from behind her. "You caused great harm to a woman I promised to protect. I promised you that you could leave. I never said how, or in who's custody. I simply thought we could have a dialogue that would save them some time before they burned you, or... hm. I never know how to say it. Do they burn your kind *alive* or do they burn you *dead* or...? It's all very confusing."

"You... you are a deceitful... lying..." she seethed as she looked first at the paladin and the other armed Messengers of Love with him... and then up at the Huntsmatron when appeared at the top of the stairwell.

"Yes, I am. Except I didn't," the thief snapped. "I told you that I would provide options for your life going forward, and I have: the Lovers take you, or I do. I honestly wish you hadn't been so forthcoming, because whatever they do with you? I assure you, it will be much faster than what I would have planned."

She lunged at him, but a shout of, "**LUMINOSO-CORSAIR**!" from Spidous ripped through the air — followed immediately by a glowing ball of pure white ether that latched onto the rotted wooden rafters overhead. The spell bathed every inch of the room in divine, pristine light that banished every shadow and ruined what little was left of Anais's glamour.

She had to cover her face with her hands and nearly tripped as the spell blinded her. Riorik, however, only suffered a fraction of the effects of the holy Words, and was able to take a full look at the broker for the first, and hopefully last, time. Every inch of her desiccated, unholy, demented form was on full display from the bones in her neck to the twisted bits of flesh that hung across her cheeks to the twisted protrusions that had grown on her arms down to the top of her thin, skeletal hands.

She was as grotesque as the lies she spun. The only thing on her that held any semblance of her haughty demeanor was her dress, and even it was stained with mud and worse. The thief felt a mouthful of bile rise up in his throat as he backed up until he hit a crumbling stone wall. "By the Gods. You are an ugly little whore, aren't you?"

That word. That insult. It was the worst thing he could've possibly said. She lunged at him with unbridled rage on her lips. "DON'T EVER DON'T EVER CALL ME – I AM NO WHORE! NO MAN'S WHORE!"

The raw ferocity in her voice set the thief back. If she'd been granted another scant second or more, her esth-atatic blade would've easily ripped his tongue out of his neck. The Paladin-Commander didn't give her the chance. Anais didn't hear the Word that wrapped silvery ropes around her arms, but their very touch burned her undead flesh with a painful sizzle.

Spidous wrenched the Bonds of Love back and caused her to spin out of control. Her body went in one direction as her scorpion tail lanced out and buried itself into a wall to try to steady her balance. A Wardkeeper followed him with an invocation on his lips that all-but sealed her fate. *"Cage thine heart so no harm can it be done/caged by Love so no harm can be caused!"*

Sizzling, almost electrically-charged etheric bars sprung into existence behind the two Lovers and blocked the hallway off. It was flashy, moreso than most of the other invocations the Order used – but for once, the spellmasters argued that presentation mattered. Sometimes, you wanted to establish the absence of hope.

Fewer better ways could be had than to project a physical cell to match a metaphysical cage. Especially when the creature you were trying to catch had little reason to hope for a peaceful return to the afterlife – a return that the Huntsmatron was only happy to provide. Anais briefly struggled free of the bonds and tried to lunge for the stairs, only to be met by a crossbow bolt that punched a hole through her left shoulder. "By Writ and by Right of the Living, you are marked for Detention and Execution by the Guild!" Elsith shouted out.

"And by Queen's Law, you are remanded unto custody to the Order of Love – now and forevermore!" the paladin shouted right along with her.

As the huntsman behind her cocked and reloaded his crossbow, the Huntsmatron stormed down the stairs with a rune-covered falchion in both hands and an eager smile across her lips. "I should've done this months ago."

"Cease your struggles and prepare to be judged!" Spidous added as he lifted the point of his sword up and aimed it at the dead woman, much as she had threatened Riorik. His other hand brimmed with the glistening, crackling etheric rope even as the broker struggled against it.

"Dead," Anais whispered, "I will see you all dead, I so swear it," she promised as the crowd began to slowly circle her. "You don't know what you're doing. Take me and he will kill you all. My death won't be forgotten or forgiven!"

"Your second death will be cheered in the streets," the master thief countered. "At least, I assume it'll be your second."

She shot him a snarling, hateful look before the stinger ripped itself free of the wall and danced in the air behind her. "You don't know him. You don't know what he's capable of. You think I'm the worst he can do? You think I'm the only one? You don't know. You don't know and you won't know until he visits! If you rid yourself of me you'll have Maelphistiphan to deal with! Trade a merchant for an assassin? I *promise*, *you* don't want to do this!"

"The Order very much does," Spidous promised. "Yet we are willing to offer penance. Whatever brought you into this world is a threat, that's true. One we'd like to know much more about."

"One I'd like to know why he's interested in one of the most sacred relics of the Guild," the Huntsmatron added. "If you use what time you have left in this world to answer, your exit may be easier."

Anais slowly looked around the room as the light from the paladin's spell continued to blind her remaining eye. She steadied herself and lifted her dagger up so that the point was pressed against her thin, cracked chin. "If you think you can, you are welcome to try. You want me intact. I have no desire to be taken as such."

Elsith circled around beside her as Spidous readied another spell. He jerked his wrist suddenly and wrenched Anais's other arm in his direction while the Huntsmatron allowed a spark of electricity to spark across the tapered tip of her falchion before it leapt across the room and struck the middle of the broker's abyssian knife.

If either of them expected their spells to do more than briefly inconvenience her, they drastically underestimated her strength — or underestimated her desire to remain free. The electrical bolt split into thin sparks as the knife repelled the attack, and her malformed tail whipped through the air and raked through the paladin's spell. The stinger ripped the bonds in half while Anais unleashed magic of her own.

Countless shadows ripped out of the walls and ceiling as she called out an invocation that was so profane that none of the spellcasters could make sense of it. Monstrous figures flooded through the room as the luminoso spell struggled to remain in place. Elsith and Spidous flashed their swords through the air while the crossbowman and the wardkeeper tried to pick their own targets through the morass of phantom flesh.

As more figures appeared, Anais thrust the point of her knife into her collarbone and ripped down the front of her chest. Her desiccated skin split away as she heaved forward. She screeched in raw pain as blackened bones and oily sand spilled out of her body, but she kept cutting until the gash was all the way down below her sternum.

For Elsith, it didn't register. She was too busy trying to land a hit on a skinless shade that moved so fast that she couldn't keep up. Her crossbowman sunk a bolt into the far wall that nearly sliced through Spidous's ear in a shot loosed out of desperation. The paladin thought he was dead when a horror made of bones and rotten dragon-scales weaved around his blade and thrust a spine-studded claw into his throat. He had time to think a prayer before the claw slid through his skin and out the other side like he wasn't even there.

Except he was. It was the claw that wasn't.

It wasn't real. None of it was, except for the monster of a woman that was trying to use the illusions to buy herself time. The paladin stumbled back from the shade as realization dawned in his eyes. Riorik, however, hadn't even flinched once from Anais's assault. What he had was his own dagger, and while the broker stayed focused on the mercenaries and holy warriors, the Guildboss took matters into his own hand.

For a man of his size, he was on the dead woman faster than she would've expected. His saw-toothed dagger slashed upward and severed the spindly arm holding her Abyssian blade just below the wrist as she continued her transformation. The sound that ripped from her chest was so fierce that it could have been from a banshee. Bloody, oily sand sprayed out from the stump as he lunged backward and avoided a clumsy swing from her other hand.

The distraction was all that Spidous needed. "**DISENCHANT!**" roared through the room and blew the phantoms away like leaves in a stiff wind. For a moment, the Crown's collective enforcers had a moment to catch their breath. But only for a moment. Her illusions shattered, all eyes turned back to Anais.

They didn't turn back fast enough.

Her stinger lanced across the room as the final shade vanished into the nothing that had given it life and slammed into the side of the paladin's forehead. The appendage throbbed once and pumped poison into his face so hard that it popped his head off of the needle-sharp tip. He didn't even scream as he fell.

Paladin-Commander Spidous Nel'don died before he hit the ground.

In desperation, Anais did the only other thing she could. As Spidous's eyes bulged from their sockets and dark red froth erupted out from his ears, she turned and dove into the fetid pool. The holy water that Riorik had poured into it coated her skin as she dove into the flooded hole, which sent a cloud of steam and boiling muck into the air.

She'd swam through it before. It was dark, it was putrid, and it flowed freely through the dilapidated warehouse's ruined foundation. It led right to the Overflow, and all she had to do was stay submerged for just a few moments and she'd be free. She just had to tolerate the ravages of the blessed water and she'd make it through the hole that...

...that had been sealed. A wall of rubble covered the egress from the other side of the building. Brackish water could flow in, but there was no chance she was going to dislodge it with roiling steam buffeting her fingers. Even as the condensed Abyssian ether that made up the hardened mass in her chest pushed back against the blessed waters, she did her best in brief to pull a few heavy stones free until she had no choice but to retreat.

Anais burst back into the basement with an agonized howl. Dead or not, the pain was all-too-real and her injuries – self-inflicted and other – had taken their toll. She landed on her hand and knees as her tail lanced wildly through the air and stabbed at anything she even thought might've been near and missed every chance to draw more blood.

The Huntsmatron's crossbow didn't.

Elsith held the weapon with a cold sneer as she braced it against her shoulder and pulled the cold iron lever on its underside. The bolt punched into the poisonous bulb right behind the stinger and slammed the malformed tail against the wall. Reloading the bow only took a few seconds. Her movements were fluid, perfectly smooth, and well-practiced.

Crossbows weren't a requirement to learn to use in most Guildhalls. In hers? Not only were they mandatory, she trained right along with the rest of her men. She wasn't even their best shot. She just wanted to hurt the bitch.

Her next round did that. The first had burst the poisonous pouch and sent noxious, steaming blue gunk all over the floor and across the broker's shoulders. The Huntsmatron took careful aim in less time than it took for her heart to beat five times and locked in on the dead woman.

Click. Clank.

Thud.

Scream.

The second bolt slammed into Anais's upper back and shattered her good shoulder. Shards of bone and clouds of red sand exploded across the room as Riorik, the remaining Wardkeeper, and the other Hunter moved into position. As Elsith lowered her weapon and stepped back, the Lover invoked Word after Word and Ward after Ward that settled down across the broker's back.

Silver runes manifested in the air around the broker and settled down on her ruined, steaming flesh and gown. "I am Isopal Reacoop — a Messenger of Love! I invoke my name and the name of the Goddess to trap your flesh as Love traps a heart!"

Nobody seemed to care what he said. The Hunters didn't even pay attention to his name. Elsith's man didn't offer his own — there wasn't a reason to. He did, however, jump across Anais's back and draped a metal-scaled belt across her mouth. She struggled and bucked to get free, but the Guildsman didn't budge until the gag was cinched around her lips.

The Guildboss had the last laugh. Wordlessly, he sauntered over with Anais's dagger in one hand and took her thrashing tail in the other. The Hunters pulled her into the center of the room as he held on to the unholy appendage like he was walking a rabid dog. As the others held her down, he took a moment to live up to his name.

Her remaining strength left her body when he sliced once and discarded the tail into the semi-noxious/semi-blessed pool. It sizzled and bubbled on impact, and the Wardkeeper was kind enough to conjure another ball of light inside the frothing flooded pit. Anais sagged to the floor, exhausted, agonized, muted, bound, and utterly defeated.

Their job done, an all-clear was sounded by the Huntsmatron. The next few minutes were a blur of Guildsmen and Lovers and Guardsmen that poured down into the basement with iron shackles, purification spells, and more questions than answers. As the Crown's combined agents worked — just this once — under unified purpose, Elsith made her way across the room and grabbed the Hobbler by his chin. "She said a name. You forget you heard it. Do you understand me? *Forget* you heard it."

"She said several names," he smoothly replied as he brushed her hand off of his chin, "and left out a few of interest."

"Don't even think about playing coy with me, thief," she seethed. "You know exactly what I mean. The Urn. You never heard of it, she never said it, *you* know *nothing* about it."

Riorik gave her a smug smile that went from ear to ear as he idly played with the broker's weapon. "I *don't* know anything about it. I can tell that it's riled you up. I even heard a gasp from the men with you that —"

"Do you want to die today, Hobbler?"

The thief looked over at Spidous's body and the Lovers attending to it. "I feel today has seen enough death. Too much of it that should have stayed dead to begin with, to tell the truth."

"Then forget you —"

He lifted a finger and lightly just... *bopped* it against the end of her nose. She was too utterly shocked to do anything except stare at him in complete bewilderment. He was lucky nobody else had noticed what he had just done, and it was only the saving grace of the Gods that she was too tired to react appropriately. "The more you protest about it, the more you should be aware I'm going to lie to you about not remembering anything about it *but* then that I will promptly have every man woman child and goat under my influence find out all they can for my personal amusement if nothing else – yes?"

"If you... you..." Elsith sputtered as she rubbed at the end of her nose, "...if you touch me again, whatever torture the Oo-los are going to put that bitch through is going to pale in all comparison to what I do to you with my own hands."

The thief just huffed in a mix of amusement or irritation, she couldn't tell which. "I'll forget I heard it if we can come to an agreement around another issue. Shall we deal?"

"Does it involve putting you in a very deep hole with a great deal of dirt over your head?"

"No," he countered slowly, "but it does allow me to continue to be useful. All I want is your backing, when the time comes to it. Your support."

Elsith stepped away from him and gave him an uncomfortable, questioning stare. "Support for what?"

"That is a question that both of us will have to discover. All I can say is that, at this moment, I foresee a time in the near future where it will be questioned if I am of use to the city and Crown or not. If you'd like me to forget what I've learned, then I'd like you to remember what I've done."

The Huntsmatron stared daggers at him but finally, after a *great* deal of thought – and no shortage of self-doubt – she agreed with a nod. "If I hear of you or anyone else in your employ ever uttering that name…"

He met her nod with one of his own. "Yes; I'm well versed with how that particular line goes. No need to repeat it. Thank you, Missus Gorosoch."

"Huntsmatron," she retorted. "You may call me Huntsmatron and *only* Huntsmatron."

"Ah, I see. Then I shall do my best to keep that in mind."

"You had best," Elsith cautioned. "Now I have request: You didn't react to her illusions. Why?"

The thief made an audible 'ah' noise from the back of his throat. "My dear *Huntsmatron*, my entire life has been spent making use of mages that know how to use spells of deception. Do you really think I'd not have learned to see through them?" He looked up the stairs as the collective officers of the Kingdom pulled her limp body up and away. "Though it was a remarkable trick. I shall assume that all steps are being taken to ensure that she won't be able to do them again?"

"I would assume as much. No shortage of thanks that are due to you."

Riorik smiled at her again and made a gesture like he was tipping his hat at her. "One does what one must do. Without her enforcer, the interests she had purchased had less reason to stay loyal."

"To her, you mean. Less loyal to her. Now they're loyal to the Fleets, I presume?" he questioned dryly.

"One does get what one pays for. One also gets what one can exert enforcement over. The one leads to the other, and in reverse."

"Speaking of control. The dagger you took from her — I want it."

The thief blinked. "Dagger? I'm afraid you're mistaken. I don't have it."

Elsith ran a hand through her hair and stopped herself from growling at the irritating Fleetfinger. "The one she was using. The one you cut her tail off with. It didn't look right."

"It didn't, did it?"

"I want it. The Lovers will want it too, if nothing else."

"I'm sure they would," he answered earnestly. "Again though, I don't have it."

"Riorik, I saw you use it."

The thief lifted both of his empty hands, and then made a show of opening his vest and turning around. He had a knife on his belt, but it wasn't the one he'd taken from the broker — nor did he have it under his coat. "What one has one moment and what one has the next are sometimes two different things."

Elsith narrowed her eyes and studied his pudgy face for the longest time. "Be careful, Riorik. The line between merely a useful thief and an enemy of the state is a short one."

"Of course, but, do keep in mind one fact."

"What?"

He pointed over at Spidous's remains and made a quick gesture of respect with the other. "That line tends to intersect with the line of one's life. If recent events have taught me anything, it's that both of those lines are rivaled by what is considered 'holy' and what is not. I may toe those lines, my good Huntsmatron, but I've lost much of my desire to cross them."

The thief shuddered in disgust as the Lovers moved the paladin's corpse and a mix of blood and toxic slush poured out of the wound in his skull. Elsith turned to leave, but before she did, added a remark in passing. "Help and lines aside? I'd steer clear of the Lovers for now. This is only going to serve to make them angrier than they already are."

***

At the best of times, the entrance to the Repository was an imposing structure. Built to house the worst of the worst of relics, tomes, and creations ever made in this world – or summoned forth from the next – it was as much a fortress as it was a place of worship. In all honestly, it was far more of the former than the latter.

The Repository ultimately served two purposes: to keep what was inside secure, and what was outside... out. In the post-dusk hour, the gold and copper gate glistened with torchlight, magelight, and the angry crackle of spell-wards that were seemingly *eager* to serve their purpose. They also shone with magic that caused the pillars they were mounted on to emit a soft white sheen that arced ever so often with tendrils of holy light.

Efforts of Order Wardkeepers had been put to task to reinforce it once word of Anais's capture reached them. Strengthen it. Turn the fortress into a beacon of light that would chase away the dark. Chase away the Abyss – and punish any brought to it. Four members of a lower branch of the Order, the Keepers of Love, stood on both sides of the gateway in preparation to lower the magic protecting the Repository and then to return it to more than its typical strength.

Those efforts to enhance the runes and wards wouldn't last more than a few hours – just enough to secure the Order's hooded captive until it was time for her excisement. That decision had already been reached:

she'd be annihilated before dawn. Nobody would speak for her, and nobody would help her.

The only thing that *might* save her from a trial by flames was if she talked. At length. And honestly. But to save her for *what*, however, was a question that nobody that possessed a faint stomach wanted to ponder.

They'd almost marched Anais through the city in a parade, and every parade has watchers. The crowd that followed made up almost every walk of life Basion, and few of the Lovers were happy about the throng of onlookers. It had a decided perk, however: *Everyone* knew who she was by the time she arrived at the Lover's base, and *everyone* knew that her influence in the city was at an end.

Everyone knew she was going to be dead before the sun rose again.

If, and only if, one of their members could be bothered to wait that long. Their captive was already bound in chains, and the only reason that Akaran *wasn't* once he heard what she had done to Seline was because Catherine had too many tears in her eyes to even care what he did. She didn't care, and anyone that took one look at him decided it was in their own best interests not to stop him.

Fury poured off of his shoulders like water. Anger radiated from him with such intensity that the few people near him could *feel* it. And if you happened to look through the world and into his aura?

Ice had seemingly encased his heart as much as anger billowed like a flaming cloak trailing his soul. "Kidnapped Sel, tortured her. Murdered Spidous," he seethed. "Don't bother to hope for survival. Time. That's all you can bargain for. Just time. Give me one reason I shouldn't mount your head on the gates right now."

Anais lifted her sack-covered head and tried to see him through the burlap wrap. "Because I know more than you do."

"Not by much. You told Riorik what you knew and quite honestly I don't give one steaming pile of fisk about it," he swore. When the news of her capture – and the circumstances around it – had reached him, he had only been out of the caves for a matter of minutes. He was filthy, he was bloody, he was exhausted, and the only thing that served to keep him upright was pure disgust.

"I still know truths," she argued as he waved away the two other exorcists that had taken the task of dragging her along the streets of the city. It had been quite the spectacle to behold, and one that was already echoing from the lowest of the cisterns to the highest of the towers around the city. "Ones I haven't said."

"Except you'd rather bullshit me and we all know it. You chose to dr..."

he snarled before he had to stop and focus his anger enough to even be able to speak. "You tried to *drown* Seline. You dunked her over and over into that pool of fetid filth. You tortured *an innocent woman!*"

The broker chuckled lightly at the accusation. "She helped you. How innocent can she be?"

Catherine must have seen the look that fell across his face and caught his wrist before he could put a blazing bolt of divine fury into her chest. "Whatever she knows, we need to know. If she's lying, I'll end her myself."

"Of course she's lying," the exorcist snapped back as the crowd around them grew in size yet wisely gave them all more space at the foot of the bridge leading up to the gates. "She needs to be punished. Now."

"She will be," the Maiden-Templar assured him as she pushed his hand back to his side. Her eyes were bloodshot and her cheeks were raw. They'd already received Spidous's body an hour back, and to say that she had not taken the news well was horribly accurate.

Akaran twisted his hand away from her and stepped even closer to their captive. The exorcists holding her up unceremoniously dropped her to the ground and moved away. Neither of them wanted to have any part in whatever their younger colleague was thinking or planning.

No matter how much they agreed with it.

He ripped her hood off and exposed her gaunt, gray face and an unexpectedly missing eye to the world to see. What was left of her neck's tail had been tied tight to her neck — so tight that the ropes used had ripped what little skin she had over her throat. If she'd been human, it would've been a miracle for her to be able to talk. Since she wasn't, he only had to assume that her words were as much magic as they were physically spoken. People gasped in revulsion and disgust at the sight, but he wasn't done yet. "If she's to be punished, then let's see what she really is."

The Templar's eyes went wide as she felt him pull ether around his eye for the spell he was about to unleash. "Not in front of the rest! Not in public!"

"They need to see," he spat. "The city needs to know what kind of monster it let rise to power. They need to work with *us.* They need to see what *we* see. So? Let 'em watch. By the Goddess, Anais — **I CALL YOU TO UNMASK**!"

His Word lunged off of his lips and slammed down onto her enshackled body. The ropes and chains didn't change, but the flesh they held did. His spell not only ripped away her glamour, it ripped away whatever pretenses of humanity she might have ever had. In the warehouse, she had ripped open her own chest to show a hardened mass underneath that was supposed to have protected her against direct spells that might have done her harm. The gash hadn't recovered in the time since.

His spell didn't cause her harm, so it didn't help.

The magic ripped away the protections that had been baked into it upon her unholy resurrection. Gray flesh crinkled, twisted, and burned away like fog dissolving under the light of the sun. As dead skin vaporized, the illusion of what she was fell away.

Her dress remained intact, though nothing underneath it did. She was more than just a walking corpse; she was a human analog built onto the shell of a monster. Her skin covered oily red and muddy sand that fell away and pooled at her feet. Dirt sloughed off of a blackened carapace that thrummed with an inky aura that made everyone's skin crawl.

When his Word finished its work, she was shown for what she was: a mass of bones mounted with copper wire and butcher's strings onto the shell of scorpion larger than he'd ever seen or that had ever existed... at least in this world. The center of the shell cracked open slightly and revealed the same kind of deformed, compressed, sickening skull that Rmaci had described seeing in Donta's chest. Some shreds of flesh remained on blotches across her face – gray, leathery, wrinkled skin.

Something to remind her that she'd once been human.

Anais's head rolled back and forth across her shoulders as the handful of tendons she had left struggled to keep it attached. Her eye was full of pain and agony even as a fountain of sand and more tried to well up and serve to hold her head upright. A long pulsing tube rolled from under the malformed skull buried in the carapace and up toward the dismembered tail just behind her throat.

The crowd reacted as expected. People screamed in horror. Others ran away. Someone threw up when the smell of ages-dead and decaying flesh wafted their direction. There were shouts for divine guidance, and cries for help.

The Order reacted with force. Someone summoned a fresh call of luminoso; someone else called for a wall of shimmering energy to push people away from the broker. Even Catherine flinched at the sight.

Akaran didn't. He stood in stoic silence with his lip curled and his left hand trembling. Magic pulsed around his fingers and palm. "I think this just made me feel better about watching you burn."

"Won't burn. Whatever you do, I won't burn. He won't let me. I know things. He won't let me burn," she promised. Her voice didn't come from her mouth this time. It came from her chest. Witnessing her 'speak' had just been another part of the illusion of life.

The exorcist's sneer twisted even harder, which was hardly possible. "He won't let you burn? Fine," he spat. "Then see if he stops *this*," he snarled as he grabbed her by the rope around her throat. Poisonous slush leaked out over his hand as he hauled her to her feet and pulled her to the Repository gates.

The metal columns seemed to swell up over her head in her eye, and she felt the divine rites of purification roll over her tattered flesh even from a distance. "No! No, don't! I know things Akaran, I know things you'll want to know!"

"Don't care," he snarled. "You have caused *pain* and I am here to deliver what you have sown."

She struggled and tried to break free of his grip. Her feet kicked at the wooden bridge with thunk after thunk as she knocked one of her boots free. "You can't do this! Please! I *know* things – I have power! Power you want!"

Catherine tried to stop him – but not very hard. Her assistant, the ever-cloaked Karaj, appeared at her side and stopped her from doing more than just shouting at her underling. Akaran could've been stopped. It wouldn't have been easy. A word, an instruction, a hand on his shoulder; that's what it would've taken to slow him down. "I don't want power. I just want justice."

He could've been stopped. The wardkeepers by the gate looked at the Maiden-Templar for instruction. She knew she should've. She wanted to have him stop. Except she didn't.

Nobody did. In their hearts, nobody objected.

Akaran placed a foot down in the gateway and pulled her close to the doors and forced her to look up the hill. From the ground, all she could see were the sparking columns, the mountain leading into the cliffside, and the statue of Miral himself that peered down from the middle of the Repository's hill. "You terrorized someone I care a great deal about, you pathetic inhuman *bitch*," he swore, "and if you're so convinced you won't *burn*, then let's see what happens when you're forced to swim in Love's glory."

The priest pulled her closer to the gate as the glowing haze in the ether began to appear in front of their eyes. The ever-after, it seemed, was very tired of waiting for her. Thin tendrils of power rolled off of the metal like steam and the edges of the black mess in her chest began to crackle. With righteous fury brimming in his eye, he pulled her up and to the very edge of the shifting shield of magic.

Two heartbeats later, and she'd have gone in.

One less than that, and she found a way to stop him. "WHERE HE IS! I CAN TELL YOU WHERE YOUR BROTHER IS!"

"My brother?" Akaran snarled. "I don't have one."

"HE THINKS HE IS – HE'S HERE! I CAN TELL YOU! THE MAN OF RED!"

The name plucked a scab off of a host of old wounds that *still* hadn't healed – and not all of them were physical. "Man of the... the asshole from Toniki? You work for *him*?!" There was one ever-so-brief moment that his rage at her abated and a cold hand seemingly clutched his heart. "He's here?"

Karaj moved in before Akaran could finish the job and pulled both the exorcist and his captive away from the gate. The broker fell onto the wooden bridge with a soft thump while the younger man tried to push past Catherine's assistant. "Of all the names you could invoke, you chose that one. You have either just demonstrated yourself as a woman very wise, very desperate, or very foolish. Mayhaps all three. If you know of him, then you'll speak truth."

"I'll speak every truth. All truths I know. All truths I can, truths that my tongue is not bound by. Please. Please don't send me back. I can't go back to the Citadel. Anything. Anything you want, anything you offer, just don't," Anais pleaded from the ground even as she struggled to push herself away from the crackling doorway.

"Get off of me," Akaran snarled as he tried to break free of the Lover's grip on his arm. "She's lying. I don't have a brother, I don't have family, I just have the Goddess. I know that I need to wrap my hands around that Sycian's throat and squeeze it until his tongue pops out but that's neither here nor there, and it isn't worth letting her live to find him today."

"There's much in this world to know and knowing more of that man is paramount," Catherine's assistant cautioned as they kept their grip on the younger priest. "Of all of his sins, delusions are one of them. I am sure he is no more your brother than he is mine."

"Delusions?" the broker spat from the dirt. "What he has is *knowledge*. Knowledge of men and knowledge of things worse. If he calls you brother – understand he gives no lies, he speaks truth and only."

The exorcist pushed back against Karaj again and would've drawn his dagger if they hadn't caught his wrist before he could. "I have the Goddess. She is my Mother. I need no other," the exorcist retorted. "The Order made that much clear."

Karaj shook their head and casually flicked a band of ether off of their wrist that wrapped tight around Anais's throat before she could struggle away. "The Order makes many things clear. Matters regarding her master are one of them; a conversation we've had already. Need I caution you further that you were found as a child bloodied and lacking of eye, found lost and with memories muddled."

"I know how I was found!" Akaran thundered. "It makes *no damn difference* in what happens to her!"

"What happens to her is what happens to him," Karaj promised. "I give my word."

"The only word I care about is the Word that *ends her*," he snarled. "Catherine! Let me have her! *Please*."

The Maiden-Templar wiped tears from her eyes and didn't say anything at first. She just stood still, and every ragged breath she took made her chest heave. "Enough. Both of you. She claims to have knowledge the Order needs – and now that everyone in *whole damn city* has heard that it can be used as a bargaining chip, I doubt we'll have much time to extract it. You'll *both* get your wishes in brief time. I have no doubt."

Akaran shook himself free of Karaj's grip and wiped sweaty grime off from his forehead with the back of his hand. "You can't trust anything she has to say. If I have a brother, fine. If I don't have a brother, *fine*. I have the Goddess either way, and I have seen no kin of mine ever at my side. Some asshole thinks he knows me? Fine. I'll beat the 'why' out of him next time he crosses my path. I still owe him an eye for Mariah's sake. We don't need *her*. We can't trust *her*."

"I... I tell you your brother is my creator and you'd still rather... rather kill me than force me to speak of what... the wealth of knowledge... I have?" Anais croaked from the ground. "You are... dangerously of single mind."

He looked down at her and spit at her feet before he turned his attention back to Karaj. "You gave me a book. Told me it talked about some city-killer from Sycio. The Man of the Red Death – that's really him?"

"Yes."

"You forget that the son of a bitch already pissed in my gruel once already? Terrorized Toniki while I was stuck in some iced-over tower dealing with Daringol?" Akaran challenged. "Much as I owe him pain, this thundering slitch needs to be banished for the sake of Love."

"She will, Akaran, I promise," Catherine offered as she stepped in closer and put her hand on his shoulder.

It didn't do a damn thing to halt his rage. She *felt* it boiling in his aura. So much anger, so much *heat* in his soul. It was the same fury she'd felt when he'd lost control at the Manor. The same rage he'd had when he obliterated a warship in Cableture.

He looked up at her, and the raw look of utter *hate* in his eye was enough to make *everyone* but her and Karaj take a few steps back. "Fine. We'll split the difference. She's a construct. Excise her and we'll use her corpse to track her creator. Same thing we've done with the vampires. We can do it for Nasta-"

The aide stepped in so close to him that the exorcist had to shut up mid-word or risk bashing his teeth on their forehead. "Names have power. That is not a power we need to have cross our door on this day," they cautioned firmly. "If she speaks truth, we need her. If not, there's worse than a Ward of Iron Hearts that awaits for her in the Vault. A day or three will make no matter."

Akaran growled a response that wasn't suitable to be said clearly, and forcibly brushed past Karaj without a direct response. "Catching this bitch doesn't solve the Annix problem."

"Or the Malik one, but we are a people capable of solving more than one problem at a time." Catherine finally chimed in. "Yet to solve problems, we need answers. So please. Tell me you found something of note in the caves."

"We found a lot. None of it good and Annix isn't working alone," he groused over at her while the crowd slowly began to dissipate at the urging of assorted Wardkeepers and other Messengers. "I need to find Telburn. The Headmaster and I need to have a *talk*."

"Not now," Karaj intoned as other Lovers marched through the gate and the spells protecting it began to fall to the side. "Night is effectively here. We have no actions to take to hunt the vampire down, and should it poke it's head out of the ground, all of us need to be ready to strike in turn."

Akaran shook his head and rejected the idea entirely. "Give me some rations and water. I'll eat as I go. I've got to find him. Annix spent a lot crowns getting a lot of magework done and –"

"And nothing, Akaran," Catherine interrupted. "You look as if you're about to collapse on your feet. Grief or not, anger or not, you need rest. You cannot serve the Goddess if you're too tired to walk."

"I'm fi-" he managed to get out before someone else rudely cut him off.

"You're fixing to speak another falsehood," Riorik chimed in as the last of the crowd scurried away to safer places with horrible tales on their lips. "Maiden-Templar. Yes, he's about to drop. I daresay I've heard more than you about what he accomplished in the caves and if I am not mistaken, don't you demand that your Messengers, as they are, take time to calm their minds after... well... they *message*?"

Catherine's jaw dropped as she looked from thief to priest and back again. Akaran just rolled his eye while she decided to address the man that she presumed would be more honest and forthcoming. "He did what? How would you know? You weren't there. I was told that you assisted with the capture −"

"Oh I wasn't *there*, but... let's just say that between our three organizations, there's a great deal of overlap between our employees as of late," he answered. "Well done, I may add. A ghoul of all things. I am not versed in the dead but even I know what grief those can cause."

"Three?" she asked, bewildered. "The Order and... yours, apparently. Who's the third?"

Karaj carefully took Akaran by his hand and peered over his palm. "A ghoul? You excised one? Does that explain why your stomach looks like it has been bleeding again?"

"Yes, yes, and I assume he means hers," Akaran sighed as he pointed at a different figure muscling their way through the dwindling crowd. "I'm fine."

"Child, those things are *toxin* defined," Catherine's aid scolded. "You should have been submerged in a vat of goat milk and ivy the moment you approached holy ground."

The Maiden rubbed at her forehead and tried not to unleash the exasperated sigh she felt building in her bones. "And he wonders why nobody takes him seriously."

"Nobody takes him seriously because he's simply too impatient to try and allow the rest of us catch up to his thoughts," the thief answered honestly. "Then he gets ignored because nobody likes dealing with the headaches that people like him tend to cause."

Akaran gave him a withering glare and shook free of Karaj a second time. "Speaking of men causing headaches," he began before he dropped his shoulders and bowed his head. "Riorik. Thank you for saving her."

"Thank me if you wish," his maybe-*actually*-a-friend replied, "but I broke a promise to her. She confessed that she had been scared for her life, and I did not act in a way that prevented harm to it. I'm quite offended by that; I expect that you're more than a measure irritated with me."

The exorcist walked back across the bridge in silence and carefully put his hand on Riorik's shoulder. "I'm not. You saved her. I didn't. I'm grateful."

"Grateful enough to rest?"

He sighed and stepped away from the thief. "Fine. I'll rest as soon as I see her. Catherine? What room is she in?"

"We do not have her here. She has been remanded to the Manor, for care," she answered slowly as the Wardkeepers pulled Anais past the gate and began to seal up the passageway with spellwork all over again.

Fury boiled up in Akaran's chest all over again and *everybody* could see it. "Are you *fisking mad*?!" he demanded. "You locked her up in the building where we know that *a fisking vampire* has been wanking his dick every night? That is the *least safest fisking place in the city to put her!*"

The Maiden-Templar cut his fury short with a softly spoken Word that seemed to take the air out of his sails even if he didn't quite hear it. "No force of ill will shall make it through the gates of the Manor this night or any night further. Henderschott is the only man in this city that is angrier than you – and he has effectively moved the city barracks into Ridora's front yard. I promise; she's safe."

"What about what Lolron said? He's some kind of... elven magical moya... master... or some... metaphysical bullshit title given to bullshit people. Can we risk it?"

"Our magics have served the Order well since the Reformation of the Order," Catherine chided. "They will serve the Order again for yet one more night."

Before he could get the energy to voice another complaint, someone else interrupted. Again. "Your medicannia may be safe, but the rest of you aren't," Elsith snarled as she finished poking her way through the last few people who had the courage to buck the Wardkeepers and watch the proceedings. "The Urn. I want it. Now."

Akaran blinked in empty confusion while Karaj straightened up like they found steel in their spine. Catherine slowly turned to the Huntsmatron and gave her a very calm, very blank stare. "The Urn?"

"Of Xabraxis," Riorik chimed in. Elsith turned her head and gave him a withering stare but he cut her off with a wave of his hand. "Oh, please. You were about to blab the name in front of all of these people and we'd be back at the, 'I need to forget what I know,' stage of the threats that would do absolutely no good and you know it."

Elsith bit her tongue and turned back to the Maiden-Templar. "That. It's Guild property. The scorpion queen over there says you have it. It belongs to the Huntsmen."

"I don't know what she told you but I promise you that the Order has no item that belongs to the Guild. Our arrangements prohibit us from keeping secrets from each other of... well I presume it's some kind of magical relic if you think we have it."

"Our *arrangements* were made by people who had one hand over their heart and the other full of shit and you know it," the mercenary charged. "I have secrets. You have secrets. Except now I know that you have one of my secrets and I can't let you keep my secret."

Riorik cleared his throat with a grin as he slowly sidled up to his confused, temporarily-befuddled friend. "It's not much of a secret if you're going to have a shouting fit about it on the lawn," he pointed out. "Now I assume that everyone knows you have secrets... of course, I can only imagine how little that's going to come as a shock to anyone that's paid the least bit of attention."

"Do you know what in the pits that Urn is?" Elsith hissed as she took a cue from the thief and edged in closer to the Templar. "*Who* is kept inside it?"

"I'd have to know what it is to know what you mean," Catherine lied effortlessly. "Since I don't, then I *don't*, and if I *don't*, then I can't help you, *Huntsmatron*."

"If I send a message to the Council of Hunters and tell them that you have it, there will be a writ in blood with your name etched upon it in my hands before dawn breaks. Understand me, *Templar*, that if you have the Urn, then I am taking it with me."

Catherine looked right into the enraged hunter's eyes and kept her face as blank as she possibly could. "Careful. You are one woman, and the Hunters of Basion are but *one* company of mercenaries – one backed by crowns, and yes, one backed by the Council of Hunters, but they are not here. *We* are backed by the Goddess and *She* is everywhere Her will demands."

"I'm willing to bet that my knives work faster than your spells, priestess," Elsith shot back. "If you have it, I want it. I want it now."

Anais called out from past the gate and tried to laugh at the pair before someone kicked her in the jaw. "Yes, the Order has it. They have a lot. They have a lot of things that benefactor wants and that Urn is one of them. Elsith, let me free and I'll tell you."

"I want the Urn. Not whatever... *you* are," the mercenary snarled. "You can't offer anything else that interests me unless you can deliver Malik."

"I already told these bastards that I can't!" the broker retorted as she nervously flicked her eye at Riorik.

"Then I expect you should prepare yourself to tell *even more* bastards the same thing," Elsith countered. "After they give me the Urn."

Akaran shook off the effects of Catherine's spell and blinked a few times to focus his sight. "Whatever you two are pissing over, I don't care. Elsith, if it's in the vault, it's not going anywhere. If not, it doesn't matter. You can fight about it after we catch Annix. I need to speak to your husband. He's been doing business with the vampire."

"Your logic is impeccable," she snapped before she tilted her head to the side. "What do you mean he's been doing business...?"

The exorcist gave a hateful snarl in Anais's direction and turned his attention back to the pair of arguing women. "There's Granalchi portal runes and mage lights and mirrors all over Annix's lair. Talk to the woman you sent with me. His people are in bed with the damn thing."

"That is... a serious accusation," Catherine remarked while the Huntsmatron tried to make sense of his claim. "What would a vampire want with *mirrors*?"

Akaran shuddered and didn't even try to hide it. "He likes to play games with his dinner. I need to speak to Telburn. *Tonight*," he stressed.

Riorik walked around and stopped him before he could take another step. "Akaran, no. I appreciate your determination, but your day needs to come to an end. Do what I am getting ready to go do, and let these ladies and more deal with the things that must be dealt with for the night."

"Do I even want to ask?"

"I am going to find a companion and a bath. Not necessarily in that order. I do suggest you do both. I can even arrange for help finding either."

"Goat's milk," Karaj added. "If you condemned a ghoul, you need to bathe in goat's milk before your skin begins to necrotize. I promise, that will be an experience you will not enjoy."

He heard the words as they followed the broker's escort but ignored the meaning as the statement clicked in the back of his head. Akaran looked back at Anais and the gathering ready to drag her inside the Repository. "The necromancy used to pull you out of the pit and let you blend in so... *humanly*. There are very few people that would know how to do that... let alone actually be able *to* do it. Where did he learn it?"

"Sycio. He must've. Nobody east of the desert has that kind of knowledge. Even if they did, they wouldn't share it."

A little shadow fell across his face as he digested her answer. "I... I can do that. I'm going to need you to do something for me first, Maiden. Please."

She looked away from Anais with tears of raw frustration in her eyes.

"What more could you possibly need from me right now? Or more importantly, would it help you calm down if I did it? I'm little more than a heartbeat away from having you put in the same chains the bitch is in."

Akaran tilted his head and moved away from their captive as the Wardkeepers worked her over. "This is an 'official request.' Not sure you're going to be thrilled."

"Official in what way?"

"You were an instructor at the training grounds of Sebbidule, right?"

Catherine frowned and nodded slowly. "Yes. What in the world would that possibly have anything to do with right now?"

He took a breath and frowned anew. "Were you able to teach Words?"

"Of course. I have access to the full body of the Templar Grimoire. It won't do you much good though – you know that exorcists are unable to channel the magic needed by those spells."

"That's not… *entirely* true," he replied with a slight grimace.

"You are very wrong about that," she scolded. "It's one of the foundations of Temple training. The spells that heal and defend are channeled differently than the Words that harm or disrupt. One does, one undoes. There are ways to cross the two for some simple things but, this is nothing you don't know."

Akaran shook his head. "Maiden, I promise, you're wrong. Listen, I –"

"No, I am not," she countered. "An exorcist attempting to use defensive or manipulative magics suffers for the cast to an extent that it's not permitted to do, learn, nor try. If you have been told differently –"

The word rolled off of her lips an instant before she realized what she had just said – and who she had just said it to. "About that whole 'permission' thing?" he asked before he closed his eye and extended his hand.

"Oh. Oh don't you even –" Catherine started to warn.

She should've known better to even try. The invocation left his tongue before she could swat his hand back down to his side, and while it wasn't complicated, it worked. "Celiouso et-vas savaline lumin," left his lips in a bare whisper. Under his tabard, a rune on his shoulder turned bright red as a ring of fire swelled up in the palm of his left hand.

He couldn't do much with it, but it worked in a pinch – if something needed to be burned badly enough. He'd used it once back in Toniki, and *once* was *enough*. Before the flames faded away, he had clutched his eye with his other fist and started swearing violently under his breath. The Maiden's headache matched his almost immediately, though her language was slightly more tame. "*That* should *not* be *possible*."

"Possible, yes. Pleasant, fisking all *no*," he whined as he fought back a few errant tears from the pain.

"How did you... where did you...?"

"Long story," Akaran countered. "Misspent youth. I *can* do it. That one, and 'allay.' I'm going to need to learn another one."

Her eyes went wide as what he was really asking sunk home. "You mean you need me to perform a Rite of the Written."

"Yeap."

Catherine took a deep breath and let it out slowly as her men finished bundling Anais up for transport. "You're asking me to etch a Word on you – put a Word on your flesh, without having the appropriate skill to channel it? You're asking me to do that even as you know you'll hurt if you ever do try to invoke it, and apparently quite severely."

"Yeap."

"You're asking me to condone you risking your health for a spell that you shouldn't be able to use, and there's no promise that you can," she went on as her voice hit a new octave with almost every sentence.

He took a breath that almost matched hers and nodded along in agreement. "Yea... I mean, yes Maiden, I am."

She couldn't stop herself from reaching up to stroke her own jaw as she tried to make any sense of this utterly *stupid* request. "You are aware that as a Maiden, my oath to the Temple is such that I shall abide by the rules of the Goddess and only provide the knowledge of Her magic and will to those that are deemed worthy of using it. That you just used a fire-call and you're asking for the imprint implies that those Words have already been placed upon your skin... which leaves me within full permission of the Office of the Holy General to remove them myself for your own good. You are aware of that, yes?"

"Are you two about done?" Elsith interrupted. "We have matters to discuss."

Akaran ignored her and rubbed the charred skin the little fireball had left behind on his palm. "Worthy doesn't have to mean pleasant," he replied. "Besides. Karaj asked where my Words are and I didn't lie to them about it."

"Willingness to suffer self-sacrifice does not mean wisdom. Yet another habit of yours I am somehow not at all shocked to discover."

"I'm a soldier," he argued. "We fight, we hurt, we suffer. It's our duty."

Catherine pointed her finger at him and forcefully shut him down. "It is your duty to *live* for the Goddess. You cannot fight if you are *dead*. Your first duty is to yourself so you can serve *Her*."

"It's my duty to do what needs to be done," he continued to argue. He rubbed at his eye again and blinked away the last few tears. "Contrary to my service so far, I really I don't like pain. I try to avoid it. But we need answers and we're going to need truthful ones."

Exasperated, she clenched her hands. "You forget that you're asking a *Templar* to train you to do a thing that a *Templar* can already do. Why ask to learn it when you can ask me to use it?"

"Because you're not everywhere I am and you may not be places I'm going. We are short-handed, the healers and Wardkeepers are up to their necks right now, and honestly, I talk to people you don't want to be caught with."

"Like that abomination? Or the dead spy that seemingly took residence in your head?" she asked as she pointed over at Anais. "Your dealings with her have may compromised all of us. Is she the type of person you want to keep me from? Or maybe your friend, the apparent *Master-Thief* of Basion?"

Riorik coughed into the collar of his offensively-orange vest. "Missus, I assure you: there's little that's 'merely' apparent about it. It is what I am. The works of the 'Lady' happened to ensure that there was a vacuum of power and nature –"

"Oh, just shut up," the Maiden seethed under her breath without even bothering to glance in his general direction. "Why you're even permitted *here* in this moment... or any damn moment..."

Akaran flinched, then steeled himself against the charge. "Yes. Like her. Like him. Like Rmaci's shade. Teach me how to use truthcall, and maybe I'll make fewer fiskups like this in the future."

"Truthcall?" Catherine repeated in surprise. "That's the invocation you're asking for?"

"It is."

"You understand why we lock that one away, don't you? To force a person to do an act against their will is a violation of self. People have the right to lie, regardless of the moral ramifications of such."

He looked over his shoulder and watched as the broken Merchant of Secrets was carted away. "She's going to be taken to a cell and interrogated. Probably violently. Are you going to use magic on her to get her to tell the truth?"

"Likely, yes," she admitted, "but we have strict rules on *how* it can be used. Knowing that spell requires that you are registered with the Crown as a psyanist, and with the Justiciar and –"

"– and it's a pain in the damn ass all around that's going to cause me to have a pain in the damn ass if I use it so I promise to only use it in event where having a pain in the ass might mean it saves me a pain that slides between my ribs. Or any other squishy spots I happen to like," he finished. "Is now really the time to have this dispute? I just need people to tell me the truth."

"This Repository is a fortress of the truth, Akaran. It can be a very dangerous thing," Catherine countered. "What plot are you cooking up in that twisted head of yours?"

The exorcist worked his leg and tried to crack his neck as she studied his face. "Honestly? If we're ever able to catch one of these assholes, we're going to have questions. We won't have a lot of time to ask them. These damn things are *smart*, Maiden, and we need every tool we have to save Bistra... damn, save the whole bloody city."

She answered with a pained sigh. "I understand the point you're trying to make, but honestly, I do not know if you understand mine. You're young. You're impulsive. You're dangerous," Catherine stressed. "I know you believe you'll only use it for reasons that are pure of heart but you lack the wisdom that comes with age and training. I fear the temptation will be there and cause you to do something you may regret."

"With all due respect, Maiden? I don't give a damn about 'pure of heart.' Annix has been cutting deals with humans. Anais has done just as many and probably a legion's worth more. This *thing* is worse than some random spirit or irritable little demon. The extra push to get someone to open their mouth might make all the difference in the world right now, and you know it."

Her response was long in coming, and she didn't give it without a feeling of disquiet brimming in her stomach. "If... *if*... I grant you this boon, I am not doing you a favor. I am giving you a spell that will cause stress, tears, and one that will give you agency over souls that may be guilty of nothing. The truth is a dangerous weapon, Akaran. I cannot stress that enough."

"A dangerous weapon?" he repeated with a disgusted little smile. "That, Maiden, is what I'm counting on."

IV. A STORY IN SHACKLES
Mid-Evening of Zundis 12ᵗʰ of Firstgrow, 513 QR

"I don't want to be here, you don't want to be here. So. Solve a problem for me, and you can go just about anywhere you like," Akaran told the prisoner as he lit a nearby sconce.

The sulfur torch cast a cool blue glow through the dungeon, and the smell it emitted only served to improve the dank hovel. It also woke up the dark-skinned man huddled in a threadbare blanket in an even danker corner of his personal cell. There was nobody else down there – this particular wing of the 4ᵗʰ Garrison's barracks had a *special* prison for 'high-value' acquisitions to be held until more suitable *arrangements* could be made. The last time that the man in the corner had a roommate was Darvol, the now headless former head of the Woodmason's Guild.

It was a fate that the Sycian native expected to befall his own neck. "You again," he sleepily muttered.

"Me again. Se'daulif Ocsimmer – a shiverdine from Sycio," Akaran remarked as he pulled up a shoddy wooden stool and sat down on it. "An odd name for a man that traffics in slaves, but, language is language. You're just a common slaver by trade, merchant by reputation, and something of a hedonist by nature. Is that about right?"

The dusky-skinned merchant sat up and scooted down the length of his cot to take a better look at the exorcist. He'd seen better days – by far better days. Between his ratty graying beard, the deep circles under his red-violet eyes, and a deep bruise along his jaw, it was painfully obvious that he hadn't enjoyed his stay in the Queen's custody. "You forgot wrongfully imprisoned. By you, one must add. Do be kind to forgive if I am not of eagerness to make a deal."

"I do, but here's the truth. I was wrong. An apology doesn't undo the circumstances you're in, but I hope it can put us on a good footing going forward."

"The one that put me in a cage comes to bargain, but does not bargain with keys-in-hand," the slaver slowly pointed out. "This leads one to think that your admission of fault is not a revocation of condemnation."

Akaran nodded in agreement. "It isn't. The mace wasn't yours. You were framed. I'm just as willing to accept that you never were in possession of the Adelin Crest I found."

Se'daulif narrowed his bloodshot eyes and stared at the priest. "I assume one then has other false charges that would necessitate my imprisonment?"

"You had an idol and certain texts in your possession that are banned under Queen's law when you were arrested. The guards found it in your belongings. *Don't* deny that – it's entirely different than the Adelin crest."

"An idol and texts? One is being held for worship?" the slaver asked as his eyes went wide in surprise. "One would expect that of all the Orders, yours is the one that would understand that persecution for belief is no crime! Especially when one worships light!"

"Nooooo," Akaran replied as he drew the word out slowly with a low growl, "because I'd agree if you were worshiping *Light*."

"Lazi *is* Light!"

The exorcist quickly drew his knife and sharply rapped the cell bars with the tip in a warning blow. "I don't exactly agree or even like the Orders of Stara or Light, but you're mispronouncing Lumina – the *actual* Goddess of Light."

"Lumina is the *bearer* of light," the slaver replied slowly but forcefully. "Lazi *is* Light. The true Creator of All That Shines. The One that births the strength of stars, the One that –"

"Enough, Se'daulif," he warned. "Regardless of how you justify it, it's enough to ensure that you're kept in a cell for a very long time. Even if not this one. My Order is tasked with stomping out cults of all kinds – and Lavi is a heresy. We have places for people like you, but I'm giving you the chance to avoid them."

"Betray one's beliefs for relief of suffering? You are as hypocritical as you are false."

Akaran snorted and leaned back in his chair with his arms crossed. The dampness wasn't doing a blessed thing for his joints, and both his knee and his gut-wound were starting to throb all over again. "I don't give a shit about your beliefs. Lazi, opposed to Lumina? You could worship Makaral or Uoom for all I care… save the argument in difference for an Inquisitor. It's not why I'm here and it's not what's going to get you out."

"An innocent man, asking to trust the priest that condemned him to prison? This does not seem like a fair request to one such as I."

"You're a slaver. You aren't interested in fair requests."

Se'daulif rolled his eyes. "Tsk. You say that as if this Kingdom doesn't endorse the trade of flesh."

Akaran frowned and gave him a dirty look in return. "Slavery exists across the world. It's not widespread here. We're better than that."

His response elicited a cold, bemused laugh from his prisoner. "Oh, you believe so? No. A good bit of my business involves supplying your military with disposable people, and your royals with forgettable helpers."

The accusation stung, but he couldn't readily deny it. "At least it isn't celebrated like it is in Sycio."

"Celebrated? No, not hardly," the slaver replied dismissively. "It is simply that my people know the value of life. The value of death, too. Both are expensive yet both have their uses in all matter and manner of commerce."

The priest answered with an irritated sigh and started to rub his eye before he remembered where his hands had been recently. "Trying to justify it isn't going to work with me. You traffic in people. Your *own* people."

"Of course! How else are the poor and destitute to find a way to leave a life of poverty on the outskirts of the sands without offering labors? I offer lodging and work — be it within the walls of the Jewels of Sycio or across the sea to this fine land of rolling green fields and woodlands. If they could survive the stress of the sun and the golden sand on their own, they would have no need to offer themselves to a man such as I. Yet there are those that cannot, and just as those that cannot, ones here that cannot withstand the rigors of woods and tunnels."

"That's twisted logic and you know it," the exorcist grunted. "You're not offering them hope at a better life. You're offering them nothing but servitude on the *dream* that they might find better when they're done."

"Do I? Is it a truth that my logic is twisted, as you say? Did you not sign your life away to a God? Did you not agree to bend your knee and serve at a whim? Do you not gain food, and water, and medicine for the service of your flesh? Do you not have a home to return to?"

Akaran shook his head firmly 'no.' "That's different. I'm serving a Goddess. Not a man."

"Ah, but 'God' is yet another name for 'Master' on the lips of those that offer themselves to service. The perks are the only real difference, and Sycio has *many* different perks to offer," he retorted smugly as he leaned against the cell bars. "Now, I must doubt that you came here to debate the morality of providing work and homes to those needing both – what questions do you have for me?"

"Let's start with the basics: what's your business here, slaver?"

"To see the wedding, of course, if I am not too late by now. The alignment of a tribe and a noble house is an opportunity for trade. But to trade, one must learn and know those he seeks to barter with."

The priest replied with a noncommittal grunt. "Barter. A Sycian wants to get into bed with the Midlanders?"

"Of course! My homeland has oft heard of the prowess of the menfolk of the Midlands," he exclaimed with a tired smile. "The idea of acquiring a few to bring to Temtu'mnot was enough to convince one such as myself to embark upon a journey to your fine lands. I assumed getting up *here* would be more comfortable than traveling up-mountain. I may have... misjudged."

Akaran felt his lip curl in disgust and didn't try to hide it. "Why am I even surprised."

Ocsimmer merely shrugged at the comment. "It is just business. You have yours, I have mine. I am sure that I find some aspects of yours equally repugnant." After he gave a quick look around his cell, he frowned and gave the priest another fake, tired smile. "I am quite sure that I do."

"Believe me when I say that as of late, in truth, my business has been just as repulsive as yours," the younger man lamented. "I didn't think it could be, but it is."

The slaver glanced down at the blood seeping from the wound on the priest's stomach and had to nod in slow agreement. "Ah, I am so glad that I do not have your job. My work is in absolutes. Yours is in entertaining the impossible to rule out the improbable. Much a headache, I would assume."

"Lots of aches," he agreed before he switched gears. "Who'd you manage to piss off while you were here? Any competitors?"

The question only served to rankle the outsider. "I am a slaver visiting a nation that both condemns those that slave and exploits the meat that I bring to the tables of the rich and the armed. *Most* people here do not look upon one such as I kindly; even more, based off of the color of my skin."

Akaran raised his eyebrow at the admissions. "Not a lot of love for a Sycian, hm?"

"Standing out in a crowd is not always a desirable trait," Se'daulif agreed. "A feeling I am sure you are well in awareness of, yes?"

"There are days. So – you've no friends here, and you don't know why Anais would have wanted to frame you for smuggling. That about right?"

"That is, I am most assuredly unhappy to say, the case," the slaver agreed before he sat up and worked his fingers nervously. "Forgive one for asking, but did you just mention the name of the secretive Lovic? She's the one…? Whatever… whatever for?"

He shrugged and rubbed at his seeping cut. "I was hoping you'd know. You're a little more inclined to talk than she is at the moment."

Se'daulif rubbed at the rough gray stubble on his chin. "I… I see. That's a proclamation of interest that holds more than one statement of fact. You would and do have to forgive one for having a measure of surprise. From your tone, I assume she's also in custody of sorts?"

"Of sorts. We'll get back to her in a moment. First…"

The dismissal – temporary or not – obviously didn't sit well with the slaver, but he took it in stride. "Yes?"

"You made your point about your profession earlier. So tell me: how involved are you in it here?"

The shiverdine didn't quite bristle, but the accusation was as barbed as a brier-bush. "Are you implying that I am making trades in the city that would be against the law of the Crown you speak so oft of?"

"I'm implying that I saw the women at your dormasil," Akaran countered. "Without getting into an argument about *their* status, yes. Have you been trading?"

"I have only –"

A raised hand and a single finger pointed to the ceiling cut the Sycian off. "Let me clarify myself. Lying about this gets you hung. Honesty gets you a pass out of the city."

Se'daulif scratched at his jaw again and tried to puzzle out the priest's meaning. "Admitting to a crime allows for a pass of punishment? Good priest, do understand if one does not feel as comfortable being forthright as you may so wish…"

"Okay, so let me try this again," Akaran replied after a moment's thought. "I just found seven dead women in a cell *far* worse than this one a little more than three hours ago. They were adjacent to a chamber where a vampire has spent years torturing people. *Someone* knows where they came from. Who built the chamber. Who supplied his tools. I have a lead on part of that. I don't have a lead on the people. *Give me a name* that might have been feeding him, and I'll let you out. If you were the one *doing it*, then we get to have a *longer* talk about everything you know about the son of a bitch."

The slaver slowly walked away from the front of his cage and sat down on the shoddy, rotted wooden cot he'd been provided. It was more than prisoners usually received in Henderschott's care, but it was far from comfortable. "You have uttered many words in a short time that I do not care for," he finally replied, "yet I feel I have begun to see the source of your irritation. It does make one question how much you will believe my honesty: I have had no such trade and no such business."

Akaran flicked his tongue against his teeth. "You're right. That makes it hard to believe."

"*However,*" the shiverdine stressed, "I may know a thing that one would find useful. Or not. Or useful in that it's not."

"If you're going to try to save your neck, make it a good story, at least," the younger man replied as he crossed his arms and leaned back. "It may be your last."

Se'daulif felt the weight of the world behind those words and tried to keep his shoulders from sagging. "You are not the first to assume that what I do comes from any kind of nefarious skill or magical method to entice a soul to sign themselves over for labors – which is most patently untrue. I merely deal in contracts; I am no different than the Guild of Fleets or the Guild of Mages and assuredly not different than the Guild of Traders... the Blackstones, specifically."

"I don't care how you do it," Akaran grumbled. "But go on."

"It was not much more than a few months back that I was approached by a woman who wanted me to engage in the... let us call it... the transactional arrangement of certain individuals. She made the case that I, with my history, would know ways to *entice* more... exotic... individuals into her service. Or at least, into her trade."

"Anais?"

"No, actually," the slaver replied earnestly. "One I had not had bidding with before. I regret that she gave me no name, but I will never forget her face. I can describe it, if you wish."

Akaran pursed his lips. "So you aren't involved, but you were approached by a mystery woman to do... what, exactly?"

The portly shiverdine rubbed his hands together nervously. "I must reiterate: I had no dealings. I declined. As we understand one another."

"I've had a really long, really bloody day, Se'daulif. Please don't make it worse by killing time."

He left the understated, *'or else I'll kill you,'* comment off of his remark, but the slaver felt it all the same. "She said she had a client who had particular tastes both in volume and in form. Oddly enough, she also had a request for gutter trash – anyone that I may have already turned down in finding otherwise gainful employment across the way."

The exorcist frowned and chewed on the idea. "Young, lithe, blonde?"

"And if possible, not of the Kingdom."

Akaran flashed back to the women he'd found stored in Annix's cave and felt his fists clench tight. "She found a dealer."

"I'm not sure a dealer is what she was actually after," his prisoner remarked. "I also do not feel as if she meant for malice. She impressed upon me that they must be in good health, and able to work. Genuinely, she did seem as if she had a way for them to earn a living. Why she approached me and not more official channels, I do not know; but, it is true that thieves that have need for hands of labor do not necessarily want to draw attention to what those labors are."

"Explain."

The sharp tone in the exorcist's voice made the Sycian cringe. "To be most honest – which is what I am being! – it felt less as if she was looking for a supplier and more for an excuse."

That caught his attention. "Someone to blame if she got found out… or if her arrangements went bad."

The slaver nodded in affirmation. "Very much that, yes. Someone with experience in the tradecraft, and someone that fingers could be pointed to should something untoward happen with her investments. As I felt that one could easily be blamed for such a failure or such an occurrence outside of one's hands…"

"…you declined in order to save your own ass," Akaran finished. "Let me guess and say that you didn't bother to pass this tidbit on to anyone in the City's Court, did you?"

"My boy, have you met the Overseer of this city? I would have done better if I had written it down on the finest parchment and then wiped my ass with it. Besides," he went on to add, "one does not buy the services of otherwise disposable souls in large quantities unless one has plenty of gold to spend. With plenty of gold often comes plenty of power, and how am I to know if such a power has sway in the places that I would go tell?"

Akaran couldn't argue the logic no matter how hard he tried. "Fisk. Just… fisk. Fine. Describe this bitch and you've got a way out of this cell tonight."

Se'daulif shook his head. "Ah, no, good priest. Not to the description – she was an older woman – tad shorter than you. Dark hair, suitable more for a chocolate desert than much else; though her eyes? Gray. Hard of a gray as granite itself. I am not deaf at all and I heard the name of the creature you uttered earlier. If I am not to consider you mad, and one would cast no aspersions upon you of the sort, then I feel that mayhaps that I would be better suited to stay where I am until the dawn arrives." As the color faded from the exorcist's face, he continued. "She also had an odd book with her. It was –"

"Thin, leather bound. Red ribbon down the side?"

"That describes many a book, but, yes. Yes, that may be it. You have familiarity...?"

Pieces of a very big, very bloody puzzle fell into place all at once. "I can't believe... Livstra, you stupid, *stupid* woman," Akaran muttered under his breath. He sat perfectly still as his mind raced to put problems and parts together one after the other, and didn't move until he had a set of answers he liked – even if he didn't want. "Alright. You're free. Tonight, tomorrow. I don't care."

"I thank you, but now I have a question of my own, if one may ask."

Akaran had already started to stand up, but he stopped himself and sunk back down to his seat. "What?"

"You mentioned that you have taken the Lady Lovic into custody. As you've alleged that she is the one responsible for my internment, I feel most compelled to ask for the why."

"I don't want to know why," the priest replied after a few long heartbeats, "but I'll tell you the truth – she's going to die. It's going to be painful, it's going to take a while, and I'm not entirely sure the specifics. But she's a dead woman walking." He snorted in brief amusement at the line. "In more ways than one."

Se'daulif leaned forward again with concern etched across his face. "Good priest, I have heard great numbers of variant ways to speak that phrase at many times in my life in the sands. It often means that the subject of discussion is bereft a pulse and oft bereft of breath."

"You'd be right," the exorcist agreed. "She's not human. Still haven't figured out what she is... but maybe you can help with that."

"I have done more favors for the one that has unjustly placed me in chains than one would expect," the slaver calmly replied, "though I suspect that should I not answer you'll seek for ways to entice my stay to be even less pleasant than it has."

"No, but it might help me make sure she stays dead."

His prisoner stretched his shoulders and craned his neck to the side slowly. "Well. One would hate to cause undue work for a man in your situation should one have a way to make it easier. A way that assuredly will be repaid in kind – yes?"

"Yes," Akaran agreed without any hesitation. "I was given a tome recently. It has an interesting name in it that I would like to know more about. Believe it or not, I trust you more than I do her."

"Many a tome have names of interest. That is the point of tomes."

"True enough. When were you born?"

The slaver peered at him quizzically. "An odd ask."

"Just a question."

"That it is," he agreed after a moment. "My eyes first saw sand in the cool-summer of Nine-hundred seventeen Full-sun. How is it you say? I believe it is… the 469th Year of Queen's Rule?"

Akaran pursed his lips. "So… you were, let me… thirty-eight by 507?"

Ocsimmer nodded his head. "Ah…? Yes, yes I believe so."

"I'll assume a well-traveled slaver by then."

"Very, I was," the shiverdine conceded. "I had been well-renown among the dunes by the age of twenty-six. Time has only been kind to me as I have aged; this inconvenience an interruption in an otherwise most stellar career."

It was Akaran's turn to lean in and rest his elbows on his knees as he scooted closer to the cell. "And you've traveled to the other six of Sycio's Jewels?"

"Of course. One cannot be well-renown unless one is truly known in each."

"So you've been to A'twol." He said it so flatly, so coldly, that it was as jarring as a punch across the slaver's face.

It had much the same effect as if the priest actually had. "Did I say six? I meant fiv…" he tried to reply before a withering stare cut his lie off before it could finish. "I have."

"What was it like?"

Se'daulif said nothing and let the question linger in the air. "I do not see why it would have bearing on my position at the moment."

"It's a question," the exorcist countered. "You want out – you answer them. That's the agreement."

"It *is* a question, but one I cannot tell the relevance of."

"Doesn't matter. It's one I'm asking. What was A'twol like?"

The very name of the city sent an uncomfortable chill down the slaver's arms. Thinking about it churned his stomach, and his discomfort was palatable. "It was like. It was a place, in a land. With people, and things. All places have things and most places have people. That city was no different."

Akaran tapped the cell bars with his knife again and let the sharp ringing noise back his words. "What else? I want details."

"Then you are asking of the wrong man. For the matter of one's interests, you are wrong in asking men. Either living *or* dead. I assure you that. You will not find any willing to broach solutions to your questions, whatever their intent may be. It is... worse than a source of shame."

The exorcist drew his lips into a smile so thin you could've cut steel with it. "Fine. Then if not a city, a man. What can you say of Addlerbatt?"

Discomfort gave way to immediate disgust. "A dead king."

"So he is dead."

"Yes."

There was so much finality to the way that Se'daulif spat the word out that there wasn't any point in trying to ask 'when' or 'why,' so the priest moved on. "What happened when A'twol fell?"

Ocsimmer bristled all over again. "It ceased to stand."

"Why?"

The shiverdine took a deep sigh and shook his head morosely. "Because of hubris? Because of lines that must not be crossed that were crossed. Because one asked questions that one does not need to know answers to, and when given, it caused the world to cease for the one that pushed."

Akaran rubbed at the edge of his knee and bit back a grunt of frustration. "Please don't make this harder than it has to be. I need to know these things."

"You ask for I not to make it harder, but you do not understand what it is you ask," the Sycian argued. "Two things and only two things befell the people of the Ruby – death."

"That's one thing. What was the other?"

"A denial of staying so."

That made the exorcist's skin bristle. "Reanimated?"

His response caused the same. "This is not a topic I can broach with an outsider. Please, master priest – A'twol fell. Neither you nor I were there. We are not of the dead, which means we are not to discuss it. Neither one of us, I presume, are of any great hurry to be without the beating of our hearts; discussing it has a habit of causing such cessations."

Akaran took it in stride. Almost. "Fine. What about the man blamed for it? Wears a red robe, I'm told? I've heard a bit about him recently. My understanding is that –"

"I know nothing," the slaver spat hurriedly. "Absolutely nothing. There is nothing to know about a nothing. I've no desire to consider more of nothing than that. Should you be wise, you will not either."

"That's a whole lot of panic for a man that's nothing."

Se'daulif scoffed at the remark. "Panic is a precursor to self-preservation. I'd rather rot in this cell than utter his name, even to a holy man."

"Well, before you interrupted me, let me finish what I was trying to say. As I understand it – and please, do tell me if I'm wrong – this 'Man of the Red' is why A'twol fell. Raised a legion of the damned and marched on the walls."

"If that is what you've heard and is what you understand to be true I am not going to seek an argument with you over it," the older man remarked as he crossed his arms and tried to hide in the growing shadows of his cell. "It is true enough."

"But is it *the* truth?" Akaran pushed. "Who is he? Where did he come from? Why did he destroy the city?"

The shiverdine nervously rubbed his hands on his arms before he gave an honest, if not hedged, answer. "It is *a* truth. As important as any other with the regards made of the people."

"Then tell me about the man that destroyed it."

"Priest, I feel as if you do not understand. That man is *not* to be spoken of," he argued in a hushed voice. "He is *not* to be mentioned. He is *not* to be invoked. To do so risks bringing down the wrath of the dead in ways that defy the imaginations of the living." After saying that, Se'daulif scooted a little closer to the priest and whispered to him like he thought the walls themselves were listening. "Whatever one has been told, understand: he did not destroy A'twol. Do not risk the same."

Akaran blinked. "That's not what I've been told. Addlerbatt's journal –"

"That book is pure *postinvt*," the Sycian grunted. "A tome unworthy of scrubbing the shit off of a camel's cunt. However one came to possess it, I offer advice: do not merely burn the book. Burn the person that handed it to you." When the exorcist didn't rise to the bait, Se'daulif grumbled in hushed annoyance. "This Man of Red? He did not *destroy* A'twol. He possessed it. Claimed it. He made the city *his* and the people were made to be *his* and the flesh was hewn from their bones as a shepherd does to his flock. The Man of the Red *was* Death. *Is* Death. And yet so much worse, so very much worse."

"So he took the city. Why does everyone think it was destroyed?"

"You truly do not know? You ask of the one that must *not* be named but you do not know the reasons why?"

"That's why I'm here."

Se'daulif muttered something in his native tongue that was impossible to understand, though the meaning was somehow felt. "A'twol fell to the Man. When he left, it still stood. Yet it had fallen."

For a moment, the priest thought he might have had something to go on. "So it wasn't destroyed."

"Oh, it was," the shiverdine countered. "The Sandkings raised their armies. They armed their militias. The six remaining Jewels of Sycio saw A'twol razed to the ground and salted the land when they left. The wells were poisoned, the wood burned, the cinder-blocks crushed, the sandstone returned to the desert in grains. It was *more* than demolished."

The priest let out a soft whistle as he imagined what that might've looked like. Sycian armies were known to be literally monstrous – loaded with beasts that defied imagination and stomach alike. Their people practiced necromancy as a matter of habit. Their Kings? Practiced it as a matter of enforcement.

The idea of five Sandkings aligning against one single city... "That's... excessive."

"Said by a man that does not understand what it was that the Sandkings found. The sins of A'twol, numerous of each masculine and feminine soul within her walls? They were repaid in full and in kind, and displayed for the world to see. Had the world seen, had the world truly seen? The petty emperors, queens, luminaries of this land and the lands of all directions north south and east would have sent their own minions! They would have done to each city of Sycio what the Jewels had to do to their own."

The conviction in his voice was enough to make the exorcist's heart skip a beat. "You expect me to believe that one man conquered an entire city and forced the rest of Sycio to ruin it?"

Se'daulif nodded in agreement. "His *name* is the Man of the Red Death, but is he a man? No. He is the one not to be spoken of. What I have said here alone is enough to justify anyone of *my* home to leave me under the sun 'till the flesh of my body has burned to dust and my bones have been scoured by the *hephasta* that gnaw through the grains of sand. Whatever your purpose is with his name and his acts? Change your ways; you are young. You have time to change of your own volition before your volition is changed for you."

Akaran took a slow breath and drummed his fingers on his thigh. "No, I don't."

"Boy. Man. Whatever you are by the customs of your people. You are one that is still young. Find a man. Find a woman. Find an overly-affectionate rat. Find a craft. A trade. Find a thing, any a thing, for you to do that does not involve asking of this man or that city or what was done or must be done to allow the dunes to keep what was done. Take the time you are granted and live a life of your control, not of his."

"Too late," the exorcist grunted. "You don't get it. He maimed a friend of mine. Killed another. My bosses have hinted that he has an interest in me, though they haven't admitted as much – though they've told me I need to take an interest in him, as if I needed the encouragement after what he did to Mariah. The dead woman that set you up to get stuck in this cage? Ask me who she says she works for. Ask me who she said *resurrected* her."

Se'daulif Ocsimmer, shiverdine of Sycio, renown merchant, and deal-maker extraordinaire, didn't even flinch. He didn't move, either, except for the corner of his mouth as it twitched. "I would ask if one knows if her hand was guided by him to turn the lock in my cell, if one would be so kind to offer...?"

"She's cut a deal with half the people in this damnable city. I can't promise, but I can't say no. From what I know about the bastard, I'd assume that if she was given instructions to have you moved out of his way we wouldn't be able to have this talk."

The slaver slowly tried to swallow down his suddenly-dry throat. "You... ah. Yes. You would likely be correct. For your own peace of mind, if he had tried to kill your maimed friend, your friend would be dead. If he wants you? Then I shall reject any word you offer me of aid, so that when he comes, I am not tainted by your curse."

The dismissal set the Lover back for a moment. "He scares you that badly, huh?"

"It is not a scare. It is the acknowledgment of a promised end that will come with a return to embrace a new beginning of nightmares and suffering unlike any you may claim to know."

"Then I think you're missing the point. Or maybe... I guess I haven't said it," the exorcist mused. "Thing is, Ocsimmer? I don't know shit about my childhood. I don't. You could tell me that the Empress of Civa gave birth to me in front of a thousand virgin maidens in a field of amber on a velvet carpet and I'd have to say it's possible. The first thing *I* remember? I woke up in an Order practionia tied to a bed. I was eight years old. They think. That's what they told me."

"Oh. That is a sad story, I do admit," Se'daulif replied slowly. "Not just presumably orphaned but maimed of memory? Tragic. To be most truthful though – I have heard much the same, said from many worse."

"I mean, I guess. I know," Akaran admitted. "Other people have it worse. I was found. I was clothed. I was taken care of. I was welcomed with open arms to an Order that has done nothing but give me purpose. Give me a home. That's better than thousands of other children. *I know this* and I am *beyond grateful* that their kindness has taken me this far even though I have been hurt, crippled, cursed, and lied to. Even though I have had to run my sword through things that would break a sane man's mind and I have spent time as of late with people that have had their minds *actually break* as of late, I am *grateful*."

The slaver shrugged his shoulders slightly but nodded along with him. "It is not outside the realm of understanding. You were given a place to stay and a task to do. You took to it. I will not argue that you will see it otherwise but I have helped many an orphan do the same, though... with fewer horrors, I will clarify."

"Maybe you have. Maybe you haven't," the priest replied. "I don't talk about my history. It doesn't matter. What matters is what's in front of me. What matters is what needs to be killed to keep other children from waking up in some stranger's bed with half their face gone."

"Except for a man who does not speak of his ills, you have just devoted a significant time to do just that."

The exorcist answered with a nod of his own. "I'm doing that because this asshole you won't talk about? Aside from killing and maiming people I give a shit about? Oh, the name Mariah. Wonderful young woman. Bit of a bitch. He took her eye. Told her to tell me hello. Acted like he knew me."

"Took her eye?" the slaver asked as he stared at the patch covering half of the priest's face. "I sense that I now have an understanding of why you may think it is a thing of a personal note yet I still –"

"He keeps calling himself my brother." As the Sycian went completely quiet, Akaran continued to ramble on. "Now, my bosses don't want to talk about it. They're telling me the same shit about 'names have power,' and 'you don't say his name without invoking wrath,' and honestly? Between us? I don't give a fisk. He's murdering people and putting my name next to his and really I'd just like to kill him."

Se'daulif tried to work words through his suddenly-dry mouth and failed at first. "Well ah... yes. I think I mentioned that you should seek out an overly-affectionate rat. Maybe instead? Find two. Distract yourself from this. People do things in the names of others since time immortal. Ask the Gods – mankind oft does things in Their names I'm sure They'd not like to have Their titles attached."

"Huh. Well. You're not wrong on that," the exorcist replied after he took a slow breath. "For what it's worth, you've told me more than I knew. At least now I know what I'm dealing with."

"You do not know a thing of him, young priest," he cautioned. "Only that you have knowledge now to avoid his hands at any cost to you. I would ignore the suggestions of one's superiors, and again — find a place, a person, a thing, far, far from his eyes."

A warning that the exorcist utterly ignored. "If he raised an army of the damned and ruined a city? Well, at least he's doing the necromancy on his own. Didn't think a single one could do that much damage on his own but..."

"Priest? I have met necromancers," he remarked with a sharp rise of his voice. "I have dined with necromongers. I have sold the unwanted and the lame to those that have demons as their pets. I have shared and bedded women with those that claim to speak with angels. What the Man is? Is none of those things. He is worse. He has objects of great power, and may well be an object of power himself. If nothing else, his name is enough to influence one."

"Then now I know he's a necromancer with relics that lets him control a *lot* of the dead. I already knew he was Sycian, so. Whatever he learned, wherever he learned it, I'm going to take a wild guess and assume it's on your side of the world. That's two more things than I knew before we started to talk."

"What makes one consider that he learned how to do any that he does in cities such as my home? What makes one believe that he learned to do any of his terrors in this world, let alone in the Golden Sands? The Sandmarshals; the Dunesires. Sandkings and Animators? Most are blessed with magic, many are blessed with the gift of lifting up past-walkers, but there is no magic in Sycio that can raise an entire army by only one man. None. Yet? This one did. Thus? He must not be a man, no matter what he titles himself as."

Akaran sucked on the tip of his tongue for a few heartbeats before answering. "Because you don't learn that kind of power without testing it. Sycio is the only place in the world where someone can learn necrosia to that extent and not get noticed."

A commotion behind him made him stop and look over his shoulder. Someone was headed down the hall, and they weren't wasting time. "He is of men but he is not a man," the slaver warned again. "What makes one as young as you, one as rejectful of past-walkers as you, believe so sincerely that one such as him must be kept to the constraints as ones such as us? No, young priest. He will consume you. First he shall feast upon your flesh, then he shall consume your soul."

"Three things," the exorcist grunted. "Cannibal. Lovely."

Se'daulif answered the remark with another deep sigh. "Priest. I was not at A'twol when it fell. I know those who were in the villages along the outskirts. Do not seek for this man. Do not attempt to capture him as you did I. I do not have any cause to like you. Yet I do not have the desire to have your fate weight upon my conscience should you think that what I say somehow gives you strength against him. It does not. It will not. You will suffer. You will be fed upon. You will die. You will return. You will suffer again. More, and longer."

"I'm suffering now," the Lover countered with a painful grunt as he stood up. "But knowing this much makes dealing with that dead bitch a little easier. I'll send someone down to work out your release. If you think of anything else that might be useful, find me."

"He'll wait," a *fully* armored guard from the 4th blurted out as he stormed into the dungeon. "Exorcist. Paladin. Whatever. I don't care. Half the damn city's been looking for you."

"What? Why?"

The guard wiped sweat off of his face and gave a dirty look at the prisoner. "Got a message for you. You're needed at the *Drunken Imperial*."

Akaran blinked in surprise. "Cel's tavern? What would...? Sirrah, you're the size of a mountain and you're standing there like you're ready to piss your boots. What's wrong?"

"Because I am," the guardsman answered honestly. "Someone just sent you a message. You, you personally, and I don't want any part of it. I don't wanna be the one giving you the message to get the message, and I will bloody the jaw of anyone that says I did."

"You aren't making sense."

The guard's chainmail clinked loudly as he shuddered in his boots. "None of it does. I don't know *what* you've done but boy, there's a whole lot of blood on the streets tonight and it's got your name on it."

"Does that mean I'm under arrest?"

"No. It means that anyone that knows what's best for themselves? They're staying away from you. I'm not going with you. I'm leaving. Going to Cableture. You didn't get told where to go by me. You got that?"

The Lover looked back and forth between the guard and the suddenly-silent prisoner. "I think I got it. Annix?"

"Don't know, don't care. The *Imperial*. Get your ass there before someone drags you to it by your cock."

"Right…" he muttered under his breath before he turned back to Se'daulif. "Well. Guess that means we're done."

"You claim he is after you? You mean this for true?"

"Yes."

The slaver looked around his cell and clenched his arms hard around his chest. "Then once I am a free man, I will be gone, and you will not see me again. Whatever direction you go, I shall go the opposite. I would warn, were I you, any of those that seek to be at your side, of what interests you have."

"Oh? And why's that?"

"The fewer around you, the fewer between his teeth."

***

The *Drunken Imperial* was not somewhere you wanted to die. Under the worst of circumstances, they'd find your body without anything you might have once held dear – life included, but assuredly not limited to. And if you *did* happen to die at the *Imperial*, odds were very good that you had run out of luck with the innkeeper. Celestine 'Cel' Navarshi kept a tight grip on her neck of the woods, and that tight grip often came with a boot in the spine.

Just this once, the deaths hadn't happened at her suggestion.

Just this once, the bodies hadn't been disturbed by the locals.

And just this once, the locals were ecstatic over the sheer number of soldiers, priests, and mages that were pouring all over the streets in Lower Naradol to address the find. They weren't even trying to pickpocket or drop a bribe or whatever else. They were all either hiding in their burrows – with the occasional head peeking out of a window or doorway.

Cel hovered by the scene. She'd been asleep when it had happened, or so she'd said. Nobody doubted her. She was furious. If she'd seen it as it had happened, she might have killed the son of a bitch herself. As it was, she had taken great pains to make sure the city at large knew what had happened even before the Orders and the Overseer's office could respond.

The other locals were telling anyone that would listen that they didn't see anything. Didn't know anything. Didn't hear anything. They'd told her the same, too.

Few were believed. Someone had to have heard something. Someone had to have seen something. A handful of them had disappeared from the streets at Cel's insistence and they were being *talked to* at length away from any witnesses. Just to be sure.

The only man that believed none of them did was the one the message was for. "A priest, a thief, and a mage. I think it's safe to say that I'm grateful none of my men are in this pile," Henderschott grumbled under his breath as he watched Lovers and Staras alike work on the corpses.

"Your men haven't been that helpful," the exorcist quietly pointed out as he sat with his head between his knees. "You're welcome. Or something."

"Akaran, I've never seen anything like this before," the Lieutenant admitted as he stared at the trio of corpses. "I'm thinking I'm fisking grateful there's not enough light for me to see it better."

The Lover didn't bother to look up. Staring at his feet was enough effort for the moment. "One nice thing about hunting them down. Aversion to the sun and all that. Don't get to see their work in the daylight."

Henderschott turned away from the bodies and looked down at the ashen-faced priest as he hid in a doorway several yards away. "I don't know what I'm supposed to do about this."

"The Pyre," the priest sighed out after a short silence. "May as well recall your men from the street. They won't find anything."

"Recall them? Are you –"

Akaran lifted his head from his hands and wiped his tear-and-grime-streaked cheeks dry. "Hender. I saw two of these men this morning. I spoke with the representative of another. Annix had someone pluck them out of *broad daylight* and drop them down on Cel's doorstep as soon as the sun dropped below the city."

"So he had help. Non-monster help."

"No. Maybe," the priest sighed. "Maybe he did it. Maybe he's strong enough that he can hide in deeper shadows without the sun destroying him. I don't know."

The Lieutenant-Commander walked over and leaned against the doorway. "That's a lot of 'I don't knows' for someone that's supposed to know these things."

Akaran swatted the edge of Henderschott's brown, woolen cloak away from his leg and looked back down at the ground. "Yeah well, tell me how certain you feel about life when you get a message like this."

"I didn't think people ever sent messages like this."

"They don't," the Lover agreed. "*People* don't."

"He made his point, didn't he? Or did I miss something? Three dead and Brother Levathil treated much the same, only he got to live through it to pass on his intent."

The older soldier looked back at the trio of bodies as a small squabble broke out over what to do with their corpses between a pair of Lovers and a handful of priests from the Order of Stara. "I think we could have gotten the intent without seeing the carnage. He wants you at the Temple of Stara Courtyard. Four candlemarks from now."

"Wow," Akaran mused quietly. "Picking a fight at the Gods' own doorstep. Say what you will, this bastard has balls."

"Are you going?"

Akaran glanced up at the guard. "Are you kidding?"

The Overseer's enforcer rubbed at his thigh. "When I was twenty-six summers old, I was hunting a privateer. Had my own ship, if you can believe it. The *Seascraper*. Thought I had a clear shot to take down one of the nastiest assholes that had poked his head up outta the surf in the Ogibus war. Son of a bitch lead my ass along on a merry fisking chase for a week before he put my dick between his shitty little sailboat and a *Drakeback* his men had stolen from the Matheians. Damn near stripped every bit of muscle from my thigh. Still don't know how I lived through it."

The story made the exorcist wince, though the point was lost on him. "Wondered how you went from the 2nd Naval to commanding a desk."

"Ballistae. Does it every damn time," he answered with a slight shrug. "Either way, point is: you get your head in a trap once, you look for them everywhere else you go."

"So what do you think I should do?"

"What do I think?" Henderschott marveled. "Akaran. We don't like each other. We admit this. Right?"

"Yeah..."

"This message was for you, not me," he pointed out. "It may not be your fault, but it's got your name on it. The half of the city that wasn't ready to riot? They're going to riot. I'm going to have to go clean that up. I'm going to have to have this cleaned up. The people these three answered to and spoke for? They're going to want answers. Lots of 'em. Isn't me they're going to come for."

Akaran took the rebuke in stride. There wasn't anything else he could do. "Then I guess I'm going to Temple Row

"Well, for what it's worth. You'll have company going there," Henderschott pointed out as he gestured over at the trio of dead as a Stara caretaker cut through the ropes that had bound them together. "I'm going back to the Manor once I patch up as much of this shit as I can. Can't fix it, just gonna try to patch it. Then I'm going to go watch over Seline."

"How is she…?"

The guard took a deep breath. "I don't know. Despondent. Terrified. Crying. Ridora has put a mountain of magic into her to get her to calm down. Whatever that slavering cu… whatever Anais did… they told me she drowned her. Repeatedly."

"That's what I heard, too. Hender, I don't know what relationship you two had but I'm sorry and –"

"Don't. Don't bother," the soldier snapped. "Whatever you got her involved in? She was trying to get away. She wanted out of the city. I should've listened. I blame you, but it's my fault."

Akaran shook his head tiredly. "No it's not. Anais used damn near all of us. We're gonna find even more bodies with her name on 'em. I'm sure of it."

"Just make sure she's one," Henderschott growled, "and don't make me throw you into the pyre with *those*. If anyone puts you in the ground it's me."

The exorcist looked at the trio again and dropped his head back into his hands. "Yeah. That's fair. I promise to try."

Three dead men.

A priest, a thief, and a mage.

Each with their heads half-shaved, throats cut, and their right eyes plucked out. Blood had been smeared around the outside of their lips and over their chins; a mockery of the rough goatee he was growing back in. A message for him and only him. A message written into the bodies of Oldstone Altund Obermesc, Austilin the Enforcer, and Adept Lolron Essinge.

Annix wanted to get his attention.

It had worked… and someone *was* going into the Pyre.

With Henderschott's help or not.

V. JUSTICE SOUGHT

Just after Midnight, Wundis, 13ᵗʰ of Firstgrow, 513 QR

During the day, the Ellachurstine Chapel was seen as a brilliant, beautiful structure. It had been built over the course of years by mages and masons and so much more. It was a labor of love, but not one designed to be a home for Love Herself – as it should've been, as far as Akaran was concerned. No matter how well-received the Order was in Basion, the Chapel was an open call to *all* the Gods and Goddesses, and as such, had been dedicated to the Temple of Stara and the Pantheon they honored.

It was hard to miss the chapel if you were ever in the vicinity of the Orshia-Avagerona Falls. Even harder if you ever spent time along Temple Row, as they called it, in the District of Chiadon. 'Hard to miss' and 'up close and personal' are two different things, of course, and this was the first time that Akaran had ever given it much more than a glancing interest. It wasn't far from the Everburning Pyre – the two were almost on top of each other – but every visit he'd taken to the Pyre had been when he'd had other things on his mind.

Until now, the Order of Stara's shrine hadn't been one of them.

Nor, honestly, had the Orshia Shallows. Both of which suddenly became the second biggest concern he had. The shallows themselves were part of the Orshia Overflow, and spread through the north-eastern section of the city. They were carefully hedged in by canals and floodwalls, except for where the three largest non-Lover shrines were located.

If you faced the Temple of Stara from the closest thoroughfare, the half-pyramid/half-semi-circle edifice stood at the end of Pilgrim's Road. Most of the building was braced atop tall marble pillars and three sets of stairs that lead up to the shrine itself. Off to the side, the Temple's courtyard was built up atop a neck-high wall and served as the open-air congregational setting for those with a mind to the Temple's daily services.

If you kept your gaze on the Temple, to the right of the edifice dedicated to the entirety of the Pantheon (shy Love, as always), Pyre Hill stood tall. Tall, lit, and ominous. The hill itself was one of the highest places in the basin proper, excluding the walls and buildings built into them. It was far enough away from the three roads that ambled around its north, east, and west sides that any trip up was a difficult slog to take.

Although knowing the Staras? It was intentional. They never missed an opportunity to make a solemn experience take *forever*. Across from it? You'd see the Ellachurstine Chapel. You'd be just as likely to see it before you saw the shrine to the Staras, given the gaudy nature of the monolith.

At night, the Chapel took on a new life. The building was arched and curved so that light cast from the braziers and magelight within would bounce across mirror-covered pylons to illuminate the building inside and out. Even in a cloud-covered night that obscured the moons above, the Ellachurstine was, without question, the singular most well-lit place in the entire city. It even put the Repository to shame.

As well lit as it was, the Stara's courtyard was downright grim in contrast. That wasn't to say that it wasn't consecrated by the Divines or that it wasn't bathed in welcoming lights from torches and magestones alike. It was; it was a bastion for peace and serenity at all hours of the day. In recent weeks, it had nearly been completely converted into a triage center for people wounded in inner-city fighting.

There was enough of that to keep them busy.

Henderschott stayed true to his word and retreated back to the Manor. The exorcist-turned-temporary-paladin didn't even mind. He was happy that Seline was being watched over, and there *might* have been a not-that-quiet order given to send a care package of weapons, armor, and Wardkeepers over with the Lieutenant-Commander's men back at the asylum.

What pissed him off was that the men that *had* shown up at the courtyard *hadn't* wanted to take instructions from anyone with the Order of Love's sigil on it. It had taken the next-closest-thing to an act of the Goddess to get them to listen. For good or for ill, that 'next-closest-thing' was Paverilak.

Drunk as he was, he also wasn't in the mood to deal with anyone's shit. "Whatever the asshole tells you to do, go do it," was all that he needed to say. It didn't make them friends, but it automatically put the Betrothed on

Akaran's good side.

Not that he had much of a good side left. The exorcism, the interrogation, and the murders? They'd all taken their toll. Even the punch that he'd taken from the Lieutenant-Commander had added to his grief. He'd been purposefully left out of the planning and response committee in order to clean up and pretend to rest rather than issue orders.

It really didn't help. He didn't sleep. He prayed. He prayed, he listened, and he made someone find a map of all of the nearby streets. He refused to admit it to Catherine, but Karaj had seen him limp up the stairs to the Chapel proper with one hand on his gut and the other clutching his cane.

Before he'd even asked, the Templar's personal assistant had a medicannia meet him in the room he'd claimed as his own. When the physician was finished, Akaran had a brand new metal brace with leather straps tied to his knee and a few extra stitches across his stomach. It was enough to support him for what they hoped would be the fight to come.

It was odd to hope for a fight, but these were odd times. It was also a much louder, much angrier screaming fit that erupted when he had to remind his superiors of one thing: that they had decided he was supposed to be in charge. It got worse when he decided to enforce it.

"Either you want me to lead this effort or you don't. It can't be both," he had growled at them.

"That was in regards to hunting him down," Catherine had protested. "Not…"

"Not trying to trap him? Isn't that the entire point?" Akaran had countered. "No. He wants *me*. He sent that message *to me*. He's picked a fight *with me*."

Karaj cleared their throat. "I would say you picked the fight with him, if you wish to be clear of meaning. You can hardly stand and I doubt you have the strength to call for magical aid, yet you want us to… what? Stand around with our thumbs in our asses?"

The exorcist grimaced. "No, but yes. Go stand somewhere, just not *here*."

Catherine ran her fingers through her flowing hair and tried not to scream at him. "This cretin is responsible for an untold number of deaths, and many of them are of men bigger, stronger, and smarter than you've ever shown inclination – and you want to challenge him alone? Are you that cocky or that stupid?"

"Perhaps a bit of both, and a bit of neither," Karaj interjected. "You know there is no way that we will leave you alone, but… this creature is not stupid."

"Not in the least. He's not going to get anywhere close enough to kill if we have a hundred people standing within fifteen feet of his head," the youngest Lover pointed out. "But as Karaj said – it's also not so stupid it thinks you're going to leave me alone, either. The difference is if you're out of immediate range and response, well."

"Then you have a chance to do something about him," the Templar agreed with a frustrated sigh. "Of course, that also means you'll be solely responsible for putting him down. You've done well, but look at you. I'm not sure you'd have the strength to excise a goat should one rise against the natural order."

Akaran shuddered in revulsion as one of the worst memories from Toniki flooded through his mind. "Don't... don't joke about goats."

"I wasn't joking."

She really wasn't, and if he was going to get her to listen, he was going to have to make some concessions – and he knew it. "Fine. Pick three people you think can handle him *and* that bitch Sherril. Messengers or Huntsmen. Mundane anyone isn't going to do shit."

Her assistant drummed their fingers against the ornate wooden railing as they looked out over one of the balconies along the edges of the Chapel into the night-covered city beyond. "We are sadly now short *Mols*. Losing both Pal-Com Spidous and Paladin Faldine... Hannock demanded that we send another to watch over the Odinals, and yet another to watch over the Tessamirch families."

"And you sent one to go sit at the Manor," Catherine pointed out. "We can't recall any of them but that one."

"Which is the only one I give a damn about right now," the exorcist muttered. "Do we have any exorcists available?"

"Yes. Seven. We have five more, but they are resting. You are not the only exorcist that put blood on their hands today," Karaj remarked. "Not vampiric, sadly, but all of the unrest has bred other things."

Akaran gave them an askance look and then peered up at the moons. "I swear if you tell me that they've found shiriak I'm going to jump off of this platform and save everyone the trouble."

Catherine started to reply, but her white-robed assistant cut her off with a quick and short shake of their head. "As we do not know what Annix intends to bring, I am not of mind to risk those that have been weakened," Karaj replied. "We would not risk you had we other options."

"Neither of us are going to give you the choice," the exorcist deadpanned. "He wants me. I want him."

"And everyone wants Malik. How sure are you that you can rescue him?" his boss asked.

She didn't like the answer to that question.

Neither did anyone else.

That didn't stop a fresh set of onlookers who weren't part of the Order, but who felt they had an exceptionally vested interest in seeing the criminal brought to justice. That put them in the way, but there was absolutely no arguing with them. They did at least decide to bring their own bodyguards, which Akaran quietly bet five crowns against for surviving the night.

Hadraie had only been happy to take him up on the deal.

The Wardkeeper hadn't left him alone since he'd limped to the Chapel, which had started to get both a little irritating and a little flattering. Eventually, he found a use for her (though someone popped in later to tell him that it wasn't the use she had in mind). At his urging, Catherine and Karaj had organized a few teams to set up on the streets and down nearby back-alleys to cover the Chapel courtyard and nearby grounds.

If she was going to keep being underfoot, then he was going to put her feet to use. Much to her disgust, she was volun-told to serve as a messenger back and forth between the various squads. They'd broken up into five, with a sixth group waiting in the rear. He'd also demanded that they send someone straight to the Overseer's office just in case the entire plot was a trap.

The only thing left to do was wait. Wait, and pray.

Hours later, Annix did as expected: he attacked.

He just didn't attack where they thought he would. By two candlemarks after midnight, a steady stream of couriers reported in. Two of those reports both came from the same woman – some footswoman from the 4th – but the rest came from nearly every district in the city. First it came by idle clouds of smoke that started to drift up over the rooftops, and then it came from witnesses and guardsmen. At first, it was hard to get answers, but as time trickled on, the scenarios all played out the same.

Groups of laughing, ashen-faced men and women were setting fire to the city. They struck without warning, they struck violently, and they killed five or six people at a time. When they were finished, they would set fire to a building. A barn. A temple. A dormosul. The attacks were at random, with no rhyme or reason to be had.

Catherine responded the only way Catherine could. The troops she had squirreled away down side streets were sent to run after the clouds of smoke and panicked cries that were erupting across the city. With an hour left before the demanded confrontation, the only choice she had left to make was to trust Akaran to deal with whatever was coming on his own or not.

She didn't. She elected to stay. Until she couldn't.

When a messenger from the Overseer arrived to tell her that the Hannock Bridge had been attacked, she didn't have a choice. If the city had just lost the main way in or out of the basin, then what fragile peace that *might* be left after the attacks tonight would be long gone and the city would fall into complete chaos. When Akaran quipped that it would help cut down on the chances that their quarry could ultimately escape judgment, Catherine nearly had him hung from the Chapel's rafters.

It was the worst choice. It was the only choice. Paverilak made it clear that he felt the entire 'meeting' was just a feint. "Annix isn't going to show up. He's going to wreck the city while *you* thundering twats sit here while the whole damn city burns! How many people *have to die* before you get off of your asses and *stop them*?"

He made a compelling argument. He also made it with the threat of imprisoning anyone who debated him. That lead to another debate as to if he had any authority to do it, but after another heated exchange, it was determined that it didn't matter. Catherine left for the bridge and Karaj stayed behind to manage the handful of troops she could leave behind.

With the Maiden-Templar gone and their forces down to a mere fifty heads — an 'over abundance' to hear Paverilak whine about it — to confront Annix when the time came to it, her erstwhile student took the lead. Except for him, taking the lead meant that he tried to manage the throng of destitute, terrified, and angry city-dwellers that began to show up at the Chapel's doorstep covered in soot and streaks of fresh blood.

"People flock to the Divine when they're scared," Karaj remarked as a crowd descended on the shrine.

Akaran took a long drawl of stale water off of his flagon and blinked slowly. His eye was bloodshot, swollen, and the stench of burning lumber from afar had started to make his nose run. "Why do I get the feeling that this is intentional?"

"Whatever could they seek to accomplish if it was?"

The footswoman that had brought the first warning of fires and chaos pulled her cloak off and exposed the ornate dragon tattoo etched into her cheek, and the blonde, high-shaved sides of her head. She extended her arm, palm out, and answered their question with a shrug.

"Witnesses," Sherril casually replied before a bolt of lightning lanced from her palm and slammed dead-center into Akaran's chest.

***

Everything was blurry, except for the pain in his chest. Akaran could hear screams and sounds of fighting. Swords clashed and meaty thunks served as a steady drum thumping in his head as the crowd descended into raw anarchy. He could see glimpses of people running through the crowd and catch fleeting moments of people getting struck down by blade and claw both.

He could see it and hear it, but couldn't do anything about it. Sherril had her hands tight around his collar, and she pulled him through the panicked throng absolutely effortlessly. He kicked and struggled, though the first time he started to utter a Word, the very next thing he felt was another blast of electricity that coursed down his neck.

Every shock made the muscles in his body spasm and sent searing pain ripping through his limbs. He pissed himself, he thought, on her third discharge. Akaran gave up entirely when she stopped, pulled him forward, and sneered down at him. "I know how much men can take before they stop breathing. I know how much it takes to stop men from simply speaking. Would you like to find out the difference between the two?"

Sherril bounded through the crowd, sprinting past anyone that might've been able to stop her if they'd noticed who she was or what she was doing. They cleared past the courtyard in a matter of minutes and bounded up the opposite hill. Between the chaos of the crowd and the attackers ripping through them, the Order was absolutely overwhelmed – which made their arrival at the Pyre even worse.

Without missing a beat, his assailant grabbed a man weakly leaning against one of the Pyre's lower pillars and picked him up in her other hand. Then, without pause or thought, she simply *jumped* to the top of the fifteen-foot tall domed structure with both of her captives in tow.

Akaran had a moment – just one – to realize that they were alone up there. She went out of her way to point out why. She dumped the other man onto the rooftop without a care, and then she grabbed the exorcist by his cheeks and made him stare at the pool of water that the Chapel proudly stood over. "Do you think your spells could stop him? Your wards? Your divine patrons?" She cuffed him across the back of his head before he could utter a response, and jerked his head again to force him to look at the small river that fed the pond and a shadowy figure standing at its shores. "You can't defend against what you can't hide from."

It wasn't the first time he'd seen Annix. It wasn't the closest he'd seen him, either. But this time, it was done with intent. It was done to make a point. The damn vampire enjoyed the theater of it all.

There was light all around the Ellachurstine. The pond glimmered below it as magelight and spells caused the silver-wrapped pillars under the Chapel to shine. All at once, all of that simply… stopped. The reflections ceased. The glimmering dulled until it was as cold and black as the skies above. Even the moonlight itself seemed to dim in the immediate area around the pond, and the river that ran beside it.

He couldn't see what happened. Nobody could. In the darkness, the pillars lost their strength. They lost whatever warmth they had absorbed through the day. The water grew cold – not freezing, not solid, but the kind of cold that would sap the strength from your bones if you soaked it in it for more than a few minutes. A thin layer of fog began to form around the dozens of stone pylons.

Cracks began to form along the pillars, and the front half of the shrine began to sway under the pounding footsteps of the terrified souls running across the raised stones. Akaran felt his eye go wide as he struggled to get control back into his limbs, but a sudden hand clamped across the back of his neck put that thought to rest. A blast of lightning made him black out again, and when the thunder in his ears faded enough that he could hear…

"You thought you could take from *me*," a rough, cruel voice growled into the exorcist's ear. "You are a child compared to me, and you thought you could steal my essence? Better *men* than you have tried."

"Better women, too, you asshole," Sherril added as she dropped to one knee on top of the domed structure.

Annix wrenched Akaran's head back, and forced the exorcist to look up into his demonic face. It was a moment that burned itself into his memory for the rest of his life, and the second time he'd been able to see the bastard clearly – the freak with the flawless pale skin and the marbled-over eye. The vampire exposed sharpened fangs and dark red gums. A tongue with just the hint of a fork to it stuck out for a heartbeat between his teeth, but it was his eyes. His eyes, and his ears.

The one blind eye that looked like a doorway into eternity. The pointed ears that both belied any notion of his perceived *humanity* and exposed him for what he had been. He acted inhuman because he'd never *been* human. He used the language of the elves in his spells because he was old enough to speak it fluently. He was as old as the First Crusade of Suns – because he'd lived through it.

A vampire. An elf. A macabre resurrection of a dead race given the antithesis of life and even less interest in mankind than his ancestors had shown while they shared the world with the Kingdoms of Men. A monstrosity that should've been lost to history centuries ago.

An abomination that would bleed the world dry if he let it.

Annix stood up to his full height and the top of the pyre groaned from the extra weight. The dome wasn't built for people to stand on it – four fourteen-foot tall pylons held it up from the base, with a circular lip that gave way to a partial roof that arched up towards the glory of the Gods in the sky. A hole the width of an average man took up the very center and top of the dome to allow both the spirits of the divine-departed and the acrid smoke of the hedonistic-fallen to ascend to the sky.

An errant column of smoke was the only thing that smelled worse than the vampire, but it was anyone's guess how long the top of the shrine would hold. The vampire clutched his other captive by the back of his neck, and Sherril clamped her fingers harder against Akaran's skin in tandem. The priest tried to get a spell loose, but another hateful, incapacitating charge danced through his bones and kept him silent.

Which was more than could be said for her Meister. When he spoke, his words carried down the cobblestone path from the pyre and across the entire courtyard. **"You came here for comfort, and as the Lovers have taken peace from me, so shall I from you."**

God-speak. It was an old spell, and not a hard one.

It worked wonders to get attention.

"The Order of Love. The followers of the Elemental Cruelty of Hearts. The Crone, the Breeder, the Whore," he spat as he blasphemed Her titles in every way possible. **"They claim to bring Love, yet they steal it from those they deem unfit."**

The crowd reacted accordingly. Most screamed in terror. Others clamped their hands over their ears. As more and more eyes turned towards the Everburning, the city finally saw the abomination that had tormented them for so long.

Even if they didn't understand it, they saw it. A dark figure against the glare of the pyre. An *evil* in the home of the *good*. The mere idea sent chills down the spines of even the most steadfast.

And there were few of the steadfast left.

While the lost and the terrified looked on in confusion and horror, the Lovers engaged in combat with the handful of fresh broodlings that had served as his vanguard. The priests felt the sting of his words and heated anger with every insult and blaspheme he invoked. The ether around Her priests soured as they heard the insults – and through them, *She* did too. Even in his stunned and befuddled state, Akaran felt Her grace go dark, and felt a surge of anger that was becoming a little *too* familiar for his personal tastes.

Annix lifted the other captive and dangled him over the edge of the pyre's roof. "**They have not kept the strongest of you safe, yet you expect them to care for the weakest? I will show you what their protections mean**," he boomed as his battlemage turned the exorcist around and made him look over at them.

There really hadn't been any doubt about the other captive, even as dazed as the priest was. Annix ripped the cloak off of his prisoner and exposed the muscle-bound strongman for everyone to see.

Malik Odinal, son of Warlord Nemok Odinal of Clan Odinal. Husband-to-be of Hylene Tessamirch, and the man that half of Basion hated. The other half hated that he wouldn't bed them. To say that he was attractive was an insult to beauty; he wasn't just handsome, he was *gorgeous*.

Except in this moment, he was none of those things.

He was pallid, gaunt, weak. His eyes were dazed and it was obvious that he couldn't tell what was going on any more than a newborn could. He didn't struggle because he didn't have the strength; and as his head rolled loosely back and forth over his sagging shoulders, more than a few bite marks were apparently across his throat.

He'd been drained, tortured, and tormented.

And now Annix had him on display like a sacrificial lamb he'd fattened before the slaughter. "**Their *protections*, the ones they offer *you*, only mean that I feast *well***," he snarled.

The fury behind his voice brought people to their knees. The chapel continued to quake as the shadows underneath it continued to rot and erode the supports and beams that held it up. The minions he had left pulled back from their fights, and began to set up a defensive perimeter around the front of the pyre's hill.

The Lovers had gained some ground and even managed to excise two of them, and the remaining three looked much the worse for wear. They were still able to fight though, and paid no heed to the bloodied and burnt wounds that they'd received so far. The Order faithful were hurt just as bad if not worse; their numbers had been depleted by an order of magnitude more.

That was the difference between fighting the living and the dead.

The dead wouldn't quit if you broke their bones.

Annix wouldn't quit until he had his glory. But not just glory. He wanted something else. Something more. Something righteous, but twisted. "**There will be no safety until I have gone**," his booming, God-like voice declared across the throng. "**I will not leave, no matter their works, until I**

**have my tvastarian. My recompense. My justice. That is all I demand —
justice for my *yomaldi*!**"

"Justice?" Akaran croaked through battered lips. When Sherril pulled
another jolt of power up to strike him down, her Meister touched her arm
and made her let the priest speak. "Kidnapping? Torture? Murder? You
call that *justice*?"

"It is but a means," the vampire retorted loud enough for the exorcist
(and only the exorcist) to hear. "I have only asked for what is mine. I have
taken what I must to survive." Before he could respond, Annix turned back
to the crowd and let his voice carry across the district with ease. "**Blood
will flow. Yours. His. Theirs. Blood will flow and I shall drain it.**"

"Lies," the priest croaked. "You've slaughtered... countless..."

Annix reached down and slashed at the priest's shoulder with an idle
strike of his claws that easily ruined his armor and drew a brief splash a
blood. "I have watched fleets of humans devastate the oceans. I have seen
millions of your mouths consume the living souls in the woods. Across
plains. I use that which I kill. Mankind cannot say the same."

Below them, the fire in the pyre erupted in a shower of sparks as one
of the broodlings grabbed a soldier from the 4th and flung the poor sod
into the burning copper bowl. The agonized screams only lasted a few
moments before the thrashing guard's lungs gave out from the flames.

As the soldier hopelessly struggled to get free of the crucible, Karaj
attempted to punish the murder. They strode through the panicked crowd
of wounded and dying with ease, and somehow with their cloak still pulled
tight around their head to hide their face. A harshly-spoken Word sent a
wave of brilliant white light from their arms that rushed up the
cobblestone street and scoured flesh away from the bloodsucker before it
could finish watching the guard burn.

The Lover almost got a second word out before Sherril unleashed a
storm of lightning from her fingertips that raked across the stones and
sent blasts of broken rocks and smoke across the hillside. Karaj melted
back into the crowd as quickly as they had appeared, but none of the
chaos stopped Annix from continuing his rant. "**When you are tired of
suffering, when you are tired of their lies and their failures — bring me
what I wish. Bistra Enil. One of theirs. They took from me; I take from
them a thousandfold**!"

There was a heartbeat, just one, when Akaran realized that the
battlemage didn't need to speak to use her spells. And another that he
saw a gleaming amulet that hung from her Meister's neck. The first was a
problem. The other was a *knowledge*.

Even in his befuddled state, he had the clarity to identify it as a Penumbra of Lethandria. It meant that he wasn't just using his own magic for the sake of his illusions, he was powering them with the essence of the Divine. It meant that they had been tracking for the wrong thing all this time... and made him wonder, albeit briefly, what *else* they'd been doing wrong.

"**The Landing of Flynn**," the vampire declared even louder than before. With every word he muttered, the God-speak spell caused the upward-facing crescent to shine with a pale black glow. "**The moment she is there, the moment that she is unfettered by their restraints and their laughable *protection*, I shall leave you. I shall leave you to rot in this pit, and let you take your vengeance on them and the Great Harlot for the pain they have caused**!"

That was an opening. A bad one. A chance, a single chance to get under his skin. "You don't... you don't know suffering," Akaran spat through bloodied, split lips. Anything right now would buy time for Karaj to act. That's all he had to do. Buy Karaj time. "Should've burned... with your people..."

Sherril grabbed the exorcist by his neck and shoved his face into the cloud of smoke billowing up the pyre's central vent before she shunted a shock into him that made him gasp in pain and inhale the dead guard's floating ash. "Burn? You before him, I promise," she hissed, "you're gonna go in next."

The chaos below and the attack from the battlemage had caused most of the crowd to disperse around the Pyre and deeper into the courtyard around the Temple. The building continued to sway as more and more of the pillars started to crumble into dust, but hardly anyone noticed it. The ones that did tried – and failed – to get people to run away from it, but the question was to run away to *where*?

"**They have known of me for years. For years you have lost. For years you have suffered. For years, they have known**," Annix declared with a lie through his teeth. "**Now? Now, you know. Now you know the cause and the cost of this curse, for I am a curse. I am *your* curse.**"

Except he wasn't the only curse in the city.

The cloud of smoke and ash faded as the burning guard crumbled into cinders and ash. In a last, desperate, futile attempt at escape, the Garrison officer flopped onto his back and reached up into the sky. If he was reaching for Akaran, it couldn't have done any good. If he was reaching for the Gods, none reached back to save him.

Whatever he reached for, it didn't reach him.

The flesh on his hand disintegrated. His clothes burned away into cinders. What skin left on his face cracked and sheered off into the heated bed of coals. His face broke away.

And revealed somebody else's.

Annix didn't know he wasn't the only curse in Basion...

...because he'd never met Akaran's.

A face he'd seen more times than not. A face he'd watched say horrific things. A face he'd watched curse him in his nightmares. A face he'd watched grow to accept her fate. A face he'd wondered if he'd ever see again since she'd disappeared.

"I am death! I am suffering!" Annix crowed. **"I am *yours*."**

Sherril dropped the exorcist and grabbed Malik by his ratty, ruined hair. She let Akaran go for a moment – a moment too long. What was left of the corpse in the pyre's bowl *smiled* up at the exorcist and very slowly, pointed to it's eye.

A frozen, shining eye, opposite a burning, Abyss-seared one. The corpse broke away into a cloud of soot and shards of bone as the fires burned hotter and faster than they should've. The body and vision vanished as quickly as they arrived, but even as it did, the rock nestled against his face *pulsed* like it *knew* what to do.

For his own sake, he hoped it did.

As the crowd watched, a hushed silence fell over the grounds. The ones that could see clearly stifled cries of horror as Sherril lifted her captives up over the flue and dangled them above the flames. Neither man put up a fight. Malik was too weak. Akaran was too busy uttering prayer after prayer.

Annix turned his head around and smiled at the exorcist. "Your people are less than the lowest of elves. You will never approach the greatness of the Elven Kingdoms, and in this lesson, I will be your one and only proctor."

The prayers were answered. Not how he wanted. Not by who he wanted. But the face – and just the face – in the flames below reappeared in the smoke just inches away and mouthed a simple statement that carried the weight of the world with it.

It was only a question of *which* world.

"No beach for you," the ashen woman crooned, *"you're not allowed."*

Nobody else heard it. Nobody else saw it. Nobody else could've. It was either a threat or a promise, and either way, he opted to make the most of it. There was one chance to get a question answered – a question that would either lead to an assassination or an all-out war. The priest let out a shuddering wheeze and looked up from the flames. "For once you... for once, just *speak truth and... and be judged*," Akaran croaked as a rush of pain erupted across his forearm. "Claiming greatness... just... you're just a Nithian dog... aren't you?"

A faint glimmer set across the vampire's shoulders and the spell did its work — for the few brief seconds it took before the elf shrugged it off and the rune on the exorcist's arm lost its shine. "Nithians? I answer to no Council, to no rule. Let them freeze where they cower. Their Kingdom is nothing — nor is yours! My rule is absolute and a rule of one among my brood! I do not serve the Cold Kingdom of Fangs and failure!"

Sherril didn't give Akaran a chance to digest his answer. She simply opened her hands and let the men fall into the pyre below. The fall was horrifying. What waited below was worse.

The crowd screamed.

Annix crowed in victory.

A massive burst of hot steam and sparks erupted from the holy crucible that bathed the vampires on the ground with ash and embers, and blinded both the woman with the dragon tattoo on her cheek and her Meister both. A hurried wall of raw force called forth from Karaj sped through the air and slammed into the half-cauldron in a last-ditch attempt to knock it over.

It didn't. It didn't hit with a clang. It didn't impact with a rush of embers and ash. It punched through the smokey steam and filled the air with a bone-shattering **crack.**

A crack that was met with a pair of etheric chains that shot out from the mist and wrapped around the neck of the closest bloodsucking monstrosity. A crack, and chains, and a vampire that disappeared into the steam with only a flash of light and a burst of burning bones that rolled away from the stairs to mark its passing.

When the fog cleared, Akaran stood atop a melting shell of ice with Malik laying in a broken slump at his side. Both men were singed, their clothes burnt and smoking, and a patch of hair on the exorcist's head had turned into a smoldering clump. The Pyre's copper bowl had shattered into broken chunks.

The Ever-Burning no longer was.

The only fire to see was what burned in his eye.

Divine, pure white rage in his left. Cold blue flames licked out from under his patch on his right. Smoke and steam rolled off of his skin and what was left of his charred clothes.

Silvery chains whipped and snapped in the air around his head and back, violent bonds of magic hunting for a victim. Raw pain and anger hunting for a release. A true Messenger of Love looking for an *excuse*.

Excuses that were only happy to present themselves for judgment.

Karaj lead the charge against the damned. The remaining two broodlings didn't know what to do or which way to turn. A gesture from Annix put their attention on the Repository's caretaker while his assassin jumped down the chimney and confronted the exorcist head-on.

She *hissed* in Akaran's face with her fangs exposed and strands of bloody bile dripping from them. He didn't bother taunting her. Didn't bother saying a word.

Didn't bother to *say* a *Word*.

The priest grabbed her by the collar of her chainmail tunic and delivered a brutal headbutt across her nose that shattered bone and cartlidge alike with a sickening crunch. In a million years, she'd never have expected it. In a thousand lifetimes, she would've never figured out how to block it.

All she did was fall over and onto her back with a hard thud. As she tried to recover, Akaran's chains whipped off of his arms and wrapped themselves around the favored son of Clan Odinal. He lunged and hauled the two of them out of the wreckage with more strength than he knew he possessed. He was broken, he was battered.

But he wasn't beaten.

Sherril couldn't say the same. A deluge of whipping strikes of magical chains lashed down across her body. The exorcist wasn't trying to grab her. He was trying to *beat* her. He gouged flesh from her arms and broke her armor. He took *special* care to strip the paint from her chainmail that marked her as a member of the Dawnfire army. Before she could get another bolt of lightning off of her fingertips, he took special care to whip his glowing bonds around her wrist.

And then he flexed his hand and snapped her forearm into three pieces. There wasn't an offer for redemption, forgiveness, or reparations. The sound of his chains hitting her body was a song of death and damnation, one punctuated by a baritone outro to end her reign of chaos.

"I CONDEMN! EXP-"

Before he could finish the word, Annix appeared almost out of thin air and clamped a clawed hand across the front of Akaran's face. The vampire squeezed and pushed the exorcist down with his bad knee pressed to the ground. A swipe of his other hand came within an inch of tearing the flesh away from the Lover's neck, but Akaran caught it with his fist.

A harsh, unspoken spell flared in his palm and scorched the Annix's wrist to the bone. A rapid second one unleashed a burning ball of light that rolled across the vampire's chest and burned the skin under his brown and black leather tunic. The sadist recoiled away, but as he did, he raked his hand across Akaran's face and ripped away his eyepatch with a splash of blood and a scorching stroke of pain.

The priest went down and the vampire lord staggered away with steam coursing off of his body. Sherril slid around on her knees and put herself between the two with sparks dancing across the fingertips of her good hand. Akaran pushed himself off the ground and took a single staggering step forward as blood pulsed down the right side of his face.

"You or the meatbag," the battlemage croaked as she pointed her finger at him... and then at Malik laying nearby. "You can't save both."

Five heartbeats. That was all the time he had to decide. Five heartbeats that turned to four, then three, as an elongated arc of energy swelled up across her fingers. Two, as he screamed out, "Luminaird!" One, as a barrier of light and ice manifested on his arm and he moved to get into position to intercept her attack.

The battlemage's arc of lightning slammed into his spell and detonated harmlessly inches away from Malik's face. A second arc formed on her fingers and followed the same path as the first across the small field, but instead of detonating, it skittered across the shield edge and discharged in the worst place possible. The bolt jumped through the steaming, rapidly melting ice and poured its full force into the metal brace on the exorcist's knee.

Searing heat unlike nothing he'd ever felt before followed a wave of what felt like a thousand bee-stings all at once down his leg. The metal flashed to a brilliant red and his leggings caught fire. His flesh followed immediate suit as the magic exploded and scoured away his skin, his brace, and his clothes all alike.

His scream was nearly inhuman.

Sherril might've gone in for the kill, if she'd been granted the chance. Karaj battered their way back into the fray with a rash of blisteringly-bright lights and defensive spells that pushed both of the vampires away. Within moments, the Lover stood between Akaran and the monsters with blades of pure lavender light stretching down from their hands. "This is over. The only thing left is your condemnation."

Annix croaked out a laugh and spat blackened blood on the street. "You think you won? You have saved two. I have devastated *generations*."

"Not all lives are made equal," the elder priest retorted. "Monsters as you even less. Yet you will submit to punishment for all."

"Will I? What makes you think they'll feel the same?" the elf mocked as he willed fresh shadows from the Penumbra of Lethandria hanging from his neck.

"They won't," Karaj admitted. "Yet they will be delighted to know that you will join them in death."

The vampires gave them a cruel little smile as Akaran writhed in agony. "But will their families feel the same when Love Herself cannot protect Her own institution?"

Catherine's assistant clenched their teeth and began to slowly trace a ward in the air with the tips of their swords. "The Repository will never fall to the likes of you."

"The vault? You believe I care about your *trinkets* and your gold?" Annix replied with a slow, guttural laugh. "Where people gather to profess Her nature, even if not Her name? Now that... that, you took from me. I take from you. The Goddess of Love *destroyed* mine. I shall grant unto that a thousand times a thousand times over!"

Karaj took a step forward. Just one. It was all they had time to do.

The elven bloodsucker reached out in opposite directions with his hands open wide. Just as suddenly, he clamped his fists closed and *pulled* at the empty air. His last remaining broodling staggered aimlessly away from a bleeding soldier and clutched at its chest. Painful glowing red cracks split open down its arms and up its neck.

With a scream, the broodling disintegrated into a cloud of churning ash that hovered in the air in defiance of gravity. With a gesture from its former Meister, the burning, glowing ball of chaotic ether and ash flew through the air and embedded itself in the shadows that quietly hung under the edge of the Stara shrine. The shadows pulsed outwards in a sudden quiet rush that battered people away from the temple's base.

Then just as suddenly, they compacted inwardly.

A third of the stone pillars followed suit.

Masonry shattered, the pylons snapped, and half of the shrine followed immediate suit. Scores of panicked, wounded, and horrified citizens fell with the collapse as chunks of rock and wooden frames gave way to the demands of gravity. Statues of the Divine fell into the water and crushed any unwitting soul that fell before they did.

People desperately scrambled across granite blocks and hopelessly wrapped their arms around flagpoles and tapestries to try to keep from falling into the rubble below. A giant canvas banner, stitched together from the flags of thirty lesser houses and families fell on the backs of a dozen terrified citizens. As it dropped, a statue of Stara herself teetered off of its platform and fell backwards into the churning pond below.

The bridge leading up from the courtyard to the Temple itself was the next part to collapse. Far too many unlucky and unwitting souls were caught under it as the rubble fell across their backs. Their bodies were crushed to gory paste as wooden beams and handcrafted tiles landed across their broken bodies. Two remaining pillars fell into the pond and across the courtyard with a final thundering crash that signaled the end of the Temple's partial collapse.

Karaj, however, didn't give it a moment's thought.

They ran across the short distance separating them from the vampires, but the damned had no interest in continuing the battle. A sudden cloud of pitch-black darkness surrounded both of them. By the time that the Lover could get a blast of light to disperse it, they were gone.

All that was left was the screaming.

The screaming and the death.

Screaming that was in no short supply from Akaran — even as he slid into the unforgiving grip of systemic shock. Karaj was at his side before the rubble settled, and for a few moments, they wondered if the exorcist wouldn't be better served to have his leg removed then and there. It was going to be a moot point if he kept thrashing and bled out everywhere.

For the battered Lover, it was all about the pain. The jolt of lightning felt like it was still coursing through his flesh as his leg flopped around on the ground of its own accord. Blackened chunks of metal seared his flesh and baked the padding wrapped around his leg into a flaky crisp.

Akaran managed to stop screaming for one tear-filled cry that croaked off of his dry, split lips. "Fisk… fisking… kill… me… *please*," he begged. "I can't *I can't* I can't!"

It was a hard request to turn down, all things considered. Instead, Karaj reached down and wrapped their hand around the top of the young priest's head and whispered an invocation. *"Surrender to Love, and be granted peace."*

Before the words were even entirely out of their mouth, Akaran ceased his struggles and sank into a blissful sleep that was deeper than simple unconsciousness. It was enough to buy time — but not much. More Words and invocations rolled off of Karaj's tongue to help soothe the burns and ease the exorcist's wounds. Magic worked miracles even as the priest worked with a knife to rip the metal chunks of the brace off of the exorcist's leg and to cut a rough tourniquet to staunch what bleeding they could.

A fresh set of healing spells and lights blanketed the exorcist as Hadraie cut through the chaotic scene and offered her own aid to the fallen priest. She tried to tell Karaj about the other victims, but they didn't let her speak until after they had finally stopped Akaran's bleeding. Once they were done, Catherine's assistant pushed themselves up off of the ground with shaky arms a small puddle of sweat under their hands.

Once she was sure that Akaran was breathing on his own, the Wardkeeper turned to Karaj and pointed over at the collapsed shrine. "We have to help them."

The Lover looked at the shattered structure for all of two heartbeats before they turned around and went right back to ignoring it. "Help them? That is a Stara shrine, not ours. We have other concerns. Gather Malik. I'll take the boy."

Hadraie's silver eyes went wide over how casually Karaj brushed her off. "But they need our help."

"These two are worth more than anyone there," the Lover retorted as they bent down and tried to lift Akaran's nearly-dead weight. When that failed, Catherine's assistant stepped back with a muttered curse. "We'll provide aid – when we have aid to provide."

She grimaced and nodded her head. More of the 4th – a *lot* more of the 4th – had started to arrive on the scene. It took a bit of doing, but once the Garrison realized that Malik, of all people, had been rescued? Even despite the rest of the unmitigated disaster, that bought a little bit of good will.

As both men were loaded onto makeshift stretchers cut from destroyed flags, Karaj laid the back of their hand and stroked Akaran's cheek gently to wipe away some of his comatose tears. "There is a fine line between Love and Hate, you know. In the elemental balance of all the worlds. It is just part of nature."

"So the Tenants say," she agreed.

The Repository's administrative officer – if you could call them that – nodded sagely. "Yes, yes they do."

Hadraie looked over and watched Karaj idly just... *pet* the fallen priest. "Why do you mention it?"

"Because we were never told we'd be able to see the line in person."

VI. A FAIR GAME
Day of Wundis, 13th of Firstgrow, 513 QR

The city burned. There was no nice way to put it. The city burned.

If Annix had left the carnage to just the Ellachurstine, it might not have been so bad. But he hadn't. The attack was worse than anyone could've imagined. Worse than anyone could've possibly expected. A bard would later call it, "The Dirge of the Mad,' a name which would be absolutely loathed by the residents of Basion but absolutely loved by the residents of the capital.

In the here and now, there was only one thing to do: pick up the pieces. Annix had struck in every district. He'd moved through them one after the other, starting sometime around the first candlemark after midnight. He'd started in Akkador West and had moved through the entire city.

He knew what to hit, too, to just... *maximize* the terror. In the mercenary district, he'd taken out a traveler's hall where wives and families of soldiers-for-hire cared to stay. In Lower Naradol, he'd sent his broodlings to wipe out a street of drunken revelers, and they'd come damn close to killing everyone there. In Upper Naradol, he'd set fire to the Wall of Gardens – and parts of the fields were still smoldering by the time the sun came up.

There was a silver lining, if you could call it that. Maybe... maybe more of a bloody leather cord than *silver*. With his acts of terrorism, his broodlings had left witnesses. They were able to put descriptions to quill and parchment in enough cases to confirm that the spawn that had ravaged the city were the same ones that had struck the Ellachurstine.

Since all of those were dead, it let the Lovers presume they had neutered most of his army. Two more had been tracked down and exterminated in the pre-dawn hours from the other side of the city – an act that the Oo-lo's bragged about with every possible breath. It did little to earn them good will, or restore *any* respect they'd lost, but it was better than nothing.

'Better than nothing' was a low bar to cross.

But still better than nothing.

The chaos and the wreckage left behind was more than anyone but war-weary veterans and a few errant followers of the Goddess of Destruction had ever seen. Except for two other women. One was just a little girl, yet she'd seen eons of devastation.

The other?

What had only felt like an eternity of suffering.

"Chose to terrify him in fire again, did you?" the little girl chirped from her perch above the panicked masses. The pair had taken roost on a tall spire – one of the Granalchi's – that overlooked the city-scape. Neither were visible to the naked eye, and both were buried behind the Veil so well that they would have only appeared as ambient sprites to a magical onlooker...

...and only if you knew to look. Nobody did. Intentionally.

"*You wouldn't let me intervene,*" Rmaci retorted as she crossed her burnt arms. "*I could've done so much more.*" She looked down at her half-frozen and half-charred spectral flesh. "*As the Lady saw fit to cast me back into this accursed form, I assume it wouldn't have had the same impact if I'd simply appeared laying back in the grass with my legs spread.*"

"You *earned* those flames. She was *pissed* after your little talk," Love's messenger remarked offhandedly. "As for the other, probably not. Understand that you were granted a *special dispensation* for that appearance. If the Others find out We let you show up down there, limited as it was, there will be grief to pay."

"*Yours or mine?*"

The girl idly flicked a lock of hair back and forth in her fingers. "You could make an argument that they are one and the same, although, I wouldn't be overly worried. They rarely care about what happens down here. Mere mortals, dealing with simple problems on an imperfect world. Why bother?"

The spy looked over and tilted her head slightly. "*If the Others of the Pantheon don't, why do you?*"

"It's simple, I suppose. Dirt and Fire and Light and Death and Water and Air and Luck and Knowledge. War. Just... all of it. All of *Them,*" she replied as she stressed the word, "They exist *here* – here among these *people*. The Elementals? They're one thing. The Lady's children and grandchildren. Born out of Love to allow souls of man and beast to prosper. The others? The *Conceptual* Elementals – and the Divine? Why does one heal another? Compassion. What is compassion but Love extended as kindness? None of this... *mess*... would even exist without Love."

"Doesn't really answer the question, does it? That's Their nature, but not why She cares."

"She didn't always. Not to this extent," the emissary remarked. "But. Her hands-off approach? Lead to Her humiliation. Blame. Distrust. All that. Her involvement now is a direct response to getting pissed off by what man and demon wrought."

Rmaci looked out over the chaos. Riots had broken out across the northern part of the city. A new faction had emerged overnight that called themselves the 'Soldiers of Ellachurstine,' and they had gone on a campaign of terror of their own against the Order of Love. Followers of Niasmis were attacked in the streets, their safe houses and way-stations taken to the torch, and the streets leading to the Repository were covered in angry protests and more.

The city had taken Annix's words to heart. Half of the damn town had decided that the only way to protect themselves was to force the Order to hand over Bistra. The other half? They directed their anger at the 4th, the Overseer, and anyone else with a Dawnfire sigil and a sword. Even some of the people in that camp had made it clear they wanted the Overseer to use the army to deliver the Auramancer Exorcist to Flynn's Landing – just in case the Lovers made the wrong decision.

"It doesn't look very hands-on to me right now," Rmaci lamented. *"It looks more like She's allowing Her people to take the blame."*

The little girl wrinkled her nose and scoffed in muted disgust. "Mortals. You're guilty of failing in the same way that they are right now. Even as you watch from your new position."

"Your Lady made it clear I had failed in many things," the spirit pointed out icily. *"Given that conversation, I have some doubts as to if She is as holy as it is proclaimed."*

"Almost exactly what those idiots think, too," the emissary returned with an errant flick of her fingers. "Our Boss doesn't have dominion over the damned. She can't control Annix from the Mount any more than you could control a fish in the sea from your chamberpot. You could arrange for a series of events to unfold around them and eventually get that fish in your hands, yes. To actually force it there by yelling at it through the window? So much harder."

"So She does have a hand in this? It was Her follower that started this war, wasn't it? Now She lets these crimes against Her people continue?"

The little girl looked up at the former spy and blinked in surprise. "You think She wants this to happen?"

"Does She? Do any of the Gods?"

Her otherworldly companion looked down on the masses and pursed her lips. After a few long moments, she decided to opt for the diplomatic reply. "She can't control the vampire. She can't control what he said. The choice is – as it always has been – how your kind... mortal kind... respond. Do they give in to fear and demand the blood of an innocent and condemn a woman based on the words of a monster? Do they fight and sacrifice for a stranger? This is *their* choice. This is *their* test. Are they worthy of Heavens? Are they so wretched to deserve the pit? They're *tested* through suffering and joy alike to see what their worth is. That they must sin against each other – or not sin! – is their burden to bear."

Rmaci nodded along in slow understanding. *"It's also a choice for the Lovers, isn't it? Do they cave, do they give in to the threats? Or do they stand their ground?"*

"Yes. It is a test created by powers not Hers, but one these people are now forced to endure. How they move forward? That is up to them, and yet, they do not realize it. Their fates will be changed with how they react; they will be judged for how they choose to overcome adversity."

"It seems that it would be much easier to simply tell them what's right and wrong without any of this... ambiguity. Show them the truth. Direct them and help them understand what price may be paid if they chose one act over another."

"Maybe," the girl admitted. "Maybe not. If that was done, they wouldn't grow. There would be a hand on their neck at every moment, with no free will would be offered. They would no more be worthy of ascension than a loyal dog to your lap; just weeds grown by the Gods and let to age in the ground without ever sprouting into fruit or flowers."

The dead spy glanced away from one of the multitude of riots and arched a single eyebrow on her burnt, blistered face. *"Given that flowers only grow when one shits upon them, I think I see your point."*

"You haven't met our Lady's kin." she asked. "I have. It's a good point."

The wraith choked on her tongue and tried not to laugh. In the World Between Worlds, it was hard to say Who was listening, and it wasn't worth the risk. *"So... what happens next? What do I do next? You could've let me work down there. I could've… made a difference. Worked to undo my sins."*

"You don't belong down there anymore, nor can you undo the harm you've caused. You can only try to make amends beyond the world, and that means going to places where those busy little idiots down there won't ever know what you're doing — until it's their turn to make amends in death themselves," the girl countered as she stood up and smoothed out her pale yellow dress and adjusted one of the perfect daisies that decorated the neckline. She looked like she was all of seven… maybe. But it was more accurate to say she was all of seven millennia… if not more. "Your essence has been, for lack of a polite way to say it, torn to bloody bits and left to befoul the wind. There's rules to follow that let the dead cross over, and you… you of *all* people… know that. Your anchor there is gone. No anchor, no *you."*

"Since when do you bother with being polite?" The girl growled low in her throat and The Burned Woman immediately walked the quip back. *"I doubt you brought me here just to wax poetic about what these cowards are doing."*

"That's true," the not-exactly-young girl admitted. "You are here for a reason, though your understanding of it is your own choice to make. Have you been banished? Yes. Are you still useful? Oh, yes."

"A banishment that I am surprised little has been said about."

She shrugged. "Well, the idiot doesn't know that you've been taken out of play. We'll have to fix that at some point, but not at the moment. As far as the idiot that did it? They'll have to answer for their choices as much as you had to answer for yours. And the rest of those idiots answer for theirs."

Rmaci felt the cracks on her back and shoulders split open as a rush of heat and tiny little flames briefly jutted out from under her spectral skin. *"I'd like to help that answer."*

"Your fate is not decided," the little girl cautioned. "There are roles for all of us in the grand scheme, and Her scheme is grander than some angry little cockroach down below. For now, you have a role — a messenger, a watcher. I would accept that for what it is, and decide if you are willing to take on more. Or not."

The Burned Woman looked down at her ruined flesh and watched as light ebbed and flowed under her skin. *"Patience is not always a virtue. Sometimes it's a death sentence. I think that asshole rubbed off on me. I want to go **do** something and not just… sit here and wait for someone to… I don't know."*

"Set you on fire or heal your hurt?"

"That. Yes."

Love's Emissary shrugged her little shoulders and adjusted the yellow poppy in her hair. "As the terrors below are the fault of men, we have to wait for men to act. You've given warnings to those that needed to hear it twice – I assure you, you'll have your chance to help someone or other again in the future, even if just once more. It just depends on what *Her* idiot does."

"Speaking of. Is he done screaming yet?"

"Does he ever do anything else?"

The spy had to admit that for once, he really had reason. The only thing that had kept him from dying, as far as she could tell, was that he'd broken that frozen curse he'd spent so much time under. He'd made it to Medias Manor before he woke up – he was deemed too 'at risk' to be stored at the Repository – and it was more than a minor miracle that he didn't go into complete shock when their resident surgeon went to work.

When it was all said and done, any hopes he'd had to be able to run before the end of the year were dashed. Sherril had done more than just burn up the skin; she'd melted his new brace almost to the bone. The damage from that alone was more than magic alone could ever help to repair.

Not that they didn't use magic. After saving Malik, he was granted all the resources of the city to get patched up. The rest of it would take time to heal. Time that he didn't have. Time that none of them did. Time, sadly, that he'd have to take – for at least a pair of days.

That was time they'd be desperate to get back.

Time that they wouldn't.

Time that someone else took.

***

The Mother Eclipsian Erine Rrah was dead.

She'd been murdered in Cableture. Her body had been found the morning after the battle in the bay. It had been found then and by Queen's Law – she was already consigned to ash. Bodies were rarely allowed to lay in rest for more than a few days at most. Souls lost to agents infernal, or ruined by monsters of this world?

The lighthouse/pyre in the middle of the Bay had been well fed.

She was gone. That was the only thing that mattered.

She was dead, and she was dead streets away from where he'd been. She was dead, and she was dead because he'd been at the docks flinging bolts of *lightning* at some giant *squid* that had taken over a warship. She had been *murdered* while he was off fighting *ghosts* instead of being at her side.

It didn't matter that everything was falling apart around the port. It didn't matter that you couldn't walk two blocks without being hit by the suffocating stench of burnt skin or smoldering timber. The refugees from Basion were drenched in it; the ones that called Cableture their home reeked of the mountainous yeshal corpse still rotting in the bay. It didn't matter that people tried to get his attention, tried to get his help, tried to get him to come provide aid or come defend him because that was his job, wasn't it? That's what he was supposed to do, wasn't it?

They scattered whenever he flicked a small shower of sparks from his fingers. Basion had seen enough of that for one night, and word had spread like the plague about the terrible woman with the terrible streaks of lightning from her fingers. Nobody wanted to pick a fight with a man that could do the same – just in case.

Port Cableture had been spared the chaos of Annix's attack on the city. However, 'spared' was an adjective used lightly. The vampires had successfully destroyed Hannock Bridge leading out of the city but that hadn't stopped people from building a makeshift ramp across the river and into Yittl Canyon. The refugees had started to stream into Cableture almost by mid-day, and when they arrived, it was nothing short of bedlam.

Bedlam in a port city already up in arms by the disaster in the bay a few days before. It had made finding information hard. Not impossible, but hard. Information that only gave rise to tears. Words that only gave rise to a cry of anguish.

Truth that only shattered his heart.

The only thing that mattered was that it was his fault.

While that was the only thing that mattered, two other things tried to get his attention. The first was a haunting laugh that dogged his steps from one taberna to the next. The other?

The trail of cruel laughs and the faint odor of corpse-rot that he'd picked up on as he wandered the streets. Every time he tried to ignore it, the sound and smell got worse. After half a candlemark of trying to put it at the back of his mind, he gave in and decided to follow along.

It was the kind of thing that Akaran would do, and frankly?

It probably meant he'd get a fight.

With who or what he did not give a single damn.

Except he wouldn't get the opportunity. The smell lead him to a burnt-out warehouse with a giant hole in the roof and a dead horse someone had pulled inside and cut in half. It was barely illuminated, daylight be damned.

Once he saw the creature hanging onto the rafters in the far corner, the lack of light was appreciated. "What in the *pit* are you?" the black-haired Specialist marveled as he stared at the inky little blob.

"[I am favored/I am Master's. I am death/death beyond end,]" the red-eyed, *multiple-eyed* abomination chittered from afar. "[Some see as beast/some see as best.]"

"Some see as target practice," the battlemage growled as he channeled raw ether down his hands and let it dance across his fingertips. "You went to a lot of effort to get killed..."

The demon chortled and simply *vanished* out of thin air before it reappeared just behind Badin's shoulder. "[Can't catch/can't kill!]"

Badin spun around on his heel and had an arc of electricity in the air before the beast could do anything to stop him — although it wasn't the beast that got involved. Before his shot could land, a chunk of the horse launched off of the ruined floor and absorbed the blast. Gore erupted around the blob of rancid meat, but instead of showering the room...

...the spray of blood, muscles, and burnt hide compacted in on themselves into a tight ball inches from his face and dropped straight to the ground. "Do take caution," another voice boomed through the ruins, "I have no desire to cause harm to you. Nor a desire to be forced into further steps requiring me to wash the stench of this city from my flesh."

More magic coalesced around the battlemage's fingers as he tried to make sense of what just happened. He only had to give the stranger one glance before he realized he was leagues in over his head just from the sheer *power* the blood-red-robed figure *radiated*. It almost *steamed* out from his cloak, and the mage was certain he saw just that when his eyes focused on the long scythe with an onyx blade that the newcomer carried at his side. "Whomever you are — I want a fight, but I don't know if it's with you."

"Oh, I know you do, Specialist-Major. You want to bring down the wrath of the heavens onto the flesh of those that have done you wrong," the other man intoned. "You have been sinned against. Yet your injury, as anguishing as a broken heart can be, is not as grievous as the harm that befell another, is it?"

Badin flinched at how effortlessly this stranger cut through him with words alone. "I can change my mind about fighting with you, asshole. Let me go, and I'll forget I saw either of you."

The other man shook his head and slowly pulled down his hood. He was Sycian, with their naturally red irises. His face was otherwise immaculate; his features were so sharp and perfect that they were nearly chiseled. His skin wasn't as dark as others he'd seen before, and not even as dark as Se'daulif; and somehow, some impossible how, he looked… oddly familiar. "Why would I wish of you to forget? My Acolyte went to some effort to guide you here so we could have a conversation."

"With a creepy laugh and the smell of death?" the battlemage spat. "You can get further with wine."

"I suppose that is true but we make good with what we have," he intoned with an unflinching, flat look across his face. "Although it is death that brings us here. The Mother Eclipsian's, to be specific."

More lightning surged in Badin's hands and the spell cast a flicker of an angry bright glow across the room. The stranger's eyes glistened from the reflection, and the mage realized that he had a belt made of metal skulls across his waist. "Keep her name out of your mouth. *Whoever* you are, you're here consorting with a demon and you look like you're tryin' to be one yourself. Pretty sure I've got friends that'd let me send you outta this shit-hole without complaint."

The other man let his lips curl into a smile that flashed his teeth – the same way a wolf would when it would look at a flock of sheep. "Oh I have no doubt of that. Except that your friends are not what you think, and by that, I do mean that you should question how 'friendly' they are."

"You don't know me. You don't know my friends. Now let me go."

"Do I not?" he asked as Rishnobia disappeared and reappeared near his feet. "You – a battlemage. You – a man who is sometimes better described as a drunk and a borderline deserter of the army. A glorified bodyguard drawing off of the Crown's purse for people the Crown has no actual interest in protecting."

The scathing assessment took all the air out of Badin's lungs and all three of them knew it. "Who in the ever-loving pits are you?"

The man in the blood-red robe didn't answer directly. "Names freely given are not names necessary. It is not a matter of who I am as it is what I can do for you – and I would like to do something for you. I would like help you right a wrong, correct an injustice, and serve ends yours and mine alike."

"I see a dead horse. I'd start with that being wrong," Badin groused as he furtively – and futilely – searched for an extra exit. "I'd believe you'd be inclined to help if we weren't *standing next to a demon*."

With a cackle, the mote flickered in and out of existence again and unleashed a stench that was worse than the corpse. The stranger, on the other hand? He simply made another observation that added even more questions to the mage's plate.

"We all walk in the presence of demons. Some of them? They manifest. Others? They are internal. Your eyes give away the ones you battle. The one that brought us together? Well. We must find ways to make our demons work for us at times. *My* demons are *much* more understanding than your friends were to your heart."

"So you know I'm a drunk. So does half the damn town," Badin retorted. "What do you mean, 'to my love?' If you know something about the vampire bitch that killed Erine…" he growled as a single arc of energy sparked from his fingers and struck a patch of dirt near the little demon.

"[Harlot's followers have you seeing fangs/you don't see the real teeth,]" the mote mocked. "[Rishnobia sees/Rishnobia knows!]"

"Rishnobia speaks out of turn," its master scolded, "even correct as you are. Sirrah Specialist: I am no friend of the Great Harlot, though I suspect you gathered that. You are, but you should not be. I have come to proffer an arrangement between us out of necessity, though I am at a loss to suggest if the necessity is greater for you than I, or I than you. Will you hear me out?"

Badin took a few steps back. "If you're an enemy of the Lovers, then you're one of mine. Why shouldn't I fry you both where you stand?"

The other man pondered the suggestion for a moment. And only a moment. "I suppose you could try, though then you would not be of any use to me. Whereas I can be of use to you. I can mend a heart in a way that they cannot. I further suspect that if you agree to listen then you will only want to break theirs."

"If you're going to accuse them of killing her, then get on with it. I'm not a fool; I can hear it in your voice."

"Good," he intoned, "that will save us some time. Then let me explain my stance: I need to know something about the Repository. It is something that they will not freely part with, and it is something that I have no further assets available to devote into discovering into at this time. I have a preference to keep the shedding of blood to a minimum, if we can."

"You want me to break into that *fortress* and tell you something?" the mage demanded incredulously. "There are easier ways to kill myself."

The stranger arched his eyebrow. "Are you so sure of that? Suicide is not as easy as one thinks — and all I need to know is something written in relative ease of view. In exchange, I offer you the name of your lover's killer."

"Annix. Annix and Sherril."

"The killers you think, but not the killers that are," the Man of the Red Death replied. "Do, hear me out. I only deal in truths."

Badin pointed at the bemused demon and shook his head. "I don't think you're dealing in truths. Not if you've got monsters like that at your service."

"On the contrary. I deal in nothing but," he countered. "Except the truths that I deal in are not the ones that are easy to stomach. Allow me to show you what I mean."

The battlemage backed up even further as Rishnobia jumped on top of the dead horse and dug its claws into its flesh. The corpse began to deteriorate at an accelerated pace; the body deflated, hair fell away, and still-fresh blood began to dry up like it had been exposed to flame. The head rolled around in the rubble all on its own, and its tail fluffed out and promptly fell apart in a cloud of dust like so much wheat chaff thrown to the wind.

A cloud of flickering gray and white ether rolled out of the corpse and crackled in the air like a small foggy storm. The air lost all warmth, and the equine's skull made a pained, unholy 'neigh,' cry that was so *obscene* that it made the mage's blood run cold. The stranger in red made a guttural, downright *inhuman* noise that echoed across the room and set the head of his scythe briefly ablaze with a stream of orange flame that was gone as soon as it came into being.

All Badin could do was curse and prepare a desperate thundercall that would've turned what was left of the roof into fingernail-sized splinters. "GODS ABOVE – A NECROMANCER?!"

The Sycian turned his eyes from the horse and rapped his scythe on the dirty broken floor with a sharp crack. "If you seek to wound me with words, that is not one that shall," he cautioned, "and this city has worse in it than those that can command the dead. But if you are willing to see truth – then please, do turn around."

Against all reason, against *any* reason, one of the best of Dawnfire's Specialist-Majors did just that and had to stop himself from falling to his knees. Erine floated in front of him, with her long hair flowing as if she was in a pool and her dark brown eyes brimming with emotion. Sadness or joy, he couldn't tell.

She didn't make a sound. She didn't move. She just hung in the air, suspended in an etheric current he simply couldn't see. When he saw the hole in his beloved's chest, however, any strength he had in him fell to the wayside. "Damn you," he seethed. "How did you... why...? No. *Damn you.*

Let her rest!" he demanded.

"Calm thyself, battlemage, and hear me out," the stranger replied. "Now I must ask, as distressing as it may be – have you known your vampires to often kill with a shortblade in the back? The work they do seems to be much more of either the neck or more flagrantly in the front."

Badin refused to look away from her blank, tear-filled eyes. "What are… they've been slaughtering… what difference does it make how they did it? She's dead and it's their fault. I swear I'll end them all."

"[Night bitch/got dead,]" Rishnobia cackled, "[By the damned/you are wrong.]"

The man in red intercepted the bolt of lighting a heartbeat before it cooked the vile mote on the spot, but just like the first time, the chunk of dead animal he used to block it crumbled inwardly and fell to the floor. Through it all, the demon just laughed. "What happened is that allies of your friend were not allies of hers. It is easier to hide uncomfortable truths when the speakers of them are no longer in this world – and so much easier more when there is another soul nearby that can easily take the blame."

With a trembling hand, the mage tried to take Erine's in his. His fingers brushed across hers, and then slipped through her phantom flesh like she was just a waking dream. "Annix… Sherril… those two didn't…?"

"No, they didn't," the man in the red replied. "Though they have made such a mess that I am now forced to make other… arrangements… to satisfy my interests. This is one of them," he intoned. "I can bring her back. For a price."

Badin turned around on shaky legs as his eyes went wide. "Bring her…" he started before the blood rushed from his ace and his stomach fell to the floor. "You're the one Akaran wants dead. The one in the red…" he rambled as the stranger watched on, utterly bemused. "You killed a friend of mine."

"I did?" the Man of the Red Death asked, ever-so-slightly bemused. "I would apologize, except that I only do it when necessary and thus, that is not something I can apologize *for*. I am sure I had a reason, and that reason doesn't impart a difference for where we are now."

"You killed him because he wasn't showing you proper *manners*," the mage seethed. "Right before you ripped an eyeball from a young woman who hadn't done a *damn* thing to you."

The stranger cupped his chin and wagged his finger once in the air. "Oh! But she did. She served to deliver a message. It was important," he replied. "As are manners. I trust that you will keep that in mind."

"[No time argue/no time fight. Listen and entreat with Master/or another will be found,]" Rishnobia cautioned from atop what was left of the poor horse.

"I'd rather kill you both right now."

"Your quaint snarls aside, my Acolyte is correct. Now that you know who I am, allow me to fill in a few blanks: my name is Nastavol DeHawk, and yes, for what your mind can comprehend, I am… something… of a practitioner of necrosia. Specifically, something that is far more than just the flesh."

Badin clenched his teeth and swallowed past the lump in his throat. "DeHawk, huh? That's Akaran's name. I'm really starting to think you didn't just pick my name out of a hat."

"Just now? That is such a pity; I had assumed you had already come to understand that this was not a meeting by chance," the necromancer replied with a little bit of mirth to his voice. "Yes, you are right, of course. It is his name. I suppose the question you need to ask yourself is if that is just poor luck, fate, or if there is blood between us."

The remark lingered in the air like it was made of lead. The Specialist shot a quick glance back at Erine and took a nervous, furious breath. "Fisk. I'm dead if I say no, aren't I?"

Neither Nastavol nor his acolyte bothered to reply.

They just looked at him like he was the village idiot.

"What do you want of me?"

"As I said, a trade. I will give you her. In exchange, you will fetch and grant me knowledge I seek. I cannot say that she will be back as you fully remember her, to warn. Unlike those you have been aiding as of late, I again state that I only deal in truths."

The mage turned around and looked at the floating specter behind him. Specter. Illusion. Soul. Mental trick. Whatever she was. She was there. The first woman that had ever made him feel like he was more than the drink, the first hand on his shoulder that made him feel like he was worth more than a few sparks on a battlefield.

Thirty-five years on this Gods-forsaken world, and she was the first one to ever treat him as more than just some conscripted weapon. They hadn't spent a lot of time together. But it'd been enough to know.

It'd been enough to know that he'd give anything to spend more.

A chaotic surge of lightning coursed across his fingers and tore through her etheric form. Her wounded vision scattered into a thousand fragments of a hundred memories. When her spirit was gone, he turned back to the necromancer and his minion with tears pouring down his bearded cheeks.

"I'll see her again soon or I won't. I won't stomach seeing her suffer at your hands."

Nastavol tilted his head in a gesture of respect to the battlemage. "What makes you so certain that she would?"

"Because I've seen enough damn things walking around that don't need to be. I've seen their eyes. I don't think that one-eyed bastard sees the pain in their faces, for all the good he tries to do. But I do. I have. Pull her back across the Veil again and we'll see which of us joins her first."

"[You I promise/you'll go first,]" the mote warned.

"Ah. Well, yes, I suppose if you spent enough time with *him* then it would tend to cloud your judgment. Still, I would say that this means I picked the right man for the job. Few would turn that offer down... and the ones that would? They would only ask for one thing instead," the necromancer remarked with a smile. "I will give you the name of her murderer. You will not be able to act against them, so I will also give you a promise."

Badin sniffled away tears and tried to work his throat. It was so tight it hurt, and the energy at his fingertips had left a few burns on his arms. "What kind of promise can a man like you offer me?"

"The kind I promise to keep," the necromancer replied. "Inside the Repository, I believe in the foyer – or perhaps the receiving hall – there is a statue. It is a large one. Gold, likely. Possibly copper. Possibly a mix. It will be of the Archangel Miral; yes, the one that open grave is named for."

Of all the things that the asshole could've asked for... "A statue? What, you want me to go in and destroy it? I won't make it past the first *thought* to summon a spark."

"Destroy? No. No such need. There will be a spell – an invocation of some kind. It will be written on it. I need to know what it is. Tell me that, and I will ensure that justice befalls those who are in sore need of it."

The mage stood still and just tried to focus on breathing. In and out, slowly. Just breath after breath. Anything else seemed like more than he could do. "You want me to turn on the Lovers. That's a damn big ask."

"They turned on you first when Karaj murdered your lady," Nastavol proclaimed.

His accusation made the room collapse in on itself. Everything around Badin simply... stopped. No thoughts, no ideas. Just a steady stare and the sound of his heartbeat in his ears. "Karaj...? I know that name. The assistant to..."

"Assistant is such a *vague* word," the necromancer countered. "Assisting *what*, however, is a much better thought to explore. Erine died at their hand as indisputable as I am standing before you."

It was a simple question that Nastavol saw coming from a mile away. It was the only question that could be asked. The poor mage said it so quietly that it was almost impossible to even hear. "Why?"

"Because Erine discovered a thing that Erine had no business knowing. Even I have to admit that. The Order is an entity that is built upon secrets and that covers them in lies. They act to 'protect the world,' and do not particularly care who has to leave it in the process. You have seen their work first hand, so I know you know that much to be true."

"That much... yeah," Badin slowly agreed. "Why in the name of the Pantheon should I believe you about the rest? Akaran wouldn't turn on me..."

The Man of the Red Death shook his head dismissively. "You presume that he has any idea. He assumes as you did until just now; that she was just another claim by the vampire. He has no other reason to assume otherwise – Karaj banished one of his other allies at the same time, of which he has an equal lack of knowledge. He had no hand in her passing. Of that, I assure you."

As his stomach churned, the mage slowly sank down to the muddy floor. Horrific thoughts spun through his head. Conflicting emotions, terrible ideas. "Why... what could she have possibly found out...?"

"Now that, I am afraid, is a truth you do not get to know," Nastavol argued. "The 'why' is less important as the 'who.' Followed by 'what you intend to do about it,' which is a matter of great interest to me."

Badin took a deep, nervous breath. "Why should I possibly believe you?"

"Because I can bring her back to tell you," he replied. "It is not as difficult as some make the idea out to be. Of course, it helps when I have this," the necromancer added as he pulled a knife almost out of thin air, "as well as the paid-for services of a very disinterested Granalchi Psyanist outside who could not care less about you or I or anything but the weight of the crowns slid into his purse."

Rishnobia jumped into the air, grabbed the knife, and dropped it down at Badin's knees. It was a simple steel blade with bits of blood staining the edge. The hilt was the giveaway – a pair of entwined lovers had been embossed into the steel where the blade met the handle. A single red ruby had been placed in the center of the acidic etching, and it briefly shimmered while the demon held it.

The battlemage stared down at it and felt the world collapse down into a single point all over again. "You don't play fair... do... do you?"

"Good Sirrah, no. I do not *play*," Nastavol countered. "I run the game."

"The psyanist... they'll... it'll need something to verify..."

"If you presume to suggest that you do not own something that has her imprint on it, I will be most disappointed. I will even so much as assume that you have such a thing on your person even now. Am I wrong? Show them that, and they can tell you if the blood on the blade belongs to the woman in question."

Badin swallowed hard and shook his head mutely.

"Then do as you need to do. Ask a Lover who it belongs to. Ask the Psyanist to verify the blood. Once you have the one and the other, you will have what you need to know."

"Describe 'justice.' I'm not..." he started before he took a shuddering breath. "I'm not going..."

"There is a thing I need and I intend to collect it. In the process, I will ensure those that have caused harm to you will have harm come to them. I do not dabble in the deaths of innocents. Only in the deaths of the necessary... and *yes*, manners *are* a *necessity*."

Rishnobia chortled. "[Things be done/things be found. You get peace/she gets justice. A deal that be made/has rewards for all involved.]"

The mage picked up the knife and ran his fingertips across the stains. "Akaran gets a pass. He doesn't get hurt. I don't care what he's done."

"I have no intention of causing him harm. Grief, perhaps, but only as a means to an end. Nothing punitive or personal. Harm, no. Nothing that will cause him disability for an extended period. Even then, only if to remove him from the field while I work – if it comes to it."

"I can't trust you. You know that."

Nastavol smiled down at him. "Of course you cannot. I would not dare ask you to do such a thing. I will tell you that with that name, and the knowledge of the party of guilt, you will have no chance of finding justice on your own. Less of course, you attempt to kill Karaj yourself," the Sycian suggested with a quiet snort of dismissal. "Which we both understand will not likely work, and we equally know no justice from the Crown will be offered if you do not approach the Overseer or army. The Lovers will merely claim she was working with the vampire, or was part of a cultist uprising against the Crown. That is what they do when they wish to hide a thing."

"Dammit," Badin swore under his breath. "Why are you doing this to me?"

"Because I need someone that can do as I ask."

"Yeah well, this *ask* of yours?" the mage grunted, "I don't think you picked the right damn person. I'm not a Lover. I take orders from them, sure. I'm in the Army. We all do. Just because I do doesn't mean I get to walk into their front door. If it that was that easy, I think you'd have found someone else a little more willing without all this effort."

The necromancer waved his fingers and a cloud of *death* floated away from the horse's corpse and into the nothingness overhead. "That is quite true, and I am aware of your limitations. I also know that a man of your stature *would* have business within the Lover's home *if* you had something of import to them... evidence, perhaps?"

Badin did *not* like the way the Sycian said that word. "Of what?"

Rishnobia vanished from sight and reappeared a few moments later with a burlap satchel in its oily little claws. "[We had arrangements/with a former. Former of many things/former of use now.]"

"In those arrangements, she kept a chronicle of her travels," Nastavol continued for the mote. "A full accounting. It is quite amazing – you went to search for a Mother of Lethandria, and what you found instead was a suggestion for where to look to find plots written by one that falsely claimed to be the same." As the mage looked down at the bag, the necromancer then quietly added, "So that I am not speaking a lie, may I suggest in your efforts to find your Eclipsian, I *suggest* you look into a bag owned by someone that falsely claimed to be one whenever it suited her. She was a great many things to many others, even if rare said in public."

He didn't have to be goaded into it more than that. Not that he wanted to look, but the idea of pushing the subject didn't feel like the greatest of ideas. The satchel was full of journals, scrolls, ledgers, deeds, contracts – and every single one of them had the same name. "Anais Lovic. She was yours."

"We had arrangements. She has not lived up to all of them. I expect you will do better," the necromancer replied. "What I also expect is that the Lovers will find much of this on their own before terribly long. Much of her work has already been undone and there are other agents of the underworld that have been gleefully dismantling the empire of secrets she put together. If you intend to uphold your end of our deal, I would ensure that you make this delivery quickly."

Badin bit down on his lip and stared into the bag. His heart pounded in his ears like a horde of bison and he wasn't sure if he was sweating from the humidity or sweating from the stress of dealing with the asshole. "If Karaj didn't do it... you know I'm going to tell them everything about this conversation. Every last bit."

"Oh, I am quite aware. I also know that I can trust you to be a man of your word. If what I say is true, and you are able to see the spell — and believe me, my jaundiced friend, I will know if you are able to enter the Repository or not — I know your desire for justice will bring you back to me."

"I assume you'll kill me if I don't," the mage snorted.

"Oh, no. Specialist. I will have no need to do such a thing."

"Thought you didn't lie?"

Nastavol smiled at him under his hood. "It will not matter if I kill you or not. My reach extends far, far past this simple world, battlemage. I will not need to kill you because *you* will eventually come to me."

As he spoke, Rishnobia flicked out of the warehouse and perched atop its broken roof and peered into the sky above. It didn't matter what his master had to say. He could say damn near anything he wanted. Whatever he said would work.

Because he didn't run a fair game.

VII. BROKEN DEFENDERS
Morning of Madis, 15th of Firstgrow, 513 QR

Two days.

It had been two long, miserable days since the attack on the Ellachurstine. Two days that he'd spent locked up in his room at Medias Manor. Two days with next to no contact with the outside world. He wasn't being punished, he was assured, it was just that, honestly?

Nobody knew what to do with him.

Nobody knew what to do with him because at this point, nobody knew what he could do. Could he walk? If you could call it that, yes. His leg had been immobilized from the hip to his ankle, his cane was firmly back in his hand, and the damn thing *hurt*.

The *only* upside, if you could call it that, was that the damage that the sparkcasting bitch had inflicted had left most of his leg completely numb. "You'll get feeling back eventually," the Manor's surgeon had offered. "You won't like it when you do, but you will."

That was Keto for you. Helpful, eager to take care of his charges, and utterly depressing. He was also talented beyond words and measure. Between his efforts and the Order healers that Karaj had dispatched, Akaran could at least stand up. Being allowed out of his room?

Allowed was such a loaded word.

The phrase, "I'm going to be a whiny bitch if you don't,' was the one that granted him an exit – even if only to the dining hall. It also landed him directly across one of three women at the Manor whom he truly did not want to see, yet couldn't help himself with trying to talk to until he could do more than just worry about Annix.

Because, right or wrong, he blamed himself for her being here.

Seline settled down across from him at the dining table. She had other options – there were three more of the long tables, with free benches, and nobody else but a pair of orderlies in the room – but she, for whatever reason, decided to sit down with him. "You're back."

"I don't want to be," he replied quietly as he looked down at the bowl of… porridge? …in front of him. "Wasn't by choice."

She nodded her head at him until he glanced up and looked her in her eyes. And just as quickly, his soul shattered for her all over again. Gone was the spunky, aggressive, assertive young woman that wouldn't take 'no' for an answer; the one who would be willing to tell him to go get stuffed into a goat if she felt like he deserved it. "You got hurt again."

"Yeah."

Whatever had taken her place? Whatever had crawled inside her hollowed-out mind and taken up residence? "Did you win?" she asked with her voice barely above a cracked whisper.

"I don't know," he admitted as he lowered his spoon and slumped his shoulders. Seline looked like an absolutely shattered husk of the healer that had been equally both his near-constant companion and thorn in his side, and he simply did not have any idea how to talk to her now. "They won't tell me. I saved someone. I think."

"But not everyone," she quietly pointed out.

"But not everyone."

Seline traced a small circle on the table and sighed. "Save some. Hurt others. That's what you do."

He winced and pushed his bowl away. She looked at it with utter disinterest before she returned to tracing small circles over and over again across the simple wooden planks. "Starting to feel like it."

The healer – *former* healer – shifted her simple cotton gown around her shoulders. She'd been put into one of the typical light-tan/dirty gray smocks that the Manor tended to hand out to its residents, and she didn't look particularly happy to have it on. "Akaran?"

"Yes?"

"I don't…" the blonde-haired girl started to say before she bit her lip and ducked her head. "I don't want you here. Can you go? Please?"

Her question felt like an utter slap across the face, but at the same time, one he was grateful to answer. He started to push himself up before he even opened his mouth. "Yeah. Yeah, I can. I'll go eat in my room. I'm… I'm sorry."

She hesitantly reached over and wrapped her hand around his to stop him. "Not… not the table," she clarified. "I don't… I don't want you here.

At the Manor. I knew you… you were here. Heard the screams. I know yours."

Akaran looked at her shaking hand and suddenly realized how *frail* the poor girl had become over the last few days. She wasn't just emotionally drained – she looked like all the strength in her body had been completely sapped out. "They won't let me out. I tried."

"They won't let me go either," she lamented as her hair fell down over her eyes. "You? You, they'll let go. Just haven't asked the right person yet."

He recognized it for what it was when she looked down at her finger and watched it like she was expecting it to move. *Cocasa*, he realized. *She's had a bushel of it shoved down her throat.* He winced again as a mix of disgust and nervousness and utter sadness churned with a burning ferocity deep in his stomach. "When they do, I'll go. I promise. I'm sorry."

Seline let go and pulled her arms around her chest. "I know. Just don't… don't come back, okay? Please?"

He nodded and tried to swallow back the sick feeling in his throat. "I'll try. How… how long are you here for?"

"I don't… I don't know. I don't want to be here. They said after… the thing. That I'd be safer? Safer here, I guess. I'm not… I'm not supposed to be out of my room but I had to come ask you to leave. Please."

"Why aren't they letting you…?"

She pointed up at the ceiling and shrugged again. "Ridora, she, well. She's upset. She's scared. Won't admit it, you know her. She's scared that she'll lose more people. She gave me belistand. Cocasa. A few… other things. My head doesn't feel… my head feels… off? I'm supposed to rest."

"You should," he agreed in a slow, soft tone of voice. He tried to make it sound comforting. He ended up sounding menacing. "I don't know what you've been through but, you need to rest. That's what you always told me.

She flinched, and then she shot him a look that lasted for a heartbeat. A heartbeat was all that was needed. It was full of anger. Nothing but raw, unquestionable anger that made him step back before he realized he was even trying to move. "Except you didn't listen. I told you…" she snarled as she fidgeted on her spot, "I… I told you again and again. Sit down. Stay here. Don't do. Just… *stay*. You didn't."

Akaran looked down at his knee and wondered, deeply wondered, if he'd have been better off if he had. It didn't matter either way, because of one simple fact. "I couldn't."

"I know. I know now," she sadly agreed. "I know you. I know you couldn't. You couldn't now I can't. That's the way it goes, isn't it?"

"Maybe. I don't know what I'm supposed to do."

"Hurt people," Seline answered without hesitation. "That's what you do. I bet… I bet you didn't save people because you weren't supposed to save people. You were supposed to hurt people."

Her accusation had merit. It didn't make it any easier to swallow. "That's not true. I'm supposed to –"

The smile she gave him had no joy to it. Just a quiet sadness. "Supposed to do whatever… whatever the Goddess tells you… you to do. You keep saying that. Except if She's not always… always telling you what to do. You just *do* and… *do* what you *do* is hurt people. *I* got hurt. You didn't do it. But I did. I got hurt because I was around you."

Akaran tried to steady himself on his cane, though her words were cutting so deep he couldn't help but feel even more off-balance than he already was. "No. You got hurt because… well… you got hurt because…"

"Because someone decided that if I hurt then they'd get what they wanted," she lamented. "That's the funny thing about it. You know?"

"Funny? What in the world do you…?"

Seline leaned over across the table and looked up at him like a helpless little kitten. "It could've been anyone. See? Anyone. It didn't *have* to be me but it *was* me and it *was* me because *you* and that squid on that ship and that burned woman and everyone and… I had to get away. I had to get away because of you. So… because of you I'm…" she explained as she gestured at her face. "I'm… I'm not myself now. I don't know what's *wrong* but I'm not *myself* now." Without missing a beat, she shifted so she sat straight up again and let that raw rage flash in her eyes again.

"You're healing. Whatever she did to you – the important thing is that you're still here. That's what you kept telling me after I first got here. That no matter what, I was still here."

"Saw how well… that worked out, didn't… didn't we?" she stammered under her breath. "Can't even talk now because… had my head under water so much that I…"

"I'll go. Don't push, Sel. Please. I'm not worth you."

She gave him a withering glare and dropped her spoon back into her bowl. "Truest thing you've… ever said," she replied between bites. "Wait. I heard you.. when you came in."

"Heard me?"

"Yeah. Scream. About… Nith? A Council? That he's not one? Who… who are they?"

Akaran blinked and scooted back on his seat. The movement made a fresh jolt of pain blossom from the side of his leg all the way up to his lower back. When he finished swearing and fighting back an errant tear, he took a long breath and started to explain. "I'm not going to lie to you. The good news is, I managed to get an answer from him when we fought. He isn't one. He's not a Nithian."

"Is that... is that good?"

He answered without even thinking about it. "Yes."

"But he has others... like him."

"Yeah. Several so far."

"Raechil... she was one of his?"

"She was."

Seline pensively prodded at her gruel. "So there may be more like him. Ones he's... made?" she asked as he answered with just a faint smile. "Why hasn't he made more before now?"

He shrugged his shoulders and sighed. "I guess because he was trying to avoid getting noticed. Why now, I'm not sure. Maybe by us. Pits, maybe even by the Council for all I know."

"You... didn't say who the Nith... who they are."

Akaran blanched and took a moment to compose himself. "I didn't know most of this; not until after Cableture. I made Catherine tell me everything she knew about these... fang-faced freaks... since apparently low-rank shits like me aren't supposed to know."

"Told... you everything? I doubt... doubt that."

He absolutely loathed the fact that her distrust felt *entirely* justified. "She told me that after the Crusade of Suns, the vampire race – the survivors – found a way to go south. *Very* south. Down to the peaks of Crys south, beyond the empires of Matheia and Atheia, beyond the seas. Nobody even knew they'd *survived* until a hundred fifty-some years later."

She listened intently and continued to roll her spoon around absentmindedly. "Dawnfire didn't... want to go down and...?"

"Nobody did," he admitted. "The Adelin Civil War erupted twenty years after the Suns. When Agromah fell... nobody cared. Too much... too much *everything* went on."

"So now... there are still vampires... in Crys? That's what you're scared... worried over? From... the bottom... bottom of the world?"

Akaran grimaced and really wished she'd drop the subject. "The Maiden is," he warned. "The Nith popped out of the ground again near the turn of the third century. Made contact with Matheia. They didn't get a great welcome," he grunted. "Turned out they'd spread. Everywhere. Alive and well with an Empire of their own. The first Crusaders missed some damn prince or something when they went culling. Apparently Order *Paladins* have been hunting them down since 392," he added as he stressed the title like it was almost offensive to say. "This wasn't a secret they should've kept buried from the rest of us, but apparently they did. Utter freaking lunacy."

"Oh. So why… why is she worried? Why… why did you… even in pain did you…?"

"I don't remember doing it, if it helps." When she shook her head no, he sighed and continued on. "Catherine made it clear: to her, there's a difference between a *monster* and a monster with *friends*. She's not wrong, and the way she put it after our *talk*…"

"But he's… he's not? He's just… himself?"

"Himself and anyone he can turn," Akaran answered gloomily. He looked around the empty room and leaned in close to whisper. "From what she told me, the Council isn't active in Dawnfire. The Order made sure of that. Down south though? I guess The Guild has their hands full of it. Nobody in the Queen's Court will admit it, but it's a problem. As long as we keep the problem *out* of the Kingdom, Her Majesty won't admit they even still exist. If the Queen won't, then the Order doesn't. Catherine said that the Holy General has a *lot* of grief she's dealing with back in Mulvette because of this… mess. It's the only reason Fire-Eyes isn't down here already."

"Except you Lovers haven't… *you* haven't. They're here."

"*A* vampire is here. It's not the same."

"One rat in the bath or thirty. Still a… a rat in the bath," Seline pointed out. "But I guess… I guess I see. Should I be grateful he… he is or isn't part of this… this Council?"

The exorcist ran his hand over his lips and sighed. "I don't know. Probably better. One rat or thirty."

"Rats… rats breed," she groused. "Akaran? Did you kill her?"

He blinked in surprise at how fast she moved from *broken* to *breaker*. "Who… oh. You mean Anais? No. They wouldn't let me."

"Are you going to?"

"Someone is."

She crossed her arms. "But not you."

The venom in her voice… "I don't know."

"You know, there's a… a reason for every soul in this manor," she lamented as the fury faded. "You broke your leg. Divitol? He… he was a Hunter," Seline replied as she calmed down and started to speak a little easier. "Got his face… burned off. By a mage. Tried to save a village.

Tanstin?" She continued as he wondered if he should stay or hobble away as fast as he could. "Tanstin? Stara. Ladjunct. Hovoth cultists. They... they ... did things to... to him. Appaidene? Just... just a mess."

"Seline..." he started before he gave up and tried to reach for her.

She saw his hand coming and the young woman violently flinched and pulled away from him so hard that she nearly fell off of the bench. "Don't. Don't... don't ever... touch me. Don't you *ever* touch me... me again, damn... damn you," she swore. "I'm not here because I... because I did something *right*. I'm here because I was scared... scared of... of *you* and then a *monster* wanted to sca... *scare* someone *else*."

"Seline..."

"And now? You can't even prom... promise me you'll kill the... that *bitch*, even for... even for *me*," she stammered. "Holy warrior...? Holy *murderer*. But you won't... for *me*. Why? Why am I... am I not worthy? Worth blood... blood on your blade? Blood on your hands... blood on your hands not enough? What did I do? Did I deserve... deserve getting... getting drowned? Again? Again? And *again*? Because I... I helped *you*?"

"No, I don't –"

She cut him off with a cutting motion and a snarl. "Helping... helping *you*. Is that... is that my sin?"

The scathing rage in her voice stripped him down to the bone. The hate, the blame, the pain. All of it. For a moment, brief as it was, he saw Mariah in her. Mariah, whom he had tried to keep safe; Mariah, who had gotten her eye gouged out because someone wanted to send him a message.

"You'll get it, I promise," he replied quietly as a tear slipped down his cheek. "I'll deliver justice for you."

Seline scoffed and crossed her arms. "No you won't. You... you're a liar. You lie. You do. You aren't a... a protector. She can't hurt me anymore. What does it matter? You can't make this... this right. You are incap... *incapable* of it. You're a liar. A failure. For all the blood you drip? You won't face... face the blood that didn't... didn't *deserve* to be spilled."

Her words broke his heart. He left without saying another word.

Worse yet? She was right. He couldn't deliver her justice.

But there would be a reckoning.

***

"In all of the years I have spent on these grounds, of all of the broken and lame, of all the combative and rude, I have *never* met a man – met anyone, really – as *unquestionably* single-minded as *you*," the voice called out behind him as he packed what little he had (and what little he could carry) in his room.

Akaran grimaced and bared his teeth out of her sight. "Ridora."

"Lady Ridora," the caretaker replied succinctly and with enough of a barb in her tone to give an arrow a run for its money. "I rarely use language this coarse, but you, 'good' sirrah? You are a cock."

His mouth dropped open. "I... I don't know how to respond to that."

"Your response has no matter and wouldn't change it even if it did. *You. Are. A. Cock*," she repeated. "You *refuse* to accept care, you *refuse* to rest, you *refuse* to stay in your room, and now, I presume, against *all possible logic and education*, you *refuse* to stay in the one place that can offer you *safety* while you *recover*."

"I thought I proved you that this place wasn't safe," he muttered as he stuffed his bloody tabard into a burlap bag and sighed as his fingers couldn't quit shaking enough to tie it closed. "But that's not saying that I don't appreciate the help."

"Oh, yes, you *appreciate the help*," the auburn-haired woman retorted as she stormed across the room and snatched the sack from his hands... and promptly began to help him work more stuff into it. "I should have the orderlies come in here, sit you down, and tie you to the bed. Just that. You sleep or you don't. Maybe gag you for good measure," she added.

Akaran took a step back and let her take care of the bag. Every single time he moved, he had to swing his leg around and brace himself on his other. He felt like his hip was about to explode, and the raw *throbbing* coming from his knee was maddening. "Except you're not."

"Except I'm not. Do you know what I've done the last two days? Aside from look after you – since you seem to be so dead-set to constantly return to my care?"

"No...?"

"Do you remember that you found a scroll in Livstra's room? You handed it to me, told me not to lose it, that it wasn't dangerous but it was important? It was right before you decided to break some windows and tear up the upstairs."

He sagged against the edge of his bed and tried to think it through. "No?"

She looked up from the bag and somehow, down at him at the same time. "You were busy stalking the halls and setting shadows on fire, so let me remind you: you stormed into Livstra's room. Destroyed a windowsill, cast a few spells. Raided her bookshelf."

"Oh. That... oh. Right. The windowsill that had Ameggenon on it."

"Yes, if that's what it was," she answered dismissively as she stuffed a book into his sack. "That scroll has been the biggest headache I've had since your arrival. Livstra had her hand in many a honeypot, it seems. I didn't realize that purgalaito was one of them."

Akaran perked up slightly at her irritated remark. "The scroll was a spell?"

"At least an active invocation of one, with a room number written on it," Ridora confirmed. "I know you have no idea nor interest in the depths of my abilities with magic, so I shall spare you my resume of spellcraft — but I did study, for a time, in the Granalchi Academy before I decided that the Order could use my talents more."

"The Order could use you or you could use the Order?"

She let that slide with nothing more than a dirty look over her shoulder. "She had penned an invocation to Solinal, except... it wasn't just. There was a reference to Stilamatheric in it, too."

The exorcist blinked slowly. "That's an odd combination. The God of the River of All-Souls and Peace being summoned at the same time as the God of the Unders?"

"That was how I felt about it, too. Translated, it wasn't convoluted. 'May the Waters wash over your skin, and set your *clobben tabboroth* to rest beneath them.' Tabboroth being purgalaito for bones. That's what I thought it said, at first."

His confused blinks turned into concern in a hurry. "And when you thought second...?"

The Lady of the Manor turned around and sat down on the edge of his bed with a deep frown. "It didn't say 'bones.' It said *clobben tevath*.' I'm sure you're aware of the difference. Her handwriting is terrible, if I do say so myself."

Akaran rubbed at the back of his neck and tried to remember his old lessons until a steady throb in the back of his head interrupted his train of thought. "Honestly? I'm feeling... not all here. Refresh my memory?"

"Not surprised," she scoffed, "given how much of yourself you left under Keto's knife." As he started to voice a protest, she shut him down and went on to explain. "It means 'clothen soul,' usually referring to someone that has taken on a shroud of sin, or who merely has decided to hide themselves under a falsehood."

"Okay... I suppose that makes sense. You want someone who is under stress and in pain to shed those worries, don't you?"

"Yes, you do," Ridora agreed. "However, 'beneath them' implies a burial. Healers never seek to bury souls. We seek to unburden them."

The exorcist nodded in uncertain agreement as he digested the concept. "Alright. Still not sure where you're going with this. You mentioned a room number?"

"Appaidene's," she pointed out quickly. "That's the room."

He pursed his lips as a sinking feeling took hold in his stomach. "Appaidene. She had a child stolen from her womb, right?"

"Yes. It's less that, as it is —"

That sinking feeling turned into a roiling inferno in his gut. "— as it is what she carries. Her doll. It's… wait. That only makes sense if it's…" he said aloud before the idea trailed off on his lips. "Please don't tell me it that it's ensouled."

The thin, grim smile that blossomed to life on her face did absolutely nothing to assuage his concerns. She reached inside a white-wool vest that hung loosely over her cotton dress and removed a ratty little cloth doll stuffed with straw and weeds. "Ensouled, no. Steeped in magic? Yes," she replied before she opened up the back of the little toy. "Lethandria's magic, and an additional aura I am not familiar with," Ridora added as she handed it over. "With a touch of Solinal's for good measure."

"Solinal… the Divine Embodiment of *Peace*?"

"I don't like what you've been hunting, Akaran. Have I said that?"

She didn't have to. "The more I learn about his tricks, the less I do," he muttered as he pried it open and saw the buried stone crest hidden inside. "We wondered how that bastard could get in. Telpid… that asshole. He said he had to keep going out past the garden in the day. Annix needed him to take things out of Appa's room or whatever and drop them off out there."

"So she would go to the garden every night looking for whatever she'd lost," she chimed in as the idea soured on her tongue.

"Then he'd use this doll as a way to sneak past the wards somehow. This is the key. I guess it doesn't matter how it worked, just that it did."

"Just that it did," the Lady answered curtly. "I would sincerely appreciate it if you made sure that *key* never graced one of my doors again. I trust that Telpid won't be able to."

Akaran grunted under his breath. "Under the Queen's Law? Any hope he had to live a long life in a prison just died my hands. So is this why you came to see me?"

Ridora gave him a sharp smile. "Yes. I don't want it here and since you seem to be so headstrong about limping out of my care, I assumed I could solve both problems at the same time. I'll even do two favors for you to help you out."

The way she said 'favors' made his skin crawl. "I don't suppose one of them is telling me where my horse is, is it?"

"That poor nag? You know, that poor thing has been handed off from one stable-master to another all over the city since you got here. Have you even given her the time of day lately? You'll be lucky if she doesn't bite you."

"She likes to bite," he retorted with a little shrug.

"Likes to bite, or likes to bite *you*?" Ridora countered. "Yes, that's one. You don't have time to meander through the city on foot and I doubt you could make it to the Stairwall even if you did. The other?" she said as she gestured out his door. "Wear that cloak over your clothes. Take off your tabard."

He looked down at the Order of Love insignia embroidered into the wool and came to the late decision that 'eating' had not been the best idea today. "Why? What did we do?"

"I told the staff not to tell you what's been going on out there for your safety — and I want you to know that I truly had your best interests in mind. Were it up to me? The most I'd allow you to do is set guard outside of Bistra's door — because I know you won't settle for anything less. But since you've decided to take the lead... again... against all possible logic and rational thought..."

"What did we do?" he repeated with a pained groan.

She glanced down at her hands, almost like she was ashamed. "The city has spoiled, Akaran. That is not an exaggeration. Annix... whomever or whatever he truly is... his words struck true. Bistra safe here for now, but it's only a matter of time before the populace realizes she is a resident of this estate. It's been discussed and decided that she cannot be moved from the Manor without great risk to her safety. As it is? The Repository? The only thing that will get through the throng of protesters outside its gates would be the full might of the 4th cutting them down."

"Shit," he uttered under his breath. "What's Catherine doing about this?"

"Are you asking me to assume what that... *woman*... is doing?"

The exorcist grunted and bit off the first remark that came to mind. "If nobody is telling me what's going on, I'm going to assume that everything has gone worse."

"I would expect so," Ridora agreed. "I do not know if this is good or ill tidings, but with the rise in civil unrest, I have not heard of any new of the condemned being sent back across the Veil. Annix assuredly has not been found, though the Order has not been able to do much to search."

"Shit," he swore a second time. When she affixed him with a withering glare, he lifted a hand in objection. "I know. No cursing. Can you really blame me?"

She pursed her lips and leveled a glare right at him. "Yes. I can. I won't, but yes. I can."

He nearly said something worse before another question popped into his head. "How's Malik? Did he survive?"

"The Odinal boy? Yes. He lived, and you've managed to endear yourself to the entirety of the Wartribe to the Order – a feat that I don't think that *anyone* thought would be possible. I do have to give you a measure of respect for that."

"How about the Tessamirches?"

"Glad for his rescue, yet less happy about the destruction of the Stara shrine. A feeling held overmuch by the Staras... and the rest of the Pantheon followers in Basion... most of which Love is blamed for. You, almost specifically."

That shouldn't have come as a shock, but it didn't go over well. "Oh," he whispered. "Then that's that. I'll get this doll to Erine. Or... one of her people, if she hasn't shown up yet."

"Erine?" Ridora asked with her eyes slightly wide. "You didn't know?"

"Know? Know what?"

The Lady of the Manor stood up and wrung her hands together. "It would seem that tragedy has befallen across shoulders of every establishment these days. She... she was found. I am sorry."

"Found *how*?" he demanded.

Ridora took a pair of steps forward, and then saw the *aura* burning around his body in the ether. "In a condition not suitable for discussion. Just outside of Cableture. The assumption, I have been told, is that the vampire's assassin may have had a hand in it. Word arrived only yesterday."

He clenched his fist around his cane and grit his teeth so hard she could hear them grind. "I swear that bitch is going to roast. One way or... another..." he growled before a painful realization struck his chest. "Badin. No. Oh Goddess, no."

"Badin? He's a friend of yours, is he not?"

"And Erine's consort. A battlemage. Another sparkcaster. He is... was... is? madly in love with her," he explained. "This is going to kill him."

"It... it may be wise to try to fix his broken heart by breaking the heart of another," she cautioned. "The city already has one man loose of caution. It does not need another."

Akaran smirked and squeezed the head of his cane again. "Was that was directed at me?"

"It was," the Lady remarked with a dismissive wave of her hand. "I am shocked you haven't asked about Bistra."

"Your people won't tell me, I can't get up the stairs to her room, and I've seen how many guards you have around here. Would you let me go even if I did?"

"Absolutely not."

He snorted and hung his head in mock-defeat. "I guess it doesn't matter. I can feel the magic saturating the whole house, too. It's... muted. I can feel it. If she's not safe and secured by now, we're all fisked anyways."

"An apt description. We did have to take some steps to ensure that the only people allowed near her are ones that would not be tempted to accept the vampire's offer. That doesn't include you, of course, but there hasn't exactly been an *ideal time* to ask about the package you sent for her."

He scoffed and rolled his head from side to side. "No, but I'm blocked from seeing her because you think I'm going to go on another rampage through the manor if I get close to her again."

Ridora didn't even bother to deny it. "Yes. I daresay you've caused enough emotional trauma to both the residents *and* the staff as of late. The solutions to her problems, I think we can both agree, will not be found in these halls."

"I hate to admit that you're right."

"Not as much as I hate to admit when you are," she countered. "As far as the muted? I'm quite surprised you haven't noticed the taste."

"Taste?" he asked with a confused blink. "You didn't... Ridora..."

She gestured at the flask next to his rucksack. "Healing magic is magic of Time and magic of Growth. Chronomancy to speed the recovery, Growth to encourage it. Even the Grand Healer's essence itself owes to those immutable elements and others – and it does come with cost. It's why you're exhausted and why you're hungry even while you're sick from the shock," Ridora pointed out. "It's why we push for spells of *relief* rather than spells of *repair*. The average mundane does not have the connection with the ether to sustain the exertion and drain as someone blessed to be a conduit to the Gods."

Akaran looked down at his bandaged and braced knee and frowned in concern. "I'm not sure I like where you're going with this."

"You're muted because you're tapped out," she noted. "Tapped out, drained, worn out, likely fighting off infection. Whatever tore a chunk out of your gut? I don't intend to have you be in the Manor when you take your bandages off because I don't want to hear the stream of profanity you're going to put out when you see the incision we had to make to *clean* it," she lectured.

"The ghoul... shit," he remembered slowly. "Goats milk?"

"There are not enough goats in the world to solve your problems. Human bodies are not made to receive the type of punishment you seem to enjoy inflicting on yourself."

"I don't enjoy –"

"You constantly put yourself into situations where it occurs and often, from what I have been told by witnesses and read in reports, without care as to your own safety. There are ways we describe people that espouse those qualities, and they are not labels you would appreciate." When he started to protest, Ridora shut him down. Hard. "Nor will I listen to you prattle about how, 'The Goddess will protect you,' or some such. Allowing you to survive is not the same as offering you protection, and you know it."

He didn't answer directly, and took the dressing-down in stride. She was *right*, dammit, even *if* it was rude. It wasn't until he noticed a familiar tremor in his left hand that grew worse the longer he looked at the flagon before he realized what she'd done. "You dosed it with cocasa, didn't you?"

"A steady diet of it, all over again," she remarked. "A side-effect being, of course, that your sense of spellwork has been dulled. For a day, nothing more. We did it both for relief, and... for other reasons."

Akaran blinked slowly. "You ran out of rune-cuffs and you didn't trust me to behave."

"I don't trust you to behave when you're in control of yourself. When you're not? I didn't even want Keto to touch you on the grounds, let alone..."

"I don't want Keto touching me regardless, if it's all the same."

"Better than the alternative. As far as the cuffs, the 4th had need of them, and we weren't sure the mood you'd be in once you deigned to wake up after the surgery," the Lady admitted as she picked up his bag and handed it over. "But that is neither here nor there. We need to speak of the package you sent to Bistra. You attempted to give one of my charges – and without my approval – a *gift* laden with all manner of arcane compounds. One covered in runes and dripping with magic of Love that I can *feel* the violence radiating from. I wasn't aware you'd suffered an injury to your skull that would have corrupted you into thinking that it would be a good idea."

"Well, it's… it's not good, and I'm going to have one made for Seline. You can have one too if you want," he answered with a half-hearted grunt. "The Granalchis made a suggestion I didn't like. This asshole has magic. They're afraid he might have some very bad magic that might make ward-work a little harder than normal to manage."

"So you decided to send her some kind of… what? Magical protection that can be activated… with magic she doesn't have? Without getting permission from I or any of her other handlers first?"

"Activated *without* magic and no, I didn't give her a shield. I gave her a weapon. I thought the instructions were clear."

"Oh yes," Ridora replied with a slight roll of her eyes. "I believe the note read, 'If in danger, merely bleed,' is that right?"

He frowned and added, "Bleed and say —"

"I am not repeating the words of a spell I don't know in front of a man that should know better than to bring magic into a place where magic is why people are in the place!" she shouted. "You *truly* are a daft individual at best, aren't you?"

"Please. It's safe as long she doesn't utter the words to activate it. I don't even know if she *can* with the way you've muted her magic."

"I muted hers the same we've muted others. A rune on her arm. So no, she won't be able to *do* anything that requires an Act of Willful Channeling to bring to focus, let alone the weight of power brought by Niasmis's Words."

Akaran shrugged. "Then maybe it doesn't matter. Maybe it does. As far as the spell? You're not going to tell anyone, she won't tell anyone, and honestly, every single exorcist we have knows how to use it. Just make sure she gets it — please. It might save her life."

"*Might* save her life? You're asking her to bleed on a bag with unknown reagents? No, I didn't open it to look because I'm not mad *myself*. Nor did I let her touch it!"

"Lady Ridora, if she needs to use it, I can almost promise you she'll already be bleeding. Her mind is rattled, but she'll know what it is. *I promise* it's safe for her and everyone around her *except* for anything that means her harm that's not part of the natural scheme. In fact, I want Seline to have one too. Are you sure you don't?"

"I am *positive*," she promised as she wrinkled her nose and finally pulled some of the venom out of her voice. "I will expect that you have a written list of everything that is in that bag left on this bed by the time you leave the Manor. If either of them are allowed to receive one after will depend entirely on what you write down – so I may suggest being nothing but utterly honest. Am I understood?"

Akaran nodded and immediately started looking for a sliver of charcoal to write with. "Fine. I agree. Don't throw it out. They're a pain to make."

"I will consider it," she growled. "With all of that said, I must entreat one favor of you."

That was the last thing he expected her to say. Now, or ever, honestly. "Lady?"

"You do no good being assigned to my care. Argue if you wish, but you don't. As *loathe* as I am to admit, you have been *right* more oft than you have been *wrong*. You seem to have been, for whatever Divinely-ordained reason that I will not fathom for the rest of my living days – and quite likely after – to be given a task. I hope that it's a Divine ordainment, and not a sickness of mind, I should say, but in either state... it does seem to be a very direct one."

The seriousness in her voice made him sober up and sent an icy chill down his arms. "You don't want me to come back, do you?"

"No, Akaran, I don't," Ridora agreed.

"I promise I'll do everything I can –"

"I don't want you to come back, and despite every ounce of the experiences I have had in my life in dealing with the sick and lame, this place of healing is the last place you need to be. I say that under a great deal of duress, but the truth?" she interrupted, "The truth is because I want you to go out there and do what you're made to do."

"Lady?"

Ridora affixed him with a stare blazing with barely-contained anger, rage, and disgust. She straightened up her dress and vestments, walked over, and did the same to his. She didn't say a word until she was satisfied he was presentable to the world at large.

"I want you to go kill. I don't care who. I want you to go *fisking* kill everyone and *everything* involved in the darkening of the soul of this city," she answered with burning venom in her words. "It has grown sick and in the worst of times? For the health of the many sometimes there are those that must be culled for the good of the rest."

He swallowed hard and nodded in understanding. "I'll do what I can."

"Do better," Ridora countered. "You need to *end this*," she seethed as she slipped out of his room, and nearly altogether out of his life, "and end it *now*."

****

A thick pallor of smoke hung over the basin, and it cast a dark shadow over the entire city. Word from the Wallmen was that they'd never seen anything like it in their lives, and further word was that there was an over-abundance of people taking advantage of the lift to get *out* of the city, since the half-destruction of the Hannock Bridge.

He couldn't push for answers, even if he had wanted them. The name of the game, he'd been told at length, was to keep his head down and mouth *shut*. "A difficult proposition," he'd heard Ridora remark as he limped out of the Manor, "but one that I trust – for once – he'll learn the gravity of and do quickly." It was almost insulting.

But she hadn't been wrong.

Everything took longer. Getting on his horse took longer. Getting his gear stored took longer. Getting past Henderschott's goons took longer. By the time he'd even made it to the wall, it had taken precious hours that he didn't have to waste.

Once he got past the lift, navigating the city proper wasn't exactly a fun chore, either. Fistfights were a common sight to see every few blocks. Wedding decorations had been pulled down, set on fire, or otherwise trampled. The same could be said of any signs of Dawnfire rule, too – flags, drapes, and even a memorial statue had all met the wrath of the unruly mob.

Of all the things it was, it wasn't the 'safest city in the Kingdom' anymore. He wasn't sure it ever would be again, or if it ever even had been in the first place. It didn't bode well for it's future, that was to say the least.

Getting out of the Manor finally gave him a chance to clear his mind. You'd figure in a place dedicated to mending what troubles you that you'd be able to just *think* your way through a problem, but that had yet to become the case in all the time he'd spent there. Traveling through the city, on the other hand, offered just enough of a din and backdrop of hushed voices and shouted irritations that he felt *safe* enough *to* think.

It was just the joy of feeling lost in a crowd. Unknown, uncared for, ignored, and left to his own devices. It was freedom of a sort, and freedom to let his mind wander. Both of which he did until he saw a red-and-gold cloak adorned with the Dawnfire crest whip down an alleyway.

That brought his mind to a screeching halt even as he dropped his hand to a sword tucked away under his own coat. *It's daylight*, he had to remind himself, *and dim as it is, there are rules these bastards have to follow*.

Rules that Annix and Sherril had taken great delight in breaking.

An act he was going to have to do something about. The sight of the cloak was enough to remember that sparkcasting *bitch* as clearly as if she'd been standing there. The way her eyes lit up with joy when she used her magic. The way her pale cheeks flushed with color as she surveyed the carnage her…

*What had she called him? Her Meister? Whatever he is to her. Just… the way she **smiled** at the* carnage he left behind.

There was absolutely no doubt in his mind that she was just as bad as he was, if not worse in her own way. She didn't hold a tenth of the subtlety Annix did, but she made up for it in raw *excitement* that put her leagues ahead of anything he'd seen so far in his life.

Never thought I'd meet someone that made me pine for Makolichi, but that's the life I live, I suppose, Akaran sighed to himself as he continued through the litter-strewn city streets. *She's good at what she does. Can't argue that. If she hadn't been at the Pyre, I think I could've killed him. He's cocky but he's not stupid… next time he makes an appearance, she's going to be right beside him.*

I need to fix that.

Walking through Chiadon had a different tone than what he'd heard and seen in Upper Naradol. Hardly even three days ago, the neighborhood had been full of priests and paupers calling out holy tidings or begging for holy donations. Now, the voices were quiet, hushed, concerned. Furtive glances were the name of the game along the normally-pristine brick-laid streets.

They're mourning, he realized with a start. *That's as plain as day. The Staras lost a single shrine, and now they're hiding behind their own shadows?* He looked over at a row of hooded parishioners as they huddled in a bread line leading to a simple taberna with a poorly-cut effigy of Solinal etched into dirty stone above the doorway. *Doesn't say much for the Pantheon if their followers run and hide after getting a bloody nose, does it?*

Scared, I understand. Tired, sure. Heartbroken? Absolutely, he pondered as he noticed a little girl in a faded pink dress scamper across the street to pick up a pile of errant flower petals. *Why aren't they rallying? Why aren't they fighting for what they believe in?*

*Why are they fighting **us**?*

A twinge of anger kindled in his gut and he jerked on Nayli's reins harder (a lot harder) than he intended to. The horse took off at a fast trot and nearly knocked an old man on his ass, but truthfully, he didn't have it in him to care. *Fight or flee. The vampires are showing more backbone than these people*, he groused as he stormed down the street.

Sherril. She's steadfast and loyal, and he was a little protective of her. He sacrificed the other broodlings with impunity, but moved to block me from ripping her to shreds. She's important to him for some reason or another, even if just for muscle.

Akaran pulled Nayli to a slow stop as he looked up at the wide wall that towered over parts of the basin's edge. One perfectly defensible pit, able to withstand anything that might come challenge the walls. *If and only if they attack from outside.*

Yeah, he decided after a long candlemark of walking, *she's next.*

By the time he arrived at the Repository gates, it was noon. Maybe. It was hard to tell through the smokey skies above, and harder to care with the mass of screaming, shouting, surly assholes demanding either the death of the Maiden-Templar or that they turn over Bistra. Possibly both.

Getting through the crowd unmolested was an adventure in and of itself. Between careless elbows, aggressive shoves, and people who seemed dead-set on terrifying his horse, it was a miracle he made it to the gates with his hood intact. Or his leg. More than a few assholes had taken it upon themselves to push up against him, and whatever steady throb he'd been able to ignore most of the way down had taken on a life of its own all over again.

Once he had muscled his way *to* the gate, his problems started all over again. Wardkeepers and Knights of Love alike stood three-thick behind the gateway, and the barricade behind it made it clear that they weren't in any hurry to open it. On the other side? The gate was still protected, but not by anyone Akaran would've expected.

A blood-red flag with green accents and an oxen's head overlaying a pair of battleaxes stood tall over the middle of the bridge leading to the outpost. Heavily armored women in a mix of steel plate and blackened leather hides stood tall and were busy protecting the path with their lives. *Warmaidens of Odinal*, he marveled as he watched one manhandle a rioter twice her size. *What are they doing **here**?*

The answer was as obvious as it was confusing. Though it was somehow not that surprising when they didn't deign to let him pass. That, he surmised quickly, was their goal, if not to block him specifically. *WHY are they here?*

Ultimately, he supposed it didn't matter.

So, as he often did, he acted first – and thought later.

He pulled the heavy cloak off of his head and shoulders with a pained grunt and straightened up on the back of his mare as firmly and forcefully as he could. Even though it wasn't by much, it was still enough to draw plenty of eyes to his direction. Eyes that collectively went wide when he lifted his hand over his head and barked a pair of short Words to clear his path. "**Luminoso – corsair!**" leapt from both his lips and the palm of his hand at the same time.

The brilliant spell erupted in a starburst over his head that illuminated the grungy, sweaty, filthy peasants (and noblemen alike, it appeared). The crowd withdrew around his horse, though the Odinals dropped into combat stances that made it *damn* clear they weren't going to move just for the sake of a few flashing lights and they didn't budge until he tugged his sigil free and let it dangle in the air. "Let me the fisk in," he swore as he stared down at the Warmaidens.

As one, all seven turned to their leader – a woman with a silver streak through her hair that began just above the center of her forehead and down the length of her locks behind her back. She locked her eyes on his and held the gaze for what felt like an eternity.

An eternity where he wasn't entirely sure his heart didn't stop.

She curled the corner of her lip into a smile and then slowly pressed the tip of her tongue against the edge of her teeth. As her hands tightened on the pommels of the twin, wickedly-curved blades at her sides, the exorcist couldn't tell if he was being judged... or hunted. Or both. "The Elemental Exorcist," she said as she drug the words out slowly. "I am Emadina Oun-Odinal. If you had asked, we would have brought you here ourselves."

"The... what?" he asked even as the Warmaiden flicked the tips of her blades in his direction.

On cue, the warriors beside and behind her fanned out and encircled his horse with plenty of room to spare. Short swords, curved blades, and an errant axe or two made up the mix. Their steel glinted from the light of *luminoso*, and not a single one of the rioters took their eyes off of their blades.

"The Elemental Exorcist," their leader repeated. "Bested the Brazier of Flame, shielded with a wall of ice, and bore the brunt of lightning. Those are elements three."

Akaran took a few nervous steps forward and the Warmaidens moved with him. The Wardkeepers on the other side of the Repository's gate and worked to spread it open. "You're protecting the Repository because of... ice?" *I swear to all shit I am never going to forgive Eos'eno for cursing me with this frost-filled –*

She interrupted his thoughts by simply stepping forward to take Nayli by her reins and guide his poor – if not equal parts confused and annoyed – horse forward. "We're protecting the Repository because we were told this is where you were," she whispered as she walked him to the gateway. "We wish to protect *you* because you have done more to save the son of Odinal than any of the so-called *men* that claimed to have power. Now you have our interest. *All* of our interests," she explained.

The blank look on his face said it all, though Hadraie's voice cut through the din before he could open himself up to anything else from the Midlander (for better or worse). "Have you *lost your damn mind*?"

"Yes?" he asked and answered as he sidestepped chunks of broken cobblestone and holes in the bridge big enough that he could see into the stream below. "But I made it here intact."

"That," she growled as she pointed at his thigh, "is *not* intact. Catherine is going to see you dead for leaving the Manor, you're aware of that, yes?"

"None will see him dead as we watched," Emadina promised from the side.

Although the statement was quickly (and intentionally) ignored by the Wardkeeper, it made the crippled priest smile inside for the briefest of moments even as he blanched and reconsidered taking another step forward. Nayli, however, didn't care, and continued to march him down the path like he owned the entire Order. "Can I hope against hope that she's not here?"

"Oh she is," the Wardkeeper scolded as she helped guide him in even as the other Lovers pushed the gate shut once more. "Be happy that none of us have the lack of self-preservation required to go beseech her to awaken."

"So you're saying I have some time to myself."

Hadraie clenched her jaw and gave him a frustrated, withering glare. "I was told – in no uncertain terms – that you were to be placed under guard. I was *promised* – in no uncertain terms – that you would be kept safe at the Manor. Yet you traveled through the city with nobody to protect you but your horse and the Goddess above?"

"More or less. Ridora gave me this cloak and –"

"You are not worth the trouble you cause," she huffed as she walked him up the winding path to the Repository's main entrance. "Though there's a chance she won't kill you because we're too short-handed as it is."

"It looked bad out there," he remarked as the looming visage of Miral lorded down from the rock-face ahead. "I don't think I saw a single one of us on the streets. Please tell me we haven't given up hunting for Annix."

The Wardkeeper shook her head slowly. "No, though we haven't gotten far. He left enough headaches in the city to cause more than a little consternation, and there have been... other elements... that have begun to exert influence."

Akaran stopped just before they hit the last flight of stairs and looked up at the edifice mounted on the cliffside. "Other... elements?"

"The Everburning Pyre was desecrated, the Temple of Light was devastated, the citizens are up in arms, and *other* things that lurk in the shadows are taking advantage of the opportunity provided to come out and play," she pointed out. "We've had reports of all-manner of Abyssian disturbances and even if a handful of them are more than the ravings of scared minds, we have *problems* out there. How was it the Maiden said it? *'One could not have placed a grander beacon in the sky to attract all-manner of ill-intent,'* I believe."

"Shit," he grunted as he caught the point. "Annix rang the dinner bell and now the city is...?"

"The ether is trembling, and we cannot tell how much of it is outside agents seeking to gain a foothold and how much of it is merely the madness of men."

"Neither make for a happy ending."

"No, neither do," Hadraie lamented. "Worse yet, the city believes that we're the ones responsible for their ills. After that monster's speech, every soul with a stubbed toe found cause to heap blame on Catherine's doorstep. We have lost all ties to the ruling factions; the Overseer has banned the Guard from taking orders from us. The Granalchi have decided that it is within their best interests to stay neutral in the upper-level fighting between factions. The Hunters... well."

"Elsith is pissed about the Urn, yeah. I know that much."

"The Urn?" she asked with a blink as she waved a pair of Lovers over to help him off of his horse. "Some relic we have buried, I presume? She is furious with the Maiden-Templar, but the *why* has been left to the imagination."

Akaran grimaced as rough hands began to untie his leg from Nayli's side. "We have something she wants, Cath doesn't want to give it to her."

The raven-haired woman cringed as he cursed at someone's errant elbow that hit the side of his braced leg. "This is not the time to be ostracizing allies. We have so few as it is."

"At least we have the Midlanders," he remarked as the Lovers helped him up and off of his horse. The landing was gentle enough, but he staggered forward until he caught Hadraie by her arm to steady himself.

"*You* have the Midlanders," she countered as she helped him straighten up. "*You* saved their prince and nearly got killed in the process. As it turns out, that means something to those honor-drenched barbarians. I don't think they give one particular wit about the rest of us either way."

"Then why are they here...?"

"It really is because they thought you were inside," Hadraie answered. "They are the *one* group in the city that's being upfront with us and honestly? I think their only interest is taking you out to stud," she growled. "You made them think you're some kind of damn grand warrior of the Crown. We simply had no reason to convince them otherwise."

Akaran looked back over his shoulder and down the hill at them as he contemplated *all* of the ramifications of *that* loaded statement. "So. Uh. Malik *is* safe, right? Recovering?"

The Lover nodded, and then she carefully cupped his chin with her white-cotton-gloved fingers. "If it wasn't for what you did to save him, this city wouldn't be rioting. It would be in open war. Yes, he's safe, yes, he's being tended to, yes, he's healing."

He started to pull back from her grip but she absolutely wouldn't let him move his head. "Then that's a good thing, right?"

"Karaj had to make a decision. Keep you two alive after that... that... *monster* ran off... or help the victims at the Temple. You have something to say to me because of it."

"I do?"

Hadraie nodded sharply. "You do. You will swear an oath right here and right now: you will make *your* life worth the cost of *theirs*," she flatly demanded, "else I will have these men return you to the mob. Do you so swear?"

The exorcist felt his stomach drop down to his knees (again) before he swallowed hard. "I swear. Their lives will be avenged."

"Not avenged. *Honored*. We *could* have saved more than you two, but Karaj said we couldn't risk it. We placed more value in yours than that of a father of three, a sister of one, a grandmother of an entire family. Children, parents, and those without family. Of the dozens we could have rendered some form of aid to, the Order decided *your* life meant more than *theirs* and we put *all* of our resources into *you* instead of the *many* that needed the help *just* as badly *just* to get you on your feet again as fast as we could."

"I didn't ask —"

"You didn't, because you couldn't, and you couldn't because you put yourself in a situation where you had to do what you did to live," she scolded. "I don't know who we could've saved, who we could've helped, or how many. I know that we could've. But we didn't, because we saved *you*."

Akaran took the scathing commentary head-on, and felt a tear of shame blossom at the edge of his eye. "Didn't have a choice. Gods only know what would've happened if we *hadn't* been there…"

"Yes, you played into his hand and yes, you saved Malik," she agreed before she turned his victory against him. "You didn't save thirty-nine others. Some of them Order, some of them 4th, some of them functionaries, some of them Staras, and some of them? Just poor sods caught in the middle," the Wardkeeper added with a sigh. "So you swear to the Goddess right now that you'll make their losses worth something."

He looked up at the edifice on the cliff, and then at the assorted busts around the final gateway. "On Niasmis's heart, and by the Invocation of the Three, I swear," he responded slowly and firmly. "I swear upon pain."

Hadraie scoffed slightly and waved her hand at someone unseen. The doors slowly swung open to let him pass. "Next time, swear it on something you're not already living with. Now. Why did you decide to risk a trek through this shit-mess you stirred up when you should be hiding under a blanket?"

VIII. LESSONS OF HISTORY
Day of Madis, 15ᵗʰ of Firstgrow, 513 QR

The Wardkeeper didn't follow him down into the Vault. She wasn't allowed, and after they'd chewed him out, he didn't want to try to force the subject. *He* wasn't allowed down there either, but he took a few cautious steps that earned him passage – and consternation. While Catherine surely hadn't intended for him to use his provisional paladinship to pull rank on anyone *in* the Order, the guards couldn't deny that he had the sigil.

Because he had the sigil, he had a pass. Nobody liked it. Nobody offered to help him. Nobody gave him even the slightest bit of encouragement, and nobody would because they *knew* he was bending the rules that they were bound by and they didn't want to get caught in the eventual fallout. It was one thing to be injured in service to the Goddess. It was another, it turned out, to use that injury for sympathy.

They also all thought he was toxic to be around, though not just because of his personality. *Nobody* wanted to be blamed for giving aid to someone that had rank but shouldn't be using it, so his friends were few and far between. One kind scribe was nice enough to give him some water, though that was the extent of it. Honestly?

He had to admit they were right.

At least nobody watched him humiliate himself as he tried to hobble down one flight of stairs after another. The Repository was full of them; thin staircases, tight hallways, and curved steps that made defending the vault a breeze. It made limping down on one leg a nightmare. It just wasn't the only nightmare that the Repository held.

Not by a long shot.

***

The contents of the lower levels were kept secret – very secret, very aggressively secret – but you didn't have to be a drug-addled paranoid problem-child to overhear the facility's caretakers dropping room titles here and there. It helped, but you didn't *have* to be. It gave him a solid idea for where he had to head, even if not necessarily on how to *get* there. Of all of the chambers in the secured lower pits, there was one name that branched over them all:

The Vault.

It wasn't just *one* room in the Repository. It was part of a network. A network that was blocked off at every turn by soldiers and spells designed to keep all but those with Order-ordained permissions away from it.

Once you made it past the upper levels – nothing but guard rooms full of twitchy soldiers and pissed-off scribes trying to take a nap – you had to scoot past the watchful eyes of the caretakers of the Grand Study. Which, unfortunately, was as stuffy as the name suggested. Beyond that?

Guard rooms. You didn't make it through the twisting halls of the outpost without passing more guard rooms than he assumed Henderschott had across the entire city proper. The last one was on the path to the Vault itself, and it wasn't just manned by a pair of very tall, very angry, men with no sense of humor *whatsoever*, thank you sirrah. No – they were backed by a very angry, very hungry (he presumed), very *snarling* dog-shaped golem made of cold sandstone and held together by thorn-bushes and vines.

By the time he successfully bullshitted his way past *those* obstacles, he made a point to write a letter back to Old Maid Hirshma back in Toniki. *An apology*, he decided, *for not giving the respect to magic from Kora'thi that it deserved*. That decision was quickly met with another question, and he wondered if anyone would tell him who had summoned the violent little hedge-hound into being in the first place.

As his questions went, it wasn't important.

The Wardkeepers and their puppy weren't exactly delighted to give him a tour of the lower halls, but they gave him enough directions that he could find his way around without more of a headache than was absolutely necessary. "Go left," one of them had remarked. "Go right, bad things. Go straight, book things."

The final hallway branched into three directions. Straight ahead would lead him to the Central Indexiary, another golem – one built to copy, sort, and store any and all reports that the Order may have wished to file for future reference. Which, by Law of the Holy General, was supposed to account for all of them.

No matter how full of bullshit they may be, he muttered to himself.

The ramp and stairs to the right would take you to three more rooms, they'd warned. They fessed up that one of them was the Vast Library, which was the *last* place he wanted to go spend time. He assumed from what he'd overheard before that the Reliquary would have to be attached to it. The Order had no shortage of 'friendlier' relics of ages-old eras, and they didn't quite need the same security.

They didn't tell him what the final room down that branch was. They just hinted that there were guardians around it that weren't as pleasant as the walking briarpatch they had been playing 'fetch' with. That, and that alone, was enough to convince him that he really didn't want to find out.

One last hallway took him down deeper into the outpost. Deeper down, and into a corridor that held a blackened miasma in the ether that made his skin crawl. The last time he'd felt anything this foul in the air, he'd been inches away from a breach into the Lower Realm of Eternity. He wasn't excited over the prospect of discovering the source, but... knowledge wasn't supposed to be easy to obtain.

'Ini Haerth, Xaphas Pa Wittundir.'

Behind him, Catherine spoke up before he even had time to ponder it. "*In Home of Heart, Cruelty Entombed*," she recited with a tired calm tilt to her voice.

The inscription was carved into the cold stone over the massive onyx slabs that kept the Repository's deepest secrets carefully tucked away. It blocked access to the remaining trio of storerooms: The Vault itself, the Tomb, and a room that sounded like the opposite of a lovely vacation spot: the 'Dreamfont.' The Vault was where artifacts and relics deemed too 'unstable' for destruction would be buried away and lost to the machinations of time itself.

The latter reminded him of a rule of thumb that Order Exorcists had beaten into their heads at length that summed up the extent of his curiosity on the matter. "*Ask yourself if you should know. Then ask yourself how painful your death might if you are wrong as to if you should,*" Brother Steelhom had intoned on more than one occasion. "*It is no sin to not know a thing if you do not have need. Only a sin to pretend you know more than those more educated you, and act in accordance with your falsehood.*"

It was a sin he had to seek forgiveness for with alarming frequency.

With that in mind? The 'Dreamfont,' he decided, would remain undisturbed. The Tomb wasn't a name that filled him with joy, either. Once again, he didn't know, and he didn't want to ask. He did, however, want to ask how to get *past* the damn doors and the lock secured by three empty slots for flat discs to be mounted across the mull down the center.

He pondered that particular problem as he sat (painfully) on the last three steps leading down to the gate with his broken leg outstretched and a sheen of sweat across his forehead. The inscription was absolutely no help, though the woman that recited it as she came down the flight of stairs might be. If she felt like taking pity on him.

"Cath, I —"

"You know, I pushed for a corollary to that to be delivered to Ridora. '*Ini Cepa, habaenth pa dichat,*' but I couldn't get anyone at the Manor to accept it."

"In Peace, Courage be Controlled?" he asked without looking up at her.

"Close. 'In Peace, Fools Be Caged.' The words mean much the same," she added with a frustrated sigh. "Obviously, she needs a stronger lock more than she needs a crest…"

He matched her sigh with a slump of his shoulders. "Really? I just got told off by Ridora on my way out, and you're going to just shit all over me too?"

"That's, 'and you're just going to shit all over me too, *Maiden*," the Templar countered as she sat down next to him. "And, no. With the storm coming for both of us, whatever shit I have to spread won't matter."

Akaran looked away from the door and gave her a puzzled look. "Both?"

"Both," she reiterated. "Not just us, specifically. The whole Repository. It doesn't matter to the Crown what we did or didn't do. We didn't do enough of it."

He grimaced as he caught the underlying meaning to her words. "The General?"

Catherine nodded and a lone lock of dirty, tangled, blonde hair fell across her face. She looked like she'd been through a war, and that wasn't much of a stretch. "I bargained with her. The Grand Temple is livid. Honestly? The only reason Fire-Eyes isn't here *now* is because the Sisters intervened."

His eye went wide. "More words from On High?"

"Or something," the Templar answered dishearteningly. "They said, and I quote, '*Ash falls when light turns dark, lest one disturbs the air in the sunken city in days by five; arrive then and bear witness to the exhumed,*' which… if they mean *us,* and the General thinks they do, then…"

"We have five days to end this?"

"Four," she clarified. "I didn't get to speak to her by Callstone until last night. So. We have to fix this before Zundis, or…"

Akaran's mouth went uncomfortably dry as she rubbed her eyes. "Or what?"

"Or I'm likely hung for my failures, the Repository will be re-staffed from the ground up, and your fate… are you familiar with the story of Shelton the Crossaxe?"

"I know the name but… the third General of the Reformed Order?"

Catherine nodded morosely. "Yes. He was exiled to the Sycian shores for six years after the Order gambled a great many lives and even more crowns that we had that he could catch the Spider King, Alinox. When he failed, he was banished."

"Oh." Akaran rolled his head across his shoulders and muttered something under his breath. "I mean it's not like I did anything to make her mad…"

"Really? You're going to take the, 'but I'm blameless' line when you personally upended the Pyre?"

He pointed his finger at her accusingly. "That bitch tried to throw me into it. That wasn't my fault."

"There isn't a priest of Stara in this province that doesn't want her to try again, just so you know," she countered. "Granted, yes, you've got fans across town now for saving Malik. I don't know how far that's going to get you… but if that's the argument you're willing to take, it's better than anything I have."

Akaran just grunted and cracked his neck. "Maybe we'll get lucky and we can *both* go on a trip. If we survive this bullshit, I might ask to go over anyways."

"I'm sorry," she began as she suddenly stared at him like he'd grown a second head. "Did you say you *wanted* to go to Sycio? You *are* aware that the Orders of Light – yes, including ours – are *banned* from the Jewels, yes? On pain of death? And you know that *pain of death* doesn't necessarily end at '*of death*' over there?"

He shook his head slowly and rubbed at the bandages on his knee. "I said that I may *ask* to go. Didn't say I was *going* to."

"Why…?"

"Because of a book Karaj gave me, and a talk I had with that slaver I arrested. The same bastard that Anais works for? He's a Sycian that wiped out a Sycian city before he came over here and started to dig around in our territory. Can you think of any better place to go look into him?"

Catherine tried to keep her composure. She really did. He couldn't tell if she was angry, disgusted, or worried. Maybe all of the above. "Karaj decided to go ahead and just *give* it to you, did they? Well, then I assume you know he's an enemy of the Order."

"Yeah, but they wouldn't say why."

"There's a good reason for that," she sighed. "Yet it opens a concern, other than the immediate and obvious. Understand: pray she's lying as to her employer. Because if she isn't, we have a new mystery to uncover that I am *certain* we will not enjoy the fruits of."

Akaran wrinkled his nose. "I have a strong feeling you're about to tell me that it's beyond the scope of what I'm supposed to know."

"It is," the Templar retorted, "but everything else has gone to shit so it may not matter. Don't tell me that's why you're down here?"

"Not entirely," he admitted as he pulled out Appaidene's doll from his coat. "This is how Annix has been getting into the Manor."

The Maiden-Templar took the ratty piece of fabric and hair from him and scowled at it. "I think I saw this when I was there... didn't some madwoman have this in her possession?"

"She did," he replied before he explained as much about Appaidene as he could. It wasn't much, but it explained why she had a doll. "So. He used a *lot* of shadow-based magic at the fight. I saw him wearing a Penumbra of Lethandria. Use this and some elven bullshit to get a foothold under the Manor's wards, and –"

"– and once he was in, he used a spell based in Ameggenon to invoke Chaos to cover his tracks," Catherine finished. "I think I owe you an apology for comments I made over some of your paranoid delusions."

"Not just Chaos. Ridora said she felt Solinal's essence embedded in it somehow. He's mixing a *lot* of different powers and I can't even begin to understand *why,* let alone *how.*"

Catherine blinked and prodded at the little toy. "Magic of Peace in such an awful creation? One would think it would dilute the effect...?"

"Or maybe just the aura?"

"Oh. Yes, maybe just... that's a thought to revisit later. Again, another one I'm not happy to hear you utter but as usual, you find a way to turn a simple thing into a complex concern."

He didn't rise to the bait, but he did take the toy back from her and gave it a hard squeeze. "I can't feel the ether around it," he admitted. "Not enough to use it to trace back to him. I thought if I brought it here, we could study it. Or at least secure it away where it can't hurt anyone else."

Catherine nodded and slowly pushed herself up off of the stairs. "Well. Once again, you did the right thing – though in the wrong way. Relics like this don't go straight to the Vault, you know."

"No, I didn't. But at least we have it now."

"At least we do. Now I suppose you're going to be a pain in my ass about seeing the Urn for yourself?"

"Only if you make me."

The Maiden-Templar looked down at him as she slowly fished a trio of flat metal discs – one copper, one gold, one silver – out of a satchel on her belt. "That paladinship is *provisional*, which I hope you'll remember. I also still out-rank you, had you forgotten."

He winced as she walked over to the door and slotted the keys into the stone. "Apologies, Maiden. I hurt and... and I don't quite feel like myself. Forgive me if I act out of the norm."

Hurt? That was an understatement. All she had to do was take a look at the way they'd wrapped his leg up to realize he was putting on a false front. That he was willing to admit that he didn't quite feel right, opposed to his usual stubbornness and bravado?

"Act out of the norm?" she slowly asked with a raised eyebrow. "Come now. You've been a pain in my ass since you got here, why should now be any different? As far as the Urn goes, well. What's the worst that can happen if I tell you?"

A lot.

A lot was the worst that could happen.

And, as often comes to pass, it was going to.

***

"So he was actually innocent?" Catherine asked with a raised eyebrow.

Akaran nodded as they walked down the grim, dank tunnels deep in the bowels of the Repository. It hadn't taken him long to understand why Altund – may the Goddess bless his soul, maybe – had taken such a dislike of the Order's efforts. "Unfortunately. Had a psyanist confirmed it."

She made a disgusted noise from somewhere in the back of her throat. "That's almost a pity. What did you do with him?"

"Set him loose," her exorcist admitted. "He didn't do much wrong."

"Aside from his occupation."

"Which is unfortunately still legal."

His boss came to a stop and stared at him keenly. "So you made the decision to simply let him go, knowing he will hurt people in the future? No bargains or deals to get him to change his ways?"

Akaran shook his head and trudged past her. "I encouraged him to get out of the city. I could've held him over for Henderschott to deal with but the result would've been the same. You know the Queen's stance on it as well as I do. I don't like it, I don't have to like it, and I can't do anything about it. Long as she likes it..."

"I understand we're constrained to the law – better than you, I would wager – but there are ways to ensure the safety of the city without being strict to the Queen's interests."

"I was always cautioned that what you're suggesting would be an abuse of power."

Catherine took the remark in stride (and calmly strode right past him). "When we are granted permissions and ability to enforce the Queen's Law, we have an obligation to *correct* it in the cases we can claim authority."

"Well, yes," he returned as they rounded a corner and approached one last archway with another solid stone door barring the way. "Right now though, let's be honest: we don't need to give the Overseer or his ilk any more reason to pick a fight with us. Se'daulif made it clear he had friends in high places here. If you have a better idea about what I could've done..."

"No, I suppose not," the Maiden finally had to agree. "Though at the very least, we didn't have to put him on the street so soon."

"Trust me, I thought about it. Though honestly, if anything, I'm pissed that it was my fault he was in irons in the first place. He wouldn't have even been there if I hadn't been so quick to jump on Anais's offer."

She placed her hand on the center of the door and uttered a quiet invocation under her breath. "For that, I don't actually blame you. Had I seen the same, I'd have done as you. Any of us would have."

"Doesn't make it right."

"No, possibly not," she admitted again. "Though, in the end, you removed the influence of a man who trades in slaves from the city proper. I do hope you won't mind if I find no reason to complain about that, even if I wish it had been for longer."

Akaran didn't quite rise to the bait, but he did deflect to the one thing he *did* blame himself for. "Makes me wonder what else I missed... whatever shit that bitch peddled," he groused as the door slowly swung open. "For what it's worth, I made sure he was given a stack of coins and sent on his way. *Strongly* suggested he head back to Sycio."

"You gave him money? Whatever for?"

"He had some go missing when he was arrested."

Catherine looked into the dimly lit room for a few long heartbeats before she turned around and gave him her full attention again. "Did he now. How did that happen? Should I notify Henderschott....?"

The exorcist blanched and turned his head away. "No. You shouldn't. It got lost. I reimbursed him."

"Out of city funds?"

"Personal stipend."

Her lips curled into a slow smirk. "Interesting."

"My fault," he argued. "Only right I should pay for it."

"Yes..." Catherine slowly drawled. "Only right indeed. Did he get back everything he had lost...?"

Akaran coughed as a small cloud of dust tickled his nose (and that was the story he'd stick to). "No. Most of it."

"No?" the Maiden countered with another long, accusatory tilt to her voice. "That doesn't seem fair."

"What was it you just said? Queen's Law? I get some leeway, don't I?"

"Just remember it is only some, and only when *just* or for *just ends*," she reprimanded. "I'll hope that whatever he didn't get back finds its way into the Temple coffers at some point."

He looked her dead in her golden-green eyes and smirked. Just a little. Just enough. "It should, shouldn't it?"

"All of that aside," Catherine replied as she gave up on trying to hold him accountable, "that bitch, as you so eloquently described, went to great pains to find out if we owned this glorified vase... and you've gone to almost as much to see it. I suppose I should say something of grandiose importance," she exclaimed as she walked into the chamber, "but honestly? I sense it would be lost on you."

"Speaking of that bitch, where is she?"

The Maiden stopped for a moment and tilted her head. "Don't go paying her a visit, but, we weren't able to stash her here. An attempt was made and it went poorly, so we have her secured in an alcove deep underground off-site. We found enough *delightful toys* with her that the scribes are positively beside themselves with excitement."

Akaran blinked slowly as he gave his boss a dumb look. "I don't think I use those words the same way you do."

She chortled slightly under her breath. "You probably don't. The Broker of Secrets is more than just an illusionist. She's an avid practitioner of necrosia, alchemy, illusions, and more. We found spell components and more that are used to briefly resurrect a dead soul and force it to talk. There were a few other communication-type spells in her arsenal, along with enough poisons and substances used to do everything from putting a man to sleep to leaving him so dazed he can't help but answer any question you pose to him."

"That's... that's a lot."

"That's worse than a lot. It explains how she's earned her title. The grave has plenty of secrets, and I suppose if you can just dig them up at will..." Catherine remarked before she let the idea die on her lips. "We're here. Now just don't fisking break anything."

The insulting rebuke stung enough to earn her a nasty remark of his own, but the words died on his lips as he hobbled into the Vault proper. It was unlike much he'd ever seen, and the little bit that seemed familiar was so overdone that he couldn't think to put words to it. The Grand Temple in Mulvette, just outside the capital city proper, had 'secure' wings where dangerous magics and other artifacts were stored, but this?

This?

The door gave way to a three-story brick-covered pit lined with wooden walkways that branched off into long hallways. Recesses had been dug out of the walls at every turn, with a mix of wooden doors and metal gates covering each of them. There weren't a lot of scroll cases or books that he could see, but there were plants.

Lots, and lots of plants.

Greenery covered almost every exposed surface of the vault. *Wveld-weed*, he realized. It covered almost every exposed inch, and what it wasn't on? Undja was. Bushes of the much-demanded 'blooded rose' were nestled in cage after cage, or planted in long rows along the walkways. It was a gardener's paradise, and utterly baffled him how any of them could grow this far underground.

It also baffled him on how he could even see. There weren't any magelights active that he could see, and no tell-tale glowing runes anywhere within eyesight. Yet the entire vault was on display as clearly as if the sun was shining through on a cloudy day.

It wasn't until Catherine noticed him absentmindedly scratching at his eye that she pointed out what should've been obvious. "The vault is enchanted with a host of spells," she answered before he could even ask. "There are relics in this room that do not respond kindly to light. Keeping them in the dark is the best choice – so we worked around the problem."

"How can you work around... light?"

"It wasn't easy," the Maiden admitted. "But one of my predecessors worked with The Family… you know. The Damian royalty. They found a way to see past the curse on their eyes to never see the light of day, and so, we found a way to do the same."

"So… wait," he replied as he realized what she meant. "Are you saying the same magic that lets them see underground or around those metal plates on their faces is letting us see without torches…?"

"It's similar, yes. It isn't just *torchlight* either, it's *light* at all, except for a few errant auras from other magics we have down here. Don't get used to it," she added when she *felt* the thought start to form in his mind. "It's not one that can be easily replicated. It took a man willing to offer his eyes so we could see with ours."

If she noticed the way he grimaced, she went to great pains to ignore it. "It's just one of a multitude of steps we've taken to secure these relics. I'll ask again that you not break anything, but I would appreciate it if you wouldn't *read* any of the plaques as well. Some of these relics are to be held in the deepest secrets that the Order possesses and forgotten with reason."

He could see why, too. Each alcove had a metal plate with names etched into them, and even with her insistence, he couldn't ignore them all as she deftly walked them through the chamber and down the first flight of stairs she came to. The wooden planks creaked in protest from every step she took, though she moved with all of the confidence in the world.

Goddess above, Akaran uttered to himself. *You'd have to be a fool* not *to know what some of these are*. He tried – he tried very hard – to follow her instructions, but, there was only so much he could do to ignore the raw *evil* locked away. *Nerian's Harp. Played by the last Civan King as he was executed by the first Civan Empress. It's said that to play it, you give life to the screams of his children… and that their voices will carry you to the void.*

Another name nearly jumped out at him on the second flight down. *The Word of Gabel. Not a book, but a sword. A hilt fashioned from the bones of his mother, a blade quenched in the collected filth and pus of a Matheian village consumed by plague. He tried to use it to carve out territory between Atheia and Matheia in the name of Neph'kor.*

"I told you not to read them," Catherine scolded.

"I spent my entire life being trained by the Temple to hunt down things like these," he countered. "Asking me not to read them is like asking me not to breathe."

"Can I at least ask you to be more cautious around the wveld? It seems to like you."

Which was accurate, to say the least. Every time he stopped to look at a plaque, one tendril or another would begin to crawl off the wall and reach for him. "Should I be worried about *why* it likes me?"

"Probably," the Maiden admitted. "Wveld-weed feeds off of wild magic, and cursed auras. Considering that stone in your eye…"

"You think it has a cursed aura?"

"I think you're dripping in magic that nobody seems to understand and you spent a few weeks carrying around a pissed-off flaming woman in your skull, which I'm sure isn't helping. Watching the vines reach for you is making me doubt the wisdom of letting you down here," she countered. "As far as the weed itself? It's thought that it's a plant created by the God of Rot – so that where He goes, He could show that He was the true God of Nature."

Akaran grunted as he pushed a questing vine away from his shoulder. "Growth from damnation. Sounds right for Him."

"An egomaniac," she agreed. "For all of Neph'kor's faults, and the Goddess knows He has many, He is part of the natural way. I wonder, sometimes, if He had not grown so mad, that He and Kora'thi could not have found a way to co-exist. Things in nature die, they fall apart, they go back to the ground. Things in decay give way to life as animals feed and flowers bloom in their passing."

"Like the way that Melia retained Her seat with the Pantheon," he countered as they entered the lowest part of the Vault that he could see.

"Yes. The Goddess of Destruction claimed the mantle of Rebirth. She embraced what She could be, rather than what She was," Catherine remarked as she approached a recess a bit shallower than most of the others. There was a wooden table in the center of it, and a cage on top.

The cage wasn't exactly remarkable, although the sheer amount of wveld and blooded-roses that covered it was more than a little impressive. It took him a moment to realize it, but it wasn't a wooden *table* – rather, it was a deep, dark brown wooden *stump* with roots that pushed into and below the thick bricks at their feet. And the object nestled inside the iron bars, set into the hollow of the stump, and wrapped up in lush green vines and brilliant red roses?

A plaque below the cage read simply, 'The Urn of Xabraxis.' The vessel itself was more ornate, though not by much. It had been crafted from a pale gray clay into the shape of a standing goblet. Two tarnished copper handles stretched across the top edge, with a trio of gold bands that wrapped around the center. It was surprisingly large for an urn; most he'd seen were only a foot tall or so, but this one was easily twice that.

Another aspect caught his eye, too. The lid was an entirely different beast from the rest of it. It was made of a solid chunk of silver, though when he bent in closer to look at it, he realized that the edges had been charred and glistened with a faint trace of oily black ichor. His body recoiled at the sight of it, though he had absolutely no idea why.

"I've never seen such a thing," he marveled aloud. "Why the tree though?"

"For someone that keeps referencing his training, I do wonder how much you slept through it," Catherine muttered. "It's an *enatch* cask."

The exorcist took his eyes off of the urn and looked up at her. "Enatch casks? Down here?"

"Of course. Why wouldn't we? The Goddess's Will is immense, but She gave us the knowledge with how to contain the evils of the world," the Maiden replied with a shrug. "A few aisles over, and there's a book submerged in a vat of holy water. Then there's a skull of a Gresheldan soothsayer in a gold-and-diamond lined box. While we bury what we can, using elements of nature to counter the efforts and essences of the damned..."

He nodded along in understanding. "So what's this...?"

"A *bellamont* tree. They're reactive to certain magics. A small one, and mostly just the stump. It's still alive and well though. It's the easiest one to store whatever relics need more than just an iron box."

"Reactive how?"

Catherine slowly circled the cask, cage and all, as she slowly ran her hands across the iron bar. "If you see a bellamont grow teeth, tell someone."

He peered down into the cage and started to reach through the bars when she swatted his hand away. "Teeth? Are you serious?"

"No, no, I'm not serious," she added with a slight grin. "Though if the petals ever turn *blue*, then the wards securing the item within the tree have failed."

"What about eyes?"

"They do not grow eyes."

Akaran reached his fingers inside again and pulled a few errant leaves out of the way. "Oh?" he asked as he moved them away – and stared down, eye to eye, with a slightly-rounded, slimy, still wad of tissue and gel. "You sure?"

The Maiden peered down with him at the lump and gagged. "What in the name of the Goddess..."

"Eye. I think," he remarked with a disgusted grunt. After he prodded at it with a gloved finger, the appendage suddenly *sat up* on a long muscular tendril that trailed behind it and turned its clay-gray iris to his face.

The eyeball flinched and slithered back into the branches and vines before he could wrap his hand around it while Catherine retched across from him. "It's not supposed to grow an eye! It's supposed to turn blue!"

"Well, it didn't. Blessed be, that's repulsive. Is this how you let the vault work…?"

"NO!" she shouted. "I mean that it's not supposed to be an eye *at all*. Such a thing has never been heard of in all the years that the Repository has stood!"

Akaran looked back and forth between her and the slithering chunk of gore. "Then if it isn't part of the tree, I'm going to guess it's not part of any spell you have down here?"

She looked down at the slimy piece of… *whatever*… and flung her arms out in a wide circle. A shimmering pale light enveloped both them and the cask with a silvery glow that made the Urn sparkle. The eyeball lurched and *jumped* up from the branches, only to slam against the edge of the spell and drop back into the fines. "*Not* ours," she spat. "I feel… oh, no. Oh, that *bitch*. That unholy *bitch*," she snarled. "Anais. It's *hers*."

Her subordinate spat something profane and furious as he thrust his fingers back inside the cage to catch the orb before it could hide in the leaves again. It struggled against his grip, but he managed to wrench it free of the vines after a few moments. When he got it loose, the blasted thing lunged at *him* and tried to dive under his eyepatch.

Catherine wasn't about to have any of it. As it landed on his face, she uttered a sharp call of, "**EXPULSE**!" that annihilated the animated chunk of gore in a shower of golden sparks that danced across Akaran's cheekbones. While he recoiled back and slammed into a wall with a mix of curses from a sudden flare of pain in his leg to the shock of the spell detonating against his skin, the Maiden fumed over the cage.

"That… that made it into the Vault. Utterly undetected. Oh. Oh someone is going to… *I* may get hung for the state of the city but I am *not* going to be the only one at the gallows, I *swear* it," she promised as she cast another spell to further illuminate the Urn's prison.

Akaran bent down and clutched his knee as he used the wall for balance. Fresh tears dripped down his face as she continued to curse, and she only stopped when he pointed at the glowing ceiling over their heads. "We're about to have help, aren't we?"

She glanced up and saw angry red and amber runes flare to life along the edges of the ceiling and the walls. Help was an understatement – in a few minutes, the might of the Repository would rush into the Vault to see what had happened. "It only means I will not have to go as far to yell at those that deserve it," she grumbled.

The exorcist, however, hoped he wasn't one of them that did – but he somehow doubted it. "So. She knows the Urn is down here. I'm going to assume that means her benefactor knows, too."

"The Urn and Goddess knows what else. *GODDESS*, who could've been this *stupid*?"

"Considering how she managed to corrupt half the damn town are you sure it wasn't an inside job?" he pointed out.

Catherine took the accusation in stride. "That's a good question. Are you volunteering your own name? I imagine there's only one way that she got her eye in here."

He blanched as he came to the same conclusion she did, and just as quickly. "No. No, Maiden. Though you may as well. Since she hid that mace with Se'daulif and set him up so I'd confiscate it... she knew what would happen." Akaran straightened up and wiped a piece of wet ash from his cheek. "And I let her. *Dammit.*"

"Then I think we need to take a closer look at it, don't you?"

"Yeah. See if she left any other surprises behind," he agreed as he looked back down at the urn. "This... I..."

"What?"

Akaran slid his hand around one of the iron bars and squeezed it gingerly. "It feels...," he started to say before he pulled away from the old relic. "Who was Xabraxis? A demon?"

"No," Catherine replied as she studied his face. "It's the name of the man that crafted it. The 3rd Granalchi Dean-Adept himself, Shol'val Xabraxis Mulvette. Yes, related to the Queen of the same name."

"Why do we have the body of a Dean-Adept in the Vault...?" he asked in utter confusion. "Or even... the Vault? Isn't there another place where bodies are stored? And why would Elsith care? Is it because of Telburn?"

"Those are a lot of questions, and questions can be dangerous," the Maiden cautioned. "Although the answers are: We don't, here is fine, yes we do, she has her reasons, and no, that isn't one of them," Catherine answered one after the other as she felt her hackles rise a little. "He made it for someone else."

Hackles that he purposefully ignored as he studied the clay-and-gold body. "As a gift for someone or to store someone else?"

"Both," she replied. "It's a relic from Agromah. Except not really."

"Is it or isn't it?" he asked before he looked up. "That Nastavol bastard wants this, whomever he is. I'd like to know *why,* since the mother-fisker's name keeps popping up every time I dig into *anything.*"

"Knowing him, we'll never understand. It's not important why he wants it, it's more of a question as to how he broke our security and –"

"Maiden, no," Akaran interrupted flatly. "When Karaj handed me *The Fall of A'twol,* they flat out said that he is going to come for *me.* Me, *specifically.* So far he's killed people I know, maimed people I know, his minion tortured someone I know, and now he's after a relic in a building where I sometimes sleep," he ranted. "I want to know who he is and why he's doing this."

She took a deep breath and opted to choose her words carefully. "His title is more apt to describe him than whatever name he claims to hold. He's known as 'The Man of the Red Death.' He's a necromancer, and a powerful one. The Order has been after his head for nearly a decade."

"The Order is after a lot of heads," he countered. "That's very much what we do around here, isn't it?"

"Well, yes. I suppose that doesn't narrow it down terribly, does it?"

"No."

Catherine pursed her lips and slowly steepled her hands. "You aren't the first Oder member that has gotten entangled in his... methodology. He's attracted to areas of great strife. It's not unsurprising you ran into him in Toniki."

"Maiden, with respect, Basion wasn't in great strife until, well..."

"Until you got involved?" she countered.

He blanched slightly. "Until Annix decided to make a mess."

"Fair – though if you think Anais is his only minion, you're mistaken. I assure you, you are *not* the first of us, and likely not the last, to have run across him." Catherine sucked at her cheek and freely added a remark that didn't go over well. "Though if he can animate and entreat entities like Anais and Donta, he may be even more powerful than we feared."

"I've met one of his others – little beast called '*Rishnobia.*' Disgusting little... almost like a hairball with teeth," Akaran remarked as he digested the ramifications of her latter statement. "Although that doesn't explain why he's after *me.*"

She sighed and rolled her eyes. "Why do madmen do anything, and why are you so certain you have gained his personal attention?" she argued. "I don't know why Karaj would have told you that he'd be after you... personally. Unless my speaks-too-often assistant has happened to come to the conclusion that since you've stated your intent to doggedly hunt the necromancer down, that you've have gained his interest… or will gain it, in the near future."

"I think we both know the answer to that."

"We do. So my point stands," she answered firmly. "I will speak with Karaj at length on the matter *if* that will help mollify you. They have a habit of speaking of more than they should about more things than they actually know. They breathe gossip like I breathe air."

There wasn't a word of what she said that Akaran believed – and damned if it mattered. He opted to just grit his teeth and turned his focus back to the urn. "So. It's a relic that is and isn't from the cursed continent. That doesn't narrow it down in the least, you know."

When she realized he wasn't about to let *that* go either, she caved – a little. "Xabraxis crafted it to hold a demoness. One of the worst ever recorded in the Order's history… and one of the first. She was one of… well. She was one of the Arch-Duke's. She was slain, but she didn't return to the pit."

"The Tyrant?"

She just nodded her head.

The name had meaning. A *lot* of meaning. Arch-Duke Belizal. The three-headed tyrant. The Ascendant Daemon responsible for the fall of the Adelin Empire. Powerful enough to be considered one step just below a God – even if it was a big step. Known and reviled among the Order, and for good reason.

Akaran pursed his lips and moved back from the cask with a concerned frown. "So it's a vessel."

"A prison," she countered. "One the demoness escaped from. We hold the Urn for her eventual return to play – with intent to use it again."

It was, at best, a miserable revelation. It didn't answer any questions, and if anything, it made him think of more. "Why does the Guild want it so badly?"

"Because she was their first hunt," Catherine answered. "They've had a very hard time holding onto it over the years. Once the Order found it, we decided that maybe… maybe it would be for the best if we didn't let it stay in their fumbling fingers."

That explained a lot. A relic from the Guild's first hunt? It had to be worth thousands of crowns to them. *Tens of thousands, at least*, he realized inside his mind as his eye went wide. "The sheer amount of gold it would be worth… do you think that's why he wants it so bad?"

"For riches? With the way that Anais pissed gold in this town, I doubt it."

There wasn't a good argument to the remark, and he let the train of thought die. "Maiden? I've never seen this before. I've never touched it. I've never heard the name."

Her eyes narrowed as she went back to searching his features again. "I can see the 'but' in your voice as if you wrote it in the air. Out with it."

Getting it out was easier said than done.

"I know it. I don't know how I know it. But I know it."

Catherine slowly narrowed her eyes into slits. "And what do you think you know? What could a neophyte exorcist know about a cup stored in a vault in a pit...?"

"When you said that this demoness was one of his... you meant the two he claimed he owned as a wife and a concubines, didn't you? And not one of his Claws?"

"The ones he owned were also titled as the Claws of the Tyrant, so you are clear in thought," Catherine corrected. "They all served as his generals, for a lack of a better word to define them."

Akaran nodded along slowly. "Alinox, the Spider King" he began to recite, "and the Winged Brothers: Solobob Balach and Salabab Boloch. The other two... The Duchess and the Mother."

A flash of anger bloomed in the Maiden's heart as he recited their names, though it wasn't just *her* feelings that triggered it. "The monsters that destroyed the world."

"The ones that destroyed *us*," he retorted. "The ones responsible for the Hardening of Hearts. The ones responsible for turning the other Gods against our Lady."

"It burns my throat to even *suggest* that they were creatures *feminine*," she pointed out as they *both* started to fume. The air felt... *poisonous* just to mention their names. "One that was once human, the lore says, with the body of an angel. The Duchess of the First Empire of the World herself. Fell to the pit when she died centuries before the fall of Adelin and grew to be a Daemon Ascendant, like her husband. The other was his consort."

"His concubine," Akaran remarked. "She with the Body of the Void." No, I didn't forget. I'm just trying to imagine which of them would be locked away in this. Duchess Alexa or..."

Catherine shuddered. "This was made to hold the other one. Abyssia. The Mother of Sin, and the Consort of the Duchery," she grimly replied. "The Urn was crafted to capture her, after her defeat at the hands of the Sons of Veritas. They blamed her for the fall of their home, and went to war to kill her. When they couldn't, they came up with the next best idea."

"Capture her and lock her away. She can't rule the Abyss if she's stuck in a vase."

"Exactly," she agreed. "So now that you know what it is, the question is: why. Why is there an eye in my vault? How did it get here? I'm very... very... curious about that."

The exorcist's face slowly went blank as he touched the lip of the urn again. "You're working with inhumans and you need to break into a fortress. You bribe anyone you can into turning the other way when you start asking questions but that isn't enough. So you dupe some idiot – me – into bringing something into the Temple that you *know* will get buried. As a result, you'll know if whatever you're after is down here..."

"...and you hide your eye with it to keep literal watch," she finished. "You know, Seline had mentioned you complained a few weeks ago that the damned in this city were 'smart.' I think I see your point."

Akaran pursed his lips and moved away from the cask. "I don't care who she might've bribed to get this past your security. If there was an active spell on that weapon, this Vault would've fallen down on top of it. Right?"

The Maiden walked over to an alcove several branches away without saying a word. As he hobbled along behind her, she knelt down and unhitched a simple lock keeping a wooden door closed. A moment later, and she had a rough iron box in her hands. "An active spell, yes. Let alone some kind of... construct? an animate? ...that can *crawl* out of storage. You are completely right."

"Well. I'm not... entirely versed on things but... you'd need to be able to activate it. A power source of some kind. Or another reaction, right? If her eye could feed on an interaction of magic to wake it up..."

She clenched her teeth as the sound of heavy footsteps and the familiar sound of rattling armor echoed down from the halls above. "You truly did sleep through half of your classes, didn't you? But yes, and this entire chamber is full of reactions."

"Or one very specific one. Moira," he realized with a start.

"Moira? Who's Moira?" she asked as she set the box down and pried it open. A flash of pale white energy rolled away from the edges of the lid as two runes on its side illuminated with a deathly-black glow.

"That, I'm assuming. The mace Anais set me on. Didn't it tell you its name when you picked it up?"

Catherine lifted the lid up and rested back on her heels. "If the next words out of your mouth are a suggestion that it sprouted lips and talked to you, you are going to have to give me a full and comprehensive list of any other inanimate objects that you may have had a conversation with before I let you out of this room."

He didn't answer, but he did make a half-hearted symbol of warding in the air. The *'Mace of Insanity's Rapture,'* it had boomed in his mind. *Moira. It liked that name more. Felt more... alive.*

Names aside, you didn't have to be a priest to recognize evil when you saw it. "Inanimate doesn't mean non-sentient," he countered. "How much shit in this pit has a taint of otherworldly *anything* around it?"

"Too much. So then tell me, oh expert-on-Abyssian-relics, what would make this weapon so special that it would cause Anais to leave her own eyeball behind so it could wake up when it got down here?"

"What makes you think it waited? For all we know it could've been popping open and looking around anytime it wanted."

The Maiden's face went an unpleasant shade of pale that quickly turned into an angry flush. "That woman never leaves our custody again."

"Was she going to anyway?"

"No," Catherine admitted, "but now I'm having whatever's left of her corpse entombed here once we're done rearranging her skull."

He ignored the grumbled threat and looked down at the mace. "This had a leather binding across the handle," he remarked. "I guess it was... oh, blessed *all*, I was holding her eye when I picked it up," he added as he gagged in the back of his throat.

"This type of weapon was common throughout the Adelin Civil War," she said after she calmed her body down from a brief shudder of revulsion. "We have... several... in here. They've all largely fallen inert. Dangerous by their existence, but most of the magic around them has faded with time. Esth-atatic metal, and there is understood to be a... draining effect, for lack of other ways to describe it... that those that wielded them were said to possess."

Akaran's eye perked up for all the wrong reasons. "Draining? We already have two vampires in the city, now we have a mace that does the same?"

"A mace, two swords, an axe... there's a reason that weapons from the Fall are destroyed or buried here if they're found anywhere on the mainland."

The fact that she said it so dismissively made him swallow back a fresh bout of bile. "Quaint. Do we know anything about it?"

"No," she admitted with a shake of her head. "Scribe Dounious hasn't finished cataloging this one," she added, "or there would be a seal etched into the lid."

"The last time I touched this, it didn't like me."

"A common occurrence for you, isn't it?" she tiredly quipped at his expense. When he didn't rise to the bait, she tilted her head slightly. "What do you mean, it didn't like you?"

The Mace – or just Moira – wasn't anything too special to simply look at. The handle was as long as his forearm, and the head had been pounded flat across twenty different sides. *That* had taken a good bit of labor, as had the four flanges that decorated its sides. The only thing that really set it aside from other weapons of its own ilk were the trio of twisted, jagged spikes that jutted out between each flat ridge.

Looks aside, it was a given that you wouldn't want to be hit by it more than once. And the first time was questionable at best. "I mean it didn't like me," he muttered as he reached into the box.

His fingers didn't even get to wrap around the cold steel handle before a shock of magic arced between his palm and the weapon. "PISS!"

Catherine jumped back a solid foot and a half and gestured a quick ward into existence in front of her as he cradled his gloved hand. When nothing came from her spell, she peered back into the box and the otherwise inert chunk of twisted steel. "What happened? I didn't feel anything out of place?"

"That *surge,* dammit!" he swore as he flexed his buzzing, tingling fingers. "Didn't you *feel* that?"

"No, nothing," she answered as she wrapped her own hand around it and uttered another Word under her breath. "Though... no. No, it feels no different than any other Adelin relic." When she picked it up, he *flinched* away from it like it was scalding his skin to even be near it. She noted his reaction and took a few measured steps across the vault floor.

As she walked, runes and shimmering walls of ether appeared along the walls and over the doors that kept other awful relics buried away. Spell after spell woke up, flared to life, and faded just as quickly. When she got close to the Urn, three distinct things happened at once:

First, the runes etched around the Urn's enatch cask erupted with a violent white light that scoured the shadows away from the lower end of the chamber. Second, a deep amber glow erupted from words etched into the vessel itself. Finally, as they watched in a mix of shock and disgust, the mace emitted a faint green glow from along the edges of each flange, and down the handle.

A heavy cold chill of *disgust* covered Catherine's hand and made her entire arm shake as she tried to hold the mace steady. "One very specific effect," Akaran repeated. "That bitch. She knew *exactly* what she was doing. Now why is the prison that held Belizal's consort *glowing* in proximity to that chunk of pit-steel?"

"I... I don't know," the Maiden answered as she stepped away from the urn and lowered the weapon to her side. "The only relics in this vault that respond to the Urn are ones that are believed to have been held by the Claws," she breathed. "There's something very wrong with that mace for it to react that way."

"Maybe worse than wrong," he countered as he nervously slipped his glove off. Before she could do anything to stop him, he grabbed the weapon and took it from her. Whatever she had to say after was lost in a raging wind that buffeted him down to his very soul.

***

Wherever his mind went, it wasn't in the Vault – and it surely wasn't in the Repository, let alone Basion City. He stood in front of a grand citadel with countless towers that reached to the stars, but they were cracked. Crumbled. Broken. They were fingers that reached for the heavens yet had been broken and twisted so that they could never stretch so high.

The sky above was haunting. Nightmarish. It was blackened and filled with smoke. It wasn't the storm of the Abyss, but it was more ominous than the worst summer storm you could ever imagine. Ash fell from the clouds like a blizzard, and the pale white flakes covered the corpse-and-rubble-strewn courtyard just as well.

Men and women lay scattered across the ruined field. Every single one of them had been brutally murdered – and where there weren't bodies, there were limbs. Their white tabards had been stained with fresh blood and covered with streaks of black filth. He realized they were Lovers before he saw what had brought them low.

Who had brought them low.

She stood in the center of the bloodbath, though there wasn't a single drop on her. Her skin was darker than the midnight sky above to the extent that she was more of a *shadow* than a tangible *thing*. Little swirls of energy faded in around her body and vanished into her flesh like her very skin was an all-consuming void. Those flickers were the only thing that gave her body any discernible definition – a flicker here, a glow there. Just enough to provide an outline if you looked at her dead on.

A different glow emanated from her fingers and her toes. Every curve of her body that was designed to entice or attract had a slight sheen to it to draw your eyes, and it was impossible not to let them linger. She was *made* that way, *crafted* to draw you in. Chiseled out of the very screams of perdition themselves. To entice you with obscenity and trap you in torment.

Crafted to create terror, and designed to spread sin.

None of it mattered. None of it mattered the second he saw her face. In a heartbeat later, he saw the blazing hair that draped down her shoulders. The fire that raged in her eyes. The burning heat that made the air shimmer from her lips. She was everything that Rmaci had been tortured with, only on a level of *perfection* that it could have only been given birth by the divine.

Her face contorted with a mix of glee and agony as the chunks of flaming coal in her eyes pulsed and billowed with gouts of eternal flame. She looked down at her closest victim and plucked the poor woman from the ground. Her lips parted and opened slowly.

As he watched, her jaw dislocated. It fell to her throat. Her cheeks billowed out. The demoness screamed in pain and delight and joy all at once as she pulled the wounded Lover up from the ground. She unhinged her mouth like a monstrous anaconda and *swallowed* the struggling woman whole.

There weren't any words he could say to explain how atrocious the sight was. Her body shrank back to 'normal,' or whatever 'normal' could be for a demon that was taller than he was by half. Flames licked around her jet black lips as she digested her prey and as her inhuman eyes searched over the carnage.

As his mind recoiled from the sight, her body started to shake. The flickers of energy around her skin crackled. The pulsing shadows she left in the wake of her every movement trembled. Before she took another step, her mouth split open again and she disgorged a mace and a pile of smoldering gore from her lips onto the bloodstained path at her feet.

A winged demon dove in from above to pick it up. It was a *chinikari* – a tall, lanky, winged beast with scales for skin and an alligator's snout for a face. If the Dukes of the Abyss had a preferred foot-soldier, *chinikari* served them well. *All* of the lore spoke of their savagery, cunning, and strength. They were as smart as the average human, and stronger than the average ox.

They were armed and armored in the forges of perdition.

And, apparently, by the Mother of Sin herself. He felt the name for the weapon radiate in the air around his head so unmistakably *certain* that he'd never call it by anything else ever again. The demonic fighter flew off with the Mace of Insanity's Rapture as quickly as it had arrived, and it left

Abyssia to peruse the rubble for a new victim to consume.

The demoness' eyes flicked over and saw him. It was impossible, but they did. She saw him standing there as plain as day, and her lips curled into a twisted mockery of a smile. Abyssia started to speak, but a different voice cut her off.

[*YOU*.]

As the Goddess's voice boomed, the world cracked and fractured. The vision broke away until there was just all-encompassing darkness around him. It too shattered, and he saw Catherine clutch at the side of her head and sink to her knees as an overwhelming *presence* pushed through the vault.

Akaran couldn't control his arm as he slowly lifted the mace up to eye-level. He spoke, but it wasn't *his* voice. *"We did not forget you,* woman," he intoned as the Maiden cringed away. *"You belong to Us."*

Catherine's voice broke through elemental *violence* raging through his body as he affixed the weapon with something so much worse than just an angry *stare*. "DAMMIT PUT IT DOWN AKARAN – PUT IT DOWN NOW!"

Rage boiled around him to the extent that he wouldn't have even if he could have. "We have not *forgotten you,* **Abyssia**," his dual voice intoned. His hand tightened upon the hilt as a raw wave of energy poured down his arm and into the handle. The weapon smoked briefly before it simply disintegrated into droplets of molten metal and pale gray ash. He looked over at Catherine and gave her a smile that chilled the Templar to the bone. "The offenders will be punished. *We so* **promise***,*" they finished as the fury left his heart and he caught himself as he slumped forward.

Catherine moved to catch him before he could fall to the ground. He sagged into her arms and slowly sunk down to the cold stone floor as the world spun around his head and his heart pounded violently in his ears. "DOWN! Lay down, right now!" she demanded as she helped guide him down to the floor safely.

He shook his head and tried to fight her, but the Templar wouldn't let him do anything but rest on the stones. "What... what in the pit was..."

"What did She tell you?"

"Put it down?" he croaked as he felt a cold chill and a steady electric tingle arc up and down his arms. It felt like his bones had been shocked, and he might not have been wrong.

"Not me," Catherine scolded. "*Her.* The Goddess. What did *She* tell you?"

He looked up at her and blinked a few times in confusion. "I don't... I..."

"She said SOMETHING," the Maiden pressed. "I could... I could *hear* you but I couldn't *understand* you. But I *felt* it. What was it?"

Akaran tried to swallow, but his mouth had gone completely dry. "She said… She said She hasn't forgotten. Forgotten what, damned if I know. I saw… I saw things. I don't want to see them again."

She matched his nervous gulp with one of her own. A moment later, and she worked her fingers in the air and a calming spell landed on his shoulders. Another spell made the air above his hands glow in a faint pink hue, and a third unleashed a wisp that hovered over the remnants of the mace.

That wisp turned a decidedly ugly shade of red before it faded away into the ether. "I would say She hasn't."

The effect of her spell made him completely droop against the enatch cask as all the strength went out of his limbs. There wasn't much left to begin with, but her efforts took the last of the wind out of his sails. "Ooookay, I don't know what just happened but my head is hurting really bad now and…"

"*You* aren't to touch any relic in this building with a gold rose stamped on or next to it," she warned before she tapped his forehead firmly. "*Do you understand me?*"

"Don't have to fisking yell," he protested with a wince. "Goddess. It feels like someone was screaming in my skull."

"Goddess? Yes. Yes, you got that part right," the Maiden scolded. "You just channeled Her. *Again*. And She's *pissed*. *Again*," Catherine stressed. "Congratulations – you may be the youngest exorcist in our history to ever successfully channel the Matron and speak with Her voice. *And more than ONCE*, for… fisk. For *Her* sake."

"Thanks…? But don't we all speak for Her?"

She looked down at his utterly bewildered face. "*For*, you daft child. *For* does not mean *with* or *as Her mouth*. I'd turn you over to the Sisters if it wasn't for the fact that whenever She talks, you're *both* so damn *angry*. The Sisters are *empaths,* you dolt. Honestly? I'm quite terrified of how they'd react exposed to that much rage." She pursed her lips and frowned. "Going to turn you over to them anyway. We're not equipped to store the living."

He shifted so he was sitting straight up and clutched his not-so-quietly screaming knee. "Okay I don't know why you're so pissed at me. I don't know why you're looking at me like you think I'm about to catch fire, but… does this headache I have tell me we learned something new or no? And where did the mace go?"

Catherine gave him an absolutely flat glare that spoke volumes as heavy footsteps and raised voices erupted from the hallway just outside the Vault entryway. "What did you see, exactly?"

It was hard to get it entirely out. Some of the vision faded into fragments right away, and the details he could offer were spotty at best. The two things he could say, without question, was that the mace he'd been holding had belonged to Abyssia, and that it was present at the fall of the Grand Temple outside Veritas.

Veritas. The last city of Agromah. The last known outpost of humanity to fall at the end of the Adelin Civil War. It was destroyed by Belizal and his minions days, if not hours, after he had his way with the Grand Temple and brought the Order to levels that were near extinction. It had been so thoroughly annihilated that the location had been lost to time.

The Temple? Despite being a day's ride from the port, Belizal had buried it so well it had been lost to time. The Arch-Duke had entombed it in a mountain and set the Spider King's unblinking eyes to keep watch for eternity.

The bodies of those within had never been found.

When he finished, the Maiden had gone completely blank. Her eyes showed comprehension, though her shoulders were slumped and her face was devoid of emotion. "One of... one of powers she... no. In the old lore," Catherine slowly started to explain as she picked her words carefully, "in the old lore, Abyssia consumed all. The Grand Devourer. She could return to this realm twisted versions of what she had absorbed... or I guess... consumed."

"She ate a person and returned a mace," Akaran grumbled. "Or at least, that's what I saw."

Catherine took a deep breath as Order soldiers trundled through the upper levels of the Vault with shouts of concern. "She ate a Warrior of the Goddess and returned a weapon," she clarified slowly. "You said the mace spoke to you once?"

"Yeah... didn't exactly say much..."

"Well then, congratulations, Exorcist," she sighed. "I think you've successfully managed to excise the soul of one of our fellows." She let the words hang in the air as she looked around the chamber with her eyes narrowing into slow slits. "If she turned one..."

"Didn't you say you had more weapons from back then stored away?"

She made a pained, strangled noise in the back of her throat as idea after idea crashed through her head. "Be even more proud of yourself," she muttered just loud enough for him to hear. "You may have just found something even *more* important than a rampaging vampire for me to focus my attention on. Do you know no end to the stress that you cause?"

Before he could ask what *that* was supposed to mean, Hadraie and a host of Lovers thundered down the final set of stairs and rushed into the basement chamber. Several of them wasted no time in pointing their weapons at the prone exorcist on the floor, though Catherine worked quickly to dissuade them from using them on him. In fact, she honestly gave him as much help and kindness as she could, even in spite of how pissed off they could *all* tell she was.

The instructions that rolled off of her tongue included, and said in no uncertain terms, that he was to be helped upstairs ("With dignity," she stressed) and set to rest in her private guest chambers. The instruction earned a few raised eyebrows and was certain to start rumors later, not that she cared in the now. He was also to be, "Given a bath, food, and an Invocation of Respite..." and the latter of which was to provided, "... without haste, and even if he objects."

Which he tried to. Immediately. The Invocation would absolutely knock him on his ass for the rest of the day, even if it would help his leg heal faster *and* restore some of his personal stores of magic. *Both* were badly needed, but the time-limit the Maiden had begrudgingly admitted to didn't lend itself to 'personal time.'

The next set of orders that she demanded included no less than three Templars, five Wardkeepers, and two additional exorcists to be dispatched to the Vault's antechamber. Several scribes were also to be tapped – and by tapped, she meant, "Pull them out of their damn beds and march them down here – *naked if you have to!*" along with any Granalchi that they could lay their hands on. Ether-keneticists and Ambianists, specifically.

It wasn't until Akaran was safely in the hands of a pair of Wardkeepers (with Hadraie doing her best to pretend she wasn't watching) that he managed to get out one last question. "Maiden? Karaj said that there was 'blood between us.' Between me and... the necromancer. Do you have any idea what's that supposed to mean?"

She flung her hands up in annoyance and exasperation. "I don't know! You mentioned he killed someone you knew – maybe that was it?" Catherine shot back as she stormed over to another enatch cask. "It doesn't matter right now. I've got to go through this and..."

"But he made it in here," Akaran interrupted. "He broke past everything and made it in *here* to find *that* and –"

She sighed and walked over as quickly as she could. Her blonde hair flowed down across her shoulders, and it didn't stop moving until she took him tenderly (albeit firmly) by his jaw with both hands. "You of all people know how dangerous raw information can be when used for ill-ends," the Maiden began, "and look at what he did to get an *eyeball* in these walls. He has discovered things. Things we'd very much not like for anyone to know, that's true."

"So what are we going to do about it?" he asked as Hadraie watched the scene unfold – and the other Lovers decided to try very, *very* hard to hear *nothing*.

"We do what we are tasked to do. We contain. We secure. We protect. We fight for what we love. He got an eye in here. That's *all* he was able to do, and all he *will* be able to do. You of all people know that a single eye alone does not make the measure of a man," she added as she lightly tapped at his patch, "nor does it define what he can do."

Akaran twisted slightly and worked his chin free of her grip. "Forgive me if I'm not mollified. After what Anais did to Seline…"

"After what she did, she has earned fires of a kind that cannot be experienced in this world, though we shall hasten her return to the next," Catherine promised. "We'll find out why he wanted to know about the Urn so badly once we have time to deal with her, but time is not our ally."

"Then why are you making me sit through an Invocation of Res –"

"Because you are not of clear mind. If we intend to do *anything* about Annix and his pet mage, then we need to be able to think. I do not know about you, but I am tired of being lied to and outsmarted every time I turn around," she retorted with a look of disgust. "You. Rest. I cannot take the time to oversee your nap – eye or not, we were breached."

He let his shoulders sag in defeat. That was the end of that, and nothing else he could say was going to change her mind in the slightest. He knew it, she knew it, and even though nobody else listening in had any idea what the two of them were going on about, *they* knew it too.

Everybody except for Hadraie, who waited.

Once Akaran was long gone and half of the troop of scribes, exorcists, and record-keepers were busy exploring the basement for any more loose eyeballs and glowing weapons, the wardkeeper pulled her boss aside and gave the older woman a very cold glare from her silvery eyes. "I don't have to utter a Truthcall to know that you just lied through your teeth to that blasted idiot. Why?"

"Excuse me?" Catherine replied with a start. "How dare you speak –"

"You just told him that there was nothing to be concerned over, that he's safe from whomever unleashed an… an eye? In here? In *here*?!" she hissed under her breath. "You told him all that and you *lied*. You didn't just lie, you *lied*."

The Maiden took the accusation with grace and didn't flinch from it. Her eyes, however, narrowed into small slits and the corner of her lip turned up into another disgusted sneer. "Because the truth would do him no good. It may later. It won't now. You don't need to know the what or the when."

"I think that he's a man who acts on what he believes to be true without questioning it which puts the lives of others at risk in the process. Lying to him, then, puts a greater danger on those in his orbit. Of which there are many souls as of late."

"We're in the middle of a war against a vampire," Catherine retorted. "Wars are nothing but lies and deceit."

"But we must avoid the temptation to speak so between allies," the younger woman pointed out. "I don't know what bullshit you're spreading, and I don't think I care to. I would just be very careful about the stories you fill his ears with."

Her superior tilted her head slightly and studied the Wardkeeper's perfectly calm, unfazed posture. "You know, if you weren't someone that had pledged their life to Love, one could consider that a threat."

"One could, I suppose, but you shouldn't," she countered. "I just think we're all tired of seeing him go off on a rampage every time he learns something new he doesn't like."

"Well. The invocation will help with that. I sense we'd be better off if we got him out of the city but with the bridge gone, that's going to be near impossible as bad as his leg's been ruined."

The Wardkeeper gave her a short smile. "I wouldn't count on him getting one."

Catherine bristled all over again. "After the instructions I gave, if he doesn't, someone is going to *wish* they were interred down here."

"Ah, but, my Maiden — he has a visitor. It seems Henderschott decided that if he's going to be a fool and leave the Manor, then he needs to have additional support wherever he goes."

"We are perfectly capable of providing support here," Catherine snapped. "I hope you left whomever it is outside in the riot."

"No, actually. He's vetted. One of Akaran's confidants *and* he brought a bag full of treasures you're going to want to see," Hadraie clarified. "Not that we let him past the foyer, but he's one that several people have spoken for across the city."

Catherine grumbled under her breath in raw frustration. "I don't like having my authority usurped. If I say we can handle it, we can handle it. What, exactly, are you even doing in here, Wardkeeper? My orders for you were that you were to pour over Lower Naradol for clues about the vampire."

"I heard he was returning to the Repository," Hadraie answered honestly — which was more than she'd done when she'd confronted Akaran at the entrance to the shrine. "I needed to be here when he did."

"Oh? And why, exactly, is that? And how did you hear when I am certain he made efforts to be sure that nobody knew he was?"

"Maiden," she began as she drew herself up to her full height and turned to leave, "if you happen to think that you're the only soul in this city that gives orders where he's concerned — *you* need to be the one to go and take a nap."

***

"Back in the caves... Kiasta," Badin began. "What she said."

Akaran settled down on a couch in the main reception hall and gingerly lifted his leg up onto it. Someone was going to come by and short order and scream at him for getting bloody bandages on the upholstery, but he didn't give a damn. "Hadn't forgotten. Were you able to find anything out?"

The mage nodded his head as he sat down across from his friend. The Lovers had eagerly snatched the bag of evidence out of his hands the minute he'd crossed the threshold, and they'd gone out of their way to make him comfortable. Hadraie had taken one look at him and simply said, "This is a home for all hearts," before she carted the package into the depths of the outpost.

"Ridora told me..." Akaran began before Badin interrupted with a sad shake of his head.

"Well. Kia was right."

The exorcist closed his eye and bowed his head. "Any idea what happened?"

His friend started to answer, and then caught himself before he stumbled over his words. "Found dead in an alley. Maybe some beggar. Or a vampire. Or whatever," Badin sighed under his breath. "The Guard didn't know. Didn't seem to care. At least... that's what they're saying."

"I'll go down there and make them care," the exorcist promised. "Help my ass up and —"

"— and *nothing*," his friend interrupted. "If Annix and his brood is responsible, then you'll kill them. If that monster at the docks was responsible, you've already killed them. If they weren't?" Badin asked with a hateful glint in his eye, "Then I'll kill them. I left the city for three damn days and you destroyed the whole damn temple of Stara?"

Akaran blanched at the ferocity building behind the mage's tone. "Not the whole… but, no. Erine. How am I supposed to be a friend if I don't –"

"If Annix did it, either he'll be dead or we will, soon enough. Am I wrong?"

"No, but –"

The mage flicked just enough of a bolt of magic at his friend to prickle at the skin of his arm. "I am going to do absolutely everything in my power to make sure the person that hurt her is left bleeding on the floor with everything they've ever held dear *destroyed*. I *promise* you that," he growled. "That's *my* job right now. Fisk the Crown, fisk the city, fisk the 4th. Fisk your Order. *I don't give a shit*. *Your* job? I respect what you do. I do. But she died while I was helping you do your job so everyone else who wants to tell me what to do can go take a piss in their own mouths."

"She did? *Fisk* Badin, *fisk*. While we were fighting Daringol?"

"While *you* were fighting Daringol," he seethed as Order caretakers and servants worked in the Hall. "While *I* was trying to keep your head up. Don't you get it? People are *dying* around you while you're blundering between fights with your head up and dick out of the surf."

Akaran swallowed as he weathered the torrent of quiet anger radiating off of the battlemage's presence. "I didn't know. I couldn't."

"Of course you couldn't," his friend snapped. "I don't blame you. I want to. I do. I want to put this on your feet. But I can't. I can't because I saw you had to do. I know if *you* hadn't done what you needed to do that *thing* would've done so much worse to so many more. Erine wouldn't have wanted that and no matter what, I guess I was destined to lose someone I've taken a damn liking to."

"Goddess. Badin I don't know what to say. I just… I don't. What can I do? How can I make it right?"

"Promise me she didn't die in vain. That's what. Promise me that because I was saving your life and wasn't there when she needed me – even if she didn't know she did! – that it meant something," he demanded as sweat glistened off of his forehead. "Promise me that fighting at your side saved more lives than just hers and promise me that if I *stay* at your side that you'll do everything and absolutely *everything* in your power to make *damn sure* that whomever did it *suffers*. Will you pro-"

Akaran didn't even let him finish the sentence before he painfully swung his leg off the couch and grabbed both of the mage's hands tight in his. "I swear on my name and my blood that whatever it takes to bring her killer to heel, I'll back you. Whomever it is, whatever you decide to do. However she was killed, by whomever, I give my word I will be at your side."

"Swear that in front of the Gods?"

"I do. The Goddess and her Guardian," the priest promised without any kind of hesitation. "I swear it upon Niasmis and by Miral, the punishment that's to be had will be had."

Badin looked up at the colossal statue of the Archangel and nodded slowly. "I'm going to hold you to that. But she's dead, and it's not like I can bring her back. So we gotta deal with the thing that's gonna kill someone else's Erine next, don't we?"

"We can't bring back the dead," the exorcist replied slowly, "even if we wanted to. I mean, we can. But you've seen how they do. None of 'em come back right. It's always, *always* something bad."

"Yeah," the mage sighed wistfully. "Just… yeah. It always is. So. You had a chance to get a lecture from the fang-faced prick before he fisked you over, huh?"

Akaran grunted and sat back on the bench. "Yeah. Think I'd rather shove my head up a bear's ass than listen to him give another one. Power-hungry little cunter."

His friend smirked and flicked another ember of lighting into the ether. "Human or not, guess it's true. You've heard the saying, right? About what men want?"

"An hour on the beach with privacy and the Queen's daughter?" Akaran equipped back.

Badin snorted and rolled his eyes. "About men with power. They want more power. And more importantly, people to do what they tell them to do."

The exorcist frowned. "Vaguely. 'The Crown demands obedience, and obedience demands power to serve those that submit,' or something, right?"

"Some shit like that," his friend agreed. "So we want to get their attention, right? Annix or his bitch? So what's the one thing nobility can't stand?"

"The poor?"

"People not doing what they say," Badin chided as a pack of bedraggled Lovers made their way through the brilliant gold-and-copper foyer – with Huntsmatron Elsith, of all people, leading the pack. "This bastard wants control. It wants to embarrass your folk."

His friend nodded. "Done a damn good job of it, too."

"Oh, I know," he replied with a snort. "There's another saying, too. Erine… Erine used to say it sometimes. Whenever we'd talk about you."

Akaran frowned slightly and felt the hair on the back of his neck rise. "What'd she say?"

"Love's an act of defiance," Badin remarked. "So if you want to piss this thing off, find a way to show that your people are going to stick through this mess no matter what he does. Quit hiding and go do something."

"Love's an… huh," the exorcist mused. "I swear I heard someone else say that lately. Not that it seems to matter. I mean, we've been defying this son of a bitch since he poked his head up. I don't see what else…"

"Have you done it in public? I don't mean running the guard through the streets. Have you stood up and proclaimed victory or put up a banner across the gate demanding he go eat a hog's ass? That's the kind of thing that pisses off people trying to rule hearts and minds…"

"Rule hearts and minds," Akaran repeated slowly. "A public defiance…"

"I know exactly what we need to do," Elsith intoned as a few Wardkeepers blocked her from walking through the Foyer. "I need an audience with your boss," she demanded to nobody in particular. "Now."

The priest and the battlemage exchanged nervous, tense looks at each other as the Huntsmatron planted her feet in the middle of the receiving hall and *dared* anyone to try to make her move. For once, the Lovers did the right thing – and several people scurried off to go dig Catherine out from the vault.

Once the first flurry of movement was over, Akaran suddenly realized that Elsith hadn't come alone. Her husband (bedraggled, visibly frustrated, and in something of a panic himself) was borderline quivering in her wake. "Telburn? Are you alright?"

The Granalchi Headmaster-Adept's head spun around so fast that it defied physics even as his eyes went wide in excitement. "OH! There you are! I need you! We need to speak. It's urgent," he exclaimed as he quickly crossed the foyer and almost shoved Badin aside.

"Yeah it is," the exorcist replied as he flexed his fingers. "I found a lot of Granalchi summoning –"

"Yes, yes, that," Telburn replied dismissively. "I've already been told. I don't have an answer for that but I have a question that has been bothering me for the longest time and you need to know it too."

Akaran glanced over at his friend as a throbbing pain began to take life (again) in the side of his skull. "Is… is this headache why people start glaring at me when I start talking that fast?"

"Probably."

"Your head can hurt *later*," the Headmaster pressed. "This Annix fellow. It is my understanding that he has haunted that poor Bistra woman for years now, yes?"

"Best as I can tell. Ever since she fought him in 509."

"Ah but Bistra didn't fight *him* directly, did she? She fought his mate, yes? That's what you've said. She excised what we would call his wife. To the elves, she would have been called his yomaldi."

The Lover nodded his head. "Her name was Zilyph."

"Yet our vampire has had all of this time to merely turn Bistra into one of his kind. He could have abducted her at any real point in the last three, yes?"

"He could've. Asshole likes to play with his food."

"Demons do what demons do, I have heard. Except I don't think it's anything that mundane," Telburn began. "Only we do have to make one assumption that does indeed have a great deal of weight to it: that this creature truly is of elven descent and isn't just a human that learned the language."

That was a hard question to answer without any proof either way, and all Akaran could do was just shrug. "Pointy ears, marble face. Lore says that vampires don't change on the outside as much as they do in their mouth..."

"Mouth and assorted other psychological attributes, yes. I've been doing research of my own. You're confident on the ears?"

"I was busy getting electrocuted but yeah," the exorcist confirmed. "Elven vampires aren't an *unknown* thing. I mean, the Council of Nith annihilated the entire elvish *race* by doing just that. It's why all of the Kingdoms of Men —"

"Yes yes, the Crusade of Suns. So assume then that yes, this mass-murderer is indeed of elven lineage. I spoke to several men who heard him speak at the battle at Ellachurstine. He said he wanted his *tvastarian* — that was the word he used? Is that correct?"

"I think so. I was getting my head bashed around at the time."

"Then that is truly his motive," the mage marveled. "This may be a difficult concept, but tell me: what do you consider justice to be? Not in a divine sense, though one would imagine they're similar."

Badin snorted and interrupted the lecture. "Justice? Revenge. Someone does something wrong, and they're punished. You can't... undo hurt. You can just stop the person from hurting again."

"Or encourage them to find the error of their ways and do more good than harm with their lives," the exorcist added a moment later. "I guess that's what justice is. Helping people get what they deserve."

You could watch the transformation take place right before your eyes. In an instant, Telburn went from an excited puppy to wizened scholar. "What you have professed is the human definition of justice. Humans *compel* justice. If a wrong has occurred, and the party involved is not willing to make amends, we *force* justice to occur."

"When we can," the Specialist spat. "Seems a lot of people act like there's no law that applies to them."

"Well, yes, but I suppose that's where men like your friend come into play," the Headmaster admitted. "Be it in this life or the next."

"Why do I sense there's another part of this. You said *human* definition."

The mage perked back up. "I did. That is where the fault is. The elven concept of justice is built upon one simple ideal: that for justice to be given, the party that caused the harm must give up a thing of their own with a willing heart."

"That doesn't sound..." Akaran began before he frowned. "Wait. No. How would that even work? I mean, I'm all for redemption and amends, but..."

"Elves had... *have...* a very long natural lifespan," Telburn answered. "Their system of justice, unlike ours, was designed to help convince people to understand how they were wrong and to fix the reason *why* the wrong occurred. Redemption, rather than other alternatives. A petitioner could file a request for cause, and the community would gather around to dissect why the wrong was done and what imbalance caused it to take place. Correction would happen from within."

"I... I don't think I follow," the exorcist replied after a minute. "So someone steals a loaf of bread and instead of making them pay for it they'd help...?"

The Headmaster clapped his hands. "Exactly! They would work to discover why the thief was hungry in the first place, and why the thief felt he or she had no other way but to steal to satisfy their need."

"Well that's fun and all, but what about murder?" Badin asked.

"Much more complicated but the truth must still come to the end. The recompense must be granted willingly and not forced. Coerced, but not required. The thief could decide that rather than making amends, they could just suffer through whatever punishment was given."

Akaran blinked. "I thought the point of it was to prevent punishment?"

"Oh, no. Hardly anything of the sort. *Coerced*, but not required. An action would be taken against the thief to *compel* them to willingly make amends but it would be up to the thief to determine how long they would be willing to tolerate being placed lower in status or disadvantaged."

"So without the criminal ever admitting fault and being willing to make amends, their justice could never be had?"

"That's the crux of it, yes," Telburn concurred. "Which I would say is why he hasn't just *taken* Missus Enil. He needs her to admit she has done wrong, and admit that she needs to make amends. Until then, he is bound by the law of his people to merely attempt to coerce her into giving up whatever he feels – as the wronged party – would be proper payment for her sins."

The battlemage rubbed at the back of his neck as Catherine made her screeching, thundering grand arrival in the foyer. "So he tortures her until she admits she's done something wrong? Forgive me, because I'm not a bright man, but isn't that the Queen does? It doesn't sound that different."

"Well, yes, *but*," the older man argued, "once the Queen has her confession then justice is taken. There is no change to the social structure to keep such a thing from happening again in most cases. There is no heart-felt effort on the part of the criminal to offer to do better because they *choose* to do better because of their shame. In our society, the criminal is executed or banished to a dungeon somewhere. *Reform* isn't a concern because the offender is removed from area of influence by force. To the elves, there was never justice without willingness, submission to the party you have wronged, and a change for how life is experienced."

"So he needs her to admit she's fisked him over. Until she does..." Akaran replied as he gestured at simply *everything*.

"Until she does, this continues. For both her and I daresay, us," Telburn agreed.

"Just a moment," Badin interjected with a frown. "Again. Not a scholar. He's been slaughtering people without care. Feeding... turning? I guess that's the word? ...anyone that he can use. Torture, murder. All of it. A lot of it against the innocent. Doesn't that... I don't know."

"Doesn't it violate the concept of tvastarian? It would, yes, *if* he was doing it to others of his kin. Elvish kin, I feel I should add," Telburn responded.

The mage shook his head. "That makes less sense."

"Does it?" the Headmaster asked. "The elves have always considered *humanity* itself to be less than they. Even at height of their empires, humans were barely little more than tadpoles in their eyes."

"So he's invoking 'justice' on Bistra to honor his wife –" Badin started to ask before Telburn cut him off.

"His yomaldi, yes."

"– but the rest of us aren't worth the same? Bistra killed his wife and he thinks it's okay to just… kill without… doesn't he expect the same? That we'll invoke his own justice on him?"

The Granalchi shook his head. "No. We do not live as long as the elves did, and we breed far faster. We do not last long enough in this world to make the concept of tvastarian worthwhile to apply to us."

Akaran grunted and crossed his arms. "I remember he said something along those lines before he tried to burn me alive. Great. Well. That's wonderful. Thank you, Telburn."

"You're gonna sit there and tell me this is the first time you've ever heard some all-powerful creature think that we're not worth anything? Akaran, you're sitting in a temple dedicated to the *Gods*."

"Yes but… c'mon. It's different when a God says it and when something that can't be outside at noon without dying takes that type of attitude," he whined. "It'd be like if a goblin made fun for how I dress."

"A goblin would be more amused by the fact that you bothered to wear pants at all," Telburn sadly quipped. "Yet to be forthright, I do not know how much import this will have on your dealings with the creature, but it is an answer to a question. One I pray I am right about."

Badin coughed and pointed over at the shouting match that threatened to spill over in their direction. "Speaking of praying, you should probably…"

The Headmaster looked over at his embattled wife and sighed. "Does the Goddess of Love grant patience? Because I suspect I will need some. My wife has come up with an idea to entrap this pest of ours, but…"

"But?"

"But it will take many people willing to do many things. Yourself included," he replied as he left the conversation.

Once he did, Akaran looked over at his friend and they took a moment to share a grimace. "My head hurts. Did that make much sense to you?"

"It doesn't matter. I just want this over with."

"Same," the exorcist sighed as he reached over and put a hand on his shoulder. "Badin? I am… I am sorry. About Erine, I'm sorry."

"Save it," he snapped. "I don't need your pity. I need your blade."

"You'll have it," the exorcist promised. "*Human* justice. Not this elven happy-go-round shit."

Badin took a deep breath and pulled the Order dagger from his cloak. "Speaking of blades. I found this one in Cableture. Recognize it?"

Akaran glanced down and frowned. "Yeah. Belongs to… yeah. That ruby? Ranking mark. Belongs to Karaj."

A dark look passed across Badin's face and his hand trembled for a moment. "Well. You should… should probably give it back. Enough blood's been spilled. Don't need to… you know. Add to it."

The exorcist took it and shook his head. "Oh, we do. We need to spill a lot more before this is done." He squeezed his friend's hand and looked up into his eyes. "Steady your hand, my friend. We'll bring them to justice. I promise."

Badin looked up and over Akaran's shoulder. The massive statue of Miral stood tall over their heads and for one brief moment, the mage thought it looked right into his soul. He soaked it in as he started to memorize the rune-marks around it. "Justice… yeah. Yeah, they'll get what they deserve."

IX. THE WEDDING OF DUSK AND DAWN
Evening of Pridis, 17ᵗʰ of Firstgrow, 513 QR

"To love, to truly love, is to merge your souls in front of the Gods. It is to bring life to the world in a way that life did not exist before. It is to grow under Kora'thi. It is to shine under Lumina. It is to war against those that would harm you with Makaral," Upper-Adjunct Risson intoned from the center of the Ellachurstine Chapel to the throngs of the Queen's citizens below. "It is to build upon all the elemental forces of the world – from Ice to Air, from Land to Sea and All Those Beyond. It is by the grace of the Pantheon that can be here, be together, and celebrate on this blessed day."

Akaran glanced over at Catherine as they watched from well behind the crowd, tucked safely away in a small gazebo with waist-high railings and enough shade to hide under. "Suppose it would've been too much to ask him to add a comment about Niasmis, huh?"

The Maiden gripped the edge of the white oak railing so hard that she looked like she was trying to break it. "I cannot believe I let you talk me into this."

"This is not my fault. It was Elsith's idea," he offered with a little shrug, "I just happened to like it."

"Of course *you'd* like it. I just can't believe you got everyone to go along with it," she growled. "Nor can I believe that mercenary had the gall to *walk into the Repository* after what she'd threatened to do..." she uttered through tightly clenched teeth.

"In the Wardkeeper's defense, you were busy."

She turned just enough to give him a scathing glare. "Because you nearly set the Vault on fire."

He shrugged and carefully pulled himself up from his seat. "You're going to hold that against me, aren't you?"

"Until the day we die. Which may be today."

It was his turn to squeeze the railing. "It's the day someone does," he muttered under his breath.

Catherine had been a hard sell on the idea. Risson, however? Risson, the Overseer, and the local Merchant-Master? That had almost taken an act of the Gods and the Maiden hadn't ruled it out that one hadn't happened. Convincing them all – let alone convincing them quickly – had been a whirlwind of deals and arrangements and outright lies.

Henderschott, however, fell in line as soon as he received a missive from Riorik (the contents of which he did not volunteer to share). To hear witnesses talk about it, the Lieutenant-Commander went from raging refusals to a simple shrug and a grunted, "Okay, whatever," before he went off to organize the troops.

"Love is many things," the Upper-Adjunct continued as the cheers from the crowd subsided. "Love is our way as a people, as a Kingdom, as *humans* to forge an *unbreakable* bond that will stand the test of time against all challengers!"

"Challengers, but not the potter's daughter," Catherine mumbled as she listened on. Akaran raised an eyebrow and started to ask before she cut him off with a gesture. "Word of advice: if you pledge yourself to a woman, don't spend time in a bath with the local clay-maker. It stains your skin, and yes, your wife will notice."

He – with a hint of wisdom – decided to keep his mouth shut.

Oblivious to the commentary behind him, Risson kept going. The Staras, of all people, had not been so hard to convince. Once Akaran explained himself (with reluctant backing from Cath and eventually Telburn), they fell in line. It helped that as part of their pledge to punish the man responsible for the destruction of the Chapel, they offered the services of the Granalchi to put things back together.

More or less free of charge.

Free of charge to the Staras, at least. The Maiden had decided that if she was going to be drummed out of the Order for her failures, that she might as well incur even more wrath from the Holy General for over-spending out of the local coffers. Her edict of, "If I have to pave the path to perdition, then let the stones be cast in gold," delighted the Headmaster.

The next problem? The chapel.

It had taken damage at the fight with Annix. Not as badly or extensively as the Stara Temple, but Annix's wrath had damaged some of the pylons holding the structure upright. That was to say nothing of the bloodstains and rubble strewn across the entirety of the Pilgrim's Road.

The Ellachurstine wasn't perfect. *Perfection* would take months of careful building and crafted spellwork. Even still, the Overseer had gone well out of his way to make sure repairs were tackled post-haste as soon as the battle had finished.

Plan in place, not only did the Order of Stone eagerly jump in to help reinforce the courtyard and repair the pylons, they were assisted by the Granalchi Academy. Telburn's geomancers came up with a new way to brace the Chapel's amphitheater and both groups worked tirelessly with the more mundane craftsmen in the city to get it done. The end result?

Two days of rapid labor that put a shine on the Chapel even where a shine hadn't previously been. They promised that once the sun went down, the shrine would positively glow. Akaran took one hard look at them and offered a quiet prayer to not just Love, but Whomever else was listening above.

Glow? he groused to himself in the back of his mind. *They better damn well do more than that.*

"It is *Love* that brings us together today!" Risson thundered. "It is *Love* that joins the Valiant of the Kingdom of Dawnfire to the steadfast Warriors of Odinal!"

That was probably the closest admission that the Staras were going to make about who masterminded the current scenario. The pair of Lovers gave each other knowing smirks and kept their eyes firmly on the sun as the last few rays it had left began to peter out over the edge of the city. The city could argue if it was Love that had brought the two blissful souls in the center of the Chapel together or not.

But they couldn't argue about who had actually rescued the groom.

"These two souls will bring together peace and joy for our people! They will bring us together as the Gods have brought them together! There will be a great uplifting – not just of hearts and souls, but of fortunes and life!"

***

A Day Prior – Day of Lithdis, 16th of Firstgrow, 513 QR

Every word out of Elsith's mouth had been a warning, even as much as she hoped he'd ignore her. "Don't pick a fight; you won't win one. Don't piss off a doorman you can't get around. Don't make eye contact with the man with the big axe. And whatever you do – don't call them *barbarians*."

It wasn't bad advice. The Midlanders were absolutely *furious*. They were angry at the city. They were angry at the Blackstone Traders, for reasons that weren't readily apparent. They were outright *livid* with the Guard. They had completely *had it* with the rioting rabble in the streets.

They were known to be a reserved people that only struck when provoked. They were also known to be driven by a desire to strike *last* when provoked. More importantly, they were known to fight to the death to protect the people they loved.

The Tessamirch family was going to experience all of that first-hand.

Even though Kee Tessamirch had been murdered and put to rest – of which there was no end to the whispered 'thank yous,' to the vampire and his minion uttered in the halls of his former manor – his mercenary army had lived on, albeit briefly. They had persisted until the moment Malik was carried to the Tessamirch's manor to recover in the arms of his beautiful wife-to-be.

About five heartbeats later, the Warmaidens and the rest of the Odinal Delegation decided that it was time for the Advensi of the Massadine to cease to exist. The ones that thought they were capable of defending the Tessamirches against all comers were put to the test when Sherril had carved her bloody path through their ranks and were subsequently found lacking by the family. A few were *recruited* into the Odinal's *Oun-clan* to see if they could earn the right to carry a shield under the Wartribe's banner in the distant future...

...but that future was not now.

Instead, the Great House of Tessamirch was blockaded and barricaded by the Warmaidens and the entire wedding/diplomatic/potentially-a-war party that had been sent south from the Midlands with the Warprince. They, with no question about it whatsoever, were completely *sick* of Basion City's *shit.* A few distant cousins and wife of a son from a third-duke's sister (none of which who knew better) were occasionally overheard to remark that they felt like prisoners in their own estate (and the immediate grounds attached).

Not so from the staff. The maids and caretakers and everyone else that didn't have a blood (or wedded) relation to the Golden Baronessa were the happiest people in the city. The Odinals weren't letting anyone in or out, they were providing all the supplies the Tessamirches could ever need, and there was no threat of the outside world upending their peace.

Until Akaran showed up.

At which point, all bets were off.

The Warmaidens took one look at him and promptly marched him right up to the oak-and-copper gates of the Great House without a single argument to be had. A few of the semi-nobility tried to express their distrust, distaste, and disinterest, but it was amazing how fast they changed their tunes when his killer escorts gently brushed their fingertips across the hilts of their swords.

It was the first (and hopefully last) time he'd have the chance to get into the Tessamirch's happy abode, and he took a few seconds to take a look around. They had a distinct appreciation for all things dragon, which was not the most comforting decorative choice. The giant beasts existed, they weren't known to be friendly, and the fact that the family had decided to hang their scales up at every opportunity did not make him feel entirely welcome.

Nor did the statues. The seven-foot golden statues of dragons adorned with emeralds and spines made of ivory. The stories he'd heard about their riches had not been overstated. Murals of dragons adorned the foyer and reception hall, and the only artwork he saw representing Tessamirches of the past were simple plaster or the rare marble busts here and there.

Kee had one, of course. It was a gaudy clay statue hastily sculpted and planted in their central hall. They'd turned it into a small shrine, complete with decorative swords and flowers in pretty vases set there to honor his memory. Wisely, he stopped himself from asking if he could leave something there to honor his passing too.

They probably would've frowned upon him peeing in one of the urns.

(Some of them would, at least. Not many. Absolutely not the staff.)

Eager to be on his way, Akaran appreciated that he was granted an audience within minutes of walking into their not-at-all humble abode. The lead Warmaiden – Emadina again, lovely as she was with an axe draped across her shoulders – cleared her throat, calmly smashed her fist into a gong, and announced him with a thundering shout that reverberated across the entire building. "THE ELEMENTAL EXORCIST HAS ARRIVED!"

That was a title he would have been just as happy to do without. Still, the announcement got *everybody's* attention, not the least of which was Hylene and her husband-to-be. There was no avoiding it when it happened, and the *look* that she gave him from on top of her dais was one he *never* hoped to be on the receiving end of ever again.

Ever since the Danse Festistanis, the Golden Baronessa had been far from his biggest fan. When she jumped up from her gold-trimmed and throne-like chair and stormed down a meticulously embroidered red aisle-runner, all he could remember of his last meeting with the beautiful brown-haired belle was that he had intimated that she wasn't exactly getting married out of love. All he could do was plant his cane, get a hard grip on the handle, and brace for the inevitable slap across the face.

She thundered across the hall, her eyes absolutely brimming with tears and her arms outstretched like she was preparing to box his ears in. She didn't say a word. Two of her attendants scurried right behind her even as everyone else in the Baronessa's court stood by with their eyes wide and faces positively *aghast* at the very *idea* that a Lover would even *dare* show his face in their House, especially *him*.

When she clamped her arms around him and buried her head against the side of his neck, holding him as close as she could, Akaran froze up. She clutched the back of his head and made him rest his cheek against the top of her head while everyone else in the room drew in a single, collective gasp of surprise. The exorcist couldn't even manage to do that much.

The Baronessa squeezed harder when he didn't move, and without looking up at him, whispered just loud enough for him to hear, "Embrace me in return or I'll have your arms broken."

He did.

"That's better," she replied with a faint whisper and a sigh as she snuggled in tight and close. "I can't have anyone think I'm not appreciative of your efforts."

There weren't words to explain how confused he was. None. There weren't thoughts he could express to explain how terrified he was. This woman, the jewel of the city, the woman people had spent months *rioting* over because she was going to leave the peasantry behind? This woman that was nearly half a foot shorter than he was, far curvier than he'd *ever* be (belian-berry tarts be damned), and who was infinitely more beautiful than anyone he'd ever met by any metric than he could imagine?

The death grip she had on him rivaled the squeeze of the very dragons House Tessamirch seemingly idolized. The dragons, apparently, should spend time idolizing *her*. "Baronessa, I'm sorry," he squeaked. "I shouldn't have sa—"

"Apologize again and I'll have one of Malik's lesser women carve out your tongue," she promised quietly. "You saved his life at great pain to yours, and that is a debt I must repay," she replied as she placed her lips against the side of his throat. "Although you should be aware – this is as close to an act of affection that you will get from me, no matter what type whore you think I am."

Words died on his tongue. Again. Which worked out in his favor — because the next person to make an appearance half-stormed half-limped up behind him and caught both of them in a much bigger, much firmer hug. "Oun-blood Brother! Akaran!" Malik thundered.

"Oun-blood broth… brother?" the exorcist managed to eke out. "What?"

"You saved my life," the *much* bigger man boomed. "You saved the life of the Son of Odinal, and now you? You are family. Family of your own or not, it does not matter. *You* are now a child of the Odinal tribe. Without a blood bond, you are Oun. But brother still the same."

Both of them squeezed their arms around him again and almost crushed the air out of the bewildered priest. It wasn't until he managed to choke out a quiet, "Please let me go," that they relented and stepped back. When he finished gasping for air as the room spun around him, he realized two different things at once.

One was that Malik had recovered surprisingly well — although he was still morbidly pale and the wounds on his throat hadn't healed completely. He stood tall and firm, and even his weakened muscles were enough to be down right intimidating. "Although," Malik intoned after he gave the younger (and smaller) man a quick look, "you do not seem to have come through it as well as I hoped."

The second was that the Baronessa's reputation didn't speak loudly enough about her willingness to display candor. "I had heard you had healed enough to not need to use a cane any longer," his fiance remarked. "Did I hear wrong?"

"I did and now… can we just agree that Sherril is a bitch?" Akaran asked as he gestured down at his knee. "Malik. Hylene. I'm sorry I couldn't have done more. What happened should have never —"

"You saved my barbarian," the Baronessa interrupted with a glower. "I will hear *no* more apologies from you on the matter. Was it pretty? No. Is life? At times it is not. It only matters what ends we reach when we are stuck in the mud."

His friend chuckled and puts his arms on the exorcist's shoulders. "The time I spent with those monsters was not what I would wish upon anyone. I am with them no more, and I am where I belong. I won't hear your apologies either, because you are the one that delivered me from their grasp."

"You can tell us what you intend to do about the cretins that dared harm him," Hylene added before Akaran could say anything else, "because apparently, *my* men are *utterly worthless* in regards to defending what matters most to our holdings."

The Midlander cleared his throat. "Hers are dulled swords. Mine are sharp, but they lack a sheath to bury their steel in. I hope you have one for us."

Akaran took a deep breath and looked around the room at the bewildered and infuriated faces staring back at him. If the gossips lining the hall didn't have enough to talk about after that hug, they were about to lose their minds *now*. "I... I think I do."

"You don't sound certain," Hylene remarked with a flippant gesture of her hand. "I am grateful for your aid, but I do not like men that do not know what they want. Be... decisive... demanding, even, if you come to my home to ask for a thing," she added as she looked up at her towering fiance. The smile she gave him managed *utterly* make the priest feel *far* too knowledgeable about what happened behind their closed doors.

"Well," he answered after her gaze lingered long enough to make him *distinctly* uncomfortable, "then I have two questions. Do you like it when it rains?"

The young couple exchanged confused glances as Akaran straightened up and grinned at them. A nervous murmur erupted from the Baronessa's entourage around her throne before Malik slowly spoke up. "It does not do so often where I am from. Snow, yes. Rain? When it hits the scrublands, it is often most miserable. I would not hope for it on most days."

"There and here both. As well as the truth that it tends to do unkind things to my hair," his bride-to-be added. "Have the weather-witches ordained something new? Please do not deign to tell us that the reason you've come here is to deliver... a report on a storm? That is... beneath you."

"Yes, but no. You two should learn to like it," Akaran quipped. "Because I came here to see if you'd still like to get married."

"Of course we would! After everything my beloved has been through, do you think that we would cancel the ceremony?" Hylene declared with a sweeping gesture. "I'll not let some... *inhuman scum* ruin my life!"

Malik nodded along slowly, though his response was much more measured. "You ask those two things together? It is my understanding that... in your culture... rain on a day of a wedding is not a sign for health and longevity."

"It isn't. But I think we can start a new tradition," Akaran answered honestly. "That asshole hurt you," he said as he pointed at the Midlander, "has hurt your family," he added as he nodded his head at the Baronessa, "has hurt me, and wants to hurt my people too. I have an idea, and it's not a good one. I'm not going to lie to you. I want to piss that thing off and I think you two may be the best way I can do it."

They started to ask him what he meant, but he beat them to the punch. By the time he finished, they were far from excited over the idea. The wedding sounded wonderful. The rest didn't. The Warmaidens, however?

The plan wasn't out of his mouth before they announced their support.

They were ready to bathe in blood.

Even if it meant a little rain on their parade.

***

As the crowd silenced themselves for her arrival, Hylene stepped out on the stage with a smile on her face. To the surprise of not a single soul, she looked absolutely beautiful. It was impossible for her *not* to look beautiful, though right now, she was positively *beaming*. Malik looked just as handsome, although entirely... *different*. She happily wore a bright peach dress that had taken weeks of cheerful underpaid labor to dye *just right* and it was lined across the neck and over the shoulders with enough pearls to feed half of the city for the year, if she so desired.

Her hair was pulled up over her shoulders in a tight bun, and a silver pin through the middle to hold it together. The whole outfit was equal parts an affront to poverty and a glorious declaration of raw talent. Most importantly, it made the bride outshine everyone else in attendance by a league.

The bright and the shine of her dress contrasted perfectly with the flowing leather vest that her Midlander husband-to-be wore. It was a sleeveless, *thick* brown vest that could've stopped a crossbow bolt with all of the extra padding and armor hidden beneath. It showed off nearly every feature he boasted, from his muscular shoulders to the way the veins in his forearms stood out if he turned his wrists just right. It didn't completely cover his chest – instead, it was closed only by three strips of fabric tied to buttons across both sides.

The fact that he had decided to go without a shirt under it was a matter of great consternation and attention from half of the assembled crowd. For the other half? *I am never getting into a fight with that man in my life*, Akaran quietly mused as Catherine's eyes sparkled as she stared at him. "Oh, come on. You too?"

"Love comes in many shapes and forms," she answered without pulling her eyes away.

"You're confusing Niasmis with Avasharti."

She rolled her eyes for a moment before she affixed them back on the Midlander's... midland. "You can find Love in Lust. They are literal cousins. Nor is it that your eye is blind, either."

"I am not drooling over —"

"The raven-haired one with the axe," she retorted.

For a moment, he didn't answer. When he did? "I, just..."

"Uh-huh."

There wasn't a point continuing the argument.

It was hard to say which of them commanded the most attention. Was it the black-haired, braided-ponytail wearing, wall of raw muscle that had caused the ladies in the audience (maidens or otherwise) to cheer and swoon when he had effortlessly mounted the stairs leading to the Chapel courtyard? Or was it his dainty companion, who seemed to effortlessly float across the stage until she was at his side? The only people that made a noise when she arrived were men that didn't know to keep their mouths shut, and women still angry that she was claiming the Son of Odinal as her own.

Her beauty commanded rapt attention and utter respect. The cheers didn't start until she bowed her head and waved her hand in the air. When they began, it almost took an act of divinity to get them to cease

She was a glowing beacon to his thundering strength.

A true wedding of dusk to dawn, indeed.

"So it is these days, these dark days, these days of test and pain. These days of challenges and fear. These days where we are lost even within the light, where the shadows have brought us low. It is even in these days that we *must* stand, we *must* cheer, we must *embrace* each other! Our faith has never faltered that this day would come!" Risson announced to the crowd.

The last sentence was an absolute lie. He'd only agreed to include it after a few threats and a promise Akaran didn't want to make. He wasn't just to marry the young lovers under the gaze of the Gods. Of course, he'd protested the entire idea of upending the wedding plans for this... *bastardization* of a ceremony (in his own words). Oh, had he *ever* protested.

The Overseer had refused to allow the ceremony proper to start after sundown. The city had spent months preparing for it. The city would need it to happen in the middle of the day. He absolutely *demanded* that the city see the planned celebrations as they occurred under the light of the sun and nothing else would be permitted. They would need to be able to sing and dance and throw flowers and all the other crap that happened at a wedding between heads of state.

A compromise was roughly worked out. They'd start the wedding proper at dusk. The rest of the day could go on as Hannock wanted with parades and cheering and whatever other bullshit he'd planned for (all of which Akaran had eagerly sat out and had done his absolute best to avoid learning about).

With the wedding slated to begin at dusk, the Overseer assumed that meant that before night fell, the couple would be happily bound hand to hand. He assumed wrong. Nobody bothered to correct him.

Intentionally.

Risson's job, point-blank, was to delay the ceremony as long as he could. To be truthful, he'd done very well at it. In fact, he'd managed to delay it *so* well that the Baronessa was ready to have his head. Or if not have his head, to make sure that the otherwise generous donations the Order of Stara received from House Tessamirch would be directed *elsewhere*.

It was a win-win for the Lovers.

"We stand in the midst of the Light even when shadows fall! With *Light* and *Love* we shall *never* be brought to an end of our hope! For as long as we have both, the Will of the Gods will never be undone!"

The Upper-Adjunct looked up at the sky and clenched his hands nervously. The last ray of sunlight faded beyond the edges of the cliff, and for a heartbeat, nothing but darkness covered the Chapel. Akaran tapped the tip of his cane sharply on the floor and looked over at his boss. "We're on."

Catherine clenched her teeth and extended her hand to the sky. She snapped her fingers once and dropped her arm sharply to the side. Light erupted across the Ellachurstine from the edges of the clam-shell and dozens of glowing magelights placed along the rebuilt platform and stairs. The underside of the shrine erupted in a bright shining golden light that reflected off of the rubble-strewn water below. Runes spread across the ground and hidden Wardkeepers planted long, standing torches at their feet.

"On this day, our celebration of love is an act of **defiance**," Risson thundered across the courtyard. His voice was bolstered by a sudden spell from Catherine that carried his words across the city in an unquestionable challenge to anyone that would do them harm this day or any other day.

The Maiden glanced over at Akaran as he cracked his knuckles. "When they show up, you take their fisking heads. This isn't a catch. This is a kill. Am I understood?"

"It won't matter even if we do catch her," he lamented. "Annix — at the Pyre? He was able to cull his broodlings. I don't know how he did it but we can probably expect the same unless we can stop him."

"We won't get anything from her then, you think?"

"If we do, we'll have to do it fast. Thank you for etching Truthcall," he added as he rubbed at his arm. "I don't think the invocation alone would draw enough power to use it otherwise."

Catherine pursed her lips. "Don't count on doing it at all."

***

The wait wouldn't be long.

As the loving couple spoke their vows, the shadows across the city were alive with death. Everyone with an interest made a move. And there were too damned many interested parties

A multitude of souls moved in unison, yet each to opposite ends. The Man of the Red Death watched with great interest — and he stood closer to all of Catherine's spells than she could have possibly imagined. His minions moved around the Chapel with impunity and with very little effort. All it took were a few words said to the right people, and he had the stage set to get what he needed.

Akaran moved out of the small gazebo and didn't bother to try to hide who he was or to conceal the sword at his waist. None of the Basion city peasants gave him any attention; they were too busy watching the ceremony to object. While he paced back and forth, his allies went to work. A Lover made a gesture and activated a ward. A watersculpt channeled a column of water from underneath the Chapel into a pylon-and-pipe system specially crafted by the Headmaster-Adept himself.

The Huntsmatron crouched down on top of Medias Manor with a crossbow in her hands and malice in her eyes. The Lieutenant-Commander rolled his shoulders and tapped the flat of his sword against his shield at the gateway leading into the Repository. The Master of Thieves had his men openly flank the Overseer despite *every* objection.

If Annix decided to strike anywhere but where he was wanted, he wouldn't find any soft targets of note. The gamble they played was simple: with a counter to his challenge so blatant, he'd have to make a splash. He'd have to strike again just as hard... or harder. It'd be a waste of his time to kill someone at random somewhere else. They counted on him being smart enough to know that.

They also counted on his assassin joining him.

He'd only open attacked once. He'd sent her every other time.

Thunder rolled in the skies overhead. A harbinger of the battle to come. An expression of anger, possibly. Or simply it was just a declaration from the Butcher of Basion that their challenge would not go unheeded.

Akaran had made sure that the weather would be clear. The Office of Divination had been oddly helpful to promise that. They'd almost bent over backwards with sworn oaths and everything that there wouldn't be the hint of a storm in the sky.

Sparkcasters didn't like rain. If it was going to storm, it might've changed Annix's response. If there was rain, he might've sent someone else – if he had anyone – or might've decided to wait and make a scene when the newlyweds went back to their estate. Of course, the vampire had sent his pet mage every other time he had wanted to make an impact, and his mage was the uninvited guest of honor for the celebration.

Thunder meant one thing and one thing only.

The Headmaster reacted to the sound before anyone else did. Defensive magics were a hallmark of Granalchi studies, and it hadn't taken more than a minute to convince him to secure the wedding. Telburn had directed the entire Academy to assist in rebuilding the Chapel – but the spells used to shield the courtyard?

Entirely his.

Entirely his, and crafted from runes designed by his friend. If an affront was going to be made to the vampire's power, then the affront was going to be made in the name of Adept Odern Merrington. The spells were written and etched with Odern's name and his signature on each one.

Akaran approved of the method, even if he thought he'd seen the signature recently somewhere else – but in the fog of cocasa for his knee and the stress of the plan, he couldn't remember where. Riorik, however, also took note. What his ally didn't realize, *he* did – and it put a nail in the coffin of someone he was going to speak to.

Soon.

As the star-struck lovers looked deeply into each other's eyes, with nary a concern in the world in front of the cheering throngs of downtrodden and beaten, the exorcist felt a moment of calm and the touch of Love against his soul. He reached over and squeezed his silent friend's shoulder as the crowd exploded with a cry of raw jubilation. "In Erine's name."

Hylene pressed her lips to Malik's.

Their kiss was met with thunderous applause.

Lightning followed a moment later.

****

Sherril struck with all the force they'd counted on. An arc of lightning rolled from the heavens down onto the crowd but it did little more than scatter across a flickering shield over-top of the celebrants that went unnoticed, at first. People flinched from the thunder that followed, but they were too entranced by the sight before them to scatter (though that wasn't to say that it didn't fray nerves).

Another bolt of lightning struck the air and detonated against the magical shell with just as little effect. Another strike, and another, followed as the battlemage probed the wedding's defenses. The spells held.

The crowd noticed. There wasn't any way to ignore more than the first two. An errant boom was one thing. A concussive salvo of them? The more lightning that struck, the more the crowd began to panic. The more they began to fear. The more they began to fear, the harder the magic struck. "Chaos magic," Akaran mused. "Amps up when people panic."

"I hate it how often you're right," Catherine muttered as she prepared herself for her role in the play.

"Same, honestly."

As the merrymakers recoiled from the booming assault, Catherine stepped up to the dais even as the newly-wedded couple walked down the huge red carpet stretched out before them. If the assault frayed their nerves – they refused to show it.

They'd been promised that no harm would come to them.

They believed it.

Riorik only gave it fifty-fifty odds.

"I am Maiden-Templar Catherine Prostil!" she called out across the gathering. "You are scared and this I know but I am here *to promise you* that you are *safe*. I know that you have been promised this before and I know that we have failed but I *beg* of you, I beg of *all of you*, to stand fast. Stand fast and **WITNESS**."

The crowd turned their attention to her. Most with scorn and open disdain. Others with mocking laughs and rude suggestions. It wasn't until Hylene lifted her hand over her head that the crowd silenced themselves – a move the Overseer couldn't have pulled off had he even tried.

"Witness the protection of **LOVE**. Lives may have been lost this week, but in the face of that? We do not *fear* the dark," the Maiden thundered. "We do not *fear* what hides from the light! **WE WILL NOT**."

The crowd booed her.

Akaran felt the presence behind him before he heard her voice. "You really should," the woman snarled just above a whisper.

Yards away, Catherine didn't notice. "The Lovers have stood with the Kingdom of Dawnfire for *centuries*. We have offered aid, alms, and *protection*!"

"Protection," the slithering voice mocked from behind the crippled exorcist. "You offer *protection* for less time than my Meister has been alive," Sherril hissed.

The priest stood still as she moved around him, with shadows that moved along in her wake. He saw a guard perk up and take a step forward until Akaran waved him away with a curt gesture. "We haven't done a great job of it lately, I'll admit," he replied coolly.

"Haven't done *any* job of it."

"The wedding happened," he countered. "The crowd's still here."

"Because we allowed it," the battlemage hissed, "and you fools will learn that the night is still young."

Catherine let her voice boom over the throng. "**I PROMISE YOU** – before this night is over, what the Order does **will be known**! We battle in the darkness, but we battle to let Love triumph! Love like **this** love between Dusk and Dawn!"

Sherril's aura moved back and forth behind him so fast it was impossible to tell where she actually was. One moment she was almost touching him, and the next, she was almost on the other side of the courtyard. A crackle of electricity danced across the ground and charred the top of his boot as she stalked her prey. "I'm going to kill you, then I'm going to kill *them*. Did you really think that we wouldn't find a way around your spells? Meister has done it for years without you ever knowing!"

"This is the Safest City in the Kingdom, and I will stand here and acknowledge that there has been evil afoot – evil we missed, evil that has allowed to fester. **But I promise you**, they will not go unchallenged in the face of Love!"

He closed his eye as her essence swelled up behind him and he felt her arms lunge out of the shadows to wrap around his. "Kinda hoped you would, honestly," Akaran admitted as he shut his good eye as hard as he could, took a deep breath, and *focused* with all of his might on the stone in his eyepatch. "What was it you said you wanted? Oh yeah..."

Sherril snarled her arms around the exorcist and latched on without remorse. He felt the electricity charging through her body as her teeth closed on his neck...

...and her fangs *cracked* on the scales of ice that appeared across his skin. Her howl of pain ripped through his eardrums and she pulled back as quickly as she had attacked. She only made it a foot away before the exorcist manifested his chains in the air around his arms and snapped them around her body.

The sudden spell caught her off guard and pinned her against the rough icy shell that had started to form over his cloak. Sherril kicked and scratched against him, but her claws couldn't find purchase and he kept his weight planted firmly on his cane to keep from falling over. She screamed in a voice so loud and shrill that it drowned out Catherine's spiel.

"You wanted *witnesses*."

Ice flowed around his throat and face as she tried to rake her jagged nails across his skin. Blood flowed freely as she laid open his cheek, but the Coldstone turned it into stinging bloody crystals. He flexed his arms and the silvery chains snapped tight enough to dig into her armor and sizzle against some of her exposed flesh.

Catherine spun around and barked out, "**LUMINOSO – CORSAIR**!" at the top of her lungs. The sudden blast of light ripped away the shadows around the vampire and exposed the fight for the whole city to see. "We will drag you into the *light*!" she screamed.

Sherril screamed something of her own.

Akaran tried, but the ice around his face choked off his air. The world swam around him as he struggled to keep her pinned. He had to. She had to be seen. She had to be *displayed*. He had to prove a *point*.

He had to stay conscious. He had to fight. He had to dig his chains around her even tighter. But not for long. Catherine condemned her from afar. The crowd cheered – their voices rising in a mix of horror, a mix of terror, and a mix of sudden *rage* that boiled in the air.

The vampire screeched as her magic surged around her skin and crackled. It lashed against the chains. It scored across the ice encasing her tormentor. Akaran wavered, faltered, and nearly collapsed.

The ice wouldn't let him.

And when a single, calm voice spoke, it didn't matter anymore.

"In Erine's name," the Specialist-Major intoned.

Sherril turned her head from the exorcist's neck, her glistening yellow eyes wide and glistening in the light. His cloak matched hers. His armor matched hers. She knew what he was the second she saw him.

"The Order of Love will summon forth what belongs in perdition..." Catherine intoned from the altar overlooking the celebrations turned battle.

"Witness *this*, you bitch," Akaran croaked past the ice.

Badin flexed his finger. Just a single gesture. Almost a twitch.

A blast of searing lighting exploded just below her throat.

The spell struck with such force that it bowled Akaran over and knocked the ice loose from his body. The chains shattered into nothingness and the vampire *bounced* up and rolled forward in a rough heap across the courtyard.

Catherine stormed over and planted her foot on Sherril's back as the monster tried to struggle up to her hands and knees. "...and the Goddess's tears shall **wash away their sins**," she finished with her voice boosted across the Chapel.

That was the signal the others were waiting for.

Below the chapel, Quinchecco and Elverich worked their own spells. Murky pondwater began to glow and shine. The Tidesinger's voice blessed it. Purified it. Turned the mess of mud and filth into a spreading lake of vibrant whites and blues as it scoured corruption and filth away down to the lakebed.

Elverich used a simple flute to cut loose with a haunting melody that lifted the shouts above with an undercurrent of longing and peace. Water flowed freely up from the pond and into the stone pipes that Telburn had crafted into the underside of the chapel. The entire shrine began to glow as the water gushed through the building and flowed through the embedded channels.

Sherril crackled with energy as she struggled underneath Catherine's leather-and-steel boot. The lightning lasted for just a few moments before the tops of the clam-shell unleashed a gushing fountain of rain to match her thunder. Water raced down the concourse, soaking the crowd.

At first, people screamed. Then they cheered. The water tasted so fresh and so pure, they couldn't help themselves. Hylene and Malik lead the throng of celebrants with delighted cheers of their own as the disgraced battlemage was exposed for what she was.

A damned soul.

A damned soul at the feet of the holy.

A damned soul that screamed in pain as the blessed water began to make her skin blister and sear. She fought against Catherine's boot enough to squirm away and briefly rise to her feet as bits of her skin began to melt away from her face. Her screams rolled through the crowd, and the crowd *roared* back at her.

The exorcist flicked his chains out again and sunk them around her neck. Catherine drew her blade and thrust it through the battlemage's back and out through her breastbone. "By command and order of the Goddess, I *command you*, **speak truth and be judged**! WHERE IS YOUR MASTER?"

Sherril just howled.

"I SAID – **speak truth and be judged**!"

"EVERYWHERE!" she screeched. "He is EVERYWHERE – EVEN HERE!"

Akaran staggered forward and sharply pulled on the chains again, and forced the vampire to arch her back deeper against the blade. The bitch choked with blackened blood spurting from her lips as her hair melted away and her scalp dissolved down to the raw bone. "For crimes against the city, for crimes against the natural order itself, *you are done*," he thundered as bits of ice melted off of his body. "BADIN! LOCK HER DOWN!"

Sherril looked back over her shoulder like she expected another bolt of lightning. But it was cold iron that the mage had in his hands – and he wrapped the shackle around her neck with eager aplomb. "Just to let you know – these things *hurt*," the Dawnfire Specialist growled in her ear as she tried to buck against the metal even as he welded the iron closed with a jolt of electrically charged ether from his hand. "I should know, thanks to you."

She ignored him.

She *tried* to call a thunderbolt down from the sky once again.

She learned to listen.

The iron collar *burned* into her throat and left bloody red welts all across her skin from the effort. The magic she tried to channel reflected inwardly and sent sparks dancing up from around her chipped fangs and barely any out from her fingers. The feedback ended as quickly as it started, and she collapsed into the steaming water with a broken cry.

"Hurts like a bitch, doesn't it?" Badin quipped as both Akaran and Catherine slowly began to circle Annix's assassin.

Sherril turned her head up and stared into the exorcist's eye. "He's going to rip that madwoman to shreds, rip her soul out, turn her against *you.* You think... you think these pathetic *shits* matter? The city has been *fed to him* for years and it's all gonna... all gonna be exposed!"

Catherine slid her weapon out of the spellcaster's back and readied it against the bitch's throat. "The only thing about to be exposed is your spine."

"Oh you don't know…?" she mocked as she struggled against the chains. Her face sizzled and flesh boiled away grotesquely and the Maiden readied a swing. "How many… how much do you think Bistra knows about you? She took Meister's wife… now we'll take the keys to your castles! How many… how many of your Order's *black marks* do you think she'll remember?"

Akaran wrenched back on the chains and moved Sherril's neck away from the edge of the Maiden's sword before Catherine could end her there and then. "What does Annix think she knows?"

"Enough," the battlemage laughed. "She knows *enough*. Once she serves him… he turns her… and he'll use everything! Everything she ever knew! He'll use *all of it* to ruin your Order! Every story. Every *lie*. The Kingdom will turn against you!"

"Lies from a dead man won't hold sway over the hearts of the Kingdom," Akaran snarled. "Either way, you won't be around to find out."

"WHERE IS HE?" Catherine thundered. "SPEAK TRUTH AND BE JUDGED – WHERE?"

The invocation had a visible impact on the vampire and caused her eyes to roll back up into her head as blackened blood pulsed down from her nose. She quaked. Shuddered. Her skin continued to steam as the sudden burst of faux-rain ended. She opened her mouth to speak, but *something* crushed her throat hard enough that they could *see* the indent on exposed muscles under the collar. "Meister…!"

Akaran loosened his chains and looked around at the rooftops nearest the chapel. "He's here. He's watching."

"Of *course* he's… he's watching! Can't… won't say…"

"Oh you will," Catherine promised. "You will. You will speak –"

Sherril flicked her eyes up to the Maiden and shook her head. "I CANNOT. I CANNOT SPEAK YOUR TRUTH. I WOULD NOT FOR HIM AND CANNOT FOR YOU."

The Maiden pursed her lips and willed a small ball of light into her hand. The ether around the vampire trembled and a thin gray cloud started to appear to their naked eyes; a little small band of smoke that had wrapped itself around Sherril's throat. "You can't speak because he won't let you. Not because you don't *want* to."

"Can't speak what I know. Won't. Not you," Sherril promised with a raspy laugh. "Not you not them not alive not dead!"

Catherine snorted and shoved the battlemage down hard onto the stones with her boot. "Then we will find him another way and your ashes can soak in my chamberpot," she spat. "Akaran, I thought I said you were to take her head."

"Go burn you accursed woman…" he grumbled as the crowd continued to cheer and jeer. "No. No that's *exactly* what we need," he muttered to himself as an idea suddenly popped into his head. "SHERRIL INYADYINE: Are you bound by spell of your Meister, or Curse of the Pit to have your tongue held?"

"Curse by Pit…?" the Maiden repeated. "What are you…?"

"We asked the wrong question," he countered as he grabbed a chunk of the vampire's sloughing hair. "ANSWER ME. YOUR MEISTER OR THE PIT! Which holds your tongue?"

She tried to give one. Only this time, her throat wasn't just crushed. Her neck began to dissolve away in a cloud of red embers and black fog. "DAMMIT. IT'S ANNIX – DON'T LET HIM! I NEED HER INTACT!"

Catherine *snarled* something under her breath and unleashed a fresh wave of light that enveloped the immediate area with a fierce blue glow. The wedding guests **cheered** at the top of their lungs as the spell kicked in. To them, it was just another part of the execution. "**LUMINA – DISENCHANT**."

To Sherril, it was a reprieve. Only of minutes, but a reprieve. Akaran's chains faded from view and the fog around the vampire's neck vanished. The rain quit sizzling against her skin, and the glow from the myriad other spells in the area died down within the shimmering blue sphere the Maiden had summoned around them.

Before his boss could even ask, Akaran spat out his reasoning. "We're idiots. She won't say truth because Annix won't let her. But she *can* say truth because she *knows* truth. Just like Rmaci. It's locked away, that's all."

"Just like Rmaci? That burnt ghost…?"

"The damned know the secrets of the Abyss and beyond. She's damned. She's a dead soul. We can force her *soul* to speak even if Annix has a hold on her *mind*," he explained in a rush. "If we can't get past the curse that gave her life, and his control with it… then maybe we can get her *soul* to talk. Or whatever soul she has left."

Catherine stared at him in confusion. "Are you… are you suggesting that we somehow make the Pit of Perdition make her tell us where to find him?"

He felt his leg give out and Badin caught him before he could land on his face. "Rmaci explained it to me. The power of the Abyss can seal the lips of the damned but if it's just some kind of curse… we don't need whatever she is *now*. We need to compel her *soul* to talk."

"A different key… you mean… No. You cannot be serious. Are you suggesting… necrosia? You would suggest that necromancy could do what the Divine cannot?"

"Vampires *hate* necromancers. It's a rule as old as the lore itself. Necrosia practitioners have agency over the bodies of the dead. Vampires are… well. Bodies of the dead. Assholes that walk and talk and bite, but still *dead*. They're animates just as much as a corpusal or a greater zombie is." He paused for a moment and felt his mouth go dry. "Shit. We need her. We need her and Anais. *SHIT*."

"The only thing you're getting is her head," Catherine spat. "This spell… won't last long."

"Then we need to get her out of here."

The Maiden kicked Sherril onto her back and *dared* her to try to stand up. "You have less time to come up with an idea than this woman has virtues. Even if we knew where he's attacking from we can't get to him — and if we could, we wouldn't need her to talk!"

"We don't know where he's at right now, just need to make sure he doesn't know where *she's* at," Akaran countered. "TELBURN!"

For once, the Headmaster didn't magically appear.

He did show up a few minutes later, but not until after Sherril had to be shocked back into submission all over again. Somehow, Badin just didn't seem to mind. Beyond the dome of blue light, the revelers were… well, reveling. From the outside of Catherine's spell, Order Wardkeepers and city guards had rushed across the courtyard with weapons drawn and spells of great and small magnitude alike brimming on their lips.

The hazy blue dome didn't offer a clear picture for the ugly conversation inside, but the wedding party didn't need it. All they needed to know was that the priests had gotten into a fight that they'd won. There were enough plants in the audience espousing the Goddess's glory that the crowd was all-too-happy to engage in cheers for the Order.

The loudest of those voices belonged to the newly-wedded couple. Their insistence that the city would stand and the Kingdom would be safe and that justice would be had — all of the heartfelt lines of bullshit that the Baronessa simply just *knew* had to be said — was enough to keep the peace. For the city, it was a win that had been desperately needed.

For Sherril…

The battlemage didn't take the time offered to come clean of her sins. If she had, it would've saved her some grief; a fact that Catherine was only happy to espouse with frequency. The change in the Maiden's demeanor over the last few days had almost been a delight to watch. *Although,* Akaran had to admit, *knowing that she doesn't give a shit anymore doesn't bode well for me either...*

When Telburn finally made it up from underneath the Chapel, he blatantly refused to step foot into the warding sphere. "These looks did not come naturally," he scolded as he smoothed an errant wrinkle away from his eye, "nor did other aspects of my health."

"Not your health I'm interested in," the exorcist grunted as he lifted the point of his cane off of Sherril's throat. "Remember when you hid Donta's arm?"

The Headmaster shuddered in abject revulsion. "I have not seen so many loose limbs that I would forget that one."

"Good. We're doing that again."

"Another arm?" Telburn asked as his jaw dropped. "No."

"Not just an arm," the exorcist replied with a smirk as he kicked the vampire with the edge of his boot. "The whole damn thing."

The mage lost all color in his face as the corners of his mouth drooped. "Good sirrah, no. *Voidiov* creates a pocket in the Veil; a box in the world between this one in the next. No living thing can survive within it."

Akaran nodded at Badin, and the battlemage pulled the defeated vampire up to her knees. "She's not a living thing. She's a dead thing. Animated corpse. Little more complicated but effectively, just ether in a corpse."

"*THAT'S* your plan?" Catherine thundered. "You're *mad!*"

"We don't know how Annix culls his brood," he countered. "We could drop her into the middle of Civa and she'd be dust when she landed for all we know. If we put her in the Veil, then she's out of reach. I hope."

"You can't... can't hide me. Won't do anything," the battlemage croaked. "I will die in service to him, one way or another."

"See?" he added. "Even she agrees."

Telburn shook his head emphatically 'no.' "Under no circumstances. Absolutely not. The Veil does not have the same rules as our world. There is no air. No food. No life as you know it."

Akaran just shrugged and tapped the vampire on her head. "This bitch isn't alive as we know it either," he argued. "Tel. If you want justice for Odern, this is it. We need to lock her away until we can get her to talk."

"Which I haven't even agreed to let you try yet," the Maiden groused. "I'm not sure I will."

"Then we can pop her back out and let the sun do it. Please?"

The Headmaster and the Maiden exchanged tired, nervous glances between each other even as the blue dome began to flicker. "What's the worst that happens?"

"Well… from what I have seen with experiments on the matter… most simply choke to death. A dog was returned to the world with its skin and fur inverted, although there was a goblin that –"

"So the worst is madness or death?" Akaran interrupted.

"Effectively. Death, if she's lucky."

"I can live with that."

Telburn looked down at the soaking wet, smoldering vampire and shuddered. "Can she? Can I? I am no executioner."

The exorcist just shrugged. "It's not an execution if she dies by accident, is it?"

The Headmaster didn't have a good answer for that.

A few moments later, and the Granalchi had the spell prepared. A hush went over the crowd as dark clouds rolled across the sky. Her Meister was still watching. Akaran could *feel* his eyes on his back, and the raw malice in the air should've made his skin crawl. Instead? It just bolstered his resolve.

Akaran took Annix's minion by her chin and slowly tilted her head up so she could look him in his eye. Her skin was trying to heal itself already; bits of fresh flesh across burnt meat had begun to blossom on her face. The holy water had ruined her down to the bone in places, yet as grotesque as she was, it didn't make him flinch. "Understand a truth: I take no pleasure in what I'm about to do. I cannot imagine how terrible this is going to feel. You have my pity, Sherril. Tell us where he is, and we won't have to do this."

The battlemage snaked her tongue out across her lips and studied the haunted, pained look in his eye as someone tied her wrists together behind her back. "Liar."

"Maybe I am," he admitted. He let her go and nodded at Catherine.

The Maiden dropped the nullification spell and gave the crowd one more look at the vampire and her would-be executioners. Telburn stretched his arms in front of his chest and opened them wide with a muttered invocation. As he did, a gateway appeared leading to an empty, fog-filled void beyond. Cobalt-blue light flickered in the beyond as unfathomable and indescribable shapes flickered in and out of existence in the World Between.

Akaran pulled the defeated battlemage up to her feet with one hand tight on her throat. "BASION CITY: MAY WOE BE UNTO THOSE THAT WILL DO YOU HARM!" he screamed.

The crowd went silent as every eye turned to him.

In that moment, Basion City knew him – and knew what he was.

"ANNIX. YOU'RE THERE. YOU'RE WATCHING. I KNOW," he continued.

A small boom of thunder — but something that *wasn't* thunder — answered his call.

"YOU WANT HER BACK?"

Thunder peeled a second time.

The exorcist smiled up at the dark skies above and very calmly emptied months of pent-up anger and rage into one single spell in the palm of his hand. The impact nearly destroyed her neck, and the force of the Word blew her back into the otherworldly void. Sherril screamed in pain and terror so sharply that it could be heard across the entire Ellachurstine yard.

The gateway snapped shut and cut her cries off instantly.

"Then go fetch, you son of a bitch," he spat just loud enough for his friends to hear. He turned away from the celebrants and marched away without a further word.

And the crowd simply *cheered*.

***

While the crowd cheered, fate did something else. Something worse. Something cold, something calm. "I suppose we should assume that if the people are that happy, then our job is done?" Tidesinger Quinchecco mused to his companion.

"I guess," Elverich replied after a moment. "Say what you will for those Oo-lo assholes, but they have a flair for the dramatic."

"They do, but. Given the nature of their lives, do they have another choice? I suspect that if they were performing for themselves they'd have much less of a concern on style and focused only on substance."

"Suppose it does them any good? People hate them all the same."

Quinchecco nodded his head slightly and reached up to tweak the end of his ear straight. "Hate, yes. But, all you have to do is listen. The crowd above — they're rejoicing. They're happy. Actions are just the music of the flesh and we both know the value of gaining the attention of the crowd."

The watersculpt sniffed in mild derision. "Their gold is good, at least."

"That it is, that it is," the Tidesinger replied with a small laugh... before it died on his lips. "Elverich... I think you should go."

The somewhat paunchy Aquallan blinked and glanced over his shoulder at the priest. "Tired of my company?"

"Of yours? Never," Quin replied with a smile. "Yet with so much bloodshed as of late, I feel the waters are getting darker. I should take the time to speak with them before the day comes to an end."

Elverich shrugged. "As you wish, Tidesinger. Hurry topside. If the Lovers did what they said they were gonna, I expect the party is going to be in full swing by now."

"I expect as much, yes," the priest of Aqualla answered with a faked smile and an encouraging nod.

Once the sculpt was on his way down the waterlogged cobblestone path nestled beneath the Chapel, Quinchecco raised both of his hands toward the roof. "You can reveal yourself. I mean no harm. I offer no threat."

The air settled even as the cheers above and around grew louder. The surface of the pond started to pulse, with ripples appearing where nothing could have disturbed them. As the sounds of the world became muffled, a single, *firm* voice called out an understated response. "Are you sure I do not?"

"I expect that you do, stranger," the Tidesinger answered as a thin sheen of sweat appeared on the back of his neck. "I have not had much luck with people approaching me from the shadows as of late."

"No, you have not," Nastavol replied as he stepped out of the shadows and seemingly manifested from the thin air. "As that luck has changed, I have some words to speak with you directly."

Quinchecco took one look at him and surrendered instantly. He knew exactly what he was looking at, even if he didn't understand how, and didn't bother putting on airs. "I... I have heard the seas speak of your kind. I thought it was only... rumor."

"Then if you know, may we be direct and to the point?" the red-robed stranger asked with the hint of a polite smile at the corner of his mouth. "I assume you have already answered my question already, even if the questioner is currently unavailable to relay it forward."

The priest swallowed slowly and cleared his throat. "The scorpion woman?"

"Yes."

"Why... why go to that trouble when... you could just come... like now?"

"Because I did not wish to have to enter the city," the Man of the Red Death replied. "Not everyone is as welcoming as you. Now I have had to do so and my question still remains."

Quin carefully lowered his hands and slipped them into his robe's pockets. "Shall I presume more of her... treatment?"

"I would prefer not."

The Tidesinger let out a slow breath. "You will forgive me if I don't seem inclined to believe that you speak truth."

"I will," he answered. "Yet, you can verify if I am offering a falsehood by answering honestly – and quickly. I prefer a great many things, yet what I prefer and what I am willing to do to expedite an answer are not always one and the same."

The priest of Aqualla looked beyond Nastavol's shoulder and realized that he wasn't alone. A ball of vile black fur had climbed on a pylon, and a rolling cloud of black fog drifted aimlessly behind them both. "She asked me a lot of questions. Which one was the true one?"

"Did she?" Nastavol asked after a moment's worth of silence. "I must offer my apologies. She was not to ask you any."

"Tell that to the girl."

"Girl?"

Quinchecco swallowed and took a few steps away, but the necromancer didn't follow. "Made me watch her torture... a young woman. Drowned her. Repeatedly. Didn't kill her, but she hurt her. The girl has friends – they're angrier over her than they are for me. They're just a scream away."

"The Lovers, hm? I see. Yet if you thought your screams would have a result, you would have offered then by now. I will say that my... associate... will be handled. I would offer my apologies but I fear they would sound hollow."

"Hollow as your soul, Harbinger," the Tidesinger replied with far more bravado than he felt. "I know what you are and I know Who you serve. The Warden of the Abyss has no business with Aqualla, and you've no business with me."

"I think it is customary for the one who seeks to ask a question to frame what the business is, water-born," Nastavol cautioned as a fog unlike anything that Annix had cursed the Lovers with began to roll under the chapel. "My business with you is simple: I need a door."

"Then I would suggest a carpenter."

Before the necromancer could reply, his most-favored Acolyte popped up from the water and sank his claws into the closest pylon. "[Master we must leave now/fools now search for him.]"

He nodded slowly and opened his right hand to reveal a thin, almost amber-colored piece of stalactite hanging from a simple cord. "What you fail to realize is that the door I need is buried. I have a Blessing of the Stonehewn to open it – but I need knowledge that only Aqualla has to find it."

As he spoke, faint pieces of bone and steel bobbed through the murky fog. Glints of torchlight reflected from the water and offered a chance to see a dagger's blade here, an arrowhead there. Quinchecco saw it, and bowed his head in genuflection. "A disciple of the Grand Warden asking for a favor of Singer of Tides while bearing a grant of passage from the Stonehewn. All under the noses of Lovers. You… you are a complicated man."

"With a simple question. One I said I do not have the desire to draw blood to answer," the necromancer cautioned anew.

"I have no desire for a war I cannot win, Harbinger. The water screams of the blood you have poured into it in the past. But I cannot give you aid. Doing so would —"

His protests stopped with a wet gurgle as blood pulsed from his lips.

As the cloud of shadows and bone withdrew the knife it had thrust into the Tidesinger's throat, Nastavol simply shook his head. "I had no desire to draw blood," he repeated as he snapped his fingers. The cloud of bones and blades enveloped the body before it could even hit the ground. "Nor do I have time to argue. Mael. Rishnobia. Collect the corpse and follow. We have work to do."

X. BROKEN DOLLS
Pre-dawn Morning of Staddis, 18ᵗʰ of Firstgrow, 513 QR

"Appaidene, please," Ridora called out into the darkness. "It is far too late to be –"

"Dolls! Dolls! Dolls!"

"Yes girl, I *know*, the *dolls*," the Lady of Medias Manor retorted with a long, drawn-out sigh. "But like you, it's time for the dolls to be in bed."

The waif called out from ahead with a simple "**CHIRP**!" followed with a "DOLL!" that echoed across the edges of the garden.

It was just one more frustration for the Lady. With her only remaining aide worth a damn taken… *ill…* that left Ridora herself to wrangle the residents effectively on her own. There was only so much the other orderlies could do, and none of them had the same empathic touch on her guests as Seline did. Now that the poor girl was busy stuffing more cocasa down her throat than Akaran ever had, that left the more delicate patients to her and her alone.

And she'd missed the damn wedding because of it.

She hadn't missed the magical thunderstorm, however. *That* would've been impossible. Even if you ignored the fact that you could see thunderbolts *falling from the sky* almost *directly below the lip of the basin*, every blast sent raging ripples of ether through the air. There wasn't a single person in the Manor that hadn't felt it or been affected by it.

The only saving grace, as far as she was concerned, was that she wasn't wading through puddles of mud while trying to corral the woman who had decided to pretend she was some kind of chaos-goblin at two candlemarks past midnight. "Appaidene, please! You know that this is when all of the guests of our home are to be in bed!"

"DOLL!"

It wasn't, however, completely lost on her that the poor girl had managed to form a word. It was only one word, and hearing it repeated every five seconds wasn't doing anything for anyone's nerves, but it was progress. "Girl, this is not the time. We can come out again once the sun rises," Ridora pleaded. Then, quietly and to herself, added, "After I have the fool that didn't lock the doors flung off of the top of the Falls…"

No response followed, but she had to keep going. It was by sheer luck (at least) that the girl had left a trail that one could spot half-blind and exhausted even if all you had was a poorly-cut torch in one hand and a bag of sweets in another. Food worked to collect the wayward child at times.

At this point, she would've settled for a leash.

For one brief moment, Ridora realized that the sky was darker than it had any right to be, time of night be damned. It was the damned that had turned the night pitch black, and the cold finger on the back of her neck was her next warning of what was to come. Her next, and her last.

A claw bit into her flesh with practiced ease as shadows swirled across her feet. The shifting darkness solidified for a heartbeat and tripped the Manor's overseer so roughly that her head spun from the impact from hitting the ground. *"Dolls are wonderful,"* the shadows themselves called out, *"and there will be plenty for her to play with – if you don't listen to me now."*

Blood trickled down the side of her temple when Ridora was finally about to push herself to her knees. She reached for her torch but in the time it took for her to lift it up, a wicked wind snuffed it out and blew back a cloud of soot into her eyes. The Lady coughed and sneezed, unable to focus her eyes on her assailant. "What… who… Appaidene?"

"A house full of little dolls. Walking, talking, mindless dolls. So many dolls in so big a house. If she can play with them, why can't I?" the shadows mocked with a cold tilt to their voice.

"Appaidene! WHERE IS SHE?!" the Manor's Lady screamed out into the void.

The void was only happy to answer her right back. The shadows *heaved* and the broken girl fell right in front of Ridora's face with a sickening wet *thud*. Her mouth had been plastered shut with a muddy, oily mass that made it impossible for her to breathe and her eyes were full of so much terror that they almost illuminated the sky on their own. *"I've loved to play games with her dolls,"* the darkness crooned, *"but we are now past the time for games."*

If that was supposed to do anything but infuriate her, the revelation failed. Ridora worked her hands together and flung her fingers out in a wide stroke with ether following in an intense, buffeting wave. "I am not some simple wretch to be intimidated," she shouted as the shadows whipped away and dispersed back into the nothingness from where they came and the air cleared once again, "if you think that parlor tricks in darkness will do anything to me!"

The shadows vanished, but the voice didn't. The *claw* didn't, and it sunk into her shoulder from behind so sharply and suddenly a second time that she pitched forward from the sudden stab. She screamed in agonized pain, inches away from Appaidene's eyes, as blood spurted up from the wound. Her right arm went completely numb as Annix's essence leaned in close. "*I don't play tricks,*" the voice crooned with an undercurrent of a purr below it. "*Yet there is much that can be done to you.*"

Appaidene tried to howl through the mass of mud and muck across her face and there was absolutely nothing that Ridora could do about it. The pain in her collarbone radiated down her back and she felt a gout of blood rushing across her dress. It was so deep and so bad that she could barely even get a single word out. "Why are you…"

"*Why am I doing this?*" the void asked. "*I wish to. I wish to, and I wish a thing from you. It will be a trade.*"

"A… a trade?" she gasped as she tried to push herself back away from her charge. "What could…"

"*Her life. Justice. I trade the one for the other.*"

"She's INNOCENT! She's done no wrong to you! Whomever you are!"

The voice behind her chortled. "*Oh you know who I am, Lady Ridora Medias,*" it taunted. "*You are not a stupid human woman. You are not stupid at all. She has done me no wrong – which is why you will give me justice to spare her life.*"

Ridora struggled back to her feet as her arm hung limply down at her side. She tried to turn, but the second that she did, the claws dug back into her arm and nearly sent her back to her knees. "Taking an innocent… it isn't justice… nobody's justice… not for an innocent."

"*She is less than I have ever been,*" the shapeless voice intoned, "*and those less than I or mine are not worth the thought. Do lambs cry for justice? Do fish? You are **beneath me** and thus do not matter. She is not worthy of tvastarian; no 'justice' as your kind calls it. She matters only because of her dolls – which is why she **is** the choice. Why she is **your** choice.*"

Her head started to spin from the blood loss and the pain in her back, and when she tried to will fresh magic into her remaining hand, another slash of razor-sharp and paper-thin blades across her spine stole the strength from her heart. "What... what is it. What is it you want from us?"

"From you only," it cautioned. *"I want tvastarian. To have, I need the one that stole my Zilyph. But she is not the only one to trespass against my House. I seek the one that has stolen my children. A crime even you can understand that is of sin – a crime this waste understands all too well, doesn't she?"*

Appaidene just sobbed. Sobbed broken, bitter tears as her mind tried to blank out what was going on. Her body curled up on itself as she lost herself in pain and fear and grief. "I can't *give* you anyone!" the Lady shouted. "I can't march them here!"

The darkness laughed again. *"Oh. No, no you can't. But what you can give – what you will? Access. I have lost a home thanks to the one that has stolen my brood. Before the moon rises once more, I know I will have lost a haven. I will have yours instead. An unsuitable trade, but I will demean myself to accept it."*

"My... the Manor? You want the Manor!?" she exclaimed in utter disbelief. "I can't give you the Manor any more than I can give you Appaidene's life! I will not trade one innocent for dozens!"

"Then you want more. More than a trade of doll-girl for doll-house. If you wish not to provide my brood with a stocked closet full of your own dolls, I will ask another concession."

The only thing more apparent than the pain on Ridora's face was the shock in her eyes. "You speak in riddles and you demand –"

"I DEMAND JUSTICE!" Annix screamed at the top of his etheric lungs. *"I **GIVE** opportunity for my justice to be **TEMPERED**. Accept my **BLESSING** of a lower price for your ilk to pay or **FEEL** what the **JUSTICE** of the elves truly is! **THAT** is the bargain I strike!"*

The ferocity of his words buffeted her body from every direction, and Appaidene shrieked in fresh terror as she reached out and desperately clutched at Ridora's ankles. The gunk around her lips sloughed off and she managed to make a single anguished cry of her own. "No doll! NO DOLL!"

Before the lady could answer, Annix leaned in close from behind her. *"I have watched you work for years, caretaker. One thing I know: Out of all of those in your home, you care for how your garden grows more than any other – except for one. Now your garden will grow and less and more now; for not all dolls are made of cloth,"* he whispered, *"some of made of the caretakers that serve the grass."*

As he spoke, Ridora heard a small rumble and watched a gasping, mud-covered face push it's way up from the dirt at her feet. Her jaw fell and she backed up as she watched the buried cretin start to push free. "Yannis… no… oh no…"

"*Those that pluck weeds may be buried beneath them, and I suspect that the loss of the caretaker of weeds is enough to ensure that I have your attention in full,*" the vampire whispered. "*He is not the only doll my child played with. He is one of many that waits to go to your house. How much faith do you have, Medias? How much faith do you have that your House is stronger than Mine? Give free or do not, I will have it. You will not live to warn if you say no — you will if you offer.*"

"If… if I surrender the Manor… you'll spare her? Spare them?"

"*I will spare except those that are due to me.*"

Ridora took a slow, shaking breath and tried to peer around the field to catch a glimpse of him. "You've slaughtered your way through my people. My friends. Ones I've loved. Why should I take your word? Why should I trust you?"

The shadows waited a moment to reply, and when they did, a single nail slipped down her spine to the top of her hips and cut through the fabric of her dress to draw even more fresh blood. "*I gain nothing from speaking lies to those beneath me. I offer truth for ease. For nothing more, for nothing else.*" Annix paused and after a moment added, "*Our people have taken much from each other. Are you truly ready to sacrifice more on such pathetic **human** notions as **trust**?*"

"I…" she began before the claw returned at the base of her neck. "No. Allow me to evacuate the Manor — and the safe travel of those within — and you will have domain over it."

"*Not all those within. You trade your House for the justice to befall two,*" the vampire whispered from all around her. "*You will not give the fool of one eye or the woman that stole from me a way of freedom, or your own bargain will be revoked.*"

The Lady nodded slowly and felt her knees start to give. "I suspect it's more than opening a door."

"*Wise in your own foolishness. There is a spell. I shall grant it to you,*" he intoned. "*Place it, and place a seal of your blood upon it. Your life, theirs, and the life of this one will all be spared from what is to come.*"

"Spoken as a prideful beast," she challenged slowly. "From what's to come, or from witnessing your fall?"

"*Of neither,*" Annix replied. "*Those your words strike true. I cautioned that passage **safe** would come with a cost. You ask me to trade food from the brood of my child for safety of the madness of your flock. Taking from them to give to yours **is** a thing of trade. There must be an even balance.*"

Ridora shook her head slowly. "I do not suspect that you know of anything that would be of balance. You are not human enough to understand the concept."

He laughed at her with that same slow, horrible laugh that made Appaidene cry even harder. *"I will never demean myself to be so low as to be human. But I grant the passage. In return? You speak of pride, as a woman with more than most. I see that in you."*

Lady Ridora tensed up but steeled herself for whatever horrible offer he was about to demand. "I am a woman of means. I am a woman that has taken her mark on the world and done what can be done to ease the suffering of others."

"A goal of admiration. We do as we must to serve those of our own. That, I will not take. Yet I shall take away the way that the world looks at the pride upon your face."

When his claws reached her lips, she screamed.

She didn't stop screaming until she passed out.

Appaidene's screams never would.

***

"Ah. Overseer? I hate to wake you at such an ungodly hour, but let's be honest: neither one of us are Godly men," Riorik said aloud from the corner of Hannock's bedroom.

Even if his voice hadn't held a bleeding edge to it, the fact that he was there was enough to drag the city Overseer out of a sound sleep – and to make him bolt upright in his four-poster bed. "What... who? YOU?! What are you doing here – in my house?! I'll have your head! GUAR –"

The thief cleared his throat with a bemused cough. "I'll save you some time: they're taking a break. We have time to talk."

"I will *not* have a conversation with *you* in my *bedroom*," Hannock hissed. "I will see you at your trial."

"Mine? Or yours?" the thief asked as he carefully lit a candle. "Because if you promise to threaten people with a beheading, you best be sure that your head and mine won't be in the same basket."

"Are you *mad*? I'm the duly-appointed Overseer of Basion City! I have full faith of the Queen in my Contract of Governance and I have done no wrong."

Riorik shook his head 'no' as he made a faint 'tisk-tisk' sound of disapproval. "Come now. What you are is greedy. You don't need to be dishonest around *me*, of all people. I'm neither the Guard or the Justiciar.

We both know that's a blatant lie."

"What possible reason –"

"Smuggling," the thief interrupted. "Of the human variety, mainly."

The comment struck an obvious nerve. A thin sheen of sweat magically appeared across Hannock's forehead as he looked over at the dagger on his bedside table… or where his dagger should've been. Riorik flashed a small smile and opened his vest to show where the silver-hilted blade had gone. "I don't… I don't have any idea what you could possibly mean."

"Again, a lie," the balding man replied with a shrug. "Though I must say I am unsurprised. Allow me then to spell it out for you – you can correct me where I'm wrong, but I do refer you to my title if you decide to continue your denials."

Hannock took the hint. "Whatever you want to say, say it. Then get the thundering pits out of my city while you can."

"I would like to. But you cannot start a negotiation without having your chips on the table. When I arrived in your humble, low-built city, the very first thing I did was *listen*. You can't act without knowing what you have to act on, and despite my more immediate interest in a mutual acquaintance of ours, finding the lay of the land was just as important. I was very dismayed to discover a problem with missing people – people that men like you wouldn't care a whit about either way."

"People come and go. A few sods from Naradol go missing, and the city is less a few moochers," the Overseer grumbled dismissively.

"People do, yet people leave a void when they leave. A void you seemed to be happy to keep expanding," Riorik countered. "You didn't attempt to work with the Shiverdine even when he came calling with Queen-granted permissions. You made a different deal, didn't you?"

The lumbering noble pushed his blanket off and rolled to his feet. "I make deals all the time. But not with slavers."

Riorik nodded his head. "Slavers, no. Caravans, yes. Farmers, yes. Lonely fishermen along the coast, undoubtedly. I doubt that a single person you traded traveled out of the province."

"Are you accusing me of selling women?" Hannock growled.

"Yes, but I hadn't specified women. Yet. Blondes though, isn't it? We found some of your forgotten stock back in the caves."

The Overseer blinked in brief bewilderment. "This is the Kingdom of Dawnfire. Blonde women are a crown a barrel," he said dismissively. "Who would trade for brunettes? Of course I assumed you meant women."

"The thing is, of course, that it was more than just young blonde maidens or slightly-less young blonde mothers that kept vanishing. That would make it too easy to detect – patterns and all that, you know. What you did was to make a deal with someone that could promise you a steady supply – and dispose of random witnesses or complaintants. I simply can't understand why. I suspect it has something to do with... oh, her name. Yes. Lady Hosheck. Sannah Hosheck, yes? Your assistant. Former, of course, may the Pantheon take pity upon the woman she once was."

"She is a wonderful woman and you'll speak no ill of her in my presence."

"She's a dead woman, twice over, and you know it. Before the second death she was a liaison for the very son of a bitch that you've been working with – I expect the two are much one and the same, aren't they?"

"She's missed."

Riorik snorted and rolled his eyes. "I bet she is. So you don't deny knowing what she was?"

Hannock gave the thief a furious glare. "The Kingdom is inclusive. Not everyone in the Queen's graces is human. She never inflicted harm or threatened my life or the lives of those around me. Who am I to judge that which only the Gods truly understand?"

"Who indeed," the other man replied with a cold grunt. "I would say you are someone who found a friend in low places. He helped you find a disposable source of income – and you found someone that could help you with your vagrant problem."

The Overseer's brow furrowed. "Even if I did, you cannot have any proof."

"Maybe I don't. Or maybe, your dearly departed – and then later painfully burnt to vampire ash – Lady Hosheck kept records. Maybe she kept names. Maybe she kept *long, detailed journals* listing every person that went through the caves and into your pocket," Riorik challenged. "*Just* the ones that went into your pocket, of course. She wouldn't want to hold evidence against her real master."

"And who do you think would believe such a fictitious document even if it did exist? She's been proven to have been an enemy of the Crown."

"An enemy of the crown you've been entertaining and working side by side with, yes?"

The Overseer waved his hand dismissively. "Have you listened to those Oo-lo cocks? They hide among us. How should I know what they are? Who they are? I'm no mage."

The chuckle that came from the thief was far from in good humor. "Cocks, yes they are. Ones that do not know the meaning of the word no. Cocks that I am, unfortunately for you, on very good terms with. I don't have to *prove* anything. I just have to give them good ideas of what to look for."

Hannock's face darkened even further, if that was possible. "What exactly do you think you know?"

"All I've said. I suspect that your personal operation was discovered by the vile little bloodsucker, and he decided to make friends in high places. The two of you crafted a deal — you'd keep the city disinterested, he'd have some reign to feed, and you'd continue to obtain merchandise. You can tell me if I'm wrong *but* I'd even wager that you were getting part of your work by way of arrangements with The Gambling Mind and Instructor-Adept Odern, given the number of Granalchi sigils with his name scribbled in them all over the caves."

That thin sheen of sweat blossomed into a full-scale stream. "Even if you were right, I wouldn't tell you. That would be suicide if he came to believe..."

"True. It's all very droll though, I must admit. A man in power is bribed by a monster. Women go missing. Few people care. You make coin. Get your dick sucked by some desperate girl or five looking for a better life before she was... hm? Shipped to a farm, sent beyond Lowmarsh to the League? Please — enlighten me. Give me a reason that is entertaining. Storybook, even."

"What do you expect me to say? This city attracts worthless bottom-feeders. You know as well as I that if someone isn't going to *buy* a product, then they *are* the product. I find employment for those not willing to pay for product of their own."

The Master Thief couldn't stop his lip from curling up. "I can only imagine what type of pay you accepted," he spat before he let the emotion drop from his face. "That is an answer that is as disappointing as it is expected, yet somehow still surprising. So you were merely bought by promise of even more coin? Livstra and Odern — did they know? Did they contract with you, or did they contract with your conspirator?"

"You tell me. You seem to know everything."

"I know most. I don't claim everything. I suppose in the end it doesn't matter, as dead *is* dead but yet. It would bother me if I was without idea."

Hannock curled his fat upper lip. "Sannah never told me the name of the person behind her arrangement. He had needs. He had means. He needed a place to conduct our work in private. I invested in his success — that is part of the Contract of Governance issued by the Crown. To ensure the *financial* success of those in the Kingdom."

"So they didn't. They worked and traded through you without knowing who gave the coin. That's... well. Professionally, I cannot gripe so loud over the nature of the business my predecessor was in if she had no ultimate idea the roots behind it. The trade in flesh I understand, almost respect. The vampire? Surely you had to have some knowledge as to what he is, even if they purportedly didn't."

"The Kingdom welcomes all kinds of people. Someone makes an offer to help rid the city of the undesirable, and I am obliged to take it. 'Ensure that the city remains prosperous' is in the contract. I found a way to ensure that people would lead a better life – elsewhere – and honored my oath to the Blackstone Trading Company and Queen alike."

"A better life for the ones that lived," Riorik chided. "I presume that you didn't bother to check the working conditions of the ones that passed through your little scheme, did you?"

"Product is product. What happens after it is purchased or otherwise acquired is not a concern of the supplier."

The thief snorted quietly. "I presume you also feel that it's acceptable for *product* to get damaged in the warehouse?"

"It happens," he answered dismissively. "I was assured that there would be no harm to the people of Basion that mattered. The ones that were claimed weren't even *people.* There wasn't a use for them in the walls, nor was there a market for them on the out. The city was made better for it."

"Until recently."

Hannock gave the Master Thief a bemused smirk. "You of all people should know that crime occurs even in the safest of places. I didn't look the other way. Others more *qualified* to hunt a monster took the task."

"I suspect that if the monster-hunters had ever sniffed in your direction, you had ways to defend yourself, yes? Or quickly leave for places southern of the border?"

"If I had done a wrong – yes. It's always a wise idea for a businessman to have a way out no matter the cause, of course."

"A pity that it took a thief, and not a hunter, to find you first." The balding, self-professed 'friend' to those that treated him well smiled with a twinkle in his eyes that was from more than just the candlelight. "Simply put, I have an offer. I even wrote it out," he clarified as he handed a tightly-rolled scroll over.

Hannock took it and started to read it in silence. He made it about halfway down the page before he threw it on the floor and stood up in an angry huff. "This is...! What is the meaning of this... this... piece of shit?"

"It's straightforward," Riorik replied with a shrug. "Buy me out. I haven't been around here long so I don't have as much of a vested interest in this city as you do. You already know that I am more than capable of providing results when they're needed, so the last thing I would think someone with your level of exposure would want to do is to continue to have me around. Buying me out is the simple solution to your problem, and far less risky than trying to have me killed."

"You don't own anything in this city! I've *looked*! The Blackstones have no record of sale of land to you, the city has nothing in the recent logs and I certainly haven't offered you an inch of the cliff wall. Buy out *what*?"

"You can buy more than land and you can possess more than physical holdings. The latter of which I *do* own but if you think I would have done it under my own name then you are truly more misguided than I thought. That paper expressly lists every 'inch of cliff' I own, as you put it, and the other avenues I have access to."

Hannock leaned forward and gave the thief a low growl from the back of his throat. "You expect me to sign this piece of... lunatic drivel... and give you... *how many crowns*?"

The balding thief shrugged. "I cannot imagine how much money you made from dealing with the vampire or your deals with your buyers. I recognize this is more than a pittance but come now – we'd be both be insulted if I asked for less. You wouldn't even believe that the offer was sincere if I did."

"What guarantee do I have that you'd even honor your side of it?"

"No more than any businessman has. If I renege on my deals, what good am I? Nobody would wish to jump into contract with me again. Certain words travel further than others, you know," Riorik answered earnestly before adding a quick cautionary remark. "Others move *faster* even still. The choice is very clear-cut, isn't it?"

The Overseer wiped a droplet of spittle off of the corner of his mouth and read the parchment over again. "I... I will need time to verify your holdings."

"Of course you will. I also expect you need time to cover your tracks, hide some bodies. Maybe add to the pile at the Pyre," the thief agreed. "I would not take my time, were I you. As you're aware, the Order made quite the impression at the wedding. I assume that if they intend to move on your *former* partner, it will be soon, and you may still have some concerns to cover before that happens."

"That son-of-a-bitch has hid from the Oo-los for years. What makes you think they're going to do anything about him now?"

Before Riorik could answer, someone slammed their fist on the

Overseer's office door. "BOSS HOB! That asshole you're worried about? He's headed to the main gate. Boy has raw murder in his eye, and he's escorting some wench in a hood."

"Really? Is it a day that ends in -dis, or is there something new?"

"Think it might be the scorpion queen you mentioned. Her, the Headmaster, bunch of others. Watchers got a feeling that some shit is gonna go down."

"I see," he answered after a moment. The Hobbler pursed his lips and turned his attention back to Hannock. "Why do I think they're going to do anything about Annix now? Because unlike years past, they have a very violent dog in their kennel these days. I suspect he may be ready to slip his leash."

The Overseer did his best to take that much in stride. "Well. The world will be better off without him if they do."

"The world will, but I wonder if *you* will?" the thief asked with a raised eyebrow. "Sirrah, do understand: you live now because it's beneficial to me, even if I have not yet completely decided *how*. I would strongly advise that you develop the idea of how you can pay me back for such a kindness before the night is over."

"You can't do anything to me," he huffed. "Kill me, and the guards will have you hung."

"There are many fates worse than simply death, Overseer. You will find yourself not in the least shocked, I am sure, to realize that I know how to enact most of them. Plus, I may add, my time with that particular dog has shown me that what I don't know to do, the next world *does*."

Hannock didn't have an answer for that, and Riorik didn't wait for him to come up with one. If Akaran had murder in his eye and the scorpion witch in his hands, then whatever he intended to do? Well then.

The event obviously couldn't be missed.

***

"Anais. You wanted a chance to earn some favor with the Order? This is it," Akaran intoned as he pulled her hood off and let her enjoy the view of the ruined city.

The Merchant of Secrets had looked better. A lot better. The only color to the little skin she had left was a dead gray and the white strands of her hair could be counted on one hand. The Wardkeepers charged with keeping her imprisoned been kind enough to let her keep her hands, though they had been encased in iron mitts that kept her from even thinking about moving her fingers – and they'd been anchored behind her back for good measure. "How am I to do that? Admire the view of the city?"

Akaran didn't look much better. Edges of his hairline had been burnt, his limp was as bad as it had been when he'd first made it to Basion. The only positive was that he'd been given/stolen clean clothes to change into after the fight, ill-fitting as the gray and silver Stara vestments were.

She was right; the view was amazing. The city gate oversaw Hannock Bridge, the river that rolled under and around it, and the top battlements offered a perfect view of Yittl Canyon for as far as the eye could see. The pre-dawn sky was a soft shade of red with tinges of pink and orange sneaking around the heavy clouds above.

He ignored the barb and rolled his shoulders back. "We found a whole lot of fun stuff you had stored. Gotta be honest: the scribes *adore* you. They haven't had access to a full stock of necrosia reagents for a while."

"I have to keep it with me. It isn't like it's sold at a corner apothecary."

"Oh, *absolutely* not. We'd hang anyone we found selling half of it," Akaran replied with no hint of humor in his voice. "They were kinda pissed when I said you'd need it back."

"I'd need it back?" she asked as she slowly tilted her head. "For what purpose? Your people have made it quite clear that I'll never cast a spell against men again."

Akaran let his lips turn into a razor-sharp smile as he gestured at one of the guards he'd brought along. The trooper eagerly unloaded his satchel onto the parapet. The top of the gatehouse was big enough to put a full detachment of archers on with room for swordsmen – so their little cluster of nearly a dozen souls had more than enough room to set up their little question-and-answer session. "Then I have some good news for you – it's not against men. I need you to speak to someone for me."

She looked at the pile of candles and other ritual supplies with only a passing interest. "To speak to the dead, I need a dead person. I don't think you're willing to provide me someone fresh."

"Fresh, no. Provide you with one? Yes."

Anais didn't bother to hide her surprise. "You must be desperate then. Desperate men do many things for what they search for. What desperate things do you intend to do for me?"

"I'm not going to set you on fire and throw you off of the ramparts," the young priest countered. "We can start there and work forward."

The casual threat set her back when she realized how earnestly he meant it. He'd do it without a thought, and she knew it. It made her reconsider what she thought of the boy, although not kindly. "You're going to kill me anyway, aren't you?"

"Very likely. Do you want it to hurt or...?"

"Point taken," she muttered under her breath. "I don't see a body. Is it on the way or...?"

"It'll be ready. What do you need to do it?"

"I need to know what I'm doing first."

"Making a dead woman talk," Akaran replied. "Truthfully."

She scoffed and flicked her cold eyes at the pile. "That infernal wraith? She got tired of you, did she?" The dark look that clouded his face made her realize she'd just struck a nerve, though she decided to hold onto the thought for later. "Someone else, hmm?"

Akaran reached over and very calmly gripped her chin in his hand. "Can you do it or not?"

The broker ripped her head away from his hand and cut loose with a growl that made the guardsman behind him drop their hands to their swords in response. "Touch me again and find out what I can do."

He didn't even flinch, but he did lower his hand and give her a short not. "My apologies."

"Thank you," she replied slowly when she realized he actually meant it. "I can make the dead speak – truthfully even, yes. But I do need the body to force the soul."

"You'll have it, won't she, Telburn?"

The Headmaster stepped forward and nodded slowly. "One way or the other, I assume she'll have a corpse of sorts."

Anais looked him over – and he didn't look much better than the exorcist. He wasn't wounded, but he looked positively ragged and beaten down. "Curiouser and curiouser. You've been getting into bed with all manner of interesting people recently, haven't you?"

Akaran snorted a laugh and leaned in to whisper just loud enough for her to hear. "I assume you know what'll happen if you try to fisk around after your binds come off?"

"I think you've left little to the imagination."

"Then imagine worse."

The broker looked into his eyes, and what he saw in hers made him take a step back. "I don't have to. I have memories."

That was all that needed to be said. A few minutes later, and the iron bands around her wrists were carefully removed and the dampening collar around her neck unfastened and set aside. Not that she was working unguarded – far from it.

Henderschott had demanded to be present; a cost of having the 4th present. Telburn had to come along, of course, for obvious reasons. The Maiden-Templar had refused to allow Anais out of her makeshift lockdown without a heavy presence from the Order, so Karaj had volunteered to come along, as had Hadraie.

Further, they forced Anais to make a couple of concessions of her own for her newfound 'freedom.' Two of the guards had brought up a heavy wooden post that was set onto the stone roof and roughly nailed to the first exposed wooden joist they could find. From there, a long chain was hauled over and wrapped firmly around her throat.

As expected, her protests were frequent and mixed between quiet mutters and outright insults. It did absolutely no good, but she tried. She was, however, filled with a great deal of disquiet about the *other* chain that was attached to the post – and the lack of any other readily available person to attach it to.

The net result was a crowd full of people ready to cut someone's head off in the pre-dawn hours and their entire group was enough to make the gate guards below collectively soil themselves at their arrival. Their terror, however, had nothing on the last guest who was about to make her appearance. Once Anais had her preparations completed, it was time for the Headmaster to do his part.

And his part he did.

As the crowd formed a circle around the broker and the enchantment she'd painstakingly drawn out on the stone rooftop, Telburn stepped up and began to etch a spell of his own in the air with the tips of his fingers. When he finished, a glowing doorway hung freely over the gatehouse. He stepped back as a trio of wardkeepers stepped forward with pikes firmly in hand – and Akaran with a burning ball of light in his.

Hadraie came over and made sure to put an extra hand on Anais's chain while Karaj made a show of preparing for a fight. Telburn uttered an invocation under his breath and swing his arms open. As he did, the gateway split open in the empty air. The broker's eyes went wide as the mage's shrieking, terrified prisoner fell out of the dimensional pocket and onto the rough-shapen bricks and planks of wood.

Sherril did everything she could to get away from them. Her desperate scrambles with her wrists bound behind her back and her feet slick with fresh blood – from where, they didn't know – made it next to impossible for her to get up off of the ground. The wardkeepers made it even harder as they moved almost as one to slam the tips of their halberds into her back and legs to pin her down.

Karaj had the chain around her neck and fastened to the anchor post before Anais could make complete sense of everything going on. Once she was secured, the Order soldiers wouldn't let up and they kept her pinned to the roof with their blades.

It wasn't until she managed to lock eyes on Akaran that she turned strangled noises into actual words. "NO NEVER AGAIN NEVER NOT THERE PLEASE DON'T!"

The exorcist ignored the terror in her eyes and passed summary judgment without a second thought. "Sherril Inyadine. You are guilty of murder, torture, kidnapping, theft, and other crimes against the Crown and the people under the Queen's protection," he declared aloud even as she continued to scream at him. "Under normal circumstances, the sentence would be carried out quickly. These times are not normal," he added before he finished with a cold, flat, "and neither are you."

"No trial?" Anais asked from behind him. "I'd hoped to get to see how you have one."

"You say that like you expect one," he shot back at her. "Don't."

Sherril shook her head violently and struggled against the halberd blades as much as she could. "Can't say won't say anything! Don't send me back there *please* don't send me back there! Never Abyss, never again!"

"Oh, honey, no," the broker chided. "That wasn't the pit. I don't know where that was but that wasn't it. Akaran — why am I here? How did you hide her away...? *Where* did you...?"

"Worlds..." the other woman whispered. "I saw them. So many worlds. So many places. I can't... I can't see them again... I'm not... I can't..."

"In the Veil," Telburn replied as she writhed against the rooftop. "I warned you she might not come out sane."

The young priest shrugged and pulled her up to her knees as the wardkeepers adjusted themselves. "I don't need her sane. Besides, doesn't seem like anyone else in this damn city is either. What do you suggest — that I take her to the Manor when we're done?"

"I think you need to tell me exactly what you want me to do, you Oo-lo *freak*," Anais stressed. "I told you that this spell only works on the dead."

"Oh you didn't realize?" he asked as he forced Sherril to look at Nastavol's minion. "Lady Lovic. I'd like you to meet the vampire that took Donta's arm." As Anais's jaw slowly fell open, he continued the introduction with an angry smirk. "Leech? Meet the... golem... that's going to take some words out of your mouth."

Anais covered her mouth with her hands and looked back and forth between them. "First, I am no golem. Second? You're mad. You are utterly aware of this immutable truth, aren't you?"

He ignored her. "Before you can object: it seems like vampires take a special pride in not being considered *alive*. They brag about how they aren't human anymore and they've gone beyond our limitations," he argued without a care of kindness in the world. "Order spells that work on reanimated dead seem to do just fine on their kind and enough lore's scattered around that suggest the same from other Gods, too."

"I will assume that you know that necrosia does not necessarily require the blessings of the Gods to work, yes? Vampires are the lowest of the low and hated by things of all rank and file of the next world as much as they are of this. I would imagine that even the vomit from a *chinikari* would cause them distress," she argued.

"Possible," he admitted. "Very possible. Except we don't *have* a chinikari and she won't... can't... tell us what we need. Her Meister has her on a short leash and he already tried to choke her to death with it once. She has answers I need and I'm willing to work with you to get it."

"Working with me implies that I have a choice."

"True. You don't."

Anais gave the priest a scathing glare from her dead, marbled-over eyes. "Care to wager? I won't do this."

Akaran bristled at the dead woman and pulled a simple steel shortblade from his hip. "Do you want to take her place? That can be arranged."

She shifted on her feet and slowly shook her head from side to side. "Do you... do you understand where I've been? What I've done?"

"We keep finding evidence –" he started before she cut him off.

"Not... here," Anais replied slowly as her voice shrank to a whisper. "There. Down *there*. I wasn't *born* into this body. I was *returned* into it. *Given* it. I was *returned* from *elsewhere*."

Karaj stepped over to the arguing pair and crossed their arms. "We assumed as much. A Black Resurrection of some kind. Knowing that you've been *elsewhere* –"

"I was from... somewhere. Somewhere before *then*. I went *there*," she stressed as she pointed up at the exorcist. "He knows. I could see it in the burned woman he kept as a pet. She showed you everything, didn't she? What awaits for those that fail the Gods?"

"Rmaci let me see enough," he flatly stated. "Enough for me to offer you kindness in your fate even after all you've done."

She huffed and cracked her neck. "Oh, there was plenty of *kindness* there, but none shown to a sinner. I spent my time – years. Centuries. Time doesn't matter there so whatever you think? Define it any way you wish. Atrocity to atrocity. Scream to scream. I spent my time serving the cousin of your Goddess. She had *tasks* for me."

"Cousin?" Akaran mouthed over to Karaj.

Catherine's assistant frowned deep enough for the younger priest to finally be able to see the bottom of their face. "A poor fate it is," they whispered back. "to be given to the Goddess of Lust."

"Her *Citadel* in the pit," Anais went on as she ignored the interruption. "The grandest. Well. Grandest only compared to Greshelda. Envy can't have anything less than the Others," Anais went on to admit. "Ava would… give me tasks. My tasks were to groom new arrivals for Her service. It was… not 'kind,' as you so put it."

"It's damnation," the exorcist grumbled. "I don't think the Gods want it to be pleasant."

She laughed weakly while Sherril squirmed under the halberds holding her down. "No… no they do not. I… I would groom new toys for the Queen of Lust. Prepare them. Deliver them. I did my time as Her plaything. I was returned to this world with the scars earned in Her service as a reminder."

"The point, woman," Karaj growled. "Assuming you have one."

Anais tilted her head up and tried to peer at their constantly-hooded head. "While the Queen gorged Herself on the desires of Her newest playthings, I would be sent to the dogs. I would be made to watch. I would be made to entertain Her guests when She wasn't present. It was part of Her *celebration* of sin. I wasn't the first. I won't be the last. She used us and made us an extension of Her will and threw us out when She grew tired of us."

"That doesn't –" Akaran began.

The broker stomped her foot as hard as she could and pointed a shaking finger at the vampire. "She speaks, you kill her, she burns. Then she burns more. She burns eternal. I will *not* groom another woman for the pit. Not for Avasharti, not for Nastavol, and not for *you*. I will *not* force her to speak unless you give me your word you will not execute her. I have killed men as I must but I will *not* subject another *woman* to the after."

"You're asking me not to destroy a dead thing," the exorcist countered. "And you call me mad?"

"I am a liv… well… *walking* example that you can choose who you kill and when. Execute her if you wish but you will not do so with my help. You want her tongue? Then spare her life." Anais fidgeted as she spoke but she kept her back straight and her stance firm.

Akaran took a deep breath and looked around the rooftop. All eyes had gone to the trio, although most of them were trying *very very hard* to pretend they couldn't hear the dreadful truths the dead woman was offering. "Then we'll kill you both," he finally decided.

The utter ease of how he made the proclamation broke her resolve on the spot. "Kill...? No. You need me," she countered. "I know things. Things about my deals, things about your brother, things about –"

"First, don't call him my brother. I don't know who he is or why he wants me. I have no family."

"You *do*, and that's a thing you need me for. If other people won't tell you, *I* will. You can't kill me. You would give up your own heritage if you do." As she spoke, the look on Karaj's face moved from bemused irritation to cold fury. The broker noticed it, even as the exorcist didn't.

"Anais, listen," he replied slowly as he started to pick his words carefully. "I don't have a lot of options here. *Maybe* you know things I *might* want to know. But I *know* she knows things I *need* to know. Right now, the more immediate threat is her Meister. The time she has left on this world can be measured in heartbeats."

"Then you –"

The exorcist shut her down with a cold stare. "*You* are an abomination. A sentient one, but an abomination. I have very few options on what to do with you. You tortured one of my friends. You played me as a fool. You've admitted to murder. You're never going to be a free woman again and the only tools the Order has to compel you of your own free will is to either offer you the Exorcist's Forgiveness or as painless a destruction as we can. Since we both know where you're headed on the latter, I doubt *painless* has much influence. So – that means I have to hope that your time *elsewhere* has given you enough cause to want to stay *here* as long as you possibly can. So which is it? Life in a storage closet somewhere and chained to the wall or an existence where you don't want to be?"

Anais licked her dry, cracked lips as she watched him stroke the edge of his shortblade over and over again. "I notice you didn't offer the absolution."

"Because you wouldn't have meant it if you had agreed to take it," he replied with a shrug of his shoulders. "She's dead either way. Not walking-corpse dead. *Dead and gone* dead. She's not leaving this rooftop. You can join her in that, or you can help save some lives by making her talk and endear yourself ever-so-slightly to the people that make the decisions about what to do with you." Akaran looked down at his sword and shrugged a second time. "Might buy you a slight reprieve in the pit. Might not. Can't hurt."

"I will not send another woman to go through what I went through. I will not. I will not be a party to it. You may end my existence now if you wish but I will not return to Avasharti's Palace with that sin on my shoulders."

"There are other ways to compel you," Karaj threatened. "You are a dead thing. Dead things can be commanded by the Goddess to do as told. I imagine it is not a comfortable experience if we invoke those spells."

The broker scoffed at the Order follower. "You would rape my mind as the Queen of Lust would rape my soul? Your Goddesses truly are cousins. Nor is that the case because if you truly could you'd do it to that wench and leave me out of the equation! Do you even know what a vampire *is*? I think you don't!"

"Then tell me," Akaran growled. "Help me understand."

"They… it is not… clean," she began with a slight tremor, "once drained? Once murdered, and left empty? The soul is gone. It crosses. A void remains."

"Don't tell me she doesn't have a soul," the exorcist interrupted. "We *know* they have an essence. We can see it in the ether."

She shook her head slightly. "What you see is the essence that fills the void. Not a true spirit, not a soul. An essence of basest impulse. The curse of The First Fang fills the shell where the soul had once been; it allows for the energies of the after to take root. It becomes a *copy* of the person, but *not* the person. The curse of the First is itself a parasite; it is the shadow of a Demi-God that burns eternal over the realm of His Father."

"So you're having this argument over something that isn't even… human?"

Anais gave him a withering look. "You say that as if being human is the requirement to have a soul! Her soul is gone but *this essence* will be tormented and tortured just the same! It isn't the soul it had in life but it *is* a creation of the Fallen that will be punished for *existing* as such by the Will of the Warden. Don't you see? You cannot offer her absolution and you cannot do anything but condemn her to eternity! She murders people, yes, but what you do is a fate to her that is far worse!"

"It is no different than the fate that the Gods —"

"The *Gods* decide who among the mortal suffer or not," the broker argued. "The *Gods* decreed that creatures such as she *will* burn in the Light of Wrath the *moment* they cross the veil! There is no chance, no chance that an idiot like you or her or *them* have for absolution once she is removed from this world. It is a *promise* of what her fate is. You send her to that fate out of some perverse notion of what is right and wrong and you are no better than she – maybe even less!"

A quiet scuffle broke out at the entrance to the stairwell near their gathering, and the Master Thief of Basion stepped onto the roof. "Oh yes, the intractable good versus evil debate. How droll. Neither of you can give an inch. I assume you need her to do something and she's balking – yes? Fine. Anais? Listen closely."

"To a thief? Why should I bother?" she shot at him.

"Because I *am* a thief, and you are a prideful woman. Pride is a thing that I can steal; and I have had much experience with that. In the time it has taken me to begin to dismantle your operations, I've come to realize that your network expands far past Basion and has tendrils embedded into organizations as far as Civa Prime to Ameressa to Ogibus Bay," he offered. "I had intended to ignore it for the most part, but I think you're quite proud of your legacy. I promise you this: the Order may kill you. The Order will kill her. I? What will I do, you may wonder?"

Anais took a deep breath and looked at him with fresh and dawning horror. "You're just a man and beneath my concern. I make a promise of my own: that the one I work for will have you dismembered over the course of years, should you cross him."

"Oh I am just a man but I know how the Crown will react to the tidbits of information I plan to feed them. If I can't rip out the adorable empire of secrets you've tried to create and burn it to the ground, they can. And I will do that. Every. Single. Last. One. Every ally you've made, every deal you've taken, every arrangement. Every recruit. Every person you've ever had an interaction with – alive *or* dead – will either bend their knee to me or bend their neck to the Crown. There's another avenue to explore, too," he added with a smile.

"If you think undoing my works is enough..."

He slightly shook his head in denial. "It isn't. Yet there is a truth among thieves. When sent to prison, we are not fond of the people that sent us there. I have no ability to offer absolution so let us assume that there's quite a few people that will die with my name on their lips – half-truths, of course – who will have cause to blame you for whatever state they find themselves in when they arrive in their individual places of perdition. How many of them do you think will welcome you with open arms as they writhe in their own torment? I can't say I know how the workings of the Abyss truly are carried out but I expect..."

Silence reigned between the two of them while Akaran and Karaj just watched on. Finally, eventually, Anais bowed her head in slight supplication as the fight left her. "You must understand why I don't want to be part of her execution."

"I do," Akaran admitted. "In recent months, I've come to understand the gravity of what we're about to do."

"You don't."

"Maybe," he replied after a moment. "But I cannot undo the truth. Sherril has massacred dozens. She's not *human* and never will be again. Even now, she holds to the demon that created her. As we talk, he's actively hunting for people to kill and feed. Or if not hunting, plotting. They are going to keep killing and they won't be stopped. We have no other option but to put her down."

Anais looked up at him and then to Telburn. "The… wherever you had her. Can't you stick her back in it? It would be an improvement to the pit. I swear it would."

Telburn shuddered in revulsion. "I would strongly suggest to think of another option. She's already gone mad from it."

"Can you not… bury her in a box somewhere? Entomb her? Keep her from ever being seen again?" she pleaded. "You've offered that kindness to me. Anything but kill her. Please. Say you won't, and I will help."

"I'd almost think that alone would be horrifying itself," Akaran muttered under his breath. "Karaj? Can we?"

The Lover mulled it over and finally slid their blades back into the sheaths at their hip. "It would take planning and arrangements. We don't have much time left to argue and this must be done before the sun crests over the lip of the basin. Yes, if that's what it will take."

Anais swallowed nervously even as Riorik's face darkened. Sherril had given up struggling by this point, and just simply kept her head down. Hadraie heard her begging in a near-silent prayer for help, begging for an end, but most importantly, begging to never be put in the Veil again. Some of the words she said weren't of mortal tongue, let alone Queen's Common. Wherever she'd learned them, the Wardkeeper didn't want to find out.

The broker bowed her head slightly and sighed. "Will you hold it against me if it doesn't work?"

Akaran answered with a blank look that said it all, but Karaj had an idea of their own. "Consider this; if not her fate, yours. As you said – vampires are the lowest of the low and reviled below the ether as they are above it. Wouldn't undoing the plans of one – and aiding in the banishment of one of his children – earn you a reduction of the weight upon your neck in the below?"

She sighed a second time and sank down to her knees by the spellcircle. "Can she bleed? I'll need some from her. It is a requirement for the spell, I assure you."

"Yes, can she?" Riorik asked as he stepped out onto the rooftop. "More importantly, do you need help doing it?"

"Thief," Karaj growled. "This is neither the time nor the place for you."

"I would profoundly disagree. I have done nothing but show kindness to your people, and now I ask that you show the same to me. Whatever you're doing that involves this bitch and that bitch together?" he asked as he pointed between the undead women in turn, "Well. I would very much say it involves me."

Catherine's assistant gave him a murderously dark look, but Akaran shut them both up. "Not now. We don't have a lot of time," he warned. "You want blood?" he asked the broker. "Then you've got it."

Before anyone could offer a quipped retort or smart-assed remark, the priest had his blade pressed to Sherril's chest and a moment later, into her heart. Steel wouldn't inflict a mortal wound unless he lopped her head off, but it did draw plenty of blood, and if he was lucky, it'd hurt.

She screamed in raw agony as the steel pierced through her ribs and into the black-blooded chunk of muscle nestled under her bones. For a fleeting moment, he worried about enjoying the look of suffering on her face. After he pulled his sword back out and let her slump to the ground on her side, he decided not to care.

Anais went to work without any further argument. The callous thrust shut her up and turned any actual words that the battlemage tried to get out into unintelligible gibberish. The broker scooped up as much of the flowing black gore as she could with an old pewter cup as she ignited the handful of candles scattered across the rooftop.

Preparations completed, the monstrous Merchant of Secrets rolled back onto her heels and began to call out a steady invocation. "*That which is dead but not dead, alive but not alive, awake but asleep, I call on you to speak,*" she whispered.

The candles flared with brilliant green flames that created a hip-high wall around the enchantment's circle. Sherril seized up and bared her collar-covered throat to the sky as matching sparks of fire jutted out from under and around the iron shackle. "CAN'T SPEAK MEISTER WON'T –"

"I'm not interested in what he'll let you do," Akaran snarled at her so violently that a small bit of foamy spittle seeped out of the corner of his mouth. "You'll speak for her or you'll speak to the sun!"

"*That which is dead but not dead, alive but not alive, awake but asleep,*

I call on you to speak," Anais repeated. *"Speak of truths known; speak of lies not; speak of what is real; speak of what is bidden; speak of what is not!"*

Sherril screamed again and arched her back so violently it thrust her sternum to the sky and her arms straight down to the ground. "HE BIDS ME TO STAY SILENT!"

"He has no power over the truth of the Abyss! The ABYSS holds your soul's tongue and I hold the Tongue of the Pit!" the broker howled in return as her mouth opened and a snake-like chunk of meat slithered out over her chipped teeth and probed the air. "I DEMAND YOUR SOUL SPEAK!"

Henderschott took one look at her, turned around, and threw up.

"Love demands your submission, unholy *thing*," Karaj snarled. "Speak truth and be *judged*."

The green flames arced up in the air around her a second time as a heavy pink glow settled across her skin from the Lover's edict. A wall of coal-black smoke erupted from her face and briefly took the form of a screaming man with red eyes and pointed ears before it faded into nothingness. Once it left her body, she stopped struggling and her head slumped forward.

Sherril stood on her feet with her shoulders bent and head hung down like a doll with her strings cut. When she finally spoke, her voice was monotone and empty of emotion and pain. *"The damned only speak in suffering."*

"They do if you're going to have that attitude about it," Anais replied with a huff. "Ask your questions, exorcist; her soul has regained agency over her Meister's compulsion. For the moment. *This* soul has the knowledge of the body, even if the Curse of the First wishes it not to."

Akaran didn't need the encouragement. "Sherril Inyadine. I need to know where Annix is."

"I cannot tell you where he is, for I do not know."

"Then come up with a good idea."

The battlemage shuddered and twisted as she tried to fight the bonds of the spell, the chain, and the other wards around her. *"He watches every night. He is smarter than you. Wants to embarrass you. Has allies across this world you cannot even dream of. He's existed for centuries, and you? Existed for less than two decades? You expect to bring him low?"*

The broker slowly rubbed her hands together and interrupted the priest before he could yell at the vampire. "Be specific. She's bound to speak the truth as she knows it, and as the Abyss will allow her. The Abyss *loves* the truth, but it also loves to be as vague about it as you can let it. Better to ask, say – Sherril? Where is Annix's lair?"

With a pained jerking twitch, the battlemage twisted her head up yet let her shoulders continue to hang. "*He rests his head in a myriad of places. The caves behind the place where the river weeps. The forest – not the once-home of Flynn. Yet near enough to be found with shovel by hovel. And with the Preparer of the Flesh.*"

"The woods?" Henderschott repeated before he made an angry, disgusted noise in the back of his throat. "I'm about to burn the forest down, aren't I?"

"Yeap," Akaran muttered. "The Preparer of the Flesh. Who is that? What is their name – where is it?"

The vampire quaked and warred with herself. She tried to keep her mouth shut but only managed to gnaw a hole in her lip as the invocations forced her to respond. "*It is in the place you call Lower Naradol. She was once said as Pramidi. She is not now. She is his.*"

"Karaj? You know that place?"

"I do," Riorik growled softly. "Anais, you do as well. She owns a tannery."

The broker looked at him and tried to ignore the half a dozen pairs of eyes that suddenly had her in their sight. "I did not know that he was that close."

"What'd I miss?" Akaran asked, bewilderment on his face.

"It's barely a block away from where we apprehended this deceitful necromancer," Karaj remarked. "She knew where he was all along, didn't she?"

"I did *not*," Anais protested. "Had I, do you think I would have attempted to hide there? I promise, the only reason I chose that warehouse was because it was close to the river. It was an easy exit, had one been needed."

"She's speaking truth," the thief replied. "At least about attempting to use the river as an exit. But I suspect now that Annix had his eyes on us the entire time when we collected her. I saw the extent of magics that your soldiers used – how did they *possibly* miss it?"

Sherril quaked in her bloody boots and answered before she could stop herself. "*How? By magic old. Magic of chaos. Chaos melds with the magic of Order. Madness exists only in the eyes of the sane. Mixed in blood. Bathed in life after life. A haven buried in chaos and bathed in blood; if you did not search for peace, you would not have found the chaos. Search for chaos itself, and you miss what it gives it strength. The magic of chaos would have hid in the wake of ether of peace, no matter the form. To mix the two? That is the way of elves and their manipulation of the eddies of the ether."*

"Because we… we didn't look for what his magic was rooted in, we couldn't find it? Is that what you're telling us?" Karaj demanded.

"His magic is balance. He takes lives. Yes. He gives them life back. He takes the calm. Yes. He gives chaos back. Of his people, their magic is of both. To undo one, you must find the other."

"Blessed…" the exorcist whispered. "I think she just explained how he was masking into the Manor. We've been blocking the city against the wrong thing."

Catherine's assistant turned to him with their mouth agape. "Are you implying that this vampire was able to avoid detection so long because we were warding against magic of madness when we should have warded against *peace*?"

"Fisking wonderful," Akaran grumbled under his breath. "I'm *really* tired of getting outsmarted by this asshole. Fine. Two more questions for you, Sherril. How many others has Annix spawned that you know of?"

The qualification to the question made the vampire twitch anew. *"That I…"* she hissed before she looked up at him. Her eyes were simply *gone*, and nothing but smoldering sockets dropping with green embers remained. Most of the assembled guards and soldiers unleashed horrified noises and gasps for air, while Telburn watched slack-jawed.

"As of the time you were captured, unless you have ability to have knowledge of even more," he added. "Excluding yourself."

"Of his and his alone: the number of fingers on a hand."

"Five. Great."

Telburn frowned and gave a short shake of his head. "The thumb is not considered by everyone to be a finger."

The exorcist turned slightly and gave the Headmaster a look so foul that Elsith's husband shut up and kept his ideas to himself. When he spoke again, he turned his attention back to the battlemage. "Why is he doing this? Why is Annix after Bistra – the real reason?"

Sherril shook and tried to fight the answer. Glowing red cracks erupted on her skin and around her empty eyes. *"The Auramancer set his eternal bride on fire. I gave aid. I am… not enough… was not what was wanted. Meister needs a partner, one as strong as he, to rule his brood. Bringing the Goddess of Love low? To him it is true justice. Elves do not see what is right and righteous as us."*

"So why not just turn Bistra?" Riorik interrupted. "He could have had this done by now."

The vampire turned to him and smiled painfully. *"He wants her willing. Submit, give herself. Willingly and fully. To be his new yomaldi. Not turn against her desire. To give reparation willingly, not at threat of force. It is his tvastarian."*

Akaran blinked slowly. "He thinks he can get that by spending years torturing her? Convince her to change to… what? Get him to stop hurting her?"

"It worked on me… and with many less moons than it has for her," Sherril admitted with more than a hint of wistful sadness in her voice.

"Well that's horrifying," Badin muttered. "Telburn? Guess you were right. So he turned you into a bloodsucker because you killed his mate?

"Because I allowed myself to be caught. Because I was willing to offer recompense."

The resulting silence made damn near everyone uncomfortable, except perhaps for Anais – who was the one person that could commiserate with her. Mutual understanding aside, the spell had begun to take its toll, and her already withered body had somehow started to look even worse. "Are you… are you done with her?"

The two ranking Lovers exchanged looks. "Motive, numbers, location," Akaran remarked. "We need anything else?"

"No," Karaj agreed. "That's enough. I am… uncomfortably disturbed… that this monstrosity seems to think it is…"

"That it's justified?" Akaran answered. "Same."

Catherine's aid nodded their head grimly. "To stop a monster is one thing. To deter someone that feels that they are enacting the spirit of law or taking retribution? Another."

"Great," the exorcist sighed under his breath. "Well. Anything else we'll rip from her sire. By force, if the Goddess grants us the opportunity."

"You're a bloodthirsty little secretary, aren't you?" Riorik mused. "I approve of that," he added as he stepped forward and brushed past the priest rudely and suddenly. "This spell – is she required to speak truth, regardless of inquirer?"

"Yes," Anais slowly croaked out.

"Good. Then a boon, please? I've done so much for your people lately."

Before Karaj could stop him, Akaran held up his hand and interjected himself. "See that sky? Soon as the sun comes up, she roasts. We're putting her back in her cage before that happens. Ask fast."

The thief gave his friend a short nod and addressed Sherril directly. "How red is your ledger, sparkcaster?"

Sherril turned her smoldering eyes up to him. *"As red as yours, thief."*

"Possible, very possible," he admitted. Before anyone could stop him, he leaned in and whispered a question in her ear. She wavered, but then answered back with her voice so quiet that nobody could make out what she said.

When their exchange was finished, he smiled and carefully adjusted his garish orange vest and turned his head back to the exorcist. "So you're done with her, yes?"

"Yeah," Akaran confirmed as he turned his attention to the Headmaster. "Telburn? Open it back up. We'll find another way to contain her later, but right now…"

"You must know I do this under strenuous objection."

"The only other thing to do is kill her, and I just promised Anais I wouldn't."

Telburn sighed — either frustrated or resigned, the exorcist couldn't tell — and began to recite invocation to open the portal back up. "I think I'm going to have my wife speak at length to your superior over this."

"I'll save you both the trouble," Riorik replied as he turned his attention back to the battlemage patted her on the cheek, and then he gave her the kindest, most loving smile anyone had ever seen. "I do thank you for your help. I apologize for any inconvenience this may cause you."

Sherril had a fraction of a second to ponder what he'd just said before he snarled his hand up in the metal leash chaining her to the roof. He calmly and quickly unhooked the club from his belt and lashed out with it in a swing that nobody could've stopped. The impact shattered the vampire's mouth in one single, furious blow that made his wrist *pop* from the force of the impact.

She fell backward with a scream and a gout of blood that burst from her ruined jaw. Fangs clattered on the rooftop as he violently pulled the dead woman around with the chain and flung her back off of the rooftop. The sudden fall only took her so far, yet the audible *crack* of her neck shattering as the iron collar around her throat stopped her from dropping to the bridge. As the priests and wardkeepers rushed to the edge of the ramparts, the thief crossed his arms and looked down at her kicking, spasm-wracked body.

"Austilin was like a son to me," he spat down at her as her arms and legs seized. "Vengeance may belong to the Gods, but I will have my pound of teeth — and none of you have allowed me to take what is mine," he growled as the Lovers as they pulled him away from the edge of the rampart.

Anais shouted a horrified scream of, "NO! THEY PROMISED!" as the sun began to peek through the eastern clouds. Sherril's body shook as smoke began to erupt across her flesh.

The thief took one look at her and hammered his club across her chest. Her ribs cracked and her face contorted with pain as she collapsed onto the ground. Henderschott moved in to grab him and pulled him away from the broker before he could do any more damage. "Expect more than promises to be broken if they let me in the same room as you, witch," he snarled. "You and yours have murdered many people that I personally knew or knew of – and you voided a promise I had offered to Missus Valdin!"

"RIORIK! THAT'S ENOUGH!" the Lieutenant-Commander thundered at their murderous *friend* – although the mention of the healer made him loosen his grip a bit.

"Oh, I *promise you*, it's not even anywhere *near* enough, my good sirrah."

Akaran looked down at Sherril as a couple of the wardkeepers tried to pull her up. He stopped them and let the sun begin to work its nature on the twitching vampire. "He's right. Hender. Let him go. Get a division of your men ready. We have an hour."

"Make that three," Karaj interrupted. As the exorcist looked over and started to ask why so long, Catherine's assistant shrugged their shoulders. "Annix will know that he's lost his minion in moments. An hour, a trio, it won't matter. If he runs, he'll run now. A break will allow you to eat, briefly rest, and be treated further. I know how little care you gave yourself overnight."

"Dammit, I don't need –"

"Time to pray, time for someone to lay hands on your leg again, and time to take a piss? Yes, you do. We have knowledge, now we need time to prepare to use it. Others can be girding their loins while you receive a blessing from the Goddess for the battle to come."

"Karaj is right, Akaran," Henderschott interrupted. "You're bleeding through your bandages again. Just tell me what you need to have done. I want this over with as bad as you do."

Overruled (repeatedly) and with murmured agreement from some of the other Lovers, the exorcist let his head sag a little before answering. "The sun's up enough to banish the shadows in the city and give some room for you to safely move up along the lip," he remarked as he gestured at the far edge of Basion. "Once you're there, turn the Fel'achir Woods into the Kingdom of Dawn-*fire*."

"Kill… killing her… did you get… at least get what you wanted?" Anais demanded as she pushed herself back up to her knees with gore dripping out of her mouth and from a hole in her chest.

"Not yet, but soon," Riorik answered smugly. "Akaran? Will you have need of the Fleets with your next move? I suspect that you have a cleansing action in mind that may demand the tunnels to be blockaded."

The exorcist pursed his lips as daylight began to pierce through the clouds. A steady stream of smoke began to waft up from the dangling woman on the other side of the wall. "Telburn, I'm going to need to talk to your wife right away. Hender, whomever you don't take into the woods, send them to Naradol." After a moment he cursed under his breath. "Someone should tell the Overseer."

"Maybe not on that one," Riorik hastily interrupted. "I think he's busy working on something else. I would suggest that you perhaps look for Paverilak… and didn't his Maiden send her Consort-Blade with him?"

Karaj nodded slowly. "Sua… yes. Yes that's a wonderful idea."

"Why would working with the Provincial Maiden's bodyguard be a good thing?" Akaran whined. "I don't *want* to have another Maiden breathing down my neck."

"Because it's either win over as many Maidens as you can *now* or answer to the General when this is done," Catherine's assistant cautioned. "Pick your battles carefully and let him participate in the fight."

The exorcist bit back his immediate response and decided to abandon the argument entirely. A small scream punctuated the air as the sunlight washed over Sherril's face. "Shouldn't… shouldn't we do something for her?" Telburn asked.

"Why?" Karaj replied with a tilt of their head. "The thief managed to save us the cost of kindling."

"But I – I mean, she's in pain. Surely there's a more humane option?" the mage started to ask.

"She isn't the first, and won't be the last," the Lover retorted firmly. "Akaran: take your leave. In three, you have the full authority of the Order to do as you see fit. Your temporary status as Paladin will continue to be respected by all agencies in the city," they added with a sharp look at Henderschott, then Telburn, and finally Riorik. "A velvet glove or a gauntleted fist…"

Behind them, Hadraie's eyes flashed bright lavendar for a single heartbeat. *"He knows which he is to be,"* she whispered with a voice that wasn't quite her own that sent an uncomfortable chill down Riorik's spine… a chill that was matched only by the sudden thick cloud of oily smoke that erupted over the rampart as the full might of the sun finally broke through the clouds above.

Akaran must have heard her speak up, because he flicked his eye over in her direction as she stood beside Anais. "You know… with Sherril gone, Annix is gonna… you know what. I think I need to talk to you," he mused as an idea slowly popped into his head.

"To me? What for?" the wardkeeper asked with a slightly demure bit of surprise.

"I'm putting you in charge of dealing with Anais right now… and I need you to do me a favor," he began. "Henderschott! I need you two to send a message to someone. But… talk as we leave. Since apparently I'm supposed to leave," he groused over at Karaj.

"Yes, yes you are," they replied with a firm nod. "Go find a bed, exorcist. Lay in it."

Riorik cleared his throat and waved at the priest before he could talk to Hadraie. "My friend? I'll help you find one but first…" he began before he walked over and whispered something dark and vile in the exorcist's ear.

When he finished, Akaran grunted something obscene and turned his attention to the wardkeeper. The thief began to make his own exit, though that wasn't to say that Karaj was done with him – because they most assuredly weren't. After Anais, Telburn, and most of the Lovers left, Catherine's assistant put their hand on Riorik's shoulder and pulled him close. "I would ask the same question as that resurrected scorpion, but I shall not be dissuaded – except I don't need to. You do understand that you cannot bargain your way out of your impending damnation? Knowing that it comes is not enough to bribe your way free of the flames."

"Ah but dear Karaj, you mighty assistant you," the thief replied with a warm smile, "I have come to understand it that your Order has need of individuals that are not concerned with such trivial pursuits as mere morality."

"We do what we must for the good of human kind, even if our methods are not always in the good of the moment."

"I respect that, I do," the thief agreed as he slowly pulled his vest open and handed Catherine's agent a rolled-up piece of parchment. "Surely arrangements for forgiveness with the other side can be made… with the right contract?"

As Karaj tilted their head in confusion, Sherril's neck finished disintegrating in the iron collar. Her head fell free a heartbeat later and dropped to the bridge below like an obscene falling star from the heavens above. Her skull rolled around on the bridge while the guards at the gate simply stared in horror as the rest of her body fell a moment later and disintegrated into nothing but bone shards and ash with a soft 'whump' when it hit the bridge below.

Badin peered down over the edge and flicked his fingers just once.

A little arc of lightning blasted the last piece of the sparkcaster away.

XI. HOME INVASIONS
Evening of Staddis, 18th of Firstgrow, 513 QR

Once again, the city reeked of smoke. But this time, it didn't smell like musty old dust or the pungent odor of burnt flesh from the pyre. No; the city reeked of wood smoke. It was constant, heavy, and it had caused a haze to settle across the Orshia-Avagerona falls on the northern edge of the city. The distant sound of flames licking at the sky were impossible to miss; they couldn't even be covered by the intermittent hacking coughs that the stench was eliciting from the locals.

Not that the Guild cared. They had a job to do. Every Hunter currently uninjured — and some that were — were on the street. A few in Elsith's employ had been sent to the woods to help the Lieutenant-Commander cleanly burn through the forest just to be on the safe side.

It had been just under three hours since Sherril's execution, and word had spread through the city faster than Akaran could chase it. People were already on edge from the night before — now that the wedding was over, the post-celebration mood was dank and dire. The riots around the Repository had stopped and Order soldiers were moving through the streets without being attacked, but there wasn't an ounce of joy to be had by anyone...

...except for those that had lost a loved one at the hands of the monsters that everyone *finally* blamed for the city's recent ills. While there was confusion about what had happened at the end of the wedding, there wasn't any left now. The lightning-flinging mass-murderess was dead and gone for good, and all credit went to the Lovers (with whispered admiration given to the Master of Thieves).

There was confusion among the populace, however, about the intent of the Hunter's Guild inside the district. They had hit the ground running as soon as they were out of Upper Naradol, and the moment they hit an area three blocks away from Madam Pramidi's House of Hides, they'd gone to war.

War, even at the best of times, had harbingers. If you had eyes, you could see the buildup of forces in Piapat and West Giffil. Soldiers on the street garnered attention. Mercenaries in the shadows earned eyeballs. Healers setting up field stations on the outer edge of the slums earned cheers at first... which gave way to nervous sweats and panic later when people began to wonder *why*.

Word spread fast through the city. Word spread faster through Lower Naradol itself. There wasn't any way to keep it secret. You couldn't. Not with a show of force, even if it was led with a show of stealth.

The Guild kept a list of names. People to visit in any particular locale in the city if there was a problem. They were the first ones found and detained. In some cases, forcibly. People were questioned. Sometimes violently. Threats were made. Information was coerced without promise of coin, but rather, with suggestion of a longer life.

Before long, Elsith had three targets. Three places were things just weren't quite right. Pramidi's Tannery was the first. The second? A small warehouse a few buildings down. It used to be busy. Then it became inexplicably abandoned. Then later, the local squatters and vagrants learned not to try to camp out inside it lest they go missing in the night. The third? Another building a block away that was quickly delegated to the second attack force to handle.

One of her companions uttered a quiet spell several yards away from their first stop. The building lit up with a pale orange glow for no more than five heartbeats. When the glow faded, small red runes pulsed around its front door and all the windows on the bottom side.

Security wards. Some to announce the presence of mundane intruders, and others that would register magical ones. It wasn't a difficult trick to pull off – but these were good. Very good. They were etched into places that no human could've easily reached. You'd have missed them entirely if you didn't know what you were looking for.

She barked an order. A different Hunter appeared at her side and peeled the hood of his cloak away to show off his disfigured face and the metal bar that covered his eyes. He looked at the building... and then he looked *past* the rough lumber and coarse stones that composed its walls.

Damians weren't common around this part of the world, but they were invaluable to the Guild. His eyes may have evaporated into nothing by the mix of molten sylverine and steel that had been poured across his face, but the spells mixed into the metal? That let the Damian see the world as it was seen in the Veil.

It was a horrible curse to endure.

Yet an *effective* one.

The Hunter traced his gaze across every inch of the warehouse's face before he lifted two fingers up for the Huntsmatron, followed by a closed fist. An open palm if the occupants were living. A horizontal, flat one if the occupants were dead.

A closed one if they were dead but still moving.

She gave him a curt nod and placed a small bag on the ground. A moment later, she had it lit and a pale yellow smoke began to emit from the fabric. Another moment later, and she sunk a crossbow bolt with a strip of red ribbon into the wall just above the doorway.

Yellow smoke meant two. A matching cloud of green from the northern side meant her men had found another nest with just one. Sherril had claimed there were at least five that she knew of. The red mark verified the inhabitants were subject to execution.

Once it was tagged, they moved past it and let it stand.

As soon as the Huntsmatron made it within yards of the nondescript tannery, she loaded another bolt and sent it into the sky back from where they'd come. It burst over their heads in a kaleidoscope of colors that amused children watching nearby, and sent a message to someone else.

A heavily-hooded face peeked out from one of the Tannery's second-story windows to see the commotion. Just a face, and just for a few brief seconds. The last seconds it had to live. She loosed a third crossbow bolt that pierced its eye like a bullseye and stopped somewhere in the back of its head. There was a soft *thump* and a wet *pop* a moment later as the small burndust-laden charge on the back of the bolt exploded – and took the vampire's skull with it.

Sherril had said there were at least five other broodlings he'd spawned.

Now there were just four.

Another green-cloaked man rushed to her side. He was dressed like a hunter, but wasn't armored like one. It was a shitty disguise, but they didn't know how many *human* watchers the sadistic bastard had on the streets and they didn't want to give away the game until it was too late. As Akaran pulled his cloak down off of his face and planted his hands on the tannery's front door, it didn't matter anymore.

"**DISENCHANT**!" thundered from his lips.

The spell ravaged the markings hidden on the wooden slats and baked into the stones. As it did, his knee buckled and he pitched forward with his shoulder coming to rest firmly against the tannery's wall. Elsith started to approach him to help, but he waved her back. Most of the strength had returned to it, but it wouldn't be the same ever again. He made it perfectly clear that he hoped to get to return the favor on anything he found in the lair.

He didn't have to wait long.

"Do whatever it takes," he'd told the first medic he could find after the bridge execution. "Whatever. However. Let me walk on it and I'll do anything you ask."

They did. Instead of taking a nap, he gave instructions. Instead of rest, he had someone splint his leg. Instead of taking time in prayer, he'd cursed and berated the Fallen below and a few of the Divine above while a pair of medicannias poured more magic into his flesh than his aura was willing to take.

It worked. Just not well.

After his Word left his lips, another call went up.

"FOR THE QUEEN'S GLORY!" thundered from the crowd of soldiers stationed blocks away. The Betrothed of Provincial Maiden Sanlian Esterveen stood with his arms crossed atop some unimportant merchant's overpriced and poorly-decorated house that was just tall enough to give him a slight vantage over Lower Naradol. On the street below?

One of the most dangerous men in the entire city waited.

City? No. In the entire *province*.

The title Consort-Blade was not given lightly, and Sua was not a light man. Akaran had only caught a few glimpses of him in the past few months – once at Cromular's Keg a few weeks after his arrival in Basion, and he'd seen the man hovering around at the meeting of the minds in the Overseer's chambers a few days prior. That was absolutely *fine* as far as he was concerned. The man was tasked to be Sanlian's bodyguard, and she'd been so *kind* to dispatch him to keep a watch on Paverilak, or so the word on the street suggested.

The word in the quieter hallways implied that he'd been sent to keep Paver sober. Either way, it kept them out of each other's circles, and the priest would've been just as happy to leave him outside of his orbit, given the choice. Even without the luxury of getting to make the decision, he'd later admit that there were worse choices for muscle.

And *muscle* Sua was. He towered over the members of the 4th Garrison marched behind him, and his blackened-steel armor was imposing on the best of days. All you had to do was just *look* at the craftsmanship on the full suit of platemail and your sword would turn away before you could even swing it at him – and that was aided by a few special enchantments placed into the metal to harden it even further.

All of that mattered when it came time to put force behind Elsith's scouting efforts with the will of the Crown. The will of the Crown, in this instance, was backed fully by the Will of the Goddess of Love – and they had their own detachment standing by. As Sua began his march down the streets of Lower Naradol from the east, Catherine lead the charge in her own way and followed hot on Akaran's heels.

She was far from alone. Even without considering the Wardkeepers and Messengers of Love behind her, their march was met by shouts of, **"LUMINOSO!"** and invocations to sense and scour for the dead... and especially those with Abyssian taint. For the first time since the Lovers had begun searching the city, their spells finally started to yield poisoned fruit.

Sherril's clue had given away what they should've been looking for. Magic of peace, not chaos; the aura of chaotic magic hid in the wake of the normal and natural peace that Basion was known for. The city had devolved into enough turmoil for the ether to be disturbed beyond the point of sensing it directly. That was the crux of their mistake, and now?

Now they worked to rectify it.

And maybe it was because of how brazen Annix had been as of late. Maybe it was because his spawn had put her own spells in place. Or maybe, just maybe, it was because that after so much bloodshed, the ether had been disturbed enough to begin to offer a glimpse of what hid beneath.

Annix hadn't gotten sloppy. That was the hope, but it quickly turned out not to be the case. The problem was that after so much raw, unmitigated violence and so many *unsanctioned* executions (a bit of blame to be tossed at Riorik's feet later), scavengers and beings of ill-intent had started to gravitate to the city.

They were found and quickly banished.

Things in the shadows were pulled out of hiding. Little lost spirits stuck between this world and the Veil were tracked down. Almost all of them benign. Most just simple echos. Normally, the Order would take their time and investigate each one. Help them cross over gently. Help them solve their woes.

Right now?

If it wasn't one of the recognized sentient races of the mainland, it was banished on the spot. Respect, honor, and the sanctity of death be damned – and the damned were exiled with extreme prejudice. It didn't take long before the ether rippled so forcefully that additional disturbances began to erupt across the city in their wake.

A shade manifested here. A wailing voice there. Word would reach Catherine soon enough, and once Lower Naradol was purged, the rest of the city would follow suit. It was the cleansing that the Safest City so desperately needed and was so very long overdue.

Henderschott's red-cloaked thugs moved like a herd of furious drakes through the city streets and locked down the area with excessive violence. They worked in from the east and the north while the Guard slowly positioned themselves to block any other overland exits off.

Anyone they saw that looked out of place?

Grabbed. Shoved against a wall. Questioned. Searched.

Anyone with a weapon? It was taken. Handed over to a sergeant or a Knight of Love on the other side of the district. If it was at all *potentially* abnormal? It was broken, slagged, or deemed to be bundled and delivered to the Repository with haste… and there was plenty of haste to go around.

Anyone with a magical aura?

They were pulled around to answer to Catherine or the Consort Blade – whomever was closer. Every name recorded. Every face described. Every ability, every hint of knowledge of the ether was jotted down on scroll after scroll. Every single one of them would have their information passed on to the Granalchis later for further review. Unsanctioned mages? Bound, gagged, and set aside for later.

No matter their age. No exceptions.

Anyone found with contraband? Anyone with a piece of religious iconography from any of the banned Orders or disgraced Fallen? One man was beheaded on the spot after he was found to have a sigil of the God of Rot in his pocket. It was a crackdown unlike anything anyone in the city had *ever* seen.

A crackdown that was met with a strike of lighting as Badin invoked a thundercall that would've done Sherril proud. The first building that Elsith marked was the target of the blast, and the roof of the ramshackle warehouse collapsed down before the resulting detonation blew it up and outwards. Shouts of terror from the street were met with a cry of pain from inside the storeroom as Badin descended on it with Catherine and a squad of pikemen immediately following in his footsteps.

There were two vampires inside.

Within a matter of moments, there were none. Pikes, the sun, and furious charges of lightning made sure of that. Annix's broodlings never stood a chance. All they served to be were announcements to their

Meister – and if the centuries-old asshole didn't already know the Order was there, he was an idiot.

And they all knew he wasn't an idiot.

From the south, Sua didn't bother with fancy spells. He didn't bother with thunderbolts or crossbow bolts. A Hunter and an Exorcist pushed ahead of his forces. They marked a building. They had the time it took to breath three times to ruin one of the protective wards Annix had placed on the safehouse.

It had been someone's home. It wasn't affluent, it wasn't pretty, and it wasn't very clean. But it had been someone's home. If Sua cared, he never showed it. His boot crushed the pathetic lock that kept its front door closed. The massive two-handed serrated longsword in his hands went in first.

The broodling inside tried to jump on him.

The Consort-Blade caught it with a single swing. Blackened-metal teeth cut into the vampire's stomach. He lifted it up off the ground and rammed it into an adjacent wall. He gripped the hilt with one hand and the tip of the blade with the other and *pushed*.

Bisection, he noted, wasn't enough to kill one of them.

But it did slow it down enough for him to take its head.

Back at the tannery, Akaran's spell stripped away the enchantments that Annix had placed across the doorway and the immediate wall. He stepped back just in time for the Huntsmatron to flex her arms and hurl a manabomb at the pair of wooden doors blocking their path. The spell was a simple one: it harnessed unstable ether into a semi-physical ball that you could throw.

When the bomb hit, it did as bombs do.

His voice boomed along with the rubble flying right behind it. "**ANNIX! BY ORDER OF THE CROWN – COME TO JUDGMENT**!"

With the doors of the tannery blown into wooden splinters, another disguised Messenger stepped through the rubble and unleashed a blistering wall of magic that burned away every shadow on the ground floor. Tanneries would *never* win awards for being *clean* even at their absolute best. This one?

This one hadn't seen its absolute best in years.

The vampire didn't answer his demand. Nothing did, except for a rush of sparks that danced through the air. A series of runes written into the floorboards glimmered and sparked in the wood. A second demand of, "**UNMASK** and **DISENCHANT**!" rushed out of his lips and shattered the spells before they could follow whatever supernatural script their caster had designed to be unleashed.

If you just glanced inside, you wouldn't notice anything out of the ordinary. A few pelts hanging to dry in one corner; a fresh skin in another that was still dripping on the floor. A cart full of fleshy waste in the corner. Empty racks waiting for a stack of leathers to be brought up from the churning pits in the basement. It wasn't anything that looked *wrong*.

It was wrong because it was right. There were skins. There were pelts. They had been carefully peeled and carved off their donors. All of them were animal.

But the tannery hadn't been in business for months.

A truth destroyed by another: humans have skin, too.

It didn't take long to realize that a few of the skins were *faces*. Oh, they weren't dangling anywhere you could see them easily. Oh no. You'd have to dig around in the dark room for a while, and even then you might not. If not for luminoso, they'd have gotten missed.

You would if you were hunting for traps — magical or otherwise.

Nothing greeted the raiders as they swarmed through the upper level. Aside from the hanging racks and crates, there wasn't much to find to the naked eye. As Elsith's Damian and another Hunter began a sweep with Hadraie and Akaran in tow, it was more the metaphysical than the physical that was the problem. Every single one of those problems had Annix's essence all over them.

His essence, and his language of choice. Akaran wouldn't have been able to decipher the runes they found for years on his own once they were forced to appear. It took multiple harshly spoken demands to, "**UNMASK**!" at the top of their lungs to get the masking spells the vampire had placed to break down enough for the rest of his work to appear.

That was how they found the faces. The *other* faces.

Faces that looked eerily similar to each other.

Elsith gripped his shoulder tight and leaned in close. "Do you need to hear me say the obvious?"

"He isn't here."

"He was recently. I can smell him in the ether," she growled under her breath. "Should we hope he was the one that they found on the eastern prong?"

Akaran cursed and carefully tapped his knuckles against a wooden support beam. "No. Whatever's here is what he wanted us to find. That said, at least I don't feel anything in wait upstairs. Good shot earlier."

"Thank you, but don't get relaxed. There's misery to be had in the cellar," she pointed out. "Ready?"

He shook his head and waved for one of the pikemen behind them. "No. If it didn't come up to challenge us, it has a reason. Bastard not being here is enough to ruin our day. Don't rush it more than we have to."

"Caution? Surprising. Figured you'd have to break your leg at least two more times to learn that lesson."

He didn't bother to answer her bait.

Even though no threats made themselves manifest in the first three rooms on the ground floor, the exorcist forbid anyone from going to the next level up. He also made two pikemen guard a stairwell leading to the basement as ether-sensitive soldiers worked their magic. There were plenty of noises coming from under the floorboards and none of them made him happy – and less when Elsith turned from the stench to investigate upstairs

It felt like it took forever to find the traps that he *knew* the vampire had left behind. Annix had carefully hidden perfectly tanned faces in piles of pelts and stacks of leather across the ground floor. The faces had been expertly skinned from their victims, and even the edges of the nose, lips, and little pieces of the eyelids had been left behind.

There was something absolutely *off* about them. While he tried to figure out what, the discovery of the fresh horrors were enough to cause three people to run outside. It was even more than the odd inscriptions that had been carved into the back of each leathery chunk of flesh that rankled his head.

That was easy to explain. It was more Ameggenon. Some unknown spell written in some dead tongue made impossible to recite for anyone without a quarter-century's worth of education – but not impossible to destroy. He obliterated each face with a Word (or a series of Words, in the case of two etchings that proved particularly stubborn) as they were handed over. That decision flew in the face of the first Rule of Excisement:

If you don't know what an enchantment, ward, or relic does?

Leave it alone.

But, he decided inwardly, *Annix wouldn't have set these out if they were to inspire long life and confidence in the living*.

No, what was off-putting wasn't just that they were faces. It was that each face had a mole on its forehead just above the right eye. That each face had a scar running across the left cheek. That each face had the same skin tone. It was just short of impossible, but he would've sworn that the seven different faces/spells that the men found were from the same person.

Once the immediate traps were gone, Elsith sprinted upstairs with two of her men right behind her. On the other side of the first floor, a trio of Henderschott's men shattered the rear wall and opened the building up to the street on the other side and the pikemen waiting behind. Nothing was getting in, and nothing was getting out without a spike shoved down its throat.

There were two different sets of stairs that went to the basement, and one latched door with an elongated ramp that trailed down. Like several other buildings, businesses, and storerooms across Lower Naradol, this one had a semi-closed opening allowing for access to and from the Overflow. It was also unlit – on purpose, of course – though if you had all of the entrances open, it could be as bright as a summer's day.

If.

The Huntsmatron's men had already identified that the lower doors and the hatch leading to the Overflow had been completely sealed off on the outside with chunks of bricks and broken wooden beams. It made a frontal assault the only *good* option.

Not that Akaran was interested in just *good* options.

He waved his hand and barked an order outside. The same call was matched three times over, and a sudden thundering **BOOM** shook the tannery from top to bottom. The rafters didn't even stop shaking before the screaming started and the barricade was destroyed.

The process of turning freshly-shorn skin into leather required several vats – at best – to soak the hides in at various steps of the process. Saltwater, urine, and lime were a tanner's best friend; and even in a defunct one like this, the vats were still full. One of them was packed with more than just mold-filled and festering fluids.

Her name, they'd later discover, was Madam Pramidi.

Her execution was not swift.

But not for lack of trying.

Akaran barged down the stairs with his sword in hand and his leg trailing with a steady limp. Even after seeing all of the other abuses that Annix had carried out so far, this one came damn close to taking the cake.

She was horrific. Not for being a monster, but for being tormented. A Wardkeeper fell to his knees in prayer once they realized she couldn't move more than a few steps in either direction. You could thank the chain on the ceiling that leashed her in place for that.

The vats had been kept out of sight of the sun for Gods-only-knew how long – which made them perfect to store another witness. The vampire chained to one thrashed in a pool of salty slush as the light of day made her skin blister and burn every time an errant beam came across it. It was torture, and torture that their entrance had caused.

A guard ran outside, retching with every breath. The exorcist had to stop and make a warding gesture of his own before getting close. Rusting iron chains dangled from ceiling were nailed through her wrists and shins so she couldn't move out of the slurry she was anchored in. A small pile of glistening wet rocks sat on the floor beside her vat – and it was obvious that until recently, they'd been holding her down.

Son of a bitch let her up before he left. He knew we were coming.

*He **wanted** us to see this.*

Annix had wanted them to see what he had done to her. He wanted her to be able to crawl out of her watery tomb if his lair was broken into. He wanted them to be terrified of what he was willing to do to get what he wanted.

She couldn't scream; she wanted to, but she couldn't.

He couldn't tell why she couldn't. But her neck was discolored. Burnt, blistered, bulging. A funnel had been implanted in the base of her throat. The exorcist took one look at it, threw up, and realized that Annix kept her alive that way. *Probably been draining into her gut the whole... oh, Goddess...*

Akaran threw up again.

She clawed at her thighs with bloody fingernails on ruined fingers as she struggled to. Weeks... months... maybe even longer... spent submerged had caused her skin to bloat in ways that defied imagination. If she'd been human, the only thing left of her would've been a few stubborn tendons holding dissolved muscles onto the bones.

But she wasn't human, and her skin hadn't dissolved. She was undead, and it kept growing back. Down to the mole on her forehead and the scar on her left cheek. It had to have been torture. It had to *be* torture. Nothing but raw torture. If she'd screamed, people would've heard her even under water. So Annix had fixed that. He kept her in the water so he could *reuse* her and never have to hear her complain about it. He kept her supple, and used his face to hide his lair.

Again. And again.

He'd done something else, too. Just to ensure her silence.

Akaran didn't realize it until he took a swing at her neck with his sword. Instead of taking her head, his blade bounced away and fell out of his hand. Her flesh gave way to expose a solid chunk of silver. He dropped to a knee and cradled his wrist with a plethora of profanity as Catherine joined him in the workshop. She took one look at the victimized monster and a look at her cursing charge as he held his wrist in his other hand before she decided to take matters in her own hands.

A singular calm Word rushed from her lungs and bathed the tortured woman in holy light. Pramidi was gone before the Maiden's voice could finish echoing in their ears. Wherever she went, the exorcist could only hope it was better than here.

The silver chunk in her throat hit the bottom of the tub with a thud, and aside form the retching noises inside and out of the tannery, everything quieted down. Footsteps from Elsith overhead were less *hurried* and more *harried*, which didn't bode well for the next few moments. Nor did the pain in Akaran's leg, although that was easy enough to forget in the middle of the carnage.

The Maiden took a long look around the room – and the vats of tanning fluid, the benches still slick with blood, the shackles on the wall and all of the *awful* things that Annix had collected over time – and stood with a grim stoicism that was more frightening than the monster he'd left behind. "There is no soul in this city that resides in a position of authority that will not be held accountable for what we have found today."

"Ours included?" Akaran asked as he tried to flex his wrist.

"Leading the pack," she answered with a dejected shake of her head. "The very idea that this hive of scum was allowed to prosper so close to the Repository..."

"Your job was to keep the things in the grave locked in the grave," he answered with a grunt. "It wasn't to look for new things to add to it, was it?"

Catherine sighed in frustration and shook her head a second time. "No, but it does show how bad we have failed to spread the Words of Love if it fell on ears as deaf as these."

The Huntsmatron barged down the stairs with fury etched across her face. "Think we're about to hear more than we wanted," he muttered as Elsith held up a woman's desiccated, almost empty head in one hand and a pile of papers in the other.

"Your asshole vampire? Wanna know how we missed him?" Elsith snarled.

"Magic? Why are you holding a head...?" Akaran asked slowly.

A woman's head; long dead, and long drained of blood. That was fine enough; the Telburn's loving, doting wife had enough color in her face to make up for it. "This fisking son of a goblin's syphilitic inbred mother has a shrine dedicated to *Pia* up there. Dedicated to Pia, and he's got embalmed bodies of Lethandria worshipers up there. Two of them. Saw a corpse that looks like a Solinal peacekeeper in there, too. One went missing after

Marduk. This scrag-humping shithead? The mother-fisker doesn't just drink blood," she seethed through clenched teeth as she flung the head down at their feet, "he fisking *uses* it. What his bitch said about 'bathing chaos in blood' — well. She was literal. Every spell he has written on the walls of this place is *in blood*."

"He's a blood mage?" the exorcist asked as his eye went wide. "Why in the utter fisk did we not think of that?"

"Because vampires *drink* it, they don't... *play* with it," Catherine replied aghast. Her eyes bounced from written spell to written spell as her stomach continued to recoil. "How many of our spells begin with a cask of wine?"

"None of them," he grumbled, "but we're gonna make some. You hear me? We're going to have to go home and *make some* because there is not enough rum *in the Kingdom* to help me deal with today."

The Maiden started to issue a scathing retort, but...

He wasn't wrong.

"A blood mage that write spells in elvish, prays to the Goddess of Madness, and has *that* shrine decorated with the bodies of the Order of the Cloaked, you mean?" Elsith shot back. "That's enough masking that I'm surprised you can even smell the tannery outside."

"If you're trying to make me feel better by throwing a head at me, it's..." Catherine began before she looked down at the dead woman's skull, "Well. It's making me feel moderately better, yes. Akaran? Didn't you say that his assassin mentioned something about basing it in the magic of peace?"

"Can you read elven? Because I can't," he countered, "but once we started to look for calming spells, well..."

For the second time in as many minutes, he wasn't wrong. "I don't know if I should ask for Granalchi assistance in deciphering this mess or if I should just burn it all down and have someone salt the ash it leaves behind."

"Tel will pout for a month if I advocate torching it," Elsith remarked as she looked around the basement. "I'll show him a tit and make it up to him. Burn it. Burn all of it."

Akaran looked around the vault chamber and focused on an otherwise unassuming crate sitting against the wall. It *radiated* death in the air around it. "Also vote for burning, but... I have a feeling we're going to feel worse in a few," he murmured as he carefully limped over to the box.

"Oh I'm not done ruining your day," the Huntsmatron called out as she pushed the parchments into Catherine's unwelcoming but outstretched arms. "He also had these up there."

The Maiden looked down at the papers – drawings, she realized – and blinked slowly. "Elsith...? That's... me. Akaran? Why does he have a drawing of... me?" she voiced cautiously as she felt a cold sweat spring into life across her shoulders. "What is this... why is there a drawing of me with a bloody mark across my mouth and stomach? When did he see me nude!?"

Elsith crossed her arms as Akaran carefully pulled the lid off of the crate that had taken his attention. As he muttered curses under his breath, the mercenary had answers. "Of you, of me, of my husband, of Akaran," she explained. "Even that cocksucker Donta, too. There's a few dead people in that pile that I recognize. Every red mark? It's how they died. A gash here, a splash there"

"But I'm not dead," Catherine pointed out as she pressed a finger to her neck like she was checking to make sure.

"Neither is one-eye over there," she countered, "but look at the drawing the bloodsucker did of him. Red marks across both of his hands, his mouth, and a blotch on his chest. I think he was entertaining himself with ideas on how to kill us."

"That's... that's blood," Catherine realized after another moment as she stared down at Akaran's picture. "Oh. There's some across his leg, too. Both knees."

The Hunter retorted with a cold bark of laughter. "Hear that? He plans on breaking your other leg," she remarked.

When he didn't answer, the two women gave each other vaguely nervous glances and walked over to stand beside him. "What did you find?" the Maiden asked even though she really didn't want to know. "More blood magic?"

"*Brood* sacrifice," he remarked as he peered into the crate. It came up to his hip and was packed to the brim of bone shards and dust. There were scraps of burnt clothes and other relics of the dead. "He was using his own kin for his sacrifices. Goddess. Turn a human, their soul goes into the ether. They come back as a vampire. The First Curse or whatever it is. He culls *that* and keeps the chances of any angry wraiths or wild Abyssian magic from breaking through. This is incredible. I found evidence of this before I just didn't..."

"That's... that's a lot of corpse-ash," Elsith finally remarked.

The Maiden tried to work her now-dry lips. "Vampire ash. We never found a trace of anyone missing because there wasn't anyone to find."

"You don't learn a trick like this overnight," Akaran muttered under his breath. "I suspected similar over at the Wall of Gardens. I guess he did the same thing here, too. Didn't have to move bodies around. Dumped whatever he didn't want in the river, and... here we have the rest. How long has this son of a bitch really been in the Kingdom?"

"Didn't he profess his age to be over two centuries?" Catherine asked. "That alone may predate him to before the Crusade of Suns itself... as an elf, he must be. This creature..." she began as his age *really* dawned on her for the first time. "Akaran, when we kill this thing – it may well be the oldest damned soul we've expelled since the *Reformation of the Order* in 296!"

The exorcist leaned back on his heels as the weight of the comment settled on the shoulders of everyone in the room, with the Huntsmatron being the only person not to look nauseated from it. "I wonder if his children knew he was going to murder them," she mused.

"Sherril did," he pointed out. "I don't know what we can do about it from here, but she did. Or at least she knew he was willing to. One and the same, I guess."

Catherine stepped away from the box and walked into the sunlight streaming in from the open doors. "We can calm our anger and surprise. Our frustration knows no bounds and nor should it, but fury will not help at this moment."

"I'm not angry," the priest muttered under his breath.

"No, you're enraged," she countered. "It could not be etched on your face more unless you drew a knife and –"

He blanched and looked over at a hanging rack of knives, hooks, and blades a few feet away. "Maybe we can not use that phrase anymore for a while?"

The Maiden followed his gaze and felt her own eye twitch. "Reasonable. Except that I recall the last time you were truly angry, and they're still burning you in effigy at the Port as a result of your temper." As he started to argue, she went on with her voice warring between a flat monotone and a calming tremble. "I don't think any of us are surprised that he isn't here, but now we have a choice to make. Do we wait for him to make another move, or do we find a way to push him further?"

Akaran ran his fingers through his short hair and tried to do as she asked. Unsuccessfully, sadly, but he tried. "We're out of options, aren't we? We're burning down the woods. Naradol is going to be a smoking crater once we leave. I cleared out the caves. If he's still in the city, he's got a hiding place we haven't discovered out."

"I would assume he's still in the city," Elsith remarked. "I left them upstairs, but…"

"But?"

"I recall you saying that this entire mess began with the slaying of a woman? A… Zilyph?"

He shifted back and forth uneasily. "Yeah. His whole thing seems like it's based on revenge."

"Then don't expect him to end this until he has his goal," she sighed in response. "He has stacks – and I do mean *stacks* – of poems, love letters, and the like up there. All addressed to his yomaldi. His 'eternal bride.' The Zilyph woman that you said… Bistra, right? …that Bistra killed."

Catherine shrugged her shoulders. "I daresay I'm not unhappy about that. As long as we have something he wants, it increases the likelihood that we'll be able to end his reign of terror."

"It does, but we actually have to catch him to do it," Akaran retorted as he heard someone clear his throat from outside. "The only thing we have left to bait him with *is* Bistra."

"Which we aren't going to do," Akaran retorted with a grunt.

"We may not have a choice," she cautioned. "If we've already taken everything else from him, then what more do you think he'll do?"

The exorcist pursed his lips and sighed in annoyance. "Since she's locked under a hundred different wards? He'll try to do something to get us to draw her out into the open to kill us and steal her. That's all he *can* do right now, isn't it?"

As the Order ripped the tannery down to the baseboards and started to work on doing the same to the adjacent structures, Akaran pondered the answer to *that* miserable question the entire time through.

An answer, which (of course), was simple. He knew it, even if he didn't know how. Or what. Or when. But the answer was just going to be two letters.

But followed by swearing.

No, he sighed to himself. *He can do more. I just don't know* **what**. *Dammit*.

***

"Ridora! What in the… the world are you… you doing?!" Seline demanded with a stammer as she pushed her way through a crowd of screaming, crying, and terrified residents of the Manor. Her old boss was too far away and the noise of the crowd drowned her voice out and left the call to no avail.

The patients being scared was one thing. That wasn't new. The fear in Seline's own voice trembled with every word she said. It was the fear in the eyes of the orderlies.

That was the problem.

Someone tried to stop her from getting close. It was one of the guards; the Saa's replacement. Sel couldn't remember his name and gave up trying. "Missus, don't," he warned as he wiped a gloved hand across his cheek to try to clean some sooty smudge off of his jaw. "The Lady, she's... she's demanding. Everyone's out."

"But WHY?" she demanded as she grabbed the guard by his collar. "What... reason... what possible...?! It was... was Akaran, wasn't it. He... he demanded she do something... something stupid and she did."

"I don't... no," the brown-haired guardsman answered plaintively. "Whatever it was? Wasn't him. She just showed up an hour ago. Been gone all night."

"All night? I... I left this morning when... when Hender came through and... she wasn't here? Where was she?"

"Dunno missus, truly don't. Wherever she was, she got hurt."

Seline's eyes went wide. "Hurt...?" the healer asked as her voice dropped an octave. "How *hurt*?"

He just shook his head and reached back behind his side to take the hand of bewildered, bedraggled resident that had started to wander away from the pack. "Hurt enough to do this. Listen, Missus. I know your old place here. I know you're worried, but just go. She said we don't have time."

"Time before... before what?"

The guard took a deep breath and leaned in close to her. "All she'd say was 'the end.' Of what, I don't know. Of how, I don't care. We're gone."

True to his word, he left.

Against his demands, she didn't.

When she found Ridora, the Lady of the Manor stood facing the wooden doors leading into the belly of her home. Of her home, and the home of hundreds of others that had come through that gate – some had stayed briefly, some had stayed years. Others never left, and their ashes helped the garden grow. "My Lady? Wh... why...?!"

The Lady looked terrible. Her gown was coated in mud and grass stains. There were streams of blood down her dangling right arm. "It's not our home anymore," she mumbled.

Ridora had never mumbled a day in her life, though it only took a glance to realize why. At first the healer thought she was wearing a red scarf. A moment later, and she realized that a thick bandage had been wrapped around the lower part of her face and tied under her hair in the back. Blood dripped off of it from all sides. It wasn't enough to muffle the Lady entirely but Seline could barely make out a single word she said.

It was worse than that.

Her former assistant and briefly-ranked medicannia hesitated and didn't walk to stand up beside her. "Akaran made… Akaran made you do this. He did, didn't he?"

"No," the healer answered morosely. "He should have. He didn't. We… he is needed."

"He's needed to get… get out of this… this be-damned… damned city and away from us," Seline stammered loudly as her hands started to shake uncontrollably, "and you need to tell me what's going on. Out with it!"

"You speak with conviction I… I didn't know you still had."

The blonde-haired woman looked around at the panicked crowd and tried to steady the shaking in her own hands. "I have a new opinion on cocasa," she admitted after a moment. "I… I don't like it but it helps. I think… I think I should be screaming in terror but I just don't have the energy to do it right now."

"Terror?" Ridora bluntly repeated. "There's no terror. He wants terror. He just wanted to bully us. It… it worked. Had to work, had to do it."

"Had to do… do *what*?" Seline demanded. "*Who*?"

Without answering her directly, the Lady of the Manor slowly pressed a scroll up against the doorway and pressed a thick tack through it and into the wood. "The one behind this. I didn't… I didn't think he was right and… he's right. That fis… that *child* was right."

"Child… you mean… Akaran. He was… right?"

"Go get him," Ridora ordered, her voice growing *wet* and more and more *muffled* by the moment. "He's needed."

Seline felt her eyes narrow as she climbed the short set of stairs and put her hand on her mentor's shoulder. "Needed by who…? You… or Annix?"

The Lady didn't respond right away. Slowly, she wiped a bloody hand across the scroll and elvish words erupted across the parchment in a dark red glow. She turned around as the bandages fell from her face and tried to give the younger woman a little smile. But she couldn't, no matter much effort she made.

A simple answer tumbled out of her lip-less mouth as fresh blood began to pour out around the ghastly, horrific wound. "Yes."

XII. CURSED ARE THE TRUTHSPEAKERS
Dusk of Staddis, 18th of Firstgrow, 513 QR

The air had a sick acrid stench to it. It wasn't just the burnt woods beyond; it was worse. There was the taste of old, half-cooked, congealed flesh just hovering over your tongue no matter how many times you took a drink from your flagon or how many times you tried to swallow around it. It was just *there*, and it wasn't going to go anywhere.

And if you had any kind of connection to the next world, you could *feel* the abominations residing in this one. Annix wasn't hiding anymore, that was for certain. Seline didn't know anything worth relaying, though she did her best to run away as fast as she could (not that they let her; Catherine ordered her to follow them back to the Manor, her own personal opinions be damned).

Nor did she come alone. At Akaran's insistence, word had been sent back for the Overseer to follow. The instructions were to simply, "Mage portal the fisker up there if you have to, but *get him here* before we do *anything*."

"You understand it's not necessary and it's one more charge to the Order's coffers, yes? We've excised monsters for our entire existence without being watched by Overseers wherever we go," Karaj had complained (their wishes be damned, too).

When asked why, the reasoning was just as sound. "Because we need to make sure the Crown knows what happened here by the person responsible for the city. I *want* to keep my ass where it is, thank you, and that means winning over the Queen's people. He's one of them."

It was a surprising show of wisdom nobody expected from him.

Thankfully, Hannock hadn't been far from Naradol, and the cost of a mage-portal was easily skirted. Even if his objections weren't. (Objections, it should be noted, that he had no shortage of, and like the ones from Seline and Karaj, subsequently ignored.)

But not as important as Ridora herself. When everyone that had tried to turn Naradol inside out arrived on the edge of Basion, the Lady of the Manor wasn't hard to find. Lieutenant-Commander Henderschott had been above and beyond useful for a change, and Seline's former boss had been both found and attended to with all of the medical support she could've wanted.

The 4th had already taken pains to set up a tent to treat the wounded. Ridora was only one so far, but nobody expected it to stay that way. The Lieutenant-Commander had thought ahead for once, and he'd forbidden anyone from entering any of the smaller satellite buildings around the Manor proper, just to be safe.

It was a testament to Ridora's strength of will that she was able to communicate with them half as well as she did. The Lady hadn't been willing to say a word to the exorcist, and had turned him away every time he had tried to get into her tent. Where he failed, the Maiden didn't – and it was just as much of a telling of Catherine's own sense of command that she was able to get her rival to open up about everything she had learned.

When the Maiden left the medic's tent, she addressed the one-eyed exorcist with a blunter tone than usual. "You're going to die, Bistra is going to be taken, and she blames herself for it. The only other available option we have is to get in and kill Bistra before Annix can turn her if it isn't already too late *and then* wait for him to find and kill you."

Akaran blinked slowly and looked around at the soldiers, healers, Wardkeepers, and friends at his side. "All the same I'd appreciate it if you offered an option number three in there." When she just crossed her arms and gave him a tired glare, he cleared his throat. "I'm starting to understand why you don't like it when I come to you with a problem."

Catherine relayed the conversation as quickly as she could, and reiterated the parts that Seline had already covered. When she reached the end, she added the parts that the medicannia hadn't been made aware of. "She relayed everything that Annix told her before he carved her face up. Ridora couldn't read the spell but the gist she could get from him is that it's designed to nullify the wards and sanctified ground around the Manor."

"I can tell that much," he grunted. "I'm half-blind but I'm not dumb."

The Maiden nodded and flicked her hand in the air like she was trying to get something off of her fingertips. "He wants you. He wants Bistra, but

Akaran, he is *mad* at you. You walk in there, you aren't walking out."

"Why aren't I? He may've ruined the protection spells but it's still bloody daylight out here for another hour, at least."

"Because he has a brood. You were wrong," the elder Templar countered with a wave over her shoulder. "That was one thing Ridora was clear on – that Annix said that his child had children."

"Shit on me," he swore. "I asked what spawn *Annix* had. Not what *she* had."

Catherine paused and sucked on her tongue. "I don't know how much control he'll have over them. Some, yes, but.."

"He planned it. If she got killed, he'd have a whole bunch of hungry monsters waiting for the next moonrise to cause chaos. *Dammit.*"

"He truly is smarter than us, isn't he?"

Akaran refused to answer as the hairs on the back of his neck went up as he started to remember the last time he'd dreamed of Rmaci. "Where and how many?"

"In the woods," she answered with a frustrated sigh. "Could be three. Could be thirty. We won't know until they wake up."

He looked off to the side where Karaj was busy barking orders and gathering soldiers and Lovers alike with very insistent demands and angry shouts. After he looked at them for a moment, he turned his head back to his boss and started to rub at his temple. "Prepping the front line or prepping to go digging?"

"Both," Catherine answered without hesitation. "Ridora spent hours with him, Akaran. She has no reason to lie about it. I don't think she's *capable* of lying about it."

The way she described the Lady made his skin crawl and he felt the bile rise up in the back of his throat. "How bad…"

She answered him by taking his hand in hers and giving it a soft, gentle squeeze. "You can't ask that question and as someone that's gotten to know you? I can't send you in there. As your friend, I'm going to ask you not to go. Please. Tell me that it's in our best interest to burn the Manor down and regroup. Just… write Bistra off and seek to avenge her soul."

A sad, haunted, tired look flickered in his eyes as she took a breath and steeled herself for what she was going to say next, so he decided to beat her to it. "But as the Maiden-Templar of the Repository, you're going to order me to go in there even as you hope I refuse."

A look of pure, sheer regret settled across her eyes and she squeezed her hand a little tighter on his fist. "Bistra refused to come out. Seline went in to get her. Came out. Said it wasn't worth the trouble. And

Ridora..."

Akaran slowly closed his eye and bowed his head. "She traded, didn't he. Everyone gets out and safe, he keeps Bistra. He couldn't find an easy way to get through the wards you set up, so he made a bargain. If she doesn't keep the bargain... what happens? He releases his brood on the city? We see how fast this goes from 'we're going to die,' to 'maybe the world ends with our dying breaths?' Does that sum it up?"

"That's the impression she got. He wants you, too," Catherine finished. "Once he's done with her, you're next."

"Huh."

Her eyebrow lifted ever-so-slightly. "Huh? That's all you have to say?"

He added a slow shrug to his tired response. "I mean Makolichi and Daringol wanted to kill me, yeah, but this... this feels *personal*. I'm not entirely sure how to feel about that. Scared? Honored?"

"It *is* personal, you daft little twa–" she began before she caught herself and tried to rein her frustration in. "I don't want you to go in but I know short of tying you to a horse and sending you out into the countryside, you're going to do it. Plus if I ignore my duty and I *don't* order you then..."

Akaran didn't answer her except for giving her a short little nod as he shifted his armor across his shoulders. "Then I'm going in right now. Gods only know what he did to overturn the protections."

"You're going to go in without trying to understand what spells he's wrought first? Did Steelhom forget to teach you that you should know the lay of the land, and the way the eddies of ether are blowing before you approach a haunting?"

He ignored the high-pitched tenor to her voice and gave her another shrug for good measure. "I'd like to be inside before it gets completely dark. If I can get a head start, I can catch Bistra before he can."

"You assume he isn't already in there."

"Sun hasn't gone down yet."

"He's a master of shadow and darkness – how much do you think he *cares* about the sun?" Catherine demanded. "This monster is more powerful than you are now and will *ever* be and you're just going to rush in and stick your dick in it and hope it doesn't get bitten off?"

Akaran shook a finger at her and balked. "I am *not* sticking my dick in *anything*. I also promise that I'm going to do my best to keep it otherwise attached."

"You know what I mean!" she shouted as she flung her arms open wide (and as more than a few pair of eyes snapped over to see what the commotion was about). "If anyone is going in there, it's me. If anyone is going in there, it's the entire damn Army of Dawn. So yes, I'm going to order you in, yes, I'm going to pray you say no, and *yes*, I'm going to –"

"Except you *aren't* and you know it," he shot back. "You – *you, especially you of all people* – know that right now, the *only* place for you is *out here* so that if I don't kill that son of a bitch, he doesn't break containment. Plus, you *damn well* know that nobody in this city would be able to sleep tonight knowing that Bistra is in there by herself with nothing but Annix to keep her company," he heatedly argued. "Sleep tonight or any other night."

She took the words like she'd been slapped across the face, but it didn't do much to dissuade her. "So we sit out here and listen to you scream with her."

"No, I expect that you'll be busy working with Telburn to make sure that the Manor gets turned into a smoking crater before midnight," he countered. "We know *where* he'll be *when* he'll be if he isn't already in there – and you're probably right that he is. You need me to *keep* him be while you put up a wall the size of the damned Equalin Mountains to keep him locked down."

"When we were worried about her being bait, it wasn't supposed to be bait to trap you!" Catherine thundered. "And *yes*, before you utter another word out of your smart-assed mouth, I *know* this fight is pointless but I don't have to pretend to be *happy* about it."

"Then why are you having one instead of getting ready?"

She ran her fingers roughly through her hair and bit back a scream. "Because I am *hoping* that if I yell at you long enough while you stare at the God of Death you'll reconsider going up there and pissing on His robe or… or…"

He pursed her lips slightly and sucked on air as he watched her struggle to contain her own frustration. She had a good point, which he had to agree about, but… "Or? What's the 'or,' Maiden?"

"Or I'll irritate you enough that you slow down and think of a way to prove me wrong and *not* get killed."

"Oh." After a moment passed, he tilted his head slightly and started to say, "You know that's an interesting –"

"I've tried ordering, I've tried yelling, I've tried bargaining, I've tried hinting," she spat back as she stepped to the side and gave him an encouraging 'welcoming' motion with her arms in the direction of the Manor. "I've about run out of ways to encourage you to try *thinking*. Now I'm going to go yell at people that'll *listen* since *you* won't," she added as she pulled his sword out of its sheath and pointed it at his chin as he stood there dumbfounded.

Akaran grabbed at her wrist but she smacked him away. "Maiden, we can't wait. He's there, or he's about to be there. We wait, and we may lose him again. This time for good."

"We won't," she promised as she started to walk away with his blade in her hands. "We won't, and I refuse to send you in as a sacrificial lamb. Go find a spot, sit down, and pray. *You* need guidance and *I* need to get the troops ready."

"We can't wait. He can take her and –"

"Then I just lose one," Catherine intoned, "and not two."

***

Seline watched the argument unfold without saying a word, though it was the Lieutenant-Commander that broke her out of her reverie. "On the list of people that shouldn't be here, you're on top of it. C'mon Sel, let's get you gone."

"People that shouldn't... shouldn't be here?" she scoffed. "You're one to talk."

The guardsman winced but didn't go anywhere. Instead, he pulled off his helmet and tucked it under his arm. He was covered in soot, ash, and filth from head to toe and the edges of his cloak had gotten singed from the fires he'd been busy setting. "I'm getting you out of Basion. Do you have any belongings back at your dormasil you want me to go get or...?"

"My life is... is there," she said as she gestured at the Manor. "I do... do have clothes back at my place and..."

"I'll gather up anything that you can use. Just tell me what you need."

The medicannia sighed and dropped her head a little. "You're being... uncharacteristically... nice."

"One of us has to be," he grunted. "Not safe for you here, '*Line*," Henderschott replied with a smirk as he pronounced it as 'lean.'

"You haven't called me... called me that since I... we... were kids."

"Because you grew up. I'd be doing a shit job if I didn't try looking after you now. C'mon. I'm gonna have one of my men run you back."

She pointed over at Catherine and the gaggle of soldiers she had under her command. "Your men... they're needed. Here. You can't send one... send one back with me. You've done... done enough."

"I can't believe you listened to me when I showed up earlier," he pointed out. "Now that I've done what that prick asked, I can't send you back by yourself and that one-eyed jackass is too busy kneeling on the ground and cursing the sky right now to be of any use. Pretty sure he's about to go do some bad shit anyway."

Seline couldn't stop the nervous laugh in her voice. "Him? Bad shit? He'd never."

"Oh no, he'd never," the guardsman replied with a deadpanned drawl. "Speaking of bad shit, heard you gave him a lot of it last time you saw him."

"He deserves it."

"Not gonna doubt *that* any, but, Sirrah Priestly Asshole is your friend, isn't he?"

A slight tremor went through her shoulders and down her arms at the word. Just the *idea* made her tongue tremble and her stammer worse. "Friend...? I have seen more... more people *die* being his *friend... my* friends die... since he entered... entered my life. Entered *our* life. I can't even *talk* right... right anymore because... 'cause of him!"

Henderschott gave her a fleeting, tender smile and carefully, gently, took her jaw in his hand and made her look up. "People would've died even if they weren't your friends or if you hadn't seen them. There still would've been funerals. Still would've been people crying in their bedrooms," he lamented. "Difference is you got to see up close and personal what the people you take care of went through before they ended up in that house."

"Now I'm... I'm one of them," the healer spat. "I can't... can't sleep. Can't get near water. Can't see bugs. I do I scream. I do I shake. I shake now because... because that bitch kept putting my head under water and I... I couldn't breathe and my head it hurt my head and my tongue went numb and my face and my head *hurt* and I don't I... I..."

"You went through shit. I get it. It happens."

"*NO YOU DON'T!*" Seline screamed. "He pulled me through his bullshit and now I'm... eating as much cocasa as he did just so... just so I can steady my hand to... to wipe my cunt when I piss!"

"You're not wrong, 'Line, but —"

"You lost all... rights to call... call me that," she snapped as she slapped at the air. "What are you... you trying to do? Make me sound... sound more like a fool? Come here to... embarrass me... in front of these people?"

Hender dodged the slap and caught her hand before she could go for his face. "I'm here, *Seline*," he stressed, "because as angry as you are at him, you know it's not his fault Anais worked you over. You know he'd have rescued you if he could. He had more feelers out looking for you than he did the vampire asshole, and even though it wasn't him that found you, I know he tried."

She jerked away and hugged herself as hard as she could with an angry huff. "I can't believe you're... you're taking his damn side. You... you don't even like him."

The guard answered with a shrug and a nod. "You're right. I think he's an absolute bastard. He's part of why I want to get you out of Basion. He makes it through this, shit is going to get really fisking miserable from the top down for a while and I don't want you to be part of it," he replied. "I also know that if he goes in there and doesn't come out, you're going to be mad at yourself."

Seline's jaw dropped to her chest. "Why on... why on anything would... would I be mad if...?"

"Remember when I nearly lost my damn leg?"

"Like... like I could forget. You remember who helped... change your bandages?"

"I do. I ever tell you what got me through it?"

The healer paused and searched her addled brain for a few long heartbeats. "No...?"

"The boys in the 2nd Naval caught the pirates responsible. I got a front-row seat to see 'em hung."

"You never... never told me."

"You were too young," he replied quietly. "Knowing that even though I'd never be on a ship again, they'd never hurt anyone else? Helped me move through it. Hoping that talking to him will do the same and honestly 'Line? I don't know if you're gonna get the chance again. Besides," he added, "aren't you supposed to know this shit? Being a head-talker or whatever they call your people?"

"Meta... metaphysician," Seline whined. "I've told you that a... a *dozen* damn times you... you..."

The guard smirked at her and extended his arm. After a brief hesitation, she ducked under it and let him drape it over her shoulders. "Yeah, yeah. Me, me," he agreed. "Gonna go talk to the dumb-ass or do you want me to send you on out? It's your choice."

"I guess... I guess there's one thing I... I can tell him," she finally admitted as she watched him stand up to go angrily confront his boss again. "But I... I'm not leaving."

"Why in the world *not*?" Henderschott demanded. "If I had any say in the matter, *I'd* be leaving."

Seline swallowed nervously but tried to give him a reassuring smile that was anything but. "Because if he... if he doesn't win I..." she tried to explain before she took a deep gulp of breath, "I want to know so I can go jump... jump off the cliff."

***

The medicianna strode towards Akaran as if the forces of the Divine were in her wake. He wasn't doing anything of note, as far as she could tell. He was just standing quietly, facing the Manor, with one hand on a stave someone had found for him to use as a makeshift cane. The exorcist wasn't about to admit it to *anyone* but the recent trend of running from one execution to the next had done his leg absolutely no favors. Even worse, this was far from the time to use even *more* magic to tire himself out trying to dull the pain radiating out from it.

She thought he was just watching the Manor for signs of life (or un-) until she stepped in front of him and realized his eye was closed and his face was half-slack like he was sound asleep standing up. The little blonde healer studied his face for a few long heartbeats and very slowly brought a piece of cocasa to her lips. When he didn't react, she bit down on it with an audible *crunch* as she chewed through the dried leaf.

When he didn't even flinch, she casually pulled her hand back and slapped him across the face so hard that spittle flew from his mouth. His not-so-casual shout of surprise and anger brought all eyes around the camp right to him even as she looked at him like nothing was wrong at all.

"Don't you... don't..." she stammered as he cursed in confusion and rubbed his stinging cheek.

"Don't WHAT?!"

"After all I've... all I've done for you... don't..." she replied as she made a strangled growl. "Don't *die* you *asshole*."

"Sel, wait," he implored as the shock of the slap wore off. "The apology... did you get it?"

Seline's jaw dropped as she looked into his eye. "Is... is that what you... you really want to... call it?"

"It's the best I can offer."

A mix of raw emotions played over her face and through her eyes as she stared at him in disbelief. "I... yes. I got it."

"Did you accept it or..."

"You are... you..." the healer replied slowly before she ran her hands through her frazzled hair. "May the Gods... Goddesses too... pity whatever woman that... ends up spreading her legs... for you if... if that's what... how you... think an *apology*," she stammered. "Ye... yes. I got... got it. I... I accepted it."

"Thank you."

"Oh... oh shove it," she spat.

Seline stormed off before he could reply with another word, and he stood there transfixed by the entire scene with his mouth agape until Catherine came up behind him. "I heard you two went to the Danse Festistanis together. It's not working out?"

He slowly rubbed his cheek again and then gave his boss a plaintive look. "Can I have my sword back? I'd like to go kill the vampire now."

"Only if you have a plan."

"I have a plan."

"Is it more involved than just walking in there, pulling your cock out and going, 'Here I am, suck on it!' or...?"

"You're thinking a lot about my dick, you know that, right?"

Catherine sighed and shook her head slightly. "You seem to do most of your thinking with your balls rather than your brain. Thought I'd try to reach you using words you understand."

He almost laughed. Almost. Instead, he turned to her and crossed his arms. "You know, a little respect at this point would go a long way. I think I've earned it."

"You get what you give," she deftly retorted as she handed him his weapon back. "Did you hear from Elsith?"

"No. Where is she?"

"Medic's tent," the Maiden replied. "You know how she rushed her way up here ahead of us? Guess she went off into the woods hunting. She came back looking rough. Culled two, but took a shot across the head. She's out of the fight. She's *lucky* she's still standing. Karaj found two more. They buried a *lot* of people out there."

Akaran exhaled a deep, nervous breath. "If those really are Sherril's spawn, Annix may not have a lot of control over them. It's the only thing that makes sense."

"Or longer, and now without their sire to keep them in place," Catherine agreed. "Either way – the Huntsmatron is hurt. We're going to sweep but..."

He swore suddenly and snapped his fingers. "No. No, you won't have to. If he doesn't have control over them, they're going to go to the closest pulse they can find. They won't wander the woods. They'll come *here*. He knew they'd come *here* no matter what Ridora decided to do. They'd either destroy the Manor, or fail and scare us into reacting – *again* – or be warded off into the city where they'd make things *worse*. Now the only thing we can do is make sure that they don't get past the line."

"Or it's a massacre that will spawn a legion of them." The Maiden felt the color fade from her face and she dropped her hand to grip the hammer dangling from her belt. "Goddess *dammit* do you have to make sense so often?"

"Yes?" he quipped. "So you don't need to go hunting. You just need to stay here and keep them out of the Manor as much as you can."

"That's the other problem," she sighed. "Elsith said she found a tunnel. It's not far out. Any worries we had *if* he's in there no longer apply. We can safely say he's already working Bistra over Or getting ready to."

"Which means I have to go in now. We can't wait."

"*We* have to go in, Akaran."

He rolled his eye and clenched his fist. "*You* are busy out here. We had that argument, and I'm standing by it. Turn the Manor to dust if you have to, but block that tunnel and secure the grounds." Before she could offer a retort, he frowned and looked at the suddenly-ominous structure as the last glimmers of daylight left its face. "I can't believe that the gardener missed it."

"Yannis? Yeah. Ridora said that he was the body she found before Annix jumped her."

"Oh. Damn."

Catherine let loose a deep sigh and followed his gaze. "You have a plan?"

"Yeah," he answered before he laid it out for her. It was short, sweet, and only vaguely more complicated than the one she had guessed at earlier. "Lock it down. Lock it all down. If he's got a tunnel, he's got a way out. He'll *be* out before we can do more than piss on the doorstep unless he's waiting in there for me."

"So you're going to go in there and make enough of a spectacle to make sure you get his full attention," she noted. "I watched you piss off an actual warship, so if anyone can do it, it's gonna be you."

Akaran glanced back at her. "I'm not sure that's as much of a compliment as you think it is."

"Good, because it isn't. And good, because I'm going to do the same thing and piss *you* off for a change."

The way she said it took his full attention, and he wasn't sure he was happy about it. "Maiden...? What did I do now?"

"Survived."

He blinked. Once. "Cath?"

The Maiden-Templar took one more deep breath to steady herself and folded her arms across her stomach. Her armor jingled as she moved, and an errant glint of torchlight made the Order sigil on her chest glimmer for a brief moment. "You wanted to know why you? Why the Red Death is after you?" she asked. "It's because you survived."

"Now?" he asked, equal parts bewildered and oddly irritated. "You picked… now… to tell me about him?"

"I did. I'm going to tell you something that's going to piss you off. It's going to piss you off and I'm doing it so you have the motivation to *not die in there*. This doesn't go beyond us and I'm still going to hit Karaj in the face with *The Shattered Ruby*, so listen."

He felt his jaw clench harder and harder the longer she talked and she hadn't even said anything worthwhile yet. "Pissing me off is how you intend to keep me going?"

The smile that blossomed on her lips had nothing to do with *joy* or *kindness*. "I've seen what you do when you're angry."

"And what, Maiden, do you think I'm going to do?"

"Get angry."

Catherine started to talk – and what she told him was the truth. A truth he didn't know. A truth he couldn't wrap his head around. The details were interesting at worst, confusing at best, and she left a lot to the imagination. Some of it he already knew, and some of it he'd guessed.

All of it about the Man of the Red Death.

Nastavol DeHawk.

A Sycian, though from which of the Jewels he hailed from was unknown. Thought to be almost a decade older than Akaran, but that couldn't be confirmed. Born in one of the nomad territories outside of the Jewels of Sycio. Father unknown. Mother unknown.

"Necrosia. That's his power base, if you haven't guessed. I have a good idea who his patron is. Can't confirm, so won't suggest it." she went on to add.

"Rot?"

"Worse. Much worse."

That made it a very short list of potential 'bad.'

Necrosia. That was one thing *everyone* agreed on. The Order suspected he had a level of mastery of the art on par with a Headmaster-Adept. The Order *feared* he had a level of mastery closer to an Orbit-Adept… a step below the Grand Dean himself. The work he'd done on Donta and Anais pushed his perceived abilities even higher.

He was blamed for the Fall of A'twol in Sycio. What Akaran didn't know? Was that he was also blamed directly for an ugly upheaval in Ogibus in the middle of the Privateer Wars. Those were bad enough, but not enough to make him an enemy of Dawnfire.

That came after he helped assassinate a man named Anod.

A man of great power. Of great respect. Of great stature and status.

A man who was literally a king.

The world could've come to an end on the spot, and Akaran wouldn't've even noticed. "I... I mean I know the stories. Anod... King Anod. Everyone loved him. There was an attack in Mulvette. His quarters and..."

"Yes. An envoy from the Missian League smuggled a small force into the Citadel of Dawn. A few men turned into an army, one that grew in size with each man they killed – and immediately raised from the dead. Anod was one of them."

"The League disavowed having any knowledge of it, too, didn't they?"

"They had to," she replied, "and still the Queen had to be begged not to destroy them in retaliation. The crown fell to her that day, and she's led Dawnfire ever since."

"But... me? Why... me? That was before the Order found me and..."

She slowly shook her head and offered him a regretful smile. "Was it? Horrific magics were used that day. There was more than one man who lost their mind. You were found not far from the city gates, bewildered, confused, bloody, hurt. It was a couple of days after. It's assumed you wandered out of one of the castle injured, though we don't know how you got in. Most of the Queen's staff that night ended up dead. You know your own story after."

"There... there had to be other survivors, right? I mean the stories say that the Queen's Guard rallied and –"

"Yes. They rallied and cleansed the castle of all malfeasance and monstrosity, and the Order purged Mulvette of anything unholy. We both know the stories. The truth that doesn't get talked about? There were other people that survived that night... who didn't survive much longer than that. You are, it seems, one of very few ones that got away."

"I don't understand. Got away from *what*?"

"The assassin's name was Rathinal Nal'Shaga. We learned that much. He didn't make it out of the throne room. A witness said one of his men stabbed him in the back and left him to die. A boy – one just a few years younger than you are now. That boy?" she asked as a sudden chill made her hands shake for a moment, "Well. He cleaned up after the League.

Honestly? He has more blood on his hands than the two of us combined, and that was before he took the title of the Red Death."

Akaran took a breath and looked over at the Manor as she continued to tell her story. "The assassin was murdered and... you think Nastavol did it?"

"We *know* he did. We know he killed the Ambassador from the League. We know he killed the Captain of the Citadel's Gate. We know he killed a stableboy. The things he did as he left the Kingdom? Every person that the Queen was able to trace to Anod's murder was dead by the time we got to them and the things he did to the corpses? He may have been an older boy but whatever he actually *was* defied *humanity*. And years later... you know about A'twol. A monster here, a monster there, and now a monster *back* in our borders."

"But... why... why not tell me? Why... hide that?" he demanded as he stepped in close. His voice had dropped to a desperate whisper while he tried to churn through the revelations.

Catherine put a single finger on his forehead and willed a small sliver of calming magic into his heart. She needed him angry, but directed. Directed *away* from her. "Because of the Queen's command. Anyone that might be involved was purged. Innocent, guilty, it didn't matter. If you were *there* and you didn't have a good excuse to *be* there, she had them killed. Though after what Nastavol did? I think she killed more innocents than *he* did, even if not by much."

"I was... I was just a boy though and I couldn't..."

"A boy age of eight is a boy that can hold a knife and you know it. You may not have had any kind of hand in it but since nobody claimed a child of your build then what were we supposed to do? '*Here is a stranger at our doorstep, he knows nothing, trust us*?' Our heads would have found a pike beside yours. The Goddess spoke through the Sisters and told us what we were to do: protect you."

Akaran shook his head violently 'no' as he struggled to reconcile what she was saying. "I knew there was a bloodbath afterward. I didn't know about Anod until... two years later? I didn't wake up in Mulvette? Why... how...?"

"The Queen made it clear that any with no excuse that could be verified were to be considered complicit. There wasn't anything to do. You were smuggled out of the province. The reason you never saw Mulvette for two winters after was because the Order was afraid to let you go there. We assume you're on his list because you're one of the few that *might* know *why* Rathinal did it. That seems to be a secret he wants to protect."

"But I don't know! I don't even know if I was there!"

Catherine shook her head slowly. "*You* may not, but does your soul? What you just did to Sherril – can it be done to you if someone sets their mind to it? Does it matter? He's killed everyone that might have been involved and now he has his sights on your head? I have to ask why and I don't think either one of us want the answer to that question."

He felt his grip tighten on the end of his cane as he tried to digest the story. "How does he know?"

"I don't know. Nor do I know what he thinks he knows. I know that you were there – or at least, near. That is the only tie that binds you. You were never in the same city in the same time at any other point in your life in the Order, and it is the only excuse we have. We could well be wrong. I do not know."

"How do you know this? Were you there?" he demanded quietly as other Lovers began to congregate around them. "Were you one of the ones that…?"

"No," Catherine answered in a hushed voice. "I wasn't. Your name is on a scroll in a very small stack of papers in the bottom of the Vault. The Order knows *everyone's* secrets, Akaran. You are far from the only person I've read about but you are quickly turning into one I don't want to have to deal with so *believe* me when I say that what I give you is the truth. I'm breaking a Seal of Order by telling you this, and I trust you're going to want to investigate it so that means you have to survive tonight to do it. Right?"

Akaran stared at her, and slowly took a single step back.

The wind whispered once, and the breeze was tinged with a foul taste of disgust. She tried to give him a reassuring smile. Tried to make it right. But he heard the condemnation on the current, and that was all he needed to know.

[Liar.]

A moment later, and he turned from her to face the Manor.

When he spoke, he didn't address her. He called out to the one friend he had that he knew hadn't lied to him. Who he knew in his hearts of hearts he could trust. One he knew would never do anything wrong, would never cross him, and who he could trust with his life.

A few yards away, Badin planted his feet. Cracked his knuckles. Stretched out his palm. The door to the Manor shattered from the force of the bolt of lighting that tore down his arm in a loud explosion of magic, thunder, and rage.

She had told him the truth. *A truth with a very big lie buried within.*

He could smell the lie in her words like the rot that covered it. He didn't know why. Or what. But he knew. Her eyes had given it away. A faint flicker in her eyes as she lied to his face while filling his heart with everything he always needed but never wanted to hear. She was right; it was going to piss him off enough to make him want to survive.

A truth, and a lie, that would have consequences.

Annix would experience them. There was no question to that.

Except there was a truth Catherine didn't know, too.

Everyone watched the exorcist steel himself, flex his shoulders, and then ever-so-casually, they watched as he holstered his sword and turned around with a tired sigh. "Well, that's all that then. Thanks everyone; I'm out."

Every minute since they'd arrived at the Manor?

It was all part of *his* lie.

Catherine didn't budge. She just froze in place, opened her mouth, and miraculously managed to get sounds out that formed a word. "What?"

The exorcist stopped and looked at her in matching disbelief. "Do you really think – do you *really think* that I'm walking into there? The Goddess only knows how many broodlings already waiting to rip my arms off. So, no. I'm not doing it."

"But you just... you..." she stammered as the entire might of the Order ground to a halt all across the field.

"I walk in there, I'm dead," Akaran replied as simply and honestly as he could. "We all know it. If you really think I am, then *you* need to be the next resident Ridora treats. Seriously Cath, how damn dumb do you think I am? You just lied to my face – and don't even try to deny *that* – and you really think *that's* going to inspire me to go kill myself? No. N. O. *No.*"

"But Bistra...! You... you're abandoning her?" she demanded in a high-pitched screech as she *desperately* tried to fathom what he was up to.

A crowd started to form around them as he watched everyone's face. Karaj had come over. Seline was on the outskirts of the stunned gathering. Hadraie stood right beside her, but it was the Overseer that spoke the loudest.

Overseer Hannock.

Just the man he'd been waiting for.

"EXORCIST! Are you forsaking your duty to the crown? You're the one that required my presence! You demanded I be here to see what – your cowardice?"

Akaran's smirk matched his sardonic reply. "I mean if that's what you think it is," he retorted as he pulled his left glove off and pulled up the sleeve on his tunic to show off a rune etched onto his arm. "I suppose I should just ask everyone to **speak truth and be judged** to save some fisking ti... OW."

The words fell out of his mouth and the sudden agony that flared from the rune in his arm and into the back of his skull nearly put him down to his knees. As it was, it was enough to make the world spin and his stomach heave. The Maiden caught him before he fell on his face, though it was a miracle she even bothered. "Exorcist, I again say –"

"Akaran have you lost your mind you fisking bloody idiot?" Catherine snarled in his ear as he struggled to keep himself together. The pain was immense, though honestly?

He was just happy it wasn't from his knee. "BISTRA ENIL. WHERE IS SHE?" he demanded. As he spoke, the rune on his arm blossomed back to life and burned so fiercely that it scorched the skin around it and indescribable starbursts of pain erupted across his sight.

A pressure fell across the shoulders of everyone within a fifteen foot radius around him. Catherine realized what it was, but she was too mad to wonder *why*. "She's in the damn manor, you... you... WHATEVER YOU ARE! Because I don't know what you are and who you are or –!" the Maiden seethed before she realized the effect his spell was having on her even she tried to keep him upright.

"Karaj?"

Catherine's assistant answered the same. Two other Lovers spoke up otherwise unbidden, as did one of the orderlies. Compelled by the invocation, they answered one after another.

Each response made Akaran sink further and further to the ground like someone was shoveling bricks onto his shoulders. Off to the side, the blonde healer, however, slapped a hand over her mouth as her eyes went wide. Her fingers flexed over her lips as she struggled to keep her mouth shut – as she made almost adorable little spluttering noises.

Hannock, however?

The one man that always opened his mouth whenever air and space gave him an opportunity? Well, he spoke alright. "Well she... she has to be in... the place she's... she's in," he stammered.

"Yes... yes she is," the exorcist replied with a growing smile even through the pain. "You seem to have some trouble talking. Let me... help with that. **Disenchant**."

The second spell undid the first as quickly and easily as unfastening a clasp on a too-tight corset. The Overseer visibly relaxed and nearly slumped forward as Seline did the same. Seline gasped for air while the Lover pushed his boss away. While Cath and his fellow Order brethren tried to collect themselves, he marched over to one of the most powerful men in all of the Province.

And then Akaran punched him in dead-center in the face.

Hannock fell to his knees and flopped onto his face as blood streamed out of his broken nose. The crowd watched in stunned silence as he put his boot on the Overseer's shoulder and pushed him deeper into the mud. "By order of… the… well… me," he spat out slowly as the effects of the invocation dissipated, "if he tries to leave, someone cave his skull in. Yeah. That's the order. Cave his head in," he added as he clutched at the side of his.

Catherine didn't move. She couldn't. Nobody could. "What did you just do?"

"Bistra isn't there. I had her moved."

"Bistra isn't… you… *you what*?"

Akaran shrugged and flexed the fingers on his hand. "Annix made a lot of moves that took a lot of money. Didn't know how, 'till after the caves. Thank Riorik for it. Hannock was supplying Annix with things he needed — a spot in the tunnels, quiet way to get food. *Home furnishings*," he added as he thought back to the mirrors and worse. "Annix would pay him off by getting him women he could sell outside the city. Lady Hosheck was the woman in the middle, while Hannock worked with Odern and Livstra. Don't think either of them knew what he was doing, but that's it. That's how. He got away with it because this fat fisk was busy selling flesh to anyone that wanted it outside the gate."

The Maiden felt her tongue try to crawl into her throat as her mouth went dry. "Oh. Oh, I… I see. That's quite… quite an accusation… that I pray, oh I pray, you have proof of? Please?"

"Enough to punch him," he replied. "I knew Annix would do something. Fisker… fisker always does. I didn't know what. I didn't know about Ridora or that she'd get targeted. As far as anyone knows, Bistra is sitting alone in the garden. Seline made sure of it. Annix isn't dumb enough to go into the Manor himself for her no matter what, because he doesn't have a way out if he does. I wasn't expecting this but I knew he'd want to do *something*."

"So you had her moved? How? Did you say Seline? But she…?"

"I… I did," the medicannia admitted. "We found a place… place for her. Akaran figured… well… she was being watched by someone in… in the 4th. Just didn't… know by who," she stammered.

"You didn't think that it would help if you blessedly let me in on this little plot of yours?!" his boss thundered as the crowd started to wilt away under her wrath. "You're alleging a crime against the city by the *Overseer himself* and you gave no thought to tell me?"

"Because I'm alleging a plot against the city and you're in enough trouble as it is," he retorted. "If I was wrong, you'd be bent over sideways. Knew I was right just... needed to be sure. Didn't want you to go down with me."

"While I appreciate that more than I think I'm going to freely admit," she replied after she stared daggers at him, "are you suggesting you have an innocent in the Manor waiting to be torn to shreds by the bastard's minions?"

He blinked and suddenly shook his head. "Oh. No. Not an innocent at all. Promise. Anything happens in there, no complaints from me. Sel? You?"

"No... no, burn... burn it down," Seline added. "Plea... please. I'll... help. Pro... promise."

"When did you... how did you hatch this...?"

"It was after Sherril," he admitted. "Karaj and I realized that Annix would expect to lose his lair in Naradol and anywhere else Sherril knew about. So I made sure that Hender and Hadraie hauled their asses over *here* and got word to Seline. Needed her help, too."

The blonde woman crossed her arms and gave a smug little look. "He made... made a deal. I couldn't... pass it up."

Catherine looked down at the Overseer and tried her absolute best to strangle every curse she had in her throat. She managed, somehow, to do it, but not easily. "Then what... he's going to know you figured it out. You just..."

"Oh, I know. I screwed everything up. So now, I'm going to assume he's going to go look for her if he hasn't started already. It won't take long and truthfully, those broodlings out there are going to be a problem. So you go deal with *them*," he suggested as he gestured his head back towards the Manor, "and I'm gonna do the one damn thing that nobody's let me do for *weeks*."

"What?" the Maiden demanded as she fought the urge to strangle the man then and there.

He straightened up and kicked the Overseer in the ribs for good measure. "I'm going to go get a drink. Don't even *try* to stop me or so help me..."

***

As he left, a cloaked figure in the Manor garden shook against the chains holding her arms and legs in place until her hood fell from her eyes. Gagged and bound, Anais looked up at the three Divine statues overhead, and felt her hair start to singe under Their gaze. Every time she tried to move, the statue of Niasmis would glow just a little brighter, and the light would warm up the broker's skin just a little more.

Truth and lies had consequences.

Annix would experience them.

He just wouldn't be the first.

XIII. TVASTARIAN
Evening of Staddis, 18th of Firstgrow, 513 QR

"Warmaiden Emadina. I'm not surprised to see you, but I am grateful," Akaran said by way of greeting along with a short bow of his head.

The Warprince's bodyguard bowed her head to match and gave him a tender smile. "It is always a pleasure to provide assistance for the Exorcist of Elements. Anything you wish, we will provide."

"She means it, too," another voice chimed in from the entrance to the *Drunken Imperial*. "After all you have done, there is no end to the thanks we can give."

"Malik," the exorcist replied with another warm smile – even if it was couched in apprehension. "I thought I asked that you stay away...?"

"No end to the thanks, but an end to the favors," the leather-and-fur-wrapped muscle-man replied with a short laugh. "Hylene suggested that I lend my blade. I am one to listen when one's wife speaks."

"She is not as... assured... of the talents of his living weapons... as she is of the talents of his personal blade," the Warmaiden added. "The former is due as much credit as the latter."

Akaran coughed and felt a slight bit of a blush creep up his neck. "Yes well. Did you have any problems?"

Her navy-blue eyes seemed to flash in amusement at the question. "We have yet had problems since we arrived, only *inconveniences*. There was one, and inconvenience no longer. The barkeep has him now."

That was about what he'd expected. On both fronts. "Good. And the woman?"

"Unhappy, and not one to do a great deal of talking," Malik replied. "Yet otherwise compliant. I can tell she is a soul unwell. Is it the city? I have heard how places like this can be toxic for souls not accustomed to them. More than half of the Odinal tribe-holders refuse to settle behind walls for just that reason."

"It's not the city, but the city hasn't been helping," the Lover admitted. "Though I appreciate that you did. It means a lot."

"I suspect you're about to ask that we take our exit, aren't you?" Malik's protector asked with a raised eyebrow. "You have the look of a man prepared to meet fate."

Akaran didn't answer her directly, but he bowed his head again at the Midlander. "Son of Odinal, I'd be acting against the Crown if I didn't ask that you leave for now for your safety. It's not that I don't want you, it's that I'm scared of what Hylene would do to me if you got injured."

"Is the fate you prepare to seek the one that nearly took him from his bride?" the Warmaiden asked.

"It is."

She stepped forward and placed a fingertip on his chest, just above the collar of his tabard. "Will it be the last time he darkens a door?"

"If I do it right."

"If you don't?"

"Then I won't be around to care."

Emadina pursed her lips and looked so deep into his eye he felt like she was stripping him down to the bare flesh right then and there. "Then do it right," she finally remarked with a hint of something that was *more* than a smile at the edge of her lips. "Son of Master of Chiefs? He shows wisdom. We should do as he asks."

Malik sighed and slowly began to button his coat again. "If it is your wish, my *lebdiaon*, we shall go. I too will join her in asking that you 'do it right,' whatever it is you choose to do."

"Lebdia...?" Akaran mouthed quietly.

"Lover of his lover," she answered in the Warprince's stead. "His new bride has not yet come to understand the meaning of the word. It gets quite cold in the north and the men are not always on hand."

The exorcist's eye went wide as a flush exploded across his cheeks. "Oh. Oh, well. I'm glad that the Goddess reaches the hearts of those outside the Kingdom, as always," he hastily answered back a suddenly-bashful gulp. Before she could find a new way to make that blush grow even further, Akaran extended his arms and offered the big man a hug — which surprised both of the Midlanders, but the prince was quick to accept it. "I choose to end this. For all of our sakes."

The Warmaiden looked between the two young men and let the

voracious smile on her face grow even wider. "Warprince? Of the lowlanders you've granted me an audience with, I prefer this one. May I keep him?"

There was something... *something...* in her voice that made the slight blush he'd had blossom up his entire neck and across his face. While the exorcist tried to stammer out a reply, Malik stepped away and draped his arm over her shoulder with a laugh. "Brother Oun-blood of Odinal, let me just say that should you ever need, you will always have a bed in the Midlands. More than one, mayhaps."

They left without another word, for which the Lover was *exceptionally* grateful for reasons he couldn't even *begin* to put a finger on. Which was just fine, because once he stepped inside the *Imperial*, Cel had a use for fingers. One, specifically.

Once she was done flipping him off and growling assorted blasphemies in his general direction, she crossed her arms and stormed out from behind the bar. "Still limpin'. I ain't even surprised. I can't believe I let you talk my fat ass into this."

"All I asked was for just a safe —"

"You asked me for a safe place two fisking hours before you set half the district on fire!" Cel shouted back. "Now I've got *nobody* in *no rooms* when there's whole damn neighborhoods that need a place to stay and they ain't got a place to stay and I ain't got a way to charge them so they can stay here since you made me promise!"

Akaran took a short step back and shook his head. "I promise that after tonight it'll be well worth your while."

"Are you at all familiar with the laws of *supply* and *demand*?" she argued as she refused to let him get further than a hand's distance away. "Now there's a host of *demand* that I can't *supply* because you promised you'd pay my normal rate! Well, the cost just went up, half-blind boy," the oft-maligned innkeep spat in his face.

It didn't matter that most of the time, she was the one doing the maligning. "Are you familiar with the *Queen's* law?" he replied as he took two steps back. "Where she *demands* that certain people *don't supply* other people with *certain things* that we both know you do?"

A very unpleasant shadow crossed her eyes and she thumped the end of her nose with the tip of her pointer finger. "You better be good for the bill. I'll have the Overseer put you in the stocks if you don't."

"He'll have to scoot over first," the priest grunted. "I promise, you'll be rewarded. One night. It's all it's going to take."

"You better be out of here by — oh. He will, will he?"

"He will."

"You?"

"Me."

Cel sucked on her tongue and tapped her foot for a moment while she thought about what he'd just said. Finally, the stubborn mule (in all the best ways) of a woman tapped the end of his nose again. "Well. Okay. Then all isn't forgiven but it is... celebrated. By the way – can you ever show up here *not* looking like a damned drowned rat? And you smell like the inside of a blacksmith's hut if they'd been using chicken shit to melt iron."

He sighed and gently moved her hand away from his face. "You'll forgive me eventually because you are a kind woman with a warmer heart than you're willing to say. And no. I'm always going to look like a drowned rat because people are always trying to kill me."

"Do you blame them?" she asked. "Really?"

Akaran didn't bother to dignify that with an answer. He just huffed.

"Not a kind woman either, thank you. I have a reputation. I'm doing this because that sick cunter Donta's gone and word on the street is that your people have the broker-bitch tied up and rotting somewhere – but you ain't getting more favors unless you start earning them."

He let out a little sigh of tired frustration as the sun started to set outside. "Can't promise, will try. Who's the idiot in the corner?"

"Oh yeah, him," Cel replied as she followed his gaze over. "Dumb-ass over there had his nose a little too close to your *package*. Claimed to be a guard. He ain't. Found the Over's sigil in his jacket, but didn't trust 'im. You said you have Hannock locked up?"

"I think I broke his nose too, if that counts as a favor."

"Yes. Yes it does."

Akaran walked halfway across the inn to confront the bound-and-gagged thug, but stopped mid-stride and looked back over at her. "You know what? I'm not even gonna try. By edict of the Order, go yell at a guard and have them drag his ass to the Repository. I'll deal with him later."

"Oh I ain't going anywhere. You may've kicked all the other patrons outta my place but if you think I'm –"

"Room rate plus ten on the side."

"Room rate plus half."

His face went ashen as he only *imagined* the dressing-down he was going to get from the Master of the Purse. "You do understand that I want to continue living after Catherine gets the bill for this, right?"

"Livin' through the night is on you. Livin' through the morning? That's on your accountant, ain't it?" she countered as she read him like an open book. "Room rate plus thirty."

"Twenty," he countered. "Please."

Cel curled her lip and agreed – with an addendum. "You break the building and you shovel shit for a week."

"Someone shovels. My choosing. Deal?"

"Deal. What about her?" she asked as she pointed at the lone, and otherwise silent woman sitting at the bar with them. "She too or...?"

He shook his head slowly. "She's needed."

The innkeep glanced back and forth between the two of them, and then scooted over to whisper in his ear. "Don't let that one get hurt. I know *damage* when I see it and you've a habit of *adding* to it."

Akaran thought about promising that.

All he did was bow his head.

A few minutes later, and the *Imperial* was empty except for pain.

Bistra hadn't changed much in the nearly two weeks since he'd seen her last. The last time he'd laid eyes on her, she'd asked for help. When he did 'help,' he'd broken a door, shattered a window, and destroyed Annix's shadow. Then? She'd looked tired and terrified.

Now she just looked tired.

The Auramancer Exorcist sat quietly with her eyes transfixed to the top of a lukewarm cup of untouched ale in front of her. Truthfully, she could hardly see it past the loose silvery hair dangling in front of her eyes. It didn't matter either way. What she saw had little to do with the physical world, and it never had. "Do not say it," she whispered.

Akaran sat down beside her and leaned against the rough wooden counter-top. Cel kept the bar clean and well lit every minute of every day, to the point that it was almost intimidating. It made even the shadiest of conversations seem above-board and on the level, yet with this poor broken woman, it somehow made it feel cold and morose. "I have to say a lot of things."

"You do, and 'sorry' is one of them. Often, isn't it?"

"It... I've been known to have to apologize once or twice."

"You've been... known to *should* apologize by... hearts and minds of men. Not... not actually do it," Bistra replied slowly. "Nor is it by the *Gods* that you should. You... there is a distinction. You will learn, if you age. If."

"I really feel like –"

The Auramancer slowly pressed one finger to the wooden counter and made a small swirl on it like she was drawing out a rune. "Years in shadows. Years in pain before I even knew what pain was," she lamented quietly. "At the place of healing, they didn't... don't understand. They say they do but they don't because they don't do what we do and if they don't do what we do how can they know what is wrong when we can't do?" she returned just under her breath.

He felt his mouth start to go dry listening to her. "Because that's what their job is. To try and make it better even when they don't know what's broken."

"Correct," Bistra mumbled. It was next to impossible to hear her, and the pain-filled tremble in her voice made his heart each. "They never apologize for theirs. We do not apologize for ours."

"Maybe we should start," he sighed. "Not you, of course."

"Years of pain delivered then of receiving. Years of giving torment. Years of receiving. We do earn what we offer," she warned. "You should know. Know your gift. Know what you give. Know what you have, know what you are. Because it's important. You are *one thing*, and what the *one thing* you are is what you have to give. That is your aura. That is your essence. That is *you*."

He looked down at his gloves and sighed. They were still caked with corpse-ash from the tannery. Smelled like it, too; Cel hadn't been off with her observation. "I don't know what to say."

"You do not comfort because you are not made to. You are a soul that needs a hand to guide, so that you may do the work you do."

"What's that?"

Bistra stood up and turned to face the stairs leading from above. "The work that's here."

He was in motion before the first shadows could barrel down through the ceiling. Akaran snapped his arm around her waist and pinned her violently against his hip. His right hand pulled a silver-bladed dagger from his belt with such ease it was almost like he'd willed it into being. The candles in the bar flickered and began to vanish one after the other and a spell slipped from his lips.

A wall of light formed around the two humans, but it lasted for barely ten seconds before a shimmering red crack in the air appeared directly in front of them and tore it to shreds. The shadow followed suit; a cold, angry, *living* blob of darkness that coated everything it touched. Coated, swallowed, and claimed all in a moment.

It stopped mere inches away from the priests, only to emit a scream of wordless rage that rattled their ears as much as it did the windows. Wordless screams were replaced by a harsh grating whisper that raked across his heart. "Did you think you could hide from me? Here? Here of all places?"

"No," Akaran replied slowly. The world stretched out off of his lips as he straightened up and put weight back on his good knee. Bistra didn't flinch; the Auramancer kept her head down and eyes focused on floor. "Didn't think I could hide from you at all. It's why I didn't."

"You lie," the shadows whispered. "You thought you could run. You thought you could take her. Moved her from her prison. Brought her where shadows live rather than where light fades."

"I did," the priest answered as he looked around the mass of darkness. The edges of the shadows ebbed and flowed against the few lights left in the Manor, and for a moment, it looked like a flat, shapeless tide. "Didn't want any more interruptions."

A face briefly appeared in the shadows and *bit* at the empty air. "You prolong the inevitable. I have bested you before, and I will best you again."

"Did you? How long did it take for you to grow your shadow back?" Akaran taunted as he turned the corner of his lip up in a snarl. "Your *assassin* bested me, but *you* didn't."

"Tell that to those you held dear. I took from you as I had taken from me. It is your turn next, to be taken from those that care for you."

The exorcist held steady and clenched the object of Annix's desire tight to his side. "Whatever it takes to get justice, right? That's what you want."

"She took from me. I take her." There was a momentary silence before the vampire spoke up again. "It is the Law. It is tvastarian. I will have my yomaldi given anew."

"Then just *take her*," the exorcist spat. He pushed on Bistra, but she didn't move – and the shadows didn't move to claim her. "Except you won't, because that's not *fun* for you, is it?"

The shadows billowed and moved around him, and they spun to cover the bar and the counter at his back. Where they went, light didn't return – candles stayed snuffed, torches remained quiet, and windows continued to be blank. "Tvastarian must be given of will. It is our way."

"The law and justice, huh?" the exorcist growled. "If that's what you want, then you must think I'm the bad guy. I've taken more than she has. Lots more. Haven't I?"

"You have not taken from me anything I cannot replace. You are not worthy of justice. You are not worth the time," Annix taunted as a single claw stretched from the flat shadows.

Akaran watched it slide through the air and didn't flinch as it began to dig into his cheek. "If that was true, you wouldn't bother playing with me. You'd take her and leave and then do all your work in private. So what do you want, Annix? What do you want from me before you go?"

The claw slipped away even as two hands took form on the floor and wrapped themselves around the exorcist's feet. "Your people took the world from me. I will take the world from them. You will give it."

"Give you the world?" he scoffed. "Asshole, I can't even give myself a night's worth of uninterrupted sleep."

"Supplication. That you can give me. You have made weaker souls look to you with reverence. You will show them that your faith is weak before your betters!"

"Which is the same shit you want from her and we've both seen how long that's taken you," Akaran spat back. "Unless you think you're going to get it from me tonight, you're shit out of luck."

The shadows withdrew, then chortled softly. "She took my world. You have taken…? Spawn? A few creatures born of your own kind's flesh? A shadow that returned? You are less than she in every way."

"Ouch," he murmured. "Maybe. Or maybe I'm just *different*," he countered as he slid his knife down the length of Bistra's arm. "But from where I sit, you need her. I don't. I can deny you justice with a single cut. See?" Akaran asked as he angled the blade and slowly cut a thin line down the Auramancer's arm and she didn't make a single noise as blood welled up.

A thin line through a rune, one not etched until she arrived at Basion.

A tattoo placed upon her skin at the Manor.

A lock. Picked.

You couldn't say the same about the vampire. A cold howl erupted from the inn and made everyone outside come to a sudden halt. Eyes from all walks of life fixed themselves on the old, two-story building. Cel waited a heartbeat before she started to walk back. The Warmaiden and the Warprince exchanged knowing looks and did the same.

The shadows lunged at the priest and snapped at his face. He felt cold pain lance up his spine and down his thigh. The claws at his feet dug in and drew a strangled scream from his throat. He didn't budge. He didn't move. "If you want justice then you must think I'm the bad guy. Don't make me prove the point."

"Every drop spilled from her will be spilled from the ones you love a thousand times over," Annix raged through the bar. His voice slammed down into the exorcist's ears and he felt the raw *anger* the beast had roiling in the fog.

Except it wasn't just anger. It was terror. Terror that he tried to make Akaran feel, and terror that it also felt. "You want her to give up her life to make up for the one she took? Fine. You like to make deals? I'll make you one."

"There is nothing you can offer that I can't take!"

"Except her. I can give you *her*," the Lover countered. "Then you leave. You leave the city, you leave the Kingdom. I don't care where you go. But leave. I feel like I've spent years of my life dealing with your shit and I'm tired. I'm tired, Annix. I'm exhausted. It's gotta end, and it's gotta end now."

For a quiet moment, a humanoid shape appeared off to the edge of the room. It flickered, with a single marbled eye reflecting what little illumination was left in the room. "You want me... to leave you? You who has cursed me, harmed me, taken my children? You must be a supplicant. Offer a thing of yours and if I accept..."

"A supplicant. Right. I give you her, and then you want something from me, huh? Thought you said I wasn't worth your time."

"You aren't," Annix seethed. "You will give me more than she. She gives her breath to have life eternal. You must give a thing you can never take back."

Akaran spit on the floor and pushed his stool away as he began to back up to the closest wall and away from a window. The shadows let him, but he knew that wasn't going to last for long. "I know about your *justice*, asshole. I get how it works. Same thing you want from her. You want me to give you something *willingly* to show you my *contrition*, right? I do that and you leave the city alone?"

Flashes of blood-red energy crackled through the shadows. They offered glimpses of what was behind. An idea of where the bastard might be standing. It wasn't enough to do anything about, but he kept his eyes locked on it. "You claim to understand tvastarian when you don't even claim your sins."

"I don't think you want to stick around here and try to educate me either," he growled. "But I got the gist of it. So. I brought something with me. I keep getting told that there's only one thing I can do so... you'll have it. I promise. That's the deal."

"Bargaining with the life of she who is to be my yomaldi. Do you think that my slake for bloodshed will be satisfied with just her? Is that the trust you offer me?"

Akaran shook his head and then flicked a droplet of Bistra's blood off of his knife and into the shadows. The red light flashed inside them again as the drop hit the floor. "Neither one of us can trust each other. But this bloodshed *has* to end. You've lost. She's lost. We've *all* lost. I will give you the one thing I have to give that isn't my life. You want something of real value? Then you came to the wrong person," the exorcist offered. "I'll give what I have to give. You get her. You leave."

The figure moved through the shadows as effortlessly as if they weren't even there. "Coward and fool. Giving your own away to spare your life."

"Oh please, don't even try that. Your entire ability to *make* deals rests on people valuing their own lives over someone else's," Akaran spat as he pushed his knife back under Bistra's chin. "Except unlike everyone else – I figured out that you won't leave until you have her. Taking her embarrasses the Order, humiliates me, puts all of us on display for you to mock as we pick up what's left of our lives when you're done. Am I wrong?"

"There is no depth to the extent of which your failures will be magnified," the vampire promised. "I see through you. I see your mind working to plot. A hope to rescue her."

"You're right. Which is why I know if I'm not willing to kill her, then you'll have everything you want without me. So. Take her and take my offering or give up any hope you have of ever getting what sick shit you call your *justice* because I'll cut her throat faster than you could kill your own bitch of a spawn when she turned on you. I *promise* that's your only option."

That earned a *violent* response from the darkness. It thundered. It shuddered. The red lights flashed. "Dare you speak of –"

"Oh, stop it," the exorcist snapped. "I spent weeks hunting down a being created from *actual shadows and darkness* that tried to swallow me whole not even six months ago. If you think this," he said with a flick of his head at the swirling gloom around him, "is going to bother me? I don't know what kind of third-rate idiots you've spent the last two centuries eating but this isn't doing *shit* to scare me."

It wasn't *entirely* a lie.

Lie adjacent, maybe, but not *entirely* a lie.

He just hoped that the bloodsucker would buy it.

As his knife started to dig back into Bistra's throat, the creature snarled in the depths of his shadows. The motion cut a thin, frayed cord holding a small pouch around her neck, and it dropped into her bloody, crossed arms. She caught it and for one heartbeat her eyes went ever so slightly wide as she felt the magic within.

She felt... magic. The binding room on her arm flickered. Faded. A rush of power began to seep in her aura, fed by the energies raging around the younger priest. The tattoo lost strength and as it did, the protections of the Manor – protections set *for* the Manor – waned with it.

Annix noticed. He just didn't care. "You are a wretch of ego and drive that would have seen you dead of your own tongue even if you had not entered my sight. There is no wisdom is debating a fool. Give me the woman."

"We have a deal? You'll leave?"

"The woman. Your supplication. Your surrender. Your shame and your pain will be your tvastarian."

Akaran snorted and looked the vampire dead in its eye. "My knee is my pain, but you want her? Will it fulfill your claim?"

"Yes. Give her to me, and I will allow her to grant me her will in her own time." The shadows flickered again. "That is my promise. You are not worth my word, but to have my yomaldi. That is worth my spoken brand."

Bistra didn't flinch. She didn't move, she didn't cry. She just looked into the waiting void, and took a step forward of her own accord as Akaran loosened his grip on her waist. "You can... do as you will. Time comes for all things. What is done to me will not change what is done to you," she replied with certainty.

She took another step forward, and another. With each step, her arm bled onto the floor. With each move, the bag soaked up more and more blood from her cut. Annix watched as her life ebbed from the cut, and the shadows *rumbled* softly with open hunger.

The vampire moved faster than even Akaran thought he possibly could. The shadows retreated away from his ankles and shoulders and *consumed* the woman in a heartbeat. She didn't scream and didn't try to get away. The figure in the void wrapped his arms around her and tucked her in tight to his chest like he had just found his lover after years of being away.

The exorcist watched as long as he could bear to.

He looked down at the knife, and let his shoulders drop.

"You want my surrender too, right? Of free will?"

"Yes. Grant it and you shall be free."

"No," Akaran sighed, "I am certain I won't. Ask for it."

The shadows rolled over Bistra's head, and Annix's face hovered just inches away from his. "I will have the gift of your pain."

The exorcist just shook his head. "Close, but that's not what I have."

"You renege...?"

"Suffering," the Auramancer called out as she pressed the pouch against her chest.

Annix wrapped a claw around her shoulder hard enough to force her to cry out as Akaran felt a fang rake across his jugular. "Suffering is what he will know. The tvastarian he shall give to me shall be the suffering he has inflicted to –"

Blood welled around her arm, and it felt so right. For the first time in years, her hand began to glow and the Word embroidered onto the pouch took on a light of its own. "No, you old fool," she whispered, "suffering is the one thing he has to give. He gives pain, and I... I *let hope burn*," Bistra invoked with her voice just loud enough to be heard.

A cold, quiet *hiss* from the pouch filled the room. For the first time in a century, humans had managed to do the impossible. Annix was, very simply, very incredulously, and very utterly...

...confused.

"What?"

Chains appeared around Akaran's wrists as a gust of hot wind slammed the front door open and barreled through the room. It filled the air of the *Imperial* with a scent familiar, and so very far away. It smelled like burnt hair. Charred flesh. Ash-covered skin. Brimstone.

Carried on a breeze that was so fresh that it smelled...

...that it smelled like it was from a beach.

Silvery, semi-etheric links fell from his arms and brushed across the floor with an eerie, otherworldly clatter. "You said once I gave you my gift, you'd leave," the exorcist replied with his voice just above a whisper. "Now I *ask that* you leave," he intoned.

He spoke. Bistra heard the voice that echoed in his mouth. Heard the feminine chime in the back of his throat. Felt the power. Felt the anger. Felt the rage. Felt it building. Felt the *wrath* as a voice on the wind gave Her own opinion.

For the first time in years, she heard *Her*.

"Now, you disgusting **little cockroach**," he repeated as the Goddess spoke through him. "Now **we** ask that **you leave**."

The hissing stopped.

Annix turned to face the Auramancer.

She *smiled*. For the first time in years, she *smiled*.

The bag in Bistra's arms exploded. The blast knocked her back off of her feet and caused her to crumple to the floor with a burning hole in her clothes. She screamed in pain as her skin briefly caught fire and tiny pieces of silver embedded themselves in her chest.

But her pain was *nothing* compared to what Annix felt.

The detonation filled the room with brilliant pulsating light that carved through his shadow and obliterated it as if it wasn't there. Sulfur flakes and silver slivers dusted every surface in the bar. Faint etheric flames erupted across the floor wherever the vampire had stood while the wveldweed sapped the strength from his veins. But the shadows were only half of it.

The vampire *screeched* at the top of his lungs as silver and spell alike set his skin aflame and melted flesh from his face. His brilliant, perfectly pale face was ruined in seconds as his skin sizzled and burned away. The Order hadn't skimped on the reagents in the emergency bags, and while it wasn't enough to kill – it was more than enough to give Akaran the one gift *he* needed.

Time.

"*We*. Said. *Leave*."

Annix screamed in shock and agony.

Akaran screamed in judgment. "**NOW**," he shouted at the top of his lungs as his chains whipped through the air and entangled the inhuman monster in their unbreakable bonds. With one single *violent* twist of his arms, Annix *crashed* through a glass window and landed on the muddy street outside.

The exorcist dropped his silver dagger to the floor and followed him through the window as the crowd outside shouted in surprise and confusion of their own. The vampire scrambled to his feet. He started to run away. A Word a heartbeat later caused a blinding white light to erupt right by his face.

The call of, "**LUMINOSO-CORSAIR**!" staggered the burning beast and made him retreat a few steps back to the inn. Blinded and confused, burning and agonized, Annix turned around and was rewarded with the one thing that Akaran had wanted to do since the first time his name had graced the exorcist's ears.

In front of Cel, in front of Malik, in front of the Warmaiden and errant guards from the 4th, the one man the city had spat upon for being lame and broken and an addict and a Lover did the *one* thing he'd wanted to do. The very *one* thing that he had kept pent up inside for *weeks*. The *one thing* he had *dreamed of* since he'd found the massacre at Flynn's Landing.

He'd done it to Hannock. Now? Now he got to do it all over again.

He punched the elf bastard in the face so hard one of his fingers broke.

Annix *dropped*.

Another Word hammered the beast. It battered him and crushed his ribs. Another bathed him in holy light that scorched away corpse-white flesh from his neck and chest. "**BONDS**!" were called out and they ensnared his hands by the wrists a second time.

"You… you can't… this is not… this is not…"

"It's not your tvastarian," Akaran replied slowly as he walked around behind the kneeling, broken monster. "It won't… fix… anything. It won't solve… anything. It won't heal… anything. And you aren't… you aren't giving it willingly. Which… which is fine. I don't want you to. I don't want you to give me *shit*," he swore.

"Then why… why go against justice? Why not fight for… correction?"

"I'm not fighting to *correct* anything. For *all* the shit you know, you don't know that. You can't because you're not human. So proud of that, but you aren't, and because you aren't then you can't understand. Annix? It's simple."

The elf looked up at him, ruined and defeated. There was a moment in his eyes that he realized he was defeated. That he knew that this was over. That centuries of his life were coming to a crashing end because of this *dog* with a *chain*. "You are… you end what you cannot fathom!"

"*We fathom* what you are just fine," he spat. "*We just* want to *kill you*."

Annix looked up at him. He looked up and *saw* the exorcist for what he was. Who he was. What he embodied. How *different* he was than the other bags of blood flesh and meat standing in hushed, terrified silence around them. "Human… that isn't the anger of a human! You aren't…!"

Rage rolled off of the young man. It burned the air around him. It wasn't his anger. It never had been. A glimmering Divine light crested around his eye as he spoke.

He spoke for himself.

But he spoke with Someone Else's voice.

"Listen to me closely: *the tasks of an exorcist are three*."

The chains *shone* with a light that matched the one around his eye. "THIS WON'T HOLD ME YOU CAN'T STOP ME! I WILL HAVE TVASTARIAN!"

Akaran ignored him and continued to speak. But it wasn't just his voice. It wasn't just his words. He said them. But he didn't say them alone. The heavens *crackled* with their weight as a woman far away and far above looked down from Her spot in the waters just beyond an eternal beach. "*To help the souls that can be* salvaged find peace…"

"No peace for you! NEVER PEACE!"

"*…to release the souls of those cursed to walk* of volition not of their own…"

The vampire surged to his feet and fell as the weight of the edict pushed him back down. "I DON'T CARE ABOUT YOUR TASKS, EXORCIST!"

The priest whipped the chains again and pulled Annix tight to his chest. "**We weren't** talking to you, **asshole**," Akaran chided with a sneer.

Annix had a *second* to see what awaited him when the priest forced the undead abomination to face his destiny. The vampire got what he wanted. He gave Bistra his heart.

She used Akaran's dagger to cut his chest clean open to claim it.

"*...and to condemn the ones that should not have been allowed to see the light of day,*" she finished. "**PURGE**."

The Auramancer had her exorcism.

Annix caught fire with a scream.

Flames raced through his ribs and up his throat. They lanced from his mouth. They spread down his body. As he burned, scales of ice erupted all over the priest to shield him from the rigors of the flame.

Akaran pinned him tight against his chest until the last inch of the elven nightmare was immolated in holy light that rolled across the exorcist's skin without singing a single hair on his arms. He held him until his bones were exposed and he squeezed him until they cracked and broke and he unleashed spell after spell of his own until the last things left of the inhuman monstrosity wouldn't fill a breadbox.

The Half-Blind Idiot. The Cripple Priest.

The Elemental Exorcist. The Guardian of Ice.

He'd have a new name before the sun would rise over the horizon.

The Wrath of Love lowered his head as the rage left his aura and the strength left his arms. Ash and bone crumbled to the street. He slowly stripped his bloody tabard off and dropped it onto the pile. With another Word, he set it on fire, too, just to get the stench off of his skin. The job was done. For the rest of the night, he didn't want to be known. In the morning, the Order would welcome him back with open arms.

A peel of thunder rolled overhead. The only rain that fell were the tears from a woman who knew her nightmare was now at an end. She collapsed to her knees and simply cried.

But hers were not the only tears to be had.

XIV. THE CHORUS
Day of Zundis, 19th of Firstgrow, 513 QR

The city changed overnight.

With Annix gone, magic they didn't know he'd worked faded with his ashes. The city began to calm down. People began to breathe a little easier. People begin to talk a little freer. Celebrations were had... and actually enjoyed.

But peace was not given. Peace had to be earned.

Peace had to be bought.

It was paid, by some, over a cup of tea.

***

The Great Holy General Johasta Fire-Eyes had come and gone. Her next stop was Port Cableture before a return to the capital in Mulvette. She would not be missed and she would not be thought of fondly of as she left. Neither would Maiden Sanlian, or her Betrothed. It was a maybe about Consort Blade Sua, though the most he added to Johasta's visit was a dirty look that prevented Catherine from taking a swing at Paverilak...

...so it was hard to fault him for doing his job.

Hard, but not impossible.

The General hadn't stayed long. She hadn't needed to. She showed up, found out what she wanted to know, remarked on things she didn't, and left before the sun could fall below the edge of the basin. Once she was confident that the disasters wouldn't be *ongoing*, she felt content to merely verbally eviscerate and leave mountains of instructions she expected to be followed.

Visitors gone – even if they hadn't made it all the way out of the city yet, she was sure – the Maiden gagged on the cup of tea she'd just been handed and spit the drink back into the ceramic cup it'd been served in. "This is the absolute worst. Where did you *get* this?"

The greatest surprise was that Catherine hadn't been marched out of the city with her... followed only by the realization that she still had a job. The same job, at that. By the time that the General got through with her, she absolutely didn't get a *promotion* but she did at least get to keep her job. A truth that, for all of his other sins, Akaran was entirely responsible for. She knew it, and the General made her admit it.

Repeatedly.

"The man you described as a danger to himself and others, a man you described as reckless, disastrous, and responsible for a tremendous drain on the Queen's accounts is also the one that brought low a multitude of enemies of the Order – and the one responsible for ensuring a bare minimum of peace between the Kingdom and the Midlands?"

When Catherine had to acknowledge that – several times and several ways over – it was Sanlian who spoke up instead. "So it seems that he has lived up to the title of Exorcist, doesn't it? We don't bring into the Order ones that are content with playing by the rules for a reason."

"Wardkeepers and Templars are the ones that are tasked with ensuring that damage is kept to a minimum," Johasta had charged. "Exorcists are tasked with ensuring damage is done. If there is an excess of the latter, it isn't the fault of the men we train to be wild and blunt hammers, is it?"

That only ensured another argument. One with foul words and heated tempers and no few gestures. What ultimately helped her keep her position was that through the blunders and failures of the Order, most of it could be placed – and summarily was – on the neck and shoulders of Overseer Hannock. Had he done his job and kept the Order apprised of the souls missing, the problems in the gardens, the areas of malfeasance and so much more, it was determined that the Order would have known to step in much, much earlier.

It was also determined that since the Order itself had lost so few – in the face of so many other deaths and dismemberment – that it could be considered at a level of 'acceptable,' if not heartbreaking. "Nor, of course, can we expect a woman who is not trained in war to understand the complexities of a wide-scale battle," was another remark pointed in her direction.

That strike against her honor was joined soon after with, "While there is ample blame to be had for not finding and excising the vampire to begin with, the failure that was exploited was less that of Abyssian causality as it was mindless breakdowns of command-level communication."

That one hurt. Not only did that one hurt, it didn't even come from the General. Sanlian had that particular nugget to offer. Johasta? "The failure of the 2nd Naval Armada to heed the warnings of an agent of an exorcist first in Gonta and then their failure to protect their port against hostile magics is another story and another source of blame. Admiral Maddon will be held accountable for both. If it truly *had been* pirates or an incursion from a mindful creature, even more lives could have been lost. It has shown that his posturing over his ability to defend the Crown against threats foreign, domestic, and beyond the natural have been grossly overstated. I do not tolerate braggarts, and I stomach fools even less."

A multitude of other failures were pointed out in the course of the days-long dressing-down. Again, and blessedly, Hannock took more blame than Catherine did. The Maiden-Templar was asked to provide a list of people she felt made the situation worse, and once the General moved on from her own failures and then skimmed over Akaran's, the rest of the list read like a roll-call of city nobility. The mere fact that there were *riots* in the face of a diplomatic wedding was addressed as if it was a sin against the Goddess Herself and assurances were made that, "The 4th will be entirely restructured and sent to other locations to learn the errors of their ways. The 9th will be mobilized to take command over the city proper until the new Overseer can be properly exert his influence."

He already has, you blazing-eyed witch, Catherine had growled to herself. To herself and *only* herself, of course. She wasn't half as stupid the General thought she was, no matter how many times it was suggested otherwise.

Johasta's promise ensured that the new few weeks would be... interesting... on a ground level, to say the least. "That is the chief reason why you are being left in charge. There is much consternation coming as the kingdom prepares itself for the future. We do not have time to train someone else to give the care to the Repository that you yourself have proffered. I would even say that now your hands are full addressing the revelations held by the esth-atatic weapons currently buried in storage. Yes?"

Nor could that be argued. Akaran's vision of Abyssia had yielded fruit, albeit fruit poisoned by the barrel. The idea that some of the weapons recovered from Agromah could hold the souls of followers of Love lost during the Adelin Civil War? As horrifying as it was preposterous, it was a *concern* for the Order that *must* be addressed as soon as possible.

So with no arguments to be had, there was one last task to do before she could start on the new migraine just waiting beneath the floor. That, sadly, was little more than to drink tea and scribble away in what was turning into less of a 'report' on the recent disasters and more an entire damn book. It might even be more than one. *No,* she promised herself, *it'll just be one. I promise, just one.* Except that the tea was less 'warm leaf soup' and more 'affront to all things in the natural creation.'

"Well?" she demanded from the white-robed man that had brought it in as a commotion erupted outside of her door. "I asked where it came from." She blinked in brief confusion as she sized him up.

Odd. Did Johasta leave behind new staff? Must be some new scribe. Wonderful, she briefly, idly whined. *A Sycian though? Odd choice.*

"From a place that is both far and wide," he answered slowly. "While I understand you are not accustomed to the taste, I would presume you would have some familiarity with the aura. Perhaps you should check?"

"I do not have time for cryptic comments and water that tastes like someone pissed in it," she snarled. "What is it?" He didn't look up and he didn't move. He just placed his hands in the sleeves of his robe and waited. After the silence drug on, she whispered a simple spell under her breath and rolled her eyes.

Her eyes stopped rolling and her irises went wide. The Sycian very calmly took a step back as the door to her office closed on its own and a scream about a monster in the washroom echoed down the halls. "The depths of the Oceans do not end at the shores of the beach. Despite your efforts to bury the damned — and bury quite well — there is a hubris to your Order. You forget that even in a place like this, no matter how deep you dig, there are always places *lower.*"

Catherine slowly stood up as a faint blue light began to flicker across her fingertips in little etheric arcs. "Who are you? How did you get in here."

"I am a man who knew to ask a question: how well do you know where your water comes from? Or should I say, *what* well?"

"That doesn't answer a damn thing."

"It does and it does not," he answered dismissively. "Though I can feel the spell in your veins ready to expose the truth you wish. Please, as you will," he added as he opened his arms at his side in a show of surrender... mock or otherwise, it was hard to tell.

"**Unmask.**"

The Word did just that. The spell washed over his chest without opposition. She stumbled backward as her magic undid the illusion he was clad in. His sleeves darkened, and then the cords across his belt changed from rough-linen to woven gold. His body didn't shift, but an almost undetectable glow appeared around the edges of his pale pink eyes.

Everything turned red before her eyes as he pulled the hood of his cloak away from his face. The Sycian offered a single, slow smile before he spoke. "I understand you have had my name on your lips as of late. Before you surrender the Urn I have need of, I would like to know why."

Catherine tried to scream.

The Man of the Red Death only allowed her a squeak.

Outside of her office, screams were in an over-abundant supply.

***

Peace. It had a price. It always did, and it always would.

For others, it was paid by justice. *Human* justice.

Revenge. Retaliation. Paid as an *example*.

Sergeant-at-Arms Telpid looked at the small gathering of friends and loved ones arranged before him. His tired, bloodshot eyes were matched with theirs. Some had tears. Others, anguish. A few, anger. He'd submitted to Annix for sake of his family. He'd offered a trade. Just a simple deal to protect them at the cost of the lives of others.

He thought he was doing the right thing. The only thing he could.

The Queen's Law didn't agree.

He'd have time to think about his choice. Time to wonder if he could have done it differently. The rope around his throat snapped tight as a lever was pulled and a door opened.

His neck broke when he came to a sudden stop.

Telpid, Saa of Media Manor, would have eternity to think it through.

***

Peace was paid in money by others.

Gold and freedom were as much of a price as they were a payment. Brother Levathil didn't say a word as they watched the Shiverdine of Basion step free of the 4th Garrison's prison. Words didn't need to be exchanged. Crowns did.

Crowns were.

Se'daulif counted the pieces of gold and silver slowly, one after another. He'd lost weight in captivity, but hadn't lost his smile. There was more, however, than the Order had promised yet no other apology offered. There was more than just a few pieces of gold with his parting gift.

There was a message to him – but it wasn't *written* to him.

It was a simple iron lock, broken in half, wrapped in a letter granting free passage from Port Cableture to any other port in the world. Any other port not under the control of the Crown.

It was all that needed to be said, without saying a word.

For others, words needed to be said.

***

"So, good sirrah, I must ask: what is it that exists between you and Seline?"

Henderschott glanced across the room at his new boss and rolled his eyes. "Akaran tell you to ask that?"

The Master-thief of Basion shook his head. "Nothing of the sort. I just can't help but notice. It isn't that I often see you two speak but I do have ears even when I'm not around. She absolutely can't stand you, yet since her rescue from Anais, you have been nothing but supportive and extraordinarily protective of the young woman."

"Does it matter?" the guardsman argued with a tired sigh. "It's not going to change anything."

"Of course not. The time for change has moved on from the interactions of a few personal natures to a time to change for the city as a whole," Riorik admitted. "It is merely that I am curious. Truly: if it's a thing of embarrassment, I won't speak of it to anyone else. You have my word."

"Your word, huh?"

"My word. You should know by now that I hold it to an impeccable standard. I have heard you have such familiarity with each other and honestly, I rarely see that outside of a marriage. Yet... I don't think that's the case, is it?"

With a tired groan, the Lieutenant-Commander walked away from the old mahogany door and peered out the window to the city beyond. The fires had died down, and the riots had stopped. The air was full with the sound of rebuilding and eager voices pushing forward. "Marriage, no. Family, yeah. We're cousins."

"Cousins?" the thief repeated incredulously as he prodded a garish new jacket emblazoned with the combined symbols of Dawnfire and the Blackstone Trading Company both. "That is... not what I expected. Which itself is impressive, as you should know it takes a great deal to surprise me."

"How much does it take to leave you speechless?"

"Significantly more. As little as she thinks of you, what could've possibly happened?"

Henderschott sighed as he peered out at the city beyond. "Her stepmother. I didn't... I didn't know."

"Didn't know what? I'm intrigued."

He cast a defeated, dirty look over his shoulder at Riorik and ground his teeth. "She walked in on me and her stepmother. Her father had just recently remarried and I didn't know who she was and... yeah. *I swear I didn't know* but that wasn't an excuse. Family kicked my ass out. Had to join the Navy 'or else,' father said. Sel was just a kid when it happened but..."

The thief blinked slowly and settled his new mantle across his shoulders. "That is... well. The love a family has for each other. We all show affection in different ways."

"I DIDN'T KNOW!"

"I meant you and the medicannia, of course," Riorik replied with a bemused grin. "So what happens to you now? Dare I ask?"

Henderschott shrugged his shoulders. "You read my letter."

"Of course. Nor will I attempt to dissuade you. You aren't even the first to ask. Granted yes, I did have to approach the Maiden's Betrothed for permission but... it has been done. With benefits to match, given how much aid you've provided."

The other man let out a breath of relief. "Good. As to where? I don't know. Elsith remarked that the Guild hunts vampires down south. So that direction is out. Not staying in this province, I assure you that. Probably not even the Kingdom."

Riorik pursed his lips. "Have you considered Gonta? I still have connections enough that I could –"

"No offense, but the idea of taking favors from you churns my stomach."

"None taken, of course," the thief replied with a fresh chortle. "There's always Ameressa. I would advise against Civa, less you're ready for a fight against your previous employer when War turns His patient eye back to the border."

"Like the Empire would take in a half-mad healer and a former Dawnfire soldier," Henderschott grunted.

"Oh, no, they'd gladly take you. It's more of a concern as to what they'd do to you after, you know. I hear their agents are quite active these days – between the rumblings of the next Imperium War that looks as if it may well begin within the next few years and more recently, an incident with our mutual friend."

"Akaran?"

Riorik shook his head. "Would you expect otherwise?"

"Not really. But why…?"

The pudgy mastermind sighed as he smoothed the wrinkles from his coat. "Word somehow reached them that he had been having conversations with one of their spies and that he may have been why she died. Then the conversations after, which further… well. Once again, he's found a way to make enemies without even knowing it. My understanding is that the Empress would like to know more about him."

"Gods," the other man groaned. "Just… Gods. Well. Ameressa is a thought, like you said. Anywhere but here."

"No, my friend, not anywhere. No matter how much you hear about New Fritan, or any of the jobs offered on Agromah's shores – no matter how lucrative the offers may be, I would not. Presumably Sycio isn't on your list, and… I daresay, your options are starting to shrink."

Henderschott nearly choked on his drink at the thought. "One waking nightmare is enough. Thanks."

"No, my friend. Thank you. Your efforts to direct the wrath of the Kingdom were not unnoticed. My understanding is that several people owe their necks to you in this period of… adjustment."

The former guardsman walked across the room and made one final nudge to the thick fur mantle stretched out across Riorik's shoulders. "Speaking of – Hannock's is being sent to Mulvette. The Queen wants a word."

"Does she? And here we spent time pitying the priest. I imagine that discussion won't be enjoyable."

"Yeah. Speaking of half-blind idiot – I haven't heard from him in days. Any idea what he's doing?"

"He took some time for himself, I understand. Spent some time laying down cursing about his leg and manage to get himself lost in assorted introspective thoughts.

"In other words, he got drunk."

"Resoundingly. Cel almost had to threaten to cut his throat to get him to leave the *Imperial*."

Henderschott answered with a guttural laugh. "Heard the only reasons he let him stay is because he made Hannock clean out her stables."

"That was a *delight* to watch, I must admit. You missed quite a show."

Riorik swiped the mug of wine from Henderschott's hand and downed the remainder of it. "But as for him now? I have someone helping him at the moment. Cleaning up loose ends or some such. With him, I must admit – it is hard to tell."

The soldier snorted in agreement and sized the thief up. "Well. That's as good as you're ever going to look. Speaking of loose ends… shall we go make your grand appearance?"

"Yes, yes we shall," Lord Riorik Dallidon replied with a warm smile. There were plenty of people to see. Heads to turn. Deals to make. He was the Master Thief of the Fleet-Fingers Guild and that brought responsibilities, but nowhere near as many as his new title.

Lord Overseer Riorik Dallidon, the Hobbler.

While he was paid handsomely for a life of crime, murder, and more, another soul paid a price…

…by asking to become an assassin.

***

It was customary for guests at lunch to knock politely at your door. Whomever the asshole outside was, he was pounding on it in any way *but*, and if he didn't tone it down, it was going to wake up one very irritable little girl. Which was why when her mother jerked the heavy wooden door open, she didn't even bother to notice who was doing it before she shouted out, "I will bend you over and shove this door's handle up your ass if you don't *stop*!"

Badin took it in stride. "Yeah. Sorry."

"Honey? Who's making that racket?" Telburn called out from the other room.

Elsith looked down her bent nose and narrowed her swollen, bruised eyes to glare at their uninvited guest. "You. You're aware that I nearly had my skull broken by those assholes. The whole damn *city* knows I'm to be left undisturbed. Why are you bothering me?"

"Because I want out."

"You're attached to the –" she started.

He interrupted her by holding up an unfurled letter with the Overseer's stamp on it. "Not anymore. You told me that if I wanted a spot, I could get one. Remember? I want one."

"I'm having trouble remembering when my daughter was born, so… maybe?" the Huntsmatron replied with a frown. "Why would you want to leave a cushy job with the Army to join… us?"

"Because the army doesn't hunt monsters and I don't want anything to do with the people in this damn Kingdom that do," Badin countered with a grunt. "I want out. And I want in. Away from here – and away from the Oo-lo."

"Have a falling out between you and blind-eye?"

He shook his head and lowered the Order of Release. "Him, I trust. His people? Whatever shit they're pushing, I don't want any part of it. So I need to go somewhere they ain't, and you're the one to make that happen."

"Whatever your choice is, battlemage, understand: it is not an easy life. If you're sick of magic and monsters, you're speaking to the wrong organization."

"Do I get to blast them with lightning?"

"Yes."

"Then I'm in. I'll take whatever pay you offer. Just one condition."

Elsith rubbed at her swollen eyes and leaned against the doorframe. "Condition, huh? This better be good."

"Can… can your husband get me out of the city tonight? I don't want to be here any more. I can't. They might be angry with me soon."

"That's a condition for sure. Expensive one, too. Why should I risk their wrath – what do you have to offer?"

Badin held up a signed letter he'd been carrying around for days. It had taken everything in his power to write it, and it was stained by tears. "The Order of the Cloaked will want to know who killed their Eclipsian. I offered… I traded to get her justice. Now I'm trading justice to get out of here. Akaran said his people have something you want. Maybe this name'll get it for you."

The Huntsmatron's eyes widened to the extent the swelling would allow. She didn't even make it halfway through the confession before she had Telburn open a portal to go across the continent. The name on the letter was going to make the Guild a lot of money at the Order's expense to keep this quiet…

…and maybe more if she didn't.

***

While Elsith recovered from her concussion, and Telburn helped their daughter go back to sleep, one more soul had another price to pay. A price paid for in lack of sleep, a price paid for in sanctions, and a price paid for by the mutually frustrating experience of 'being punished for not following

Order protocols and spending more crowns than rank would grant,' and being 'rewarded for service to the Goddess above and beyond the call.' The combined result?

Akaran had an utter lack of desire to rest at the Repository, and not enough of a stipend left to afford another stay at the *Imperial*. Especially after Cel put her rates through the roof as a result of, well... Damage to the roof. And the bar. And a window. And every wall on the ground floor. He'd been advised to avoid the area regardless of status until the General left, and she'd be gone in the morning.

The question was if Catherine would still be there or not.

"So why are we here, exactly?" Hadraie called out.

It wasn't a terrible question by any stretch. *Here* was all the way down in Port Cableture, and *getting there* had taken several permission slips from not just the Order, but the 4th, *and* an officer from the 2nd Naval Armada just to be allowed to move around town. The latter of whom *really* wanted a word with him.

A word, he decided, that they'd never get. "I'll tell you that once you tell *me* why you've been following me around for days," Akaran countered. "Cath told me she hasn't given you instructions to do anything more than pick up dog shit, so save the bullshit on the line you gave me back in town before we trekked out here."

The Lover stopped cold and nervously looked around the alley. "Uh. You waited until we were completely away from people and away from the Order before you –"

"I didn't bring you down here to kill you," he sighed. "Agreed to bring you down here so in case you needed a place to speak freely, you could. You're *Order*, but not *just*. So, who?"

"Oh. Well, that's... appreciated," she mused. "You're right. It wasn't because of the Maiden-Templar. She doesn't actually like me."

He shrugged and leaned up against the side of some ramshackle building. "Join the club. So – why? Who's been having me followed? *Why* are they having me followed?"

"Who hasn't?" she quipped.

"That isn't the kind of answer that's going to get you out of this. I know you've been lying; I just don't know to who."

"It's not a lie," the wardkeeper protested. "It's the truth. You spent weeks walking around town yammering away to some dead Civan bitch, you've been working closely with the Fleet-Fingers, and you sank a ship of the line. On top of that, you've spent time in one dankest pits under the Queen's rule and it made people step back and look at you. Carefully."

That earned her a frown as he crossed his arms. "The Queen isn't a fan of the Repository? I assumed —"

Hadraie shook her head. "That, she's okay with. It's controlled. The Manor? Many secrets are buried in the garden up there, and many more wander around loose on the lips of people that cannot keep them closed for no fault of their own. If she had her way…"

The half-troubled, half-wistful look on her face made the hair on the back of his neck stand straight up. "Why do I get this feeling you'd have been happier if it'd been burned to the ground?"

"I would do no good for those of us in the Order if it had, and you know it. Of anyone at this point, *you* know it."

"And you *are* Order, right?"

"Of course. I couldn't call upon the Words of the Templars if I wasn't," the slightly-older woman countered. "Yet in this life, we are all many things. You have enough titles for three of us. Why can't I?"

He rubbed his back against the old wooden wall behind him and slowly let his gaze slide up and down her body. Suddenly, this 'healer' and 'defender of Love' looked a *lot* more dangerous and not a single thing about her had changed. "Because one thing we're told is that serving more than one master is a damn dangerous game for people like us."

"In the Order, we all serve two, Akaran," she replied after a moment. "We serve the Goddess, and offer aid to the Heavens above. We also have to serve the Queen; some of us just do it with a little more formality than others."

His jaw went slack as he steadied his footing. "You're one of the Queen's spies, aren't you?"

"We prefer the term, 'members of the Queen's Corrective Diplomatic Corps,' if it's all the same," she retorted. "And… really? You're surprised? A dead Civan — one of the *Empire's* spies, since you want to throw that word around — spent months in your head while you've been spending time in *two* places where the Queen has secrets entombed. Do you really think that Paver or Sua *wouldn't* have had someone watch you?"

"Well, no, but —"

"Riorik, for that matter."

"Thought you said *two* masters?"

Hadraie walked over to him and carefully put the end of her white-gloved finger on his forehead. "A girl's gotta eat. Speaking of which, why are we here? I'm hungry."

For some reason, knowing he'd spent the last week under the watchful eye of one of the Queen's spies didn't do anything for his stomach. Or the cold sweat on the back of his neck. The Queen's *Corrective* Diplomats had a simple job, and something about the way she'd been so honest and forthcoming didn't make it any easier to handle. If they thought you were a risk to the Crown, you wouldn't get a chance to appeal your case.

That made the next words out of his mouth even harder to say. "Anais sent me here."

It did make her eyebrows rise in a spectacular fashion. "Oh did she now? Were you going to admit that if I hadn't told you who I worked for?"

"Yes. And no, I don't know why."

"You seem to have a habit of following the advice of dead women without question," she candidly pointed out.

He just answered with a grunt as he turned around and continued walking down the alleyway. The only door he could see that matched the description the broker had left him with was dead ahead. "Oh I have questions. But considering what the Order has planned for the bitch, it's in her best interest to answer them with honesty."

The wardkeeper took that in stride and followed along a few feet behind. "So what did she tell you?"

"That if I made it down here and lit some candles, I'd find something I'd want," he replied. "I know. It's vague. It got me away from the General. I took the chance."

"Can't say I blame you for wanting to do that," Hadraie agreed as he tried to jiggle the door's handle open. When it wouldn't budge, she walked over and put her hand on it. "Allow me."

With a whisper, the handle *popped* open and fell apart. The door swung in of it's own accord after, and he couldn't help but stare at her in stunned silence. When he finally did speak up, it was less a question than it was an accusation. "That wasn't Order magic."

"Diplomacy in action," she replied with a shrug. "I can teach you."

When no other responses were forthcoming, Akaran slipped inside the dilapidated storehouse and looked around. Nothing jumped out at him – either literally or figuratively – but there was one annoyed mouse that squeaked once and promptly vanished from view.

The warehouse was full of sacks, boxes, and barrels enough to put the Blackstones to shame. What they were full with was a mystery, and one that both of the Lovers were happy to ignore. Legal or otherwise, nothing *reeked* of death or Abyssian auras or otherwise took their attention. The only thing that looked vaguely out of place was a dusty but otherwise gorgeous desk-turned-table with a trio of candles and an empty spot in the middle.

"Why do I think there's more here than just dust?" the Wardkeeper mused aloud as she walked over and ran her hands across the smooth top.

"Because there is. With Anais, there always is," he retorted with a mutter. A hushed command of, "**Unmask**," flowed across his lips and washed over the desk with ease. Hadraie jerked her hand back as the spell caused half of a mark on her hand to become visible for a brief moment, but far more interestingly than giving away her Crown-cast allegiance, the spell also made an old onyx bowl appear as if from thin air.

A bowl that was – and what really felt predictable at this point – filled with a blood-like substance. "Don't drink it," Hadraie warned quietly.

"Why would you possibly think I... no, on second thought, no," the exorcist muttered under his breath. "At least it's not fresh."

A handful of tiny etched runes appeared along the lip in a language he recognized even if he didn't want to. "You know, before Annix, I'd have gotten upset at seeing a bunch of Lythrivol scrawled on a spell crucible."

"You're not now?"

"It isn't elven. If I die before reading that crap again, it'll still be too soon. Curious about what it's supposed to summon more than anything," he admitted as he read the inscription over. "Oh. Weird. It's a mirror-portal." When she stared down into the oily congealed mix, he clarified by adding: "It's a mix between a callstone and a summoning portal. Brother Steelhom back at the Academy absolutely *hates* them. Most of them take a sacrifice to activate."

"Disgusting... why not just... use a callstone?"

He shrugged and began to fish supplies out of his belt pouch. "Depends on who you're gonna call, I guess," he mused. "Set up a defensive ward. Your pick. Put some salt down along the windows and the doors. I'm gonna get to work on this."

The wardkeeper slowly ground her molars together as Akaran started to get to work. "You can't be serious."

"What? It's here. She said it'd be something I want. She even offered an Inquisitor the spell to, and I quote, *'Let Akaran see that which he will be overjoyed to lay eye upon.'* Which is vague even for her, I know."

"But you don't know what it is!"

"If it tries to kill me, then everyone is going to know she did it. Like I said: she's got a lot more riding on being honest than I do," he pointed out for the second time. "Catherine promised she'd pick her brain over it. If she'd found something terrible, she'd have told me by now, so... if whatever this is doesn't kill me, then my interest is piqued."

Hadraie rolled her eyes and started to pull supplies of her own off of her belt. "You are the type of person that will either be the savior of any army or the bane of a Kingdom if we're cursed to see you grow old. I hope you understand it's far more likely to be the former than the latter."

"Why not a savior of both?"

"I didn't say which army."

As he worked his way through that thought, she went off and setup her spell walls in silence. Akaran worked just as quietly and diligently, though in his case it was less a spell *wall* and more of a spell last-ditch-effort. One he hoped wouldn't be needed, but one he wasn't willing to put past Anais to require.

When it was all said and done, the two Lovers had runes etched across the building from top to bottom. The only thing left for the wardkeeper to do was to stand behind the younger priest and watch as he lit the three candles one after another. Akaran gave her a short nod, and she began an invocation that caused the chalk-and-charcoal runes to take on a faint blue light that bathed the warehouse in a pleasant glow and emitted a light crackling sound in the air.

Once she was finished, it was his turn. He recited the spell verbatim from the broker, and she'd made sure he said it right five different times before he left her cell. "*Ill dust of the Lower, hide hidden of its own kind from its own kind, this is a call to thee to spread the Essence of Eberenth. Ill dust of fang and fur, come and speak in the name dead of Madeline Hummadalt, in name beyond death of Anais Lovic.*"

Spell said, nothing happened right away. He almost repeated it a second time, but the candles quickly extinguished themselves and the smoke from their wicks rushed into the bowl and spun around in a little tornado. The puff of smoke quickly gave way to a bloody, oily waterspout that spun almost five feet into the air in a display that would've done the watersculpt proud.

A black ball of gross *fur* popped out of the top of the disgusting fountain of gore and landed on the old desk with an unceremonious *thump*. It spoke before either Lover could react, though its grating, nails-on-slate *voice* cut through their eardrums with ease. "[Escape you did/this one surprised! Was with Master to find/would have soon have you! Would have...oh.../You aren't... damn...!]"

"You *ugly* little *asshole*," Akaran whispered as a long chunk of phantom chain appeared in the ether and fell across his arm. "Flowers. I'm giving her flowers... kill her after but flowers first..."

The wardkeeper gagged and made a warding sign in the air even as her spell started to take on an even brighter light. "What is *that*?"

The mote blinked a multitude of eyes in unison and turned around to face the two priests. If 'shock' or 'surprise' could have registered on its mottled slick fur, it would've. "[You aren't her/you're different bitch,]" the demon crooned before it locked eyes on the smirking, *delighted* exorcist. "[You are.../...oh no. Oh/no.]"

"Rishnobia!" Akaran crowed. "I have been looking *forward* to seeing you again!"

"[Shouldn't/don't,]" the mote replied hastily. "[Won't be wise/make things worse.]"

The priest pursed his lips as the little demon backed up and singed its fur on a protective wall of light hovering right behind the desk. "It might, or it might not. Either way..." he replied as he slowly licked his lips and let a spoken Word of Bonds drop phantom chains to drop across the old stone floor even as he pulled his blade free of its sheath. "We're a *long* way from Usaic's Cabin you ball of fetid grease, but I am gonna *enjoy* this."

Rishnobia *tried* to jump into the rafters, but it bounced into an overhead dome of pristine ether and bounced back down onto the gore-filled bowl with a sickening splash. "[Won't might!/Will certain! Master already moves/don't do this!]"

"Don't?" he asked slowly. "After all the shit he's put people through? People I love, people I care about, you're asking me *don't*?"

"[Oh yes/I am!]" it crooned back as it sunk its old cold claws into the wood.

The Lover sighed happily and rolled his shoulders. "Really? After what Anais did to Seline. After what Donta did to half the damn town. After what Nastavol did to Mariah," he stressed, "and after all your Master has done, you're asking me to *let you go*? Really?"

The exorcist just laughed and stepped over the closest rune mark on the floor and pointed the tip of his sword at the little demon. "[Oh./Shit.]"

The blade flashed once in the spell-light as Akaran felt the edges of his sight start to blur as all he could see was the irritating, foul-smelling, rude little cretin. "Really. You didn't think it was *over*, did you?"

Hadraie's eyes glassed over for a heartbeat, and the words that came from her lips were not her own. "*Because it isn't,*" the voice of Love replied as Akaran smiled ever so happily...

***

As for two other souls?

The price for peace was a debt they each owed to the Man in Red.

"You did not think it was over, did you, Anais?" Nastavol demanded loud enough that she could hear it through the stone door they'd stuffed her behind. "After all you have done – after all you have caused? Did you think I would forsake your efforts in the end and leave you like… this?"

The voice calmed her mind; or what was left of it. She'd asked not to be killed. They'd agreed. She didn't get a say on what happened next. Catherine had told Akaran that she intended to pick the dead woman's brain.

It was a euphemism, the exorcist had thought.

The top of her skull floated in a solution of quicksilver in a bowl on a table behind her, which left her brain – and the silver rods embedded in it – on full display. Her arms and legs had been fastened tight to an old iron chair with leather straps and heavy metal locks. Similar anchors had been stretched across her naked chest and thighs. She'd screamed at them, cursed them. Told the Maiden and later the General herself that there was nothing that they could do that would ever be worse than what she had experienced in the pit. That it had taken the human equivalent of centuries to drive her beyond her mind in perdition – centuries they wouldn't have.

Johasta had agreed.

Sua hadn't.

Sua *tried*.

When the Consort-Blade was done, Anais did indeed lose her mind. Some of it had been taken away and hidden in a cask in the Vault. A few pieces still decorated the floor beside a steel sword with the Order sigil embossed on the bottom of the blade. A significant portion remained in her skull, but not all of it.

It didn't kill her outright, and she hadn't lost all of her functions. She could still make noises. Her eye could track you across the room. She could still hear, presumably, because she'd flinch when someone would shout or make a promise for whatever was to come next.

Her tail was gone too. All that was left of her neck was just a few tendrils that should've been veins. A couple of ligaments. The vertebrae of her neck had been fused together at her resurrection so well that she didn't need muscles to hold her head up; the bones alone sufficed. There was evidence that magic had let the bones shift and move as needed to maintain the illusion of her humanity, but stripped of her spells? Even if she *wanted* to have turned her head, she *couldn't've*.

It was grisly work. If she'd been living, it would've been criminal.

Except she wasn't. Because she wasn't, the Queen's Law had no sway over what the Lovers could do. As she discovered, there was no apparent end to the things the Lovers *would* do to ensure that the people they cared for were protected. That was the entire *point* of the Reformed Order: to allow no harm to those whom are *loved*.

Even if not well.

When the door opened, Catherine's bloody body limped inside – but it wasn't really *her* anymore. She'd lost agency when her throat had been slit from side to side. She'd lost power over her own flesh when the necromancer had infused her corpse with just enough of his essence to keep it upright. As soon as she made it through the door, her body fell in a lifeless heap even as pale gray light radiated away from her eyes in a smoky haze.

Nastavol stepped through the doorway as torchlight flooded into the sealed chamber. "You gave my name. You explained my interest. You worked against me as much as you did for me," he intoned.

Anais's eyes went wide as they flickered back and forth between the Maiden's reanimated body and her benefactor.

"Did you presume that you could bargain your way to safety? That you could give them some of my thoughts and wishes and that it would grant you freedom?" he asked as he walked into the room as if he belonged there.

For all she knew, he did.

"I asked for one thing above all others. Loyalty. I promised to you that I would see you delivered from suffering if you only offered loyalty," the Man of the Red Death continued. "I have never uttered a lie – least of all to my Acolytes. Yet you never saw yourself as one. You saw yourself as an *employee* rather than a *devotee*. Your flaw was assuming that you could bargain with me as much as you could others."

Her mouth tried to work. Her tongue flicked against one of her few remaining teeth. Her hands trembled in the chair as he walked closer. She couldn't see his face or look into his eyes. But Anais didn't need to.

She could feel his intent even before he stepped over the Maiden's body. "As I have not lied, then I am forced to complete our bargain. *You* put *yourself* here, Broker. I did not. You should know that. You should know where your blame is to be placed. It will not save your life, but it may change your fate."

In a way, it did.

In another, it didn't matter.

She didn't scream, which was fine. Honestly? He detested them. The sound flesh made when he worked on it was comforting. The sound of ribs cracking? The sounds of tendons coiling under skin when sliced? The little wet chops as he practiced his craft? A cut. A tender pluck here, and a push there. A gentle tug. Those were the sounds that gave him peace and eased his mind.

The screams were not.

There were enough of those regardless, even if not from her.

Nastavol held her chacos in his hand and studied the oily, sand-covered misshapen lump carefully. His work had held up remarkably well, all things considered. Sua had been given strict instructions to avoid it… just to be safe. They promised Anais she'd live, and that meant they'd avoid the necrosia-infused anchor holding her together.

As it turned out, the Lovers decided to break the deal in the end.

The chacos dissolved in a torrent of burning blue flames and sparks as Karaj unleashed a spell from the hall beyond the dungeon. Their cloak was torn and their androgynous, flame-blistered face was covered in fresh cuts and blood. "How?" they croaked as they stopped at Catherine's body. "How did you…?"

"How did I enter, I presume?"

"How did you bring… defiled here?"

"It is not as if I brought many," Nastavol retorted. "Only enough to ensure that I could work undisturbed. You will also find that none of your people have been needlessly killed. Wounded, of course; it would not serve to steal your attention without some damages I am afraid. My creations and conscripts were educated quite clearly on the matter."

Karaj took a staggering, pain-filled step closer, and slumped to their knees with their hand on Catherine's neck. When they looked up again, their tired gray eyes were brimming with tears. "Liar."

The necromancer shook his head slowly. "Needlessly implies 'without need,' by nature of the word. Before suggesting a falsehood, perhaps you should ask for a truth."

"Why?"

"Because I need a thing you had," he replied slowly as Karaj glanced down at the Urn hanging from his belt, "a thing that you have made clear to other people you had no intention of parting with. I have only taken four things from you this day, which I will demand you remember for the future. I could have made this so much the worse."

The Lover slowly stood up on shaky legs and drew both of their swords off of their waist. Both were slick with blackened ichor and clods of gore along the edges, and Karaj's hands were bloody and coated in grime. "I will see you burn for this. Maiden Prostil… Catherine… she was a wonderful woman. She did... did no wrong."

Nastavol spread his arms open wide, invitingly. "Of course. She was innocent of wrongdoing but for a few choice lies. You need not worry; we cleared the air. She even offered a great deal of help with getting through the interesting set of controls you have in this establishment – the Vault? A masterclass of spellwork. I am utterly impressed and I do wish she could have been left alive, but. Her death was a point in and of itself. It would not have mattered to you otherwise."

"To... to me?"

"Of course. You. Why do you think I allowed you to get past my minions to confront me otherwise? You are a skilled fighter, but not one so skilled to win in combat with my assassin unless I had given Maelphistiphan specific instructions to allow you to do so. You did meet – yes?"

Karaj looked back down the hallway and felt their arm go numb as their shoulder slipped loosely in and out of its socket. "Assassin? What sort of man makes a demon an *assassin*?"

"One who needs a dedicated killer," the Sycian answered with a simple shrug. "I could have had him do to you what he has done to countless others in the past but I made the choice not to. This is your punishment for your sins. It is also the answer to another question."

The Lover looked down at his friend and then back up at the necromancer with fire blazing in their eyes. "You talk so damn much."

"A poor habit, I admit," Nastavol agreed. "Yet I am willing to answer, if you are willing to hear me out. If you would prefer to simply fight, that can also be arranged – but I would think you would like to know how I did it. Would you not?"

"I don't care," Catherine's assistant seethed. "You took her from us. I will have your head!"

Karaj made it three steps before Nastavol made a blindingly fast gesture with his fingers and one of Catherine's hands grabbed the Lover's ankle. They fell hard onto the gore-strewn floor and cracked their chin against the stone. The world spun around them but not so much that the Maiden's assistant couldn't realize what was going on.

The corpse's fingers dug so hard into Karaj's boot that even with a broken jaw, the Lover had to scream. Their scream was soon matched with one from her body as a red line erupted down the center of Catherine's face.

"You took the love of a battlemage. A Lover, stealing love. It is almost poetic," the necromancer lamented, "but absolutely tragic. I offered the battlemage a bargain – I gain knowledge of spells inscribed inside your wonderful mausoleum, and in exchange, I promised justice. I promised them as I promise you: no one has died without need. You took a love; an innocent. I took yours; also a... relative innocent."

Karaj looked up at him and tried to talk, but their broken jaw kept them from uttering anything intelligible. Just a mouthful of mashed-up words and mumbled curses. Their eyes said it all though; a demand, an accusation. A mixture of loathing and promises of revenge.

Nastavol gestured to Catherine's body, and the red line splitting her face opened to expose the bones of her skull. The corpse made a keening, pained cry as skin split and muscles were frayed. "She is in there. She does feel this. She needs to feel this, even with her soul no longer truly part of her flesh. She needs to feel it because you need to know she feels it so you can hurt for her. That is the pain I promised to deliver."

Karaj friend couldn't hold back the tears in their eyes. They rolled and fought against the dead Maiden's grip but couldn't break free. The only choice they had to get loose was to do the unthinkable, which made the necromancer smile even wider as he walked past them both.

"You could get free if you cut her hands off. You have a sword; two of them. You could. You could slice them off and maybe have a chance to press blade against my chest – but she would feel it. She would know. Maybe she would want you to. Maybe she would be angry at you if you chose not to. Do you want to take that risk? Can you?"

Karaj looked into the Templar's white, vacant eyes. They watched her as the skin peeled back away from the bone seemingly of its own accord. They watched as her skull glistened in the torchlight from the hallway beyond. The Lover rolled up and did as the Man of the Red Death taunted them to do, and Catherine's corpse unleashed a fresh peel of agony from her chest as her arms were cut in half.

As her long-time assistant started to stand and lunge for him, Nastavol clapped his hands in delight. "You could! You can! How delightful!" he crooned as he made another gesture with his fingers. "Even if not in time."

Catherine's skull separated from her neck and ripped free of what was left of her face. The chunk of bone shot the short distance between corpse and corpse-killer at lightning speed before it crushed Karaj's nose into paste. The Lover fell down and didn't so much as twitch.

"If you can still hear me," Nastavol began, "I have taken four things from you. I have removed the Urn, which belongs to you no more than it belongs to the Guild. I have removed your friend, which upholds my bargain. I have removed your prisoner, who owed her very existence to my will."

Before he could finish, a cloud of bone and smoke drifted down from the ceiling to float beside him. *"Master. The last of yours are gone."*

"Yes, I noticed," the necromancer sighed. "Rishnobia has been destroyed as well. A shame. I almost wish I could feel sad."

"Were you capable, you would feel much."

Nastavol replied with a wistful glint in his pink eyes. "So true, Maelphistiphan. So true." As he turned to leave, he paused and addressed Catherine's assistant one last time. "Oh, and the fourth thing that I have removed from you? For your sake on this day, I strode into your home unmatched and undeterred – and I took your hubris."

***

"She was the only fatality."

The statement was probably supposed to offer some relief. It didn't. A procession of stretchers marched out of the Repository's main gate, carried by men and women covered in blood and grime alike. If it had come from almost anyone else in the world, it might've. But not her.

Never, ever her.

Never, ever the Holy General herself.

Johasta Fire-Eyes. She lived up to her name. He didn't know if Fire-Eyes was her family-given surname or if it was a nickname, but it was accurate. She watched the procession leave the outpost one after another with her arms crossed and her raven-black hair pulled back into a tight braid at the back of her neck. She wasn't a tall woman, but she *projected* height. Pits, she projected *power*.

Pure might. Strength. Nobody would ever look at her and think *weak*.

It was more than just her armor. It was her eyes. Her blazing, simmering eyes with something that was beyond fury and not quite hate that lived deep inside them. There was something very elemental in her aura, something that couldn't be touched or even seen in the ether.

She'd rushed back to the Repository as soon as the attack was reported, and luckily, she'd only made it as far as the first leg through Yittl Canyon. Honestly? There wasn't a single person that felt any safer with her present.

Right now, whatever elemental energy she had in her aura?

For the moment, it was entirely directed at Akaran.

"You didn't do this, but it happened," she stated flatly. Simply, to the point. Direct. That was who she was. "Karaj has placed the blame fully on a Specialist-Major Badin. *Former*. Efforts are being made to ascertain his whereabouts."

"He… he's not here," the exorcist replied as he worked through his dry mouth. "He was… he told me he was taking a contract with the Guild and… they were going to send him away. Said he had something they needed and he… was going to go get… get a post somewhere. Elsewhere. I don't know where."

"The Guild? Fine. We will negotiate with them directly."

Akaran shook his head slowly as he watched a shroud-covered body be walked out of the shrine. It was surrounded by armor-clad soldiers as they marched in lockstep, one heavy footfall after another. "I can't… why? Why would he…?"

"A question he had best pray to have an answer for," Johasta replied coolly. "He may not have done the damage but Karaj made it clear that he's the one that offered the keys."

It was almost too much. Catherine's death. The fall of the Repository. The Maiden's assistant beaten senseless. Nineteen people wounded. Badin's apparent betrayal, if what the Man of the Red had told Karaj was true. Nothing felt quite real – not a single word of it made sense. "He saved my life so many times. I don't understand. I *don't*. How did Nastavol even…?"

"Magic is… fickle. Divine magic even moreso," she answered slowly… almost condescendingly. "Corrupt it, and you weaken it. Know the nature of the spell itself? You can unwrite it once you are in a position to do so. Combine that knowledge and that action? You can undo it. Our spells are designed to withstand manipulation but Words are just rules and changes demanded by the Goddess. Speak against them in the right way, and they can be countered. We are blessed that there are few that know the right way."

"Cursed that he's one of them."

"With knowledge you can do anything. With knowledge, you can find an aqueduct. With knowledge, you can find your way through the stone it was set in. With knowledge, you can animate creatures of the deep to burrow out a hole big enough to walk through. With knowledge from a traitor to crown, friendship, and oath?" she asked, "With that, you can break down any wall. Once you're behind a barricade, it is so much easier to tear it down."

Akaran shook his head and wrung his hands as he watched people carry out carts full of corpses. The horrifying thing? None of them belonged to the Lovers. Nobody knew where they came from – but

Nastavol had delivered an army of the dead *into* the damn Repository. "All of this. I just can't... I can't fathom it, General. I can't."

"Once Badin provided the necromancer with information about our protective spells, he found a weakness in it. The weakness was exploited. That's how. Coupled with what he knew from the eye in the Vault and what he learned from the Anais... woman...? He gained knowledge. The one responsible for protecting knowledge is dead. Nothing more can be done there."

"Just by overcoming... General, with respect, I've watched monsters cut through our protective wards like they were butter recently. Here, the Manor. What good are they if they're not... working?"

Johasta turned away from the Procession of Honor and locked her gaze on his face. "A lock is only as good as the ability to hide a key. Or dissuade a pick. This city grew complacent. The Order the same. With complacency, failure. With trust in the wrong people?"

"Disaster," he sighed.

"Unmitigated. Unforgivable."

The General turned her back on him and slowly dropped her hand down to the hilt of the golden sword at her side. He took the hint and shut up as he watched Catherine's body be escorted off to the Pyre. "I'm... General, I'm –"

"Apologize to her. If it does any good, come back and offer one to me." The words were a fresh slap across his cheek and he couldn't even begin to formulate a response to it before she cut him off. "Maiden-Templar Catherine Prostil. Paladin-Commander Spidous. Paladin Faldine Golanstav. Wardkeepers Mentriane and Humaal. Carehandlers and Messengers Tipson, Bandis, Nevionsa."

The names lingered in the air until he asked about the latter five. "General, I'm sorry, I don't...? I thought you said Catherine was the only fatality here...?"

"Here, yes, across the city? No. In Cableture? No. You didn't bother to learn the names of everyone that died in the hunt for the vampire?" she scolded. "I am far from surprised," Johasta remarked with her voice in the same flat monotone it'd been in the entire time. "Those are just the ones of our Order. I won't bother giving you the names of the ones outside of it. If you don't know who of your own kin died, then you wouldn't know the rest."

"General, that's not fair, I –"

"You are pledged to defend the people of this world against all matter of damnation and consternation. You effectively saved two lives. *Two*. The

Auramancer Exorcist and one of those barbarian savages. How many more were lost? How bright have the Pyres burned? Don't style yourself a hero, child. You're barely the length of a finger above a self-centered mistake."

Akaran flinched again and this time, the condemnation brought fresh tears to his eye. "I won't let it happen again."

Fire-eyes turned to face him and grabbed his chin with her hand. With a single, simple move she locked his head in place and forced him to look into her blazing eyes. "You will. I will. We both will. The difference, Exorcist, is in what we intend to do about it whenever it happens. Stand around and grieve, or…"

"I'll kill him," he answered without a moment's hesitation.

That must've been the answer she wanted. Or at least, the expediency she demanded. She searched his face for a heartbeat longer before she let go of his chin and gave it a little push to remind him of his place. "You won't. He's more powerful than you are. He will grind you into paste. He's done as much to your betters before."

"They didn't know he was coming for them. I do. All men die. Just a matter of when and how."

Johasta answered with a little murmured sigh. "Are you so sure he is? A man, true. Human? Are you so sure of that?"

"Then if he isn't a man, he's against the natural order. He can't be permitted to exist in our world. And if he's not a man, then we're the best ones to put him down."

"We, yes. You? To be seen," she countered. "Still. An astute observation," she agreed. "This is twice he's bloodied the Crown's nose in the public eye. First with his involvement in King Anod's murder, and now this. I don't care what he did in Sycio; those heathens can burn under the sun they glorify their hedonism in for all I care. But here? Make sure there isn't a third time."

"There won't be."

"Don't make a promise you don't know if you can keep," the General snarled back. "When we have a lead, you will be sent for. Until then, I have a task for you."

Akaran looked away from the procession and hurriedly bowed his head. "As you command, General. What am I to do?"

She turned around and drew her sword from its sheath. The hilt was solid gold wrapped with braided leather cords. The blade was a metal he didn't recognize – silvery, but not silver, sharp, but not like steel. "A weapon is defined by the forge it is cast in. It is common to presume that weapons of the Order are all cast in Her image with Her gifts. But that isn't true. If we were all of the same mold, then breaking one of us would show the world beyond how to break all of us. I have this sword. You have something else."

"That's why some of us can use magic of the other Gods, isn't it?"

"Yes," Johasta replied freely. "It came to my attention that you have made arrangements with the Granalchi to learn to control that magical rock in your eye. Do so. If you intend to go after the Man of the Red Death, then you will need all the tools you can master."

The exorcist blanched at the idea. "General, if I may. Surely we have elementalists in our ranks that understand how to use cyromancy? The ways of the Adepts aren't... I don't think that I would fit in very well."

"You say that as if you fit in anywhere," she countered, "other than within the ranks of the thieves of the Kingdom. I'd be concerned if that wasn't such a useful relationship to cultivate. No. You made a bargain with the Granalchi. Live with it."

"But General, it's going to take weeks... months... Goddess knows even longer. I could be out hunting for him instead."

She snapped her fingers. Once. He shut up. "The Order has hunted for that necromancer for as long as you've been in the Temple. He takes what he wishes and then he leaves. When he leaves, he leaves no trace. You *will* have time as we track him down because these bodies? These shells? I only bother to show an investigation for the masses as to not let them lose hope for retribution. I assure you – we will find nothing. We never do."

"Have we ever searched in Sycio?" Akaran blurted out. "It seems like the one place the Orders of Light as a whole are unwelcome would be a great place for him to hide. Plus his history..."

"That does play a role. The Queen has forbidden it before now to avoid upsetting the Sandkings..." she began before the corner of her lips curled up in a slow smile, "...but losing treasure here may mean gaining it elsewhere and the Jewels do glisten pretty in the sun. Yet if we do cast our eyes to Sycio? Be assured, you need to know how to protect yourself from the heat."

His knee started to throb at the very thought of it. "As... as you wish, General. I don't think you're giving me any choice in the matter."

"I'm not," Johasta agreed, "and I promise: this is not the end."

EPILOGUE
A Timeless Day in a Timeless Month, in a Timeless Realm

"….because for you, I promise, it's not."

"What?" Anais called out. "Who said that?"

Nothing responded.

At first, *nothing* was there. She remembered a voice in the dark that promised… disappointment. She had been in a cell… with the Lovers? Yes, them. Then someone had cut something from her head and there was darkness. Just empty darkness.

A lifetime later, there was fire.

When the fire faded, there was less than darkness. There was nothingness. No sounds, no pain, no *feeling*. Just her own voice, and after a time, even that stopped.

"It's just beginning."

"Beginning? What's beginning? *Where am I?*"

Nothing responded.

Nothing gave way to a field of alabaster-white grass under a bleak, cherry-red sky. *Nothing* gave way to a soft breeze that made her hair flutter; hair that she couldn't believe had been restored. It was a miracle; a miracle in a land of nothingness. A *nothing* gave way to rolling hills that stretched on for no end in sight.

As the *nothing* became *something*, a wave of heat descended across her shoulders. It was as oppressive as it was brief. It was stifling, and made her skin recoil. Skin that she knew she had lost before the darkness had swallowed her whole – skin she had felt be scraped away from her bones.

The grass under her feet prickled at her naked soles. The blades didn't move when she touched them; they weren't crushed under her weight.

They didn't react as if she was there at all. They were perfectly spaced – a sixth of an inch away from each other, all at the same exact height, all with the same exact mound of dirt at their base.

The Broker swallowed dry air and touched her parched lips. Her body was intact. Naked, but intact, and as youthful as it had been since the day she had been resurrected. But where? This place was unlike any she had ever seen or could have ever imagined.

Time stretched. Time stretched because there *was* no time. She existed in one moment – a moment that didn't cease. Every time she tried to count the heartbeats between gusts of wind, the number died in her mind. Time didn't exist because time didn't *want* to exist.

The moment lasted – unceasing and unchanging – until she felt the first chains drop across her shoulders. They fell with a sharp thud that she felt in her bones. She tried to yelp in pain, but no sound would come from her lips. There were five lengths of them. Four wrapped themselves around her legs and arms, while the fifth reforged itself into a collar around her neck.

The rusted iron dug into her flesh and forced her to scream. It came out as little more than a whisper. The weight of the metal pulled the strength from her lungs, and the cold links trailed off into the grass and the endless field beyond.

No sounds. No noise. Just an errant blast of heat from time to time. Anais tried to stand, but she couldn't. All she could do was rise to her hands and knees, and that alone wrecked what little willpower she could claim. After another silent struggle, she *felt* a pull behind her.

When she was able to turn, she saw a hill in the distance. An angry, unholy orange sun burned in the sky over it – the source of the burning winds. The sun hung motionless, except for the flames she could see that licked across it's surface. The longer she stared, the more she realized that she could see... see so clearly... that the flames were not just flames.

They were people.

A face flashed in the fire, once. A face with elven ears, a face in indescribable agony. A face that earned his place in the light, even if the light was not the light of the Origin. It was the light of the Fallen, and the light created to entomb those created of the First Curse.

She screamed. The weights of the chains across her back couldn't hold it down. She *knew* where she was – this was the pit. This was... this was the bottom of the pit. *Which* bottom...

It didn't matter. It wasn't Avasharti's Palace. It wasn't the City of the Harbingers. The one was a blessing, the other was a mistake. This *wasn't* where she was supposed to be. She wasn't supposed to be on this side of the Veil. The Oo-lo assholes *promised* they wouldn't kill her. Even if they had, Nastavol — he'd promised that she'd spend her time away from torment. He *promised*.

"I SERVED YOU! I DID WHAT YOU ASKED!"

Nothing responded.

At first.

"Ah. There you are," another woman's voice called out. *"Madeline Hummadalt. I've been looking for you."*

Anais recognized her. She'd met her once; just the once, in Port Cableture. "Burned Woman…" She was different. She came into focus slowly, but even as she came into full view, she was blurry. Unfinished.

She was simply *shattered*. *"Broker of Secrets,"* Rmaci replied with a faint smile across her shattered face. *"I can't say I'm happy to see you."*

"You… why? Why am I here, why you?"

"Why are you here — in the pit? The answer to that is legion. The names, the deals, the lies you told. They're etched into each link. Each length a sin, each sin a name. Each name an action.."

She looked down at the thick pieces of iron and rust and shook her head slowly. "I… I had permissions. Do you know who I worked for? What I did?"

"I know exactly what you did," Rmaci countered as she gestured down at the chains. *"I can read your sins as easy as you. **Every. Single. One.**"*

"But the man that gave me purpose…"

"….did not see fit to extend it," the spy replied with a sad little smile. When they'd first met, she'd been covered in festering burns and smoldering cracks that sank to her bones. Now she was like a broken statue of walking glass; an imperfect projection splintered and cracked but given agency to exist.

"I… did everything for him… I did what he asked."

Intact. That was the word. Rmaci wasn't *intact*. Her body was a mass of broken shards held together by a faint pale glow. It was like looking at a broken mirror in the shape of an unburnt corpse. *"You did what he asked until you decided not to do it further. Thus he allowed you to be banished anew, and thus, you are here, and thus, our interests are entwined."*

Nastavol's minion shook her head violently back and forth. "No. No. I served. I did as my benefactor asked. I know what he is. I know why. I did what I did because of who he is. A Harbinger. Don't taunt me, woman; his wrath is unlike anything —"

Rmaci quieted her with a single wag of her finger. *"You **don't** know* *why. I do. I know you want to know. That's is why I came to you. You betrayed him. You offered the Lovers things that he did not wish for you to know. You betrayed the Abyss itself to save your own skin. It does not think fondly of you for that, and thus, you fell."*

"That's not –"

The spirit held her hand down in front of Anais, and the glass of her body allowed the broker to see a reflection of the collar in it. The words of condemnation were spelled out as clear as they could be across the iron; one last sin to anchor her in this realm. *"You fell."*

"I... I couldn't. I am bound. I am bound to the World of Mortality. I belong there."

"You belong where the Gods determined you belong, as do I. We aren't so different, you know. You traded in secrets and lies to aid your master. I traded in them to aid my Empress. We both thought that our sins would be rewarded. We were both wrong, Madeline."

The broker didn't reply. Every word Rmaci said made the chains feel all the heavier. There wasn't any way to break free of them. There was barely any way to *move* from them. "But I am bound to him. He was... I remember he was there, he held my heart in his hands..."

"You trusted a man with your heart? And I thought I was a fool," the broken woman scoffed. *"You **were** bound to the place above. Your master intervened but he did not save you from your second death. He allowed you to be destroyed, as you failed him."*

"He'll... he'll bring me back. He did once. I won't... I'm not staying here," Anais whispered as tears flowed down her cheeks. "I don't belong here."

A lump of dirt bulged up from the ground a few feet away from where they stood, and a short blast of sulfurous smoke pulsed from inside it. *"That is not entirely correct. You do, and yet, you will not remain. This is not your fate, but it should be. Be grateful that I have come to change it."*

"No. It *can't* be. I served him. I was promised that even if I failed, I would earn a spot in Purgatory! That was the deal!"

*"That **was** a deal. Yes. Yet in your failure, you sought to turn away blame from your flesh to his. You presumed that the children of Niasmis would offer you greater – and they did not."*

"I served a Harbinger. I served he who serves the Warden. The One who rules over all of this!"

Rmaci bent down and picked up one of the chains in her shifting, unstable grip. *"And I now serve the Goddess that sits even higher than He. A Goddess you crossed. A Goddess that is very angry, Madeline. I hope you understand the difference."*

Anais couldn't swallow around her own tongue. Her mouth was too dry. Her flesh hurt from the fury of the sun above. Her hands trembled as the ground shook and a steaming hole opened beside her. "I did what I had to survive. You would have done no different!"

The accusation stung, but it wasn't wrong. *"I failed almost exactly as you did, Madeline. In every way. But once I understood how wrong I was I **begged** for a chance to do right. You aren't even begging for that. You're expecting to... what? Walk away? Be brought back for a second chance? Not only did you pass blame and pass his plans, you even gave up one of his Acolytes to try to save your own skin!"*

"WHAT DO YOU CARE?" she screamed in response. *"You* of all souls? *You* serve the Pantheon now? Never. It's him. This is his game. Another one of his tricks. He is a *manipulator*. Worse than I will ever be."

*"Yes he is. It this his game? You blame him when you can **see** that it is your sins that hold you down?"*

The broker raged at the chains and struggled against them. No matter how she moved, they wouldn't budge. "Do you serve him now? Is that it? Did he send you here to harass me until I begged and offer contrition? Fine! Whatever he needs to hear! I won't stay here. Nastavol will —"

"Do absolutely nothing, Madeline!"

Anais lurched to her feet. Her strength lasted a moment, and only a moment, but it was enough to lunge for the spy — and miss. "That is not my name! Madeline was weak, pathetic! I am greater in death than she ever was in life! I am Anais Lovic and I do not accept that this is my end!"

Rmaci floated back and dodged the desperate woman with ease. *"You were greater, now you are less. You compounded your sins even after knowing what awaited you if you crossed the Gods, and you did so a second time! You're right. This argument is not your end but your plans and hopes? They are done."*

The ground split open beside the broker with a rumble and a fresh cloud of burning embers exploded from the surface. Pieces of pristine alabaster grass danced across the field in a perfect display of uniformity. "I have a plan. I am going to —"

"Your plans don't matter. You failed the being that allowed you to return to walk the World of Mortality. Sin is merely a debt owed to the Gods that must be paid in death through the actions of one's life. You've been to the pit before, Madeline. I thought you knew what happened to the dead that cannot honor their debts?"

Anais screamed in terror as a figure pulled himself free from the ground. The pit opened to expose a stone sarcophagus wreathed in flames and filled with a pile of thrashing corpses. She recognized every single one. Every single corpse had the name of one of her victims on their head. Men she'd forgotten. Women she'd never cared for. A thief from Basion was the first one she could remember – Raes. He thrashed in a bed of embers that scorched his naked flesh.

But the souls in that casket weren't just ones she had claimed. They also belonged to another man. *Her* man. The man that had done her bidding for years as she did Nastavol's.

"The dead get buried."

Donta surged from the ground. He was on fire and wrapped in twisting chains that ripped through his flesh and bones in a furious display of blazing red flames and embers. ***"YOU CONDEMNED ME****! **YOU ARE MINE****!"*

His molten flesh latched onto her neck and he *pulled* her into his embrace. She screamed in agony as it seared her flesh and annihilated her collarbones. Her bodyguard howled in a wordless rage that encapsulated the *pain* the Abyss thrived on.

He pulled her down into the white-hot tomb.

Rmaci yanked on the chains and pulled her back.

Most of her body came free. Donta kept her right arm no matter how hard the spy pulled. When the bone snapped, the flesh of the limb tore free seconds later and the screaming assassin fell back into his prison. The ground quaked and swallowed the nightmare alive before he could try again.

As Anais cried in agony, the grass sprouted up around the scar in the ground. Once again, it was perfect. Each piece a sixth of an inch away from the next. Each piece the same height. Each piece unchanged. It was as if nothing had happened, because the Lord of the Realm wished it to be so.

He wished for the antithesis of His nature: silence.

"You're in Covorn's Quiet," the spy whispered down at the damned woman. *"A place for souls full of rage and wrath. That's all you are. A soul of rage and wrath. Wrath against yourself, wrath against your benefactor, wrath against the souls you helped condemn. You deserve that box, but you are not going to be in it."*

Anais barely understood her. She cried as she rocked back and forth as blood spurted from the stump of her shoulder. The ground inhaled it eagerly and didn't let a single drop go to waste. "My arm *my arm* my skin my arm he took my...!"

"He lost one serving you. That is one debt you have honored. Now it is time for another."

Blood turned to sand. Sand turned to bone. Flesh re-knitted itself but the burns stayed the same but her arm did not grow back. "No I... no. I can't. This can't be where... *no*. What...? Why...? Who... who are you? Truly?"

Rmaci wavered and her body briefly *pulsed* and collapsed on itself, like the pieces of the glass puzzle that gave her form were trying to rearrange themselves to fit... better. *"I was a spy. Now I am a courier. There are places on this side of the Veil that Love cannot go. Places where Love is absent by design and nature. Love has no home in Hate. Love has no home in Rot. Love has no home in a Void that is defined by the absence of Her essence. I have earned an existence in suffering, so I am able to walk it in Her stead."*

The broker looked up through her tears as the skies above them began to darken. Were clouds hadn't been, gray masses of smoke erupted out of nothing to cast shadows on the field at their feet. "You... a messenger of the Gods? I... no!"

"Yes, Madeline. Now I serve to earn existence beyond an eternal... painlessness... I was offered if I had chosen not to act."

"Dammit you bitch, TELL ME! **WHY AM I HERE**?"

"Because you are needed," Rmaci replied honestly. *"Now listen, because this will not be repeated. The Abyss offers truth, and to have you serve your use to me, I must tell you what that truth is – so you know."*

Anais fell back on her heels and looked up at the shifting spirit with nothing but anguish across her features. "I don't deserve this. I did as I was told."

*"You were **told** to aid an Emissary of Damnation. You **chose** to aid by embracing sin anew when you could have worked towards a different path even under his eyes. Now? Now you will know the why of the reason you were told. You want to know, don't you? What reason there was to put you on this path of fate and pain?"*

"YES! TELL ME! WHAT CURSE HAS MADE THIS... WORTH IT?!"

Rmaci sank to the ground and placed a hand on the broker's chin. Her touch was cool, calm. Pleasant. It was a comfort that broke Anais even further. *"The why of Nastavol. The why of Akaran. They are brothers by blood – yes. But importantly, above all else – they are brothers **in** blood. They wish the same goal. Nastavol knows it. Akaran does not. That was your mistake; assuming that there was only one player moving on the field. A game demands two, be they witting... or not."*

"The sa... the same goal? What could... what could a priest of *Hers* have to do with... an Emissary of *His*? Is that why my benefactor... is that why he forbade me from doing him harm?"

"Yes," the spirit replied without hesitation. *"Nastavol needs him to survive. Akaran will need Nastavol to succeed. Without each other, they're going to fail."*

The stump sealed itself shut as a chunk of chain crawled out from Donta's hidden grave like a snake. She didn't even try to escape it as it lashed back around her throat and upper body – and the weight of her sins was so grand, she failed to notice that Rmaci had picked up the other end like it was a leash. "Fail at... what? Tell me. I... I have to know."

The broken wraith slowly wrapped a length of the sins Anais had forged in her life around her left arm. *"I wanted to know too. I've changed; I am no longer a spy. I am a courier; a messenger for Love. But I wasn't the first. The first was the sister of Miral."*

"Mir... the Repository?"

"The Guardian of Love," Rmaci confirmed, *"the same one who's home you just spent a year shitting all over."*

The red sky above *thundered* with a low growl.

It was a warning. The first and the last one they'd receive. The air began to feel heavy on their shoulders. It was more than just the weight of Anais's sin. It was as if the entire realm was turning against them. The God of Wrath demanded perfection in His realm.

And silence in His home.

"The goal of the Brothers by Blood? They are tasked with the rescue of Li'Orla – the Archangel of Love's Message," she explained. *"Held captive by the Daemon Ascendant that brought Love to Her knees before the Pantheon. The Great Offender that rejected The Warden's edict of punishment. Their very lives are to exist for one reason: to bring an end to Arch-Duke Belizal."*

"That's... that's why? All of my suffering... for an angel?"

"For a being greater than we shall ever be, and purer than we could ever imagine," Rmaci agreed. *"Now you know the truth. What your sins were in service to: blood, lies, torment and worse. All to save an emissary of the Heavens."*

For a timeless second, Anais entertained hope. Hope that there was one more bargain to make. The spy – no, the *courier* – hadn't let her sink into Donta's grave. That meant she had a chance. That *must* have meant she had a chance. "To save an angel... yes. I'm willing. Yes. Tell me what you need from me. To save an angel, I'll do anything."

"Will you? Anything that is asked?"

"**YES**!" the broker thundered.

Her cry begat another – an echo of a laugh from the sky above. Another rumble began to erupt from nowhere and everywhere at once as a gold and copper gate shimmered into existence off to the side. It looked painfully familiar, and Anais couldn't stop herself from cringing away from it even if she didn't understand why. *"Thank you for your consent."*

That word. The implications of that word.

It wasn't lost on the broker.

"To what? What does this story of bloody brothers mean to us?"

"Us, as a pair?" Love's courier asked in surprise. *"Nothing. You? Just an answer. For me? My Lady needs me to deliver a message, but the recipient demands a concession. Family squabbles, if I understand correctly."*

On the other side of the golden gate, silken banners fell with words of welcome. Flowers erupted of their own accord across the metalwork. The red sky behind the metal bars vanished, and a black sky filled with magnificent stars took its place. As they watched, a citadel so tall that it defied understanding appeared in the distance and *glistened* with desire. It *called* to them with an otherworldly quality that made them *want* to go.

Even when one of them assuredly *didn't*.

"...concessions...?" Anais whispered.

"The Fallen decreed that you should be entombed in the Quiet for your sins, and Their word is law. But you, Anais? You murdered a Paladin of Niasmis, and Love is not as forgiving as the Soul of Wrath."

The golden gates swung open wide as the iron chains tightened around the broker's flesh. Rmaci stood up and walked through the open doorway and into another realm without a second thought – and she gave a sharp tug on the leash of sins wrapped around the damned woman's neck.

"N... no... no... not there... no..." Anais began to whisper as she dug her fingers into the dirt. "Donta. I'll go with Donta. Let me burn with Donta. Please. Please don't. Please. You're better than this. You're better. You don't know what She'll do to me."

"After what you did? Love thinks you're a bitch, so... come along little Madeline," Rmaci replied as she forcibly pulled the damned woman along. Anais planted her hands into the field and tried to hold on for dear life, but all she did was leave divots in the dirt. *"Come now. Be a good puppy for your once and future Missus."*

Divots that vanished just as quickly as her fingers slid through them.

The grass returned as Anais Lovic, born and died as Madeline Hummadalt, victim of a vampire in life, victim of a Harbinger in death, and condemned by her own sins, did the one thing she never wanted to do.

She went home.

"NO PLEASE DON'T DO THIS!"

"Why not?" Rmaci purred with a little smirk. *"I'm told they have plans for you, a party?"*

Anais broke down into horrified sobs as the gates closed on the Quiet.

"…something about a celebration of sin?"

END
INSANITY'S REQUIEM

BOOK IV (AND FINAL)
OF THE AURAMANCER'S EXORCISM

And that, as they say, is a wrap.

Making it this far means you've come to the end of the Auramancer's Exorcism, and the end of Akaran's journey – for now. Fresh horrors will await the intrepid exorcist as he begins to hunt for the Man of the Red Death… and to find the truth behind his own legacy.

But before then, may I please ask a favor?

I honestly hate to ask, but indie authors like me need reviews and feedback from our readers. They help us know what we got right, what we got wrong, and if we've made a fan out of you. They also help us advertise this book (and others!) to new readers, and readers that may have forgotten about us from time to time.

I would sincerely appreciate it. Even just go click upon a few stars to let me know what you thought (if you don't feel like typing something out) makes a difference for the Almighty Algorithm.

https://www.amazon.com/review/create-review?&asin=B09QNSTGQ3

So what happens next?

A lot. A lot happens next.

Akaran is going to take a short break, but plans are already in motion to put him back on a printed page after I try my hand at a new story that's begging to find the light of day. To see what my next project will be, be sure to follow me on Facebook, IG, and Twitter!

https://www.facebook.com/sagadmw

https://www.twitter.com/sagadmw

https://www.instagram.com/sagadmw

THE SAGA OF THE DEAD MEN WALKING

Year 512 of the Queen's Rule
The Snowflakes Trilogy
Book I: Snowflakes in Summer
Freshly minted by the Order of Love, a young exorcist is sent to the edge of the Kingdom of Dawnfire to deal with a 'small, simple haunting.' Between a winter that won't end, a girl that doesn't belong, and people being eaten in the woods, only one thing is for sure: he's over his head, and utterly out of luck.

Book II: Dead Men in Winter
As the search for the Coldstone continues, new allies enter the fray in the mountains around Toniki, and in the streets of the City of Mud. But new blood only means new bodies, and Makolichi seeks to provide those in excess...

Book III: Favorite Things
It's time for Usaic's Tower to ascend. Truths will be revealed, blood shall be spilled, and suffering shall become legendary. But it's not just the living who should fear the Coldstone being set loose. For though the dead will rise, the damned had best be ready for Who comes next...

Year 513 of the Queen's Rule
The Auramancer's Exorcism
Book I: Insanity's Respite
Beaten, broken, and battered, Akaran is sent to the Safest City in the Kingdom to recover from his battle against Makolichi, Daringol, Rmaci, and the rest. What he expects is peace and time to heal. What he finds instead is that insanity knows no bounds and offers no respite...

Book II: Insanity's Rapture
In life, the woman in his dreams had been a spy – a murderess, a liar, a fraud, and a thief. Sentenced to burn for her crimes, her screams have haunted his sleep since the moment she was set aflame. As both the city and Akaran's mind descend into chaos, only insanity offers rapture.

Book III: Insanity's Reckoning
The most dangerous man in the city is about to get his magic back – and he's got a murder on his mind. As he prepares to hunt a sadistic vampire, his past is about to come back to haunt him in a way he never could have imagined.

Book IV: Insanity's Requiem
It's time for the madness to end, but the insane have no desire to find peace – and

peace will only come when Basion City is turned into an open grave.

Origins of the Dead Men Walking
Year 510 of the Queen's Rule
Blindshot (Release date: TBA – it's a newsletter exclusive when it launches!)
A self-professed Merchant of Secrets enlists the help of the Northern Hunter's Guild to trek to the Cursed Continent of Agromah to recover a relic lost to time. In this land of the dead, what chance does a blind man have against a demon king?

Year 512 of the Queen's Rule
Slag Harbor (An Interruption in the Snowflakes Trilogy)
After battling Makolichi in Gonta – and before facing him down for the final time in Toniki – Akaran decides to leave Private Galagrin behind in the City of Mud to make sure that nothing got missed in his sweep. What he finds is more than just stray shiriak; it's an answer to an unasked question...

Year 513 of the Queen's Rule
Lady Claw I: Claw Unsheathed
Who's to blame when a young girl is accused of murder? Did she do it, or did her father? And when she's cornered and the claws come out... does it matter?

Year 516 of the Queen's Rule
Fearmonger
Years after Toniki, a grizzled Akaran serves as a peacekeeper to the Queen – and nothing wants the peace to be kept.

Year 517 of the Queen's Rule
Blindsided
Stannoth and Elrok couldn't be any more different. Trained mercenaries in the Hunter's Guild, they absolutely hate each other – but they don't have a choice but to work together.

WELCOME TO A WORLD WHERE GOOD THINGS HAPPEN TO BAD PEOPLE,
AND THE GOOD PEOPLE ARE QUESTIONABLE…
…AT BEST.

Good things come to those who wait, but I'm impatient as the fires in the Abyss are hot (or cold, depending on Frosel). I'm working on the next book as fast as I can (I promise!) and I've got some stuff for you.

Please be sure to follow me on social media to find out where I'm going, what I'm doing, how I'm doing it, and the occasional stupid meme just to laugh. Plus, get some random business insights on the self-published side of the coin AND see what I'm doing when I cosplay as a Ghostbuster (and other characters!) for charity purposes, too!

There's a newsletter you can sign up for!

You can expect free stories, character information, special promotions, extra information about the World of the Saga, and more! Be sure to visit and subscribe (it'd mean a lot to me if you did)!

Amazon.com:
https://www.amazon.com/author/sdmw

Facebook.com:
https://www.facebook.com/sagadmw

Website:
http://www.sagadmw.com

Twitter:
https://www.twitter.com/sagadmw

Instagram:
https://www.instagram.com/sagadmw

Dead Men Emailing Newsletter
http://www.sagadmw.com/email/

ALSO!
Please don't forget to leave a review. Your opinion on the story (and the series!) MATTERS. Loved it or hated it, thought it was amazing or thought it was garbage, your feedback helps me be a better author and helps me provide the best experience that I can for not just you, but other readers in the future. Let me know on any media platform – just be sure to tag me if you can, but a review anywhere is awesome!

www.ingramcontent.com/pod-product-compliance
Lightning Source LLC
Chambersburg PA
CBHW070759120726
47910CB00001B/227